One Little Mistake

Emma Curtis

BLACK SWAN

TRANSWORLD PUBLISHERS
61–63 Uxbridge Road, London W5 5SA
www.penguin.co.uk

Transworld is part of the Penguin Random House group of companies
whose addresses can be found at global.penguinrandomhouse.com

Penguin
Random House
UK

First published in Great Britain in 2017 by Black Swan
an imprint of Transworld Publishers

A CIP catalogue record for this book
is available from the British Library.

ISBN
9780552779791

Typeset in 11/14 pt Sabon by Jouve (UK), Milton Keynes
Printed and bound in Great Britain by Clays Ltd, Bungay, Suffolk

Penguin Random House is committed to a sustainable future for
our business, our readers and our planet. This book is made from
Forest Stewardship Council® certified paper.

1 3 5 7 9 10 8 6 4 2

To Rose and Brian Knox-Peebles

Prologue

JOSH'S DOOR OPENS SOUNDLESSLY. SIX MONTHS AGO I removed it from its hinges and planed a centimetre off the bottom to stop it rasping against the carpet. And I mean 'I'. I am very good at that sort of thing. A DIY expert. The room smells of my son; of talcum powder and baby shampoo. It's warm and dark and seems to breathe with him. The blinds are blackout ones and the curtains interlined so that no light peeps through and it takes my eyes a moment to adjust. He is clutching the paw of his panda; profoundly and sweatily asleep.

I stoop to pick him up, but as soon as I touch him he kicks a foot out and purses his lips. I step back into the shadows. If he wakes now there will be fallout and I'm too tired and emotionally blindsided to deal with it. Instead I go to the window, lift one corner of the blind and watch the raindrops hit the cars and scatter in rivulets across their roofs. The gutters are barely able to cope with the sheer volume of water and puddles are forming around them. The tight feeling in my chest won't go away, or the sense of urgency that almost certainly diminishes my ability to make good choices.

Behind me, Josh's breathing settles back into deep-sleep mode.

I check my watch then turn around and walk out, closing the door behind me and hurrying downstairs. Josh never wakes during his morning nap. Never ever. He makes up for his bad nights by sleeping soundly for an hour and a half, so I'm safe for a good while yet and I'm only going to be twenty minutes.

I put on my coat, grab my umbrella and step out into the rain.

1

One Day Earlier ❧ *Sunday, 3 January 2010*

AN IMAGE, SHARPLY FOCUSED AND PAINFULLY RIDICU-lous, gatecrashes my mind as I pull on to our forecourt: it's me in my underwear and a naked man with a middle-aged body and a naughty-boy smile. I'm grabbing my clothes and pulling them back on, getting tangled in the sleeves, apologies and excuses tumbling from my mouth as his initial amusement turns to bewilderment and consternation.

I open my eyes. I'm home now. It's OK. Nothing happened.

Our Christmas tree, stripped of its baubles, leans forlornly against the dustbins and above me the street lamp throws an eerie glow over the old magnolia tree. It's coming into bud. I remember when we first viewed this house I was enchanted by the ivory-streaked, blush-pink petals.

In the front window the light from the television flickers across the faces of my family. The four of them are snuggled up on the big red sofa; my husband Tom lounging back, a daughter tucked under each arm; Josh flat out asleep on his father's chest, his fingers curled round the collar of Tom's shirt, his legs splayed. He looks like a frog.

What in God's name was I thinking? I grip the steering wheel, close my eyes and swear. When I look up again Polly has climbed on to the back of the sofa behind Tom and has her arms around his neck. Tom finally registers that I'm here. He deposits her on top of her big sister and jumps up to open the door, Josh in his arms. This is my husband: Tom Seagrave; a funny, occasionally annoying, warm and sociable man. And he loves me. So why?

I blow my nose vigorously. Emily and Polly have pressed their faces against the window, their noses squashed upwards like pigs' snouts. Tom comes to the car in his plastic gardening clogs. I get out and take the baby from him before reaching up for a kiss.

'Have you been good?'

I scoop Polly up and hug Emily against my leg, hide my blushes in children's babble.

'We went to the playground with Daddy and Amber,' Emily says.

'Did you? That must have been lovely. Where was Robert?'

'Working his socks off, apparently,' Tom says. 'Amber left him to it.'

The house still smells of Christmas, a comforting, mixed spice smell overlaid with pine from the needles that the vacuum cleaner has missed. There are still scraps of tinsel stuck between the banisters and the Christmas cards have been left in a neat pile on the kitchen table for me to check before they get relegated to the recycle bin.

I pick them up and absently flick through them. 'You have been busy. So what did you and Amber talk about?'

'Nothing much. This and that. School stuff, mostly.'

I glance at him, wondering why he seems to be holding something back, but he forestalls any further questions, asking, 'So how was my darling mother-in-law? Still baring her breasts and howling into the wind?'

I laugh, relieved and reassured by the familiarity of his joke. Tom pretends to have fixed views on my mum. He's extremely attached to the idea that she's living some sort of eccentric alternative lifestyle, that she spends the solstice on the South Downs with a coven of like-minded souls, that her B & B is in fact a front for what is actually a harem of male sex slaves. He pretends to think this because she favours dark colours and loose layering, is prone to extravagant gestures and gross exaggeration, and has worked her way through half a dozen lovers since he's known her.

'Don't mock. It's mean.'

'Sorry. I was only kidding.'

'I know.' I give him a contrite kiss. The skin on his face is different from David's. More vulnerable somehow. 'She misses Peter.'

The lies flow easily, helped by the fact that I phoned her this morning and that I've heard it all before. My mother was seventeen when she had me and her boyfriends have been creating havoc with her emotions and

11

upsetting our routines for as long as I can remember. To think I nearly threw all this away for some ridiculous fling. What does that make me? My mother's daughter?

'Shame about that. I liked him.'

I dump my bag on the floor. 'Hah. But you like everyone. God, I wish she would grow up.' For a moment I wonder if I'm talking about Mum or myself, but then Tom wraps his arms round me, crushing the girls between us, and pushes the thought out.

'Don't be so pious. She's only forty-seven.'

'Forty-six,' I mumble happily. I tip my head back and kiss his chin, then think I might be overdoing it and pull away. The girls escape and throw themselves on to the sofa.

'Tired?' Tom asks, stroking my hair.

I nod. 'Knackered.'

'Do you want to cancel Robert and Amber? I can always do his passport renewal another time.'

'No. It'll be fine.'

I feel an enormous sense of relief. Everything passes. That's what I learned from my mother.

2

'WHERE'S THAT GLASS OF WINE THEN?' AMBER GIVES me a hug then looks at me. 'You OK?'

'I'll tell you later,' I whisper as her daughter Sophie, who arrived in stripy pyjamas, white fluffy dressing gown and bunny slippers, pounds upstairs to find Emily.

I pour her a glass of red wine and get Robert a bottled beer and we lean against the kitchen island dipping Kettle Chips into a tub of taramasalata while Tom and Robert go through his application at the table. They're soon done and move on to the subject of football, Tom leaning back, his arms locked behind his head, Robert hunched over the form, lazily scratching one arm.

I roll my eyes at Amber and she scoops up a handful of crisps.

'So?' she says. 'How was beautiful Bognor?'

'Chilly.'

I can feel myself going pink. I've kept the truth from her and I'm not even sure why. A mixture of shame and schoolgirlish excitement at having a big scary secret, I suppose. Honestly, sometimes I make myself cringe. 'I haven't shown you the new curtains in Josh's room, have I?'

Her glance is questioning. 'No, dearest, I don't think you have.'

We go up to the children's floor and Amber dutifully admires them, commenting on the neatness of my stitching. They have blue and white vertical stripes with boats painted on top. I sit on the single bed while Josh breathes noisily beside me in his cot.

'So what's the great mystery?'

I rub my nose and look away, smooth and fold a muslin square. I shouldn't tell her, but I can't help myself.

'You have to swear you won't say anything to anyone. Not even Robert.'

'OK. I swear. Vicky, what is it? You're starting to worry me.' Her eyes widen. 'Oh my God. You're not pregnant, are you?'

I glance at my nine-month-old son. 'No, I am not. I've done . . . well, nearly done . . . something really stupid.'

'What?'

'I've, um . . .' I feel her eyes on my profile. 'There's this man.'

She squeals and claps her hand over her mouth. 'Please don't tell me you're having an affair.'

'I'm not. But I very nearly did. That's where I was today. With him.'

'You didn't go and see your mum?'

I shake my head.

'Bloody hell, Vicky.'

'I know. But I . . . we . . . both realized how much we were risking. Amber, I love Tom. I really do.' I cover my face with my hands and groan. 'I must have been mad.'

'You didn't do anything?'

I sigh heavily. 'Nope.'

That isn't exactly true. We kissed and talked when we could and exchanged texts when we couldn't. But that doesn't count as 'doing'.

I get up abruptly and lean over Josh's cot. He is so adorable when he's asleep. He snuffles and I touch his head gently, stroking his hair with the edge of my thumb.

'So come on – spill. Who made the first move? How far did you go?'

'Far enough, OK. But not actually . . . you know.'

'No penetrative sex then?'

We morph into two idiotic, giggling schoolgirls.

'Will you shut up! No there was not. There was kissing and a bit of fumbling, followed by total panic on my part and confusion on his.' I stop laughing and say more soberly, 'It wasn't one of my finer moments. I am so, so thankful nothing happened.'

Amber's face is alive with curiosity. 'Who is it?'

'I am not telling you!'

'Well, I'll guess then. Does he live around here?'

She thinks I'm not serious. 'No comment.'

'I'll take that as a yes.'

'Amber, please. Honestly, it's over and I really don't want to talk about it. It's embarrassing enough as it is.'

'Don't you trust me?'

'It's not that. I don't want anyone to know.'

'Even me?' There's a pause, and then she says, 'How long has it been going on?'

I know what she actually means is, How long have you been lying to me? I hang my head and take a deep breath. 'It was nothing at first. Just eye-contact stuff,

15

nothing I'd even admit to myself. It was months before either of us acknowledged it.' My mouth feels dry. 'Three months ago.'

She sighs and then shrugs.

'I'm sorry.'

Hours later, I crawl into bed, close my eyes and sink into sleep.

I dream violently, of coming home to find half the neighbourhood crowding my hallway and the stairs. I push my way through them, laden down with bags of groceries, and they pull at my arms and shoulders and try to hold me back. But there's ice cream and frozen peas in the bag so I have to go in and I shout at them to get out of the way. When I finally burst into the kitchen, Tom is kneeling over Josh, blood spreading across the stone floor.

I wake with a start of horror, disorientated and scared. Josh is crying and I press my mouth into the pillow so that Tom can't hear my heavy breathing. I used to think my violent dreams were to do with pregnancy hormones but, unlike with the girls, they haven't stopped since Josh's birth. They leave me profoundly disturbed, heart pumping.

I pull the pillow over my head and clamp my crooked arm on top of it. I can't do this any more. I can hear him through the pillow; feel his upset turn to anger. His cries vibrate through my body and I close myself up, tucking my thighs into my stomach, hunching my shoulders, willing myself not to give in to instinct; reminding myself that, if I go up and hold him, comfort him, hug his little body to mine, he'll have no reason to stop.

I fell pregnant during my last term at Bristol University in the post-exam haze when life was all about picnics and balls; unworried, lazy days. Tom and I and our friends had been full of plans, buoyed up by euphoria, careless, young and naïve. Then term ended, along with that part of our lives. We went to India for three months but my brain only engaged with the clues, including morning sickness, which I convinced myself was Delhi Belly, about a week after we returned.

I was about to start teacher training, and Tom had been planning to spend a year in South America; he had already lined up a job in Buenos Aires. But that night, sitting on a bench in Brockwell Park, autumn leaves drifting at our feet, the moon a white ball in the sky above us, we decided to get married. We were twenty-one years old. Emily was born when I was twenty-two, Polly, the only planned baby, when I was twenty-four. Josh, the surprise, arrived six months before my twenty-eighth birthday. He's a cranky little soul, and it was a shock to the system, but I adore him.

The radio alarm goes off. Tom rolls over and gives me a sleepy smile. Time to get up.

3

Monday, 4 January 2010

THE GIRLS ARE BOUNCY THIS MORNING, UP EARLY AND
in their regulation maroon sweatpants and sweatshirts,
excited to be seeing their friends again after a three-
week absence. It's the first day of term and early signs of
spring are beginning to appear, daffodil spears visible
now like dark-green teeth in the lawn. Tom thinks I'm
an idiot for planting the bulbs where they risk being
crushed underfoot but I love the idea of flowers growing
randomly from the grass as if they've escaped their beds,
and enough survive each year to make it worthwhile. He
appreciates them once they flower.

A ginger cat jumps over the fence and I bang on the
window. It turns and looks at me before wandering
away leaving footsteps in the dew. Today marks a new
start but I'm too groggy to think about it. I know it's
going to hurt – it hurts already – but beyond that I don't
know. One day at a time.

Tom comes downstairs with Josh in his arms, shaved
and dressed; pink-and-white stripy shirt, leather trousers

and paisley socks. His tailored suit and fashionably narrow brogues are kept at work because he goes in by motorbike. Tom is in advertising, a career he never planned on, but has embraced. He is a producer at a production company called Marzipan and works in Soho. It's a great job but it has its drawbacks. The summer is a very busy time for him so we have to cram our family holiday around Easter. In the summer holidays I rent a bungalow on the beach in Pagham and the kids and I decamp down there for August. The girls would love to stay in Bognor but even though Mum always offers to have us at the B & B, I'd only be losing her money.

The bombardment begins. The girls squabble while Tom tries to talk over their noise and the radio while I make up the mush that passes for baby food. Strapped into his high chair, Josh yells at me, his hands shoving at the spoon, his face twisting away, his feet kicking the side of the table. Political pundits argue immigration while Polly and Emily fight over the breakfast cereal. Tom roars at them and then laughs at the consternation on Polly's face. He rushes to comfort her, overwhelmed by guilt when two cartoonish tears spill from her big brown eyes. I try so hard to keep it together; I get some food into Josh, although the bulk of it lands on the floor, my shirt, the table and Emily's hair. I dampen a muslin and clean myself up, then Emily, leaving Josh till last because that's another fight. When we are done, when Emily has finished demanding 'What's wrong with Josh?', when Polly has stopped crying and Tom has finished charming his way back into their good graces, I shoo the girls upstairs to brush their teeth.

We were the world's smuggest parents when Emily was a baby. When friends complained about how shattered they were, how hard it was, we caught each other's eyes and shared knowing smiles. We simply couldn't understand what the fuss was all about. She slept through the night at eight weeks and during the day was a delight, rarely complaining and diligently meeting all her milestones. Polly too was a cinch; a gorgeous baby who, unlike her more independent sister, was happiest when she was being cuddled, fitting like an infant marsupial into our bodies. We congratulated ourselves all over again.

And then Josh came along and turned our self-satisfied assumption that we were naturals at this on its head. We use the same routines, the same inducements as we used on the girls, but he's a fighter, not a stickler for rules like Emily, or placid like Polly. It'll stand him in good stead in adulthood but right now it's hard work and there are times, like this morning, when I almost despair.

Hannah, Tom's older sister, once said to me, 'Tom was more like the girls as a baby: a big sleeper and so sweet-natured. Josh must take after you.' And my mother said, 'You were exactly the same, a little horror. But don't worry – you calmed down by the time you were four.'

'Are you all right?' Tom asks.

'Crappy night, but I'll manage.'

He leans forward and kisses my forehead. 'I do understand, you know.'

I smile unsteadily.

'Try and get some rest. And buy yourself a jam doughnut.'

I laugh at that, but as he turns away I whisper, 'I love you.'

He doesn't hear me because Polly has thrown her arms around his legs. He swings her up into his arms and they gaze at each other with unconditional, slavish adoration.

'Can I have a Penguin Biscuit for break?' Emily asks.

Tom left an hour ago; seven thirty and out of the door, clean-shaven and smelling of soap, rangy in his black leathers, the boots making his feet look clownishly big. I've taken Josh into the sitting room for a bit of time out while the girls make their beds. The weather is vile. Schoolchildren draw stick figures on steamed-up windows from inside cars that sluice past our house. The front door opposite opens, expelling children and dogs. Jamie Boxer heads off under his black umbrella towards the station while his wife Millie juggles book bags, her feet tangling in leads as the two dachshunds cross and criss-cross in their excitement to be out. The baby is in its pram, the two boys still eating toast, their hair still mussed from bed. I should get a move on. Further down the street a car revs its engine over and over.

What is David doing now? Much the same as Tom probably, kissing his wife and daughter goodbye and setting off for work. A memory of his wicked smile, like a sharp stab, makes me blink. I need time to get to grips with what's happened but as I am not a teenager I don't have the luxury of shutting myself in my bedroom and listening to maudlin love songs. More's the pity.

* * *

Josh is playing with coloured plastic blocks on the floor behind me. He throws one and it bounces against the fireguard and rolls under the armchair. He's starting to get mobile and before long he's on his side, peering into the dark space beneath it. I crouch down and retrieve it for him.

'Mummy!'

How long has Emily been standing there? I focus and remember the question I only half heard. Penguin Biscuits.

'Yes. Get one for Polly as well, will you? And put your shoes on and find hers. We're off as soon as I've got Josh ready.'

'Polly should look for her own shoes. She's not a baby.'

She is defiant; her chin raised, a scowl forming. I itch to touch the grooves and smooth them out. Emily makes me want to laugh; her self-righteousness, her air of superiority, her fierce stances on the smallest things, her overriding sense of what is fair and what is not, are hilarious. But I don't laugh because she has no sense of humour where her own dignity is concerned.

'Please, Emily. You'd be helping me. If we wait for Polly to find them, we'll be late.'

Emily's face falls. 'I don't want to be late!'

She runs out of the room yelling for Polly and I pick Josh up and manhandle him into his snowsuit. It enrages him and I get a thump on my ear for my trouble. It brings tears to my eyes.

By the time we arrive there are more people coming out of the school gates than are going in. The teaching assistant shivers under her brolly, holding her hand out for the children to shake. I look round for David sur-reptitiously, but I'm not overly worried: the chances of him being down at the school in the morning are virtu-ally nil.

'Vicky!' Imogen Parker strides towards me, her twins in tow. 'How was your Christmas?'

I switch on a smile. 'Lovely. We had a fantastic time. How was yours?'

And then Millie wanders over, and Charlotte Grunden looking ready to drop her third baby, and Amber, dressed for work in a smart trench coat, high black boots, hair caught up in a ponytail, and suddenly it doesn't seem so bad any more. These are my friends. I can slot back into my old life, reprieve in hand. The relief makes me feel giddy.

'Good morning!'

Amber scrutinizes my face. 'Good morning to you too. Did you get any sleep last night?'

'Not much. He woke up at two.'

The four of them chip in with suggestions, all of which I've tried before. In fact, I've tried so many things that I've made matters worse. Josh and I are as confused as each other. Pick him up. Don't pick him up. Go to him. Don't go to him. Say something so he knows he isn't forgotten then leave. Let him see you but don't speak. Ignore him entirely. Never ignore your baby. Sometimes I think I'm going out of my mind.

And then there they are; David and Hellie North with Astrid between them holding their hands. My smile dies. I should have thought of this. Parents who both work and aren't able to do the school gate stuff often make an exception at the beginning of a new term.

I have done the worst possible thing and allowed myself to be drawn into a relationship with the father of one of my pupils at the school where I both work – although I am on maternity leave – and send my children. Never mind that we didn't go the whole way, or that the reason we desisted was because I pulled the plug, it was still a crappy thing to do. Grey Coat School is within walking distance of where we live; a sweet one-class-entry local primary. I have pissed in my own backyard, as they say. I am a teacher. Families rely on me for support and guidance. They do not expect me to destroy them.

Imogen and Charlotte wander off to greet other friends but I keep Millie and Amber talking until the Norths leave the cloakroom and cross the playground to the back doors of the school. Then I take my two in, divest them of coats, scarves and gloves, fold up their brollies and stick them under the pram, wrestle Josh out of his straps and into my arms and whizz them up to their classrooms. I hover near the door to Emily's class, waiting until I'm sure the coast is clear, and then hurry down the stairs and run smack-bang into David coming up the other way.

We stare at each other, both of us pressing into the wall to let others get by.

'Sorry.' I try and move on but he blocks me.

'It's good to see you,' he says. 'You look lovely.'

I know perfectly well that I don't but my lips give a traitorous twitch. Josh stares at him and reaches for his nose. 'I've got to go.'

'I want to talk to you.'

I shake my head. 'No. That wouldn't be a good idea.'

Hellie appears and smiles at me. 'How are you, Vicky?' Her accent gives everything she says a formal twist. I wonder if she suspects, especially since David has done this before. For a horrible moment I imagine I intercept a look between them. *Is this the latest one then? Is this her? Not a beauty, is she?*

'Oh, I'm good.'

'And the little one?'

She looks at Josh, whose cheeks are red and stained with tears.

'Not a morning person.'

'I see that.'

'I'd better go. I need to put him down for his nap.'

Amber is waiting for me. I give her an uncertain smile but hers is at full volume when she returns it. Relief at being forgiven for keeping secrets floods me. We set off towards the corner where our paths will diverge, me going home, her off to Tennyson Street where she works three mornings a week for an estate agent.

'Are you all right?' she asks, pushing the button at the pedestrian crossing. The green man flashes and we start walking. 'You're very pale.'

I can't tell her who I bumped into. 'I hate myself.'

'No you don't. You're just exhausted. Try and sleep when Josh does. Promise?'

'I promise. I've got Magda cleaning this morning. She'll keep me sane.'

* * *

25

A text pings at me as I'm unlocking the front door. I pull my phone out of my bag and read it, not understanding at first and then getting it.

Hello Vicky. Sorry but much vomit this morning and diyareorr. Will make new later. I call. Magda

I read it again and cry where I stand, in my thick coat, still holding the pushchair.

Fairhaven Young Offenders' Institute

July 1992

ADULTS WHISPERED WHEN THEY TALKED ABOUT HER. Why did they bother? Did they think she was too thick to know what they were on about? The child psychiatrist had arrived. He wasn't how she had expected. She'd imagined him in a suit and tie, with silver hair and glasses and that she would have to call him Doctor Someone-or-other. This bloke had brown hair and no glasses, and wore jeans and a stripy shirt with a jacket over it that he'd taken off. When she asked, he said he was a doctor – Doctor Adam Kozlowski – but he didn't expect her to remember all that and she could call him Adam.

Katya sat on the squeaky black leather sofa in her grey tracksuit and hoodie, feeling frightened and alone. She wasn't talking to anyone. Why should she tell them anything? No one listened to her before, so why would they listen to her now? Adults only heard what they wanted to hear, otherwise they were stone deaf. Where was Maggie? Why hadn't she come?

27

She was starving. She could smell the canteen; boiled greens and chips and maybe burgers. Her mouth watered as she wrapped her arms around her shins and hugged her thighs into her belly. She squished her nose down on to her knees and tried to think about being somewhere else. She was good at that. She used to do it when her mum was busy in her bedroom: curl up and take her mind right away, into a fairy tale usually. When things got bad there was always a prince to come galloping over the horizon on his jet-black steed. She wished he would hurry up, but sometimes she wondered if she would even recognize him if he did come. Because princes didn't exist in real life, or if they did, they didn't usually know they were one.

Somewhere in the building someone was laughing, the sound bouncing round the walls. And inside that sound, wrapped in it, the clatter of cutlery and a boy yelling and swearing, the language going on and on like a poem. Fucking, you fucking. Fucking cunt I'll fucking have you, you shit head wanker you.

Adam put his head out of the door and shouted, 'Could somebody please keep him quiet?'

Silence fell like a slap and he closed the door again.

'Would you like some lunch?'

Her stomach rumbled but she shook her head. She wasn't going out there. Not with all those kids. She wondered if they knew, if word got round.

'Has Maggie come?' she asked.

It hadn't been many days. Only a week, she thought, although she wasn't sure. So much had happened.

'No. I'm sorry, she hasn't. Is she important to you?'

28

Maybe they were keeping Maggie from her. Maybe this was part of the punishment. She felt furious at the injustice of it, but suppressed her anger in case it went against her. It seemed so unfair that she was stuck in this dump, practically in prison, all because she couldn't say the right words and no one even bothered to find out the stuff in her head. She glanced up from her hands to find Adam waiting.

'I will be good,' she said. 'If you let her come.'

'Katya, if Maggie wants to see you, she knows she can contact your supervisor. No one is keeping her away.'

She had thought Maggie was her fairy godmother but it turned out she was just an ordinary grown-up. But even that didn't hurt as much as Emily's silence had. Why didn't she say something? Perhaps she was scared too. Maybe she thought that Katya wanted to take Maggie away from her. She wished she'd had a chance to explain that all she wanted was to belong to them and Maggie loving her wouldn't mean she loved Emily any less. She started to cry. It was such a relief to let the tears flow; to be comforted; to be allowed to be a little kid again.

4

JOSH BELLOWS FROM BEHIND HIS BEDROOM DOOR AND I lean against it, my hands pressed to my face. If I give in he won't sleep and he'll be bad-tempered and miserable for the rest of the day. The crying is merely a symptom of his tiredness.

Downstairs I shut the kitchen door, switch the baby monitor off – I don't need help hearing him – make myself a black coffee and take it to my computer, where I enter my favourite property site with a click of the mouse. This is my guilty pleasure and something of an addiction. Tom rolls his eyes whenever I call his attention to an interesting opportunity but I have perfectly valid reasons for keeping my eyes open. When we bought this house it was a wreck, but it meant that we could afford to live in an area that was already on the up. We were lucky, coming in before prices went stratospheric. I would do it again like a shot, never mind the upheaval. It's to do with increasing our equity and creating a cushion if anything ever goes wrong; like Tom being made redundant or me not being able to go back to work after my maternity leave ends.

Tom doesn't really get the point about security because

he's always had it, but I know how precarious life can be. He's more like his mother-in-law than he realizes. Their mantra is, Don't worry until it happens. Mine is, Plan against it happening. I've had my life turned upside down in the space of a few days, my belongings thrown into binbags. No warning and no chance to say goodbye. The feeling that there are forces beyond my control has never left me.

Things happen. We can't assume that the good times will last for ever.

I sip my coffee. Upstairs, Josh's cries are fading, the gaps between each howl lengthening.

He goes quiet.

I hold my breath. Count to ten. Nothing.

I let it go with a sigh of relief.

Two minutes later I'm scrolling through estate agent's details when I spot a candidate five minutes away in Browning Street. My antennae twitch. It has *NEW LISTING!* splashed in red across the corner of the photograph and it's being marketed by Johnson Lane, the agency Amber works for. It's completely unmodernized and I know it well. The house is cheap for where it is, which means it needs a lot of money spent on it and months of dust and toil; but the long-term potential is huge. If we budget carefully, we could make it amazing. Adrenaline kicks in as I reach for the phone.

Sarah, Amber's boss, answers. 'You're not the only one,' she says. 'To be honest, Mrs Seagrave, it's not going to hang around. Developers, you know?'

I did know. We had to fight developers for Coleridge Street. 'Can I see it today?'

'We're booked up, I'm afraid. You know what it's like after the holidays finish. People start putting their houses on the market almost immediately. My phone literally has not stopped ringing. It's the Christmas Curse.'

'The what?'

'Statistically, more marriages fall apart at Christmas than any other time.'

'Oh.' I ponder this depressing statistic. 'Surely Amber could squeeze me in.'

'Give me a minute.' She sighs and I imagine her bright-pink fingernails tapping the desk as she checks her diary.

I take a pen and scribble Browning Street on a scrap of paper and underline it. This is the one. I feel it in my bones.

'OK,' she says. 'Amber's there now. If you can make it in ten minutes she can zip you round between viewings. I'll give her a call.'

I glance up at the ceiling. 'Can she do any later?'

'Not today, sorry. Take it or leave it, I'm afraid.'

I hesitate. Bloody Magda.

'Are you still there?'

'Yes. That's fine. I'll run round now.'

And I do . . . I do just that. I make the worst mistake of my life.

5

THE RAIN IS TORRENTIAL. I FORCE MY UMBRELLA UP
and as the wind catches it and turns it inside out I look
back up at the house, at the gabled window to Josh's
bedroom. He'll be fine. I'll hurry. By the time I reach the
end of my road I'm already lost in a developer's fantasy;
picturing myself with plans and builders, opening out
spaces and letting the light flow in.

This is a great area; sprawling enough not to feel
claustrophobic, limited enough to be a cohesive community. It isn't the best part of south east London, but it
has the usual signs of gentrification; a 'village' label shame-
lessly bandied about by estate agents, a couple of niche
cafés, a specialist wine shop and a gastro pub beside the
Common, which boasts a playground and a duck pond.
A McDonald's, KFC and kebab shop still do a roaring
trade on the London Road and make for a jolly, mixed
community. I spent my early years in Streatham, so it
was the obvious place for us to begin the search for our
first home. We moved outwards from there – hoping for
a bargain – and chanced on a cluster of streets named
after English poets where big houses that had been

converted into flats in the seventies and eighties were gradually being turned back into family houses. It's also handy for getting out of London to visit my mother on the coast.

When I turn up, Amber is saying goodbye to a couple with a child in a pram and a little girl of about two sitting on her father's shoulders, her rainhood pulled down over her eyes and nose. Amber shakes their hands and they set off towards me, obviously discussing the house, the woman excited, the man more circumspect. As they cross over the road and pass me I glance down at their baby. He's older than Josh, fast asleep, slumped in that sack-like way that only babies manage, his chin tucked into his chest, his arms and legs lolling, utterly relaxed.

'Oh God, I want it, Nick,' the woman says. She reminds me of me.

I don't hear Nick's reply because I'm already hurrying towards Amber, the image of Josh fast asleep in his cot lodged in my head and a worry starting to nibble at the edge of my good mood.

The house is double-fronted and semi-detached. It's in a state of acute disrepair but the two smarter versions that flank it have had a lot of money spent on them. They boast plantation shutters and black-and-white tessellated paths leading up to front doors painted in heritage shades.

Six years ago Tom and I stood outside Coleridge Street with Emily in her pram, almost speechless with anticipation, gripping each other's hands while Sarah Wilson from Johnson Lane battled with the lock, muttering about it being an agent's nightmare, and finally, triumphantly, pushing it open against a pile of mail that slithered out across the floor like the tide coming in. We pushed Emily's pram into a patch of warm sunlight. Sarah kept her distance, probably aware that she didn't have to sell it while we naïvely thought we were putting on a good show, Tom making critical remarks that sounded positively hammy, me standing with my hand cradling my modest bump, gazing up at a patch of damp where the corner of the sitting room met the ceiling. We moved through the house like small children discovering a new secret and when we came out into the garden where the birds were singing, climbing roses casting long stems heavy with buds, I flung my arms around him.

'Can we afford it?'

Tom laughed. 'No, but we'll find a way.'

It was a wonderful, crazy time, camping in the rooms that were liveable, working nights and weekends with Emily crawling around in the dirt, and then with Polly as well, tiny and new. I was trying to paint windows between feeds and replace floorboards, put up curtains and restore damaged original features. I spent the long summer days in decorator's overalls, finding cheap ways of making an impact. Growing up without a father, in a crummy seaside house that my mother filled with lodgers, we developed an impressive range of skills. Between the two of us, Mum and I can fix pretty much anything.

Tom and I put up with a makeshift kitchen for two years and walked on bare boards, but we didn't care. We were in love with each other, in love with the future, in love with our babies and our house. I had no idea how useless Tom was at DIY, but it wasn't all bad. If he couldn't do anything that required a particular skill he was at least willing to sand for hours on end.

My tools are lying unused in the cellar now. I miss them.

'Oh my God, this rain! Let's get inside.' Amber leads me in, checking her watch. 'I can only give you fifteen minutes, so we'd better crack on.'

I follow her and breathe in the smell; a heady blend of old carpet and damp and that musty scent of decay. I run my fingers along the brown-painted dado rail and gaze up at the cornicing. The paint is flaking off but it is generously wide; the pattern of ridges and grooves elegant and understated.

'Nice?' Amber says, raising an eyebrow.

'I love it.'

Something flits across Amber's face, a wisp of despondency darkening her eyes. It's only a tiny moment but it reminds me to pare back my enthusiasm.

'Do you think this is transferral?' she asks.

'Sorry?'

'I mean, do you think you're doing this because you're looking for an outlet for all that pent-up sexual frustration?'

She's joking of course. 'No. Well, maybe a little. But you know I like smelly old wrecks.'

'Are you talking about the house or your mystery man?'

I laugh. 'The house. Categorically.'

Amber pulls me towards the staircase, where grubby mahogany banisters lead the eye up three floors to a skylight. Even though it's too dirty and splattered with bird shit to let in more than a milky light I can imagine how wonderful it would be on a sunny day or a moonlit night. She takes me to the kitchen, a yellowing room at the back of the house with a door to the garden and a small window. A sink clings to the wall between ugly beige units encrusted with filth. When Amber flicks the switch a strip light stutters on.

'Thank God you didn't bring Josh. That last couple? Their little girl was a nightmare.'

'Their baby was asleep.' Hiding my blushes, I bend to tease up a corner of brittle lino. Underneath, the floor-boards look sound.

'Yes. But they left them both downstairs with me. Can you believe it? I'm not a bloody babysitter. And you know what she said?' Amber snorts. *Don't take him out of his pram.* As if he was too cute for me to resist. Honestly.'

My smile is strained. 'I've never seen anyone coming in or out. How long has it been empty?'

'Not long. The lady who owned it went into care last week. She's ninety-three and reclusive, apparently. Probate's going to take a while, but I doubt it'll hang around. To be honest, Vicky, if you want it, you're going to have to sharpen your elbows.'

I touch the brown wallpaper and pick at a torn edge. 'Tom will take some persuading. If it was down to him we'd still be in the flat.'

Amber's face falls.

'Sorry. I didn't mean it like that.'

'Don't worry about it.'

37

But I do and I can tell she's offended. Robert is self-employed and they're paying a huge rent to be in the right catchment area and haven't been able to scrape the cash together for a deposit. It's something I try hard to ignore, but when you start out in your career at the same income level as a friend, only to leave them behind financially, it can be awkward and you have to be sensitive. I blame my lack of tact on last night.

'You'll get what you want in the end. You're the most determined person I know.'

She rolls her eyes. 'I suppose . . .'

'Come on. It's only a matter of time.'

'Let's hope.'

We go into the next room and she waits while I look round. I can feel that she wants to say something, that I've struck an ill-judged note.

'You mustn't take what you have for granted,' she says.

'Do you mean Tom or the house?' Her words are discomforting but I suppose I deserve it.

'Both. You don't know how lucky you are.'

'I do.'

'Then why risk it?'

'Because I take risks! That's why I got pregnant at twenty-one. That's why we own Coleridge Street. We couldn't afford it, Amber, but we just did it. You and Robert can do it too.'

'Maybe.'

'Amber . . .' But she's left the room ahead of me.

I follow her into the sitting room. This is in better condition, the marble fireplace grander than the one we have in Coleridge Street. A large Persian rug lies spread across wide floorboards, the gaps between them imprinted into the weave. There's more damp above the curtain rail, but otherwise it's perfect and I can see myself living here. I do a rapid calculation. We could do it. Mortgage rates are still low and Tom has inherited a useful amount from his grandfather. It would be a strain, there's no doubt about that, but worth it in the long run. I'm tempted to put in an offer then and there. For the first time in days I feel excited, drawn into the romance of the place, the lure of the project.

'Keep moving,' Amber says, all professional now. 'I'll show you round upstairs and then you can poke your head outside.'

At first I don't hear it above the sound of the rain. We are in the master bedroom, inspecting some water damage to the window frames, Amber saying how wonderful the room will look once the shutters are restored. It's only faint, but it's such a familiar sound that it makes me turn and prick up my ears. I walk to the door and listen. It's coming from upstairs. A baby is crying.

'Vicky?' Amber says, touching my arm.

I ignore her and go up. The stairs to the top floor are uncarpeted and dusty, as if the owners stopped bothering with that part of the house a long time go. An eclectic collection of pictures line the walls: old-fashioned hunting prints, nondescript watercolours, uninspiring oils; the kind of things that turn up in job lots in auction houses or stacked forlornly against the walls of charity shops. The wailing draws me like a magnet. On the landing I stop, confused. The rooms are devoid of furniture but I can hear it clearly now, the hiccupping sob of a child who no one has come to comfort.

'It's only next-door's baby,' Amber says. 'They've got a little girl too. That noise really gets to you though, doesn't it?'

'I've got to go home,' I say abruptly.

'But you haven't seen the garden yet.' It's as dark out there as a November afternoon, the rain coming down in sheets. A fat pigeon sits on a branch looking miserable.

'I'll come back tomorrow, when I don't need an Ark.'

I'm in such a hurry I slip on the stairs, scraping my elbow against the wall. Amber reaches under my arm and pulls me up.

'Slow down. What's the panic? My next lot aren't due for a couple more minutes. Tell me what you think of the place.'

'It's great. I'll call you later. I've got to get back. I can't expect Magda to babysit when she's supposed to be cleaning.'

'She's babysitting for us tomorrow evening,' Amber says, moving away from me and brushing a speck of dust from the bottom of her trench coat. 'Honestly, I don't know what I'd do without her.'

Shit. What if she tells Amber she didn't come to me? I shouldn't have left him. What the hell was I thinking?

'Oh, and just to warn you, I've already booked her to babysit Sophie for the Forsyths' drinks party.'

She stares at me, waiting for a reaction.

'Sorry,' I say, opening the front door. 'The house is

wonderful. I need to have a think and talk to Tom, but I'd love it, obviously.'

As I leave, she shouts after me, 'Do you want me to come and value your house? Would that help?'

There's something in her voice, a touch of desperation that hangs in the air as I run into the rain.

Amber, standing in the doorway, watches Vicky as she runs out, wincing as a car drives through the puddles, splashing her. She's puzzled but she shakes it off and looks away, peering through the rain at a car slowing down. Her next appointment. The woman in the passenger seat gesticulates at the driver. Amber forgets about Vicky and waves cheerfully at them, puts up her umbrella and hurries over.

'Mrs Tarrant?' she says. 'Hello, I'm Amber Collins.'

Mr and Mrs Tarrant know exactly what they want and don't need Amber's sales pitch. Not that the house needs one. Seventeen Browning Street sells itself. Amber runs her fingers over the chipped woodwork on the windowsill of one of the upstairs bedrooms. She feels like she's in love, as though the smell of the house is male musk, its walls arms waiting to embrace her. She has a fanciful idea that she could touch her lips to the peeling wallpaper, lean into it. Why can't she and Robert have a place like this? Perhaps she should do as Vicky says and take a risk. She looks around, imagining herself climbing newly carpeted stairs, lying in a claw-foot bathtub, wafting round a sleekly beautiful kitchen. She couldn't. Could she? Vicky would never forgive her.

She nibbles at her bottom lip. Perhaps that doesn't even matter. Vicky has broken the first rule of their friendship. She lied. Amber has always aspired to be like Vicky, but now she's not so sure. She can't believe her friend was prepared to risk it all for a sordid fling. Poor Tom. Poor children.

'So what do you know about the local schools?'

She jumps – she hadn't realized the Tarrants were there – and turns with her brightest smile.

'Are you looking for private or independent?'

'Private.'

They talk education and small children, the innocuous conversation a comfort to Amber. Mrs Tarrant moves around the room, looks out of the windows and frowns at the swollen frames. Amber's phone rings.

'Your eleven o'clock,' Sarah says. 'They've cancelled.'

Amber glances at her watch. She's going to have over half an hour to kill in this freezing house. Great.

My bag knocks against my hip and I'm out of breath before I reach the end of the next street. I slow down, panting, and power-walk the rest of the way. My mind feels overheated.

Amber will guess.

Maybe I can bribe Magda?

But that would mean someone else knowing.

Maybe I should text Magda and advise her not to mention the upset stomach. Then she would have to avoid saying she hadn't been to my place.

Yes. That would do it.

* * *

42

Josh is crying. I hadn't expected that and it chills me; the noise loud enough to be heard across the street. As I shove my key into the lock the telephone starts ringing. I'm supposed to be in so I sprint to the sitting room and grab the phone off the sideboard.

'Vicky?'

'Mum. I can't talk now. I'll call you back.'

'It's just a small thing, I . . .'

'Mum. Josh is having a paddy. Please. I'll call you back.'

Something is wrong. The sitting-room door was open when I left earlier. It's rarely closed. I put the phone down slowly. The French windows are ajar, splinters of wood and glass on the floor beside them.

'Shit.'

I sprint upstairs and charge into Josh's bedroom, come to an abrupt standstill and scream with fright. There's someone there: a large figure in the gloom, shockingly out of context. He's dressed in dark clothes and he's holding Josh clamped against his chest, his hand covering my son's mouth. Josh has frozen. He isn't fighting or protesting but his eyes are big and confused and shining with tears.

'Don't hurt him.' My arms hang by my sides. 'Please.' I have never felt terror like this before. It is physically numbing and mentally degrading.

Downstairs the phone starts to ring again and the sound changes the atmosphere instantly. The man runs forward before I'm ready. He barges past, thrusting Josh at me and I'm propelled violently backwards against the sharp edge of the half-open door, whacking my elbow on my funny bone, fuzzing the nerves that lead into my wrists, so that as I try to catch hold of Josh I clumsily misjudge and he slips to the floor with a sickening thud. The man has to pull the door open behind me and I try to get out of his way and scoop Josh up at the same time, but somehow I clash with his feet and Josh lets out a cry of pain. And then it's over and he is gone, charging down the stairs, and I'm cradling my son, rocking him against me as he bellows.

Seconds later I feel something, another presence. I slowly straighten up and turn my head. Amber is holding the door wide, staring down at me, her mouth open in horror. My relief at seeing her is tempered by shame. I hold her gaze and plead silently with her.

Please don't judge me.

6

'VICKY!' AMBER SAYS, DROPPING DOWN BESIDE ME. 'Oh my God. Are you OK?'

I stare at her and whisper, 'No.'

'Why don't you give him to me before you faint?'

She tries to take him but I shy away from her, covering him with my arm. She backs off immediately, then holds out her hand for mine and with her help I stagger to the rocking chair. I lay Josh carefully on my thighs, with his toes against my stomach. He has gone worryingly quiet.

'I need to get him to A & E. I think he's broken his arm.'

Amber opens the curtains and blinds and the grey morning throws a washed-out light over the scene. Josh's face is pale, the skin blue around his lips.

'I'll take you.'

I focus on her properly. 'What happened to your viewing?'

She strokes Josh's forehead and his eyes widen as he gazes up at her. 'They cancelled, so I thought I'd nip round. What on earth happened? I saw a man run out of your house.'

'He broke in. I didn't know he was here.'

'Jesus.'

His smell lingers on the landing. Stale cigarettes and sweat. We go downstairs and I stop outside my bedroom. Amber goes in first, stands with her hands on her hips. The little wooden drawers that form part of my dressing table have been pulled out, their sparkling contents strewn across the bed. None of it is of any value.

'He didn't find your safe. That's something.'

It isn't a safe. Nothing so grand. Anything precious is kept in a concealed cavity built into the skirting under the wardrobe. There isn't much in there, just rings that Tom has given me to mark special occasions.

'I thought you said Magda was here?' Amber says as she closes the door behind us and we make our way downstairs.

'She's . . . she's around somewhere.' It's patently obvious that there's no one else in the house but I stammer on regardless. 'She was here. Perhaps she's left already.'

Amber glances at her watch as I go down the next flight. I pick up Josh's snowsuit from the end of the banister.

'You can't put him in that,' she says. 'You'll hurt him. Hang on.'

She disappears into the sitting room and comes out with the blue tartan rug we keep over the back of the sofa and carefully tucks it round him.

I pull out my mobile and she grabs my wrist. 'What are you doing?'

'I'm calling the police. What did you think I was doing?' I pull away and for a moment we look at each other.

'Don't,' she says. 'Not yet at least. We need to think about this.'

After a second's hesitation I push the phone into my pocket and she ushers me towards the front door.

'We'll talk about it on the way to the hospital. You can call the police as soon we get there, if you like. Tom as well. Where're your car keys? I'll drive. You look after Josh.'

She indicates that I should get in the car while she calls her office and explains there's been an emergency, an accident. I can tell Sarah isn't happy and I worry that Amber's getting into trouble because of me.

'Right.' Amber's tone is so businesslike that I immediately sit up straight and listen. 'Tell me exactly what happened and we'll work out what to say.'

I shiver even though the air conditioner is blasting out heat. My jeans are still damp. The sound of the rain battering down on the roof and the windscreen wipers swishing back and forth hypnotizes me.

'Vicky! Please. Concentrate.'

Her voice is enough to break the spell and words burst out of me. 'I left him. But it was only for fifteen minutes. He was sound asleep and he never normally wakes up. I thought it would be OK.'

'Have you done anything like this before?'

I don't reply. When Tom and I lived in the flat I was so bored, so claustrophobic, so lonely and frustrated and so young that I did things I shouldn't. I used to go out and walk round the block. Stretch my legs and ease my mind. Buy a newspaper. Emily would sleep right through it and because it was a flat in an anonymous mansion block, no one was any the wiser. It was, now I think about it, a compulsion. I stopped after Tom came home early from work and caught me returning from one of my mini-forays. I told him I'd nipped across to the corner shop. This time I don't have youth and isolation as an excuse.

'Come on,' Amber urges. 'We can't mess around.'

I have to raise my voice to be heard. 'Only once or twice: to get the papers or a pint of milk. It's never been an issue.'

'Christ, Vicky.'

I hang my head. 'I know.'

'OK. What's done is done. Why don't you tell me exactly what happened today and we'll take it from there.'

I tell her about the impulsive decision I made and I don't spare myself. I'm in trouble and every word I speak damns me.

'You can't say that,' Amber responds, catching my eye in the mirror with a frown. 'You need an alternative story.'

'I'm not lying. I can't.' My heart is thumping so hard I feel sick. 'It would be better to be honest, wouldn't it?'

'Don't be ridiculous,' Amber snaps.

My knees are trembling. 'It's not ridiculous. I—'

'This is not 1990, Vicky. This is 2010. Social workers have learned from past mistakes. If you tell them you left Josh alone in the house, he will be taken into care. You won't be given a chance to explain or get legal advice; they'll take him out of your arms and criminal charges will be pressed against you. Do you really want that?'

I stare at her, cowed. This is a version of my friend I don't recognize. 'I can't . . . I can't live a lie. They'll find out.' My voice rises. 'They'll understand that it was a mistake; that I was exhausted and stressed.'

'For fuck's sake, Vicky. Do you know how many exhausted and stressed mothers there are out there? Or do you think it's only you? Seriously? Are you stupid or just naïve? Pull yourself together or I'm going to dump you outside the hospital and leave you to dig your own grave.'

'Amber, please,' I sob. 'Don't do this.'

There's a long silence before she speaks. 'I'm sorry. I shouldn't have yelled at you.'

I've never seen her like this, never known her to lose her temper so violently. The deep breath she takes before she speaks is audible. 'Try and understand. You cannot tell the truth about this, not if you want to keep your baby. It's as simple as that. So please, trust me.'

I cannot speak so I reach between the seats. She takes my hand and encloses it in hers.

'This is what you're going to say and you say the same thing to the doctors, the police and Tom. Do you understand?'

I cry silently, but I listen.

Amber shouldn't have lost her temper back there but she's disappointed in her friend. Very disappointed. To do that; to leave her little boy, not to mention her infidelity to Tom – because, let's not split hairs, Vicky was unfaithful even if they never actually did it – takes an astounding degree of selfishness.

She hates this, hates not feeling in control. It was weak to shout and swear at her. But how could Vicky do it? Amber would never leave a child on its own. Even if she didn't know what that felt like herself, she wouldn't. Children are vulnerable, completely dependent on the decisions adults make. It tears her up inside to think about it.

She digs her thumbnails into the leather steering wheel, leaving crescent-shaped dents, suppressing her anger and resentment. Josh's sobs are more like hiccups now, racking his little body. Amber gives herself a moment and then turns to smile reassuringly. Vicky looks like she's about to throw herself out of the car.

'Nearly there,' she says.

'OK.'

'Good girl. You're going to be fine. I'll drop you outside A & E and come and find you when I've parked.'

'You have back-to-back appointments,' Sarah says. 'You're really dropping me in it here, Amber. Are you sure she needs you? Where's her husband?'

'I'll leave as soon as he turns up. An hour at the most. Honestly, I wouldn't do this if I had a choice, but I'm really worried about her.'

Sarah sighs. 'So what happened exactly?'

Amber leans back into the car seat, the tension easing from her shoulders. 'The poor thing. She was at home with the baby and some guy got in and all hell broke loose. I'll tell you about it properly later. And thanks, Sarah. I owe you.'

'Where are they?' Tom says.

He's arrived out of breath and frantic, still in his wet motorbike leathers, big boots clumping on the rubber floor. Amber hears his voice before Vicky does and goes to meet him, leaving Vicky standing over the cot where Josh is fast asleep, a bruise ripening on his cheek.

'Is he all right?'

'No, he's not.' Vicky runs over and collapses sobbing into his arms.

'Shh,' he says. 'It's OK, darling. I'm here now. Tell me what happened.'

Amber feels Vicky trying to catch her eye but she avoids looking at her.

'I . . . we had a break in,' Vicky says. 'He had Josh. He shoved him at me and I dropped him.'

She starts to cry again, so Amber takes up the story, handing him the leaflet that the radiologist gave them.

'It's his arm. Josh has a super . . . supracondylar fracture. He's going to be in overnight. Look, I'd better get back to work,' she stammers. 'I'll leave your car outside the house and put the keys through the letterbox.'

Vicky turns her head but doesn't let go of Tom. 'Thank you.'

'You'd do as much for me.'

She catches her eye and is reassured to receive an almost imperceptible nod. Vicky is going to be sensible.

'Bye,' she says, but they are not listening.

She turns in the doorway to watch them and something

51

deep inside her opens and closes, startling her in its intensity. She recognizes that feeling of wanting to belong, to be known. She hasn't felt like this since Emily Seagrave's christening. But now she feels an itch niggling at her. Vicky's actions have triggered this, along with feelings of tightness and frustration. She thought the friendship was enough to assuage the emptiness, that she had what she needed, but it wasn't. It won't ever be now.

She pulls her jacket over her head, runs to Vicky's car and gets in, turning to glance at the hospital. Walls of glass reflect grey back at her.

She cares about Tom. She hurts for him. Vicky is so careless of other people's feelings. If she places so little value on her husband, then she doesn't deserve him. Amber has always fancied him but she's never taken it seriously. They have an undeniable connection, but she wouldn't go there. She's not like that.

It's only pheromones, she tells herself as she shoves the key into the ignition. Not love. Love is what Robert gives her; it's a solid, thick-walled thing that keeps the bad side of her out. And love is Sophie.

She puts Tom Seagrave out of her mind and thinks about Browning Street instead. She saw how much Vicky loved it, could sense her imagination painting the walls and polishing the floors, because she has done the same. That beautiful old house, proudly wearing its neglect like an aristocrat fallen on hard times, could change her life.

Could she? After what's happened, yes. The thought is thrilling but she packs it away. She needs to sleep on it.

March 1992

'YOU MUST BE KATYA.'

She had lost count of how many people had said that same thing to her in the last week. It was beginning to annoy her. Of course she was Katya. Who else could she be?

'My name is Maggie Parrish and I'm from Lambeth Children's Services.' She left a long enough gap for her to fill and then added, 'How old are you, Katya?'

This one was young, much younger than the social worker who used to come when Linda was still alive. She was tall; big without being fat exactly. Katya's mind said, *generous*, when she looked at her proportions. Big boobs. Big hips. Big eyes.

'Ten.'

'Ten! Well, I have a daughter your age.'

'What's her name?'

There was a slight, almost imperceptible hesitation. 'Emily.' Maggie paused again. 'I'm so very sorry about your mum, Katya. Would you like to tell me something about her?'

Katya found herself quickly falling for this stranger. She felt a desire to please her, to be pleasing, so she tried, pushing her mind into the maze of memories, hoping to avoid the dangerous ones. It was hard to remember a time before it got bad, but it was there all the same. Her memories were like petals, beautiful but too fragile to hang around for long. She remembered holding her mother's hand. She remembered her mum crouching down to hug her and the scent of her fine blonde hair. She remembered the earrings Linda wore; gold hoops in different sizes. Then that changed and she saw the mess in their flat, the clothes strewn across the floor, the dirty ashtrays and the beds that smelt like school dinners.

She was an orphan now; or as good as one since she had no idea who her dad was and doubted he knew he was her dad. In the books, good things happened to orphans and they often turned out to be special children. Like Annie and Oliver Twist, Cinderella and Snow White. In the stories there was often someone who would see their specialness and help them find what they needed – a fairy godmother or a kind stranger.

'She used to take me to the playground.'

She tried to conjure up an image but failed and she wondered if it ever actually existed. There was somewhere, blown with litter, where she wasn't allowed. Linda said people left dangerous stuff there, like needles and condoms. She kept those things in the flat though, where Katya could easily get at them. So she was a hypocrite too.

'Good. That's good. Was it in a park?'

'Yes.' She stared at Maggie's boots. They were black with laces; like the ones Victorian women wore.

They struggled for a few more minutes, Katya coming up with memories that were a mixture of truth and fable, things she thought normal families did, things she'd seen on television, when they had one. It broke when one of the boyfriends tipped his beer down the back. Smoke had come out of it. Then Maggie told her about a couple she knew; good people who fostered children short-term. The Bryants. Luke and Sally.

'How long do I have to stay with them?'

'Not long. A month or so. While I look for a permanent placement.'

'Do they have a telly?'

'Yes. That'll be nice, won't it?'

She wished her mother could have been more like Maggie Parrish. Even a little bit. Self-pity and a sense that she had been unfairly used brought the threat of tears. Maggie hugged her. It was unexpected and overwhelming. Katya tensed at first and then sank into her embrace.

'It'll be all right, Katya. I know that someone will want to adopt you very soon.'

Katya gazed at her, wide-eyed and hopeful. 'Who?'

Maggie smiled and stroked her hair. 'Just someone. You are a very special little girl.'

But Katya didn't hear the last bit. Her mind had already rushed off down a new avenue. If Maggie adopted her she could be Emily's sister and live with them for ever. She would be Katya Parrish. She could see

Emily in her mind's eye. Running across the playground, ponytail flying, turning to laugh and beckon at her. They would be best friends. Katya had never had a best friend because she had never spent enough days in a row at school to get one.

'I'll get things organized soon,' Maggie said. 'But first let's see how you get on with the Bryants.'

The feeling she was left with, the imprint of Maggie's body against hers, was a magic spell that couldn't be broken. Emily. She whispered the name to herself. There was something about it that felt right. She knew that she and Emily were meant to meet one day. That they would be friends.

7

Tuesday, 5 January 2010

WE ARE HOME. IN MY ABSENCE, TOM HAS DONE A temporary job on the French windows. Quite a feat for him. He's nailed a piece of hardboard over the broken window and screwed a strip of two-by-one across the bottom panels to keep them closed. Otherwise he's been careful to leave everything as it is because we've been told to wait for the forensics team. I have no idea where he found the wood, but he probably asked either our next-door neighbour or Jamie Boxer. Either way, the news is spreading.

The kitchen is untidy. There's a frying pan and a saucepan in the washing up bowl, the dishwasher is open, the racks pulled out. There are toys on the floor, which hasn't been swept. My eyes are drawn to a baked bean lying underneath the chair where Polly normally sits. None of this matters.

Tom doesn't say anything but I know how he's feeling. This house was our sanctuary and now it's been desecrated and it doesn't matter what we do, the stain will not rub off. I wish the girls were here to distract us.

'Tea?' he asks and I nod, grateful to him for being one step ahead of me.

I move into the front room and collapse on to the sofa, curling up and cradling my head in my arms. I only slept a couple of hours last night, and that fitfully. I kept having nightmares about the social worker, with her clipboard and lanyard, informing me that she had a duty to share any concerns she might have with the relevant authorities and a right to remove Josh from my charge if she considered he was in danger.

Because this is how it works. Amber is right. This is what happens when a baby's injuries cannot be explained satisfactorily. The woman was only doing her job. Her questions were detailed and intrusive but I played compliant and humble, aware of Amber sitting nearby, reading a magazine, listening to my lies.

The image changes to an X-ray of white bone against a milky fog of flesh and muscle, and I experience that shock of guilt and disbelief all over again. My son's bones are so small and so fragile. There's a fine line across the base of the humerus close to the elbow.

The radiologist told me he'd seen a lot worse. It was a common enough fracture in children and would mend quickly. He told me not to worry. That there was no great harm done.

But there was. How could I have left him? How could I have been so cruel and thoughtless and downright negligent? My breath was audible and the radiologist's smile slipped. He steered me towards a chair and pressed me into it then fetched a plastic cup of water from the dispenser. I took it gratefully.

'He won't remember a thing, Mrs Seagrave,' he says. 'Please don't blame yourself.'

'Vicky? Are you awake? The police are here.'

A cup of tea sits on the coffee table, undrunk and cold. I must have been asleep for at least an hour.

DS Grayling is in his late thirties; black with a shaved head and craggy bone structure; handsome in a rugged outdoorsy way. I wonder if he has a wife and children and glance at his left hand, hoping he does because then he'll understand the stresses that come with it. He isn't wearing a ring, but Tom doesn't wear one either. He smiles at me and pulls out his notebook.

'Can we start from before you took the children to school yesterday morning?'

I have no problem recollecting that. Monday morning is imprinted vividly on my mind. I can feel my heavy eyes, my sluggish body, and I can hear the radio jabbering and Josh crying, Emily demanding biscuits and Polly taking her sweet time over everything. Lack of sleep is like a disease that makes your bones, joints and muscles ache; it tears down your defences and warps your judgement. I remember the feeling of walking out into the rain without Josh, as illicit as the kiss of a lover. And I remember the fear that came over me when I heard the baby in the house next door crying. Does Grayling know what it's like? Does he have a tired wife and a wakeful baby? Does he know the difference between that sort of tiredness, where something has sucked the energy from your body and then demanded more, and the tiredness that comes after doing a full day's work?

'I went to a viewing at a house round the corner. While I was there, Amber, my friend who works for the estate agent, had a call to say she had a cancellation. So she came back here with me.'

Grayling stops writing and looks up and I meet warm brown eyes. Disconcerted, I shift my gaze to the bridge of his nose.

'Wouldn't they have expected her to go back to the office?'

'Ordinarily, yes, but I was upset about something and she had a gap between viewings, so she cleared it with her boss.'

'What were you upset about?'

I wait, chewing my lip. Tom gives my hand a squeeze.

'I'm finding it hard with the baby. I'm not sleeping and it's affecting me. I needed to talk to someone. I don't like moaning about it to Tom when he's working so hard.'

Grayling nods as if he understands. 'What happened when you arrived back here?'

'Well, Josh had fallen asleep in his pram, so I took him upstairs and put him in his cot. He usually has a nap in the morning. Then I came back downstairs and made coffee.'

'You didn't notice the broken French windows?'

'No. I had no reason to go into the sitting room. We went straight to the kitchen. I put the coffee on. Then we heard Josh crying and I went upstairs to see what was wrong.' I frown, pretending to replay the scene in my head, and tell him the story I've agreed with Amber, finishing at the moment Josh slips from my grasp.

'Did either of you speak?'

'He didn't. At least, I don't think he did. I don't really remember. It all happened so fast and I was in shock. I know that I begged him not to hurt the baby. Amber heard him and came out of the kitchen in time to see him rush out into the street. I was in a terrible state so she drove us to A & E and called Tom and the police from the hospital.'

'It must have been exceptionally traumatic for you.'

'It was horrible. I see that man every time I close my eyes.'

His eyes sharpen. 'You saw his face?'

'Yes. No. I mean, not clearly. I saw a man holding Josh in the dark.'

The policeman's smile is benign but behind it I sense scepticism. Tom must do as well, because he turns to me and releases my hand.

'I only ask because there was a similar burglary in Graves Avenue two months ago.'

'Yes, I heard about that.'

'You and Amber were totally unaware this man was in the house?'

'Yes.'

'Even though you went upstairs and put Josh to bed? Didn't you notice the mess in your bedroom?'

'No.'

'What do you think happened?' the policeman asks.

'I think he was hoping to find jewellery and when Josh started to cry he panicked and went upstairs to try and quieten him down.' This, at least, was probably true.

The flicker of a frown crosses the policeman's face and then it's gone. He transcribes my words. He thinks it's far-fetched, I know he does.

'Do you think you would recognize him, Mrs Seagrave?'

'I don't know. As I said, it was dark.'

'Was there anything about him that you do remember?'

'He wasn't particularly tall. I don't think he was young. Possibly late thirties.'

'Black or white?'

'White.'

'When he came out of the shadows, when he was close to you and the door, presumably the light from the landing fell on his face?'

'I was only looking at Josh. I didn't take in his face. He was pretty ordinary.'

'Ordinary in what way?'

Exhausted, I lean forward and rub the space between my eyes. 'I don't understand.'

'Well, what do you call ordinary? Am I ordinary, for instance?'

He looks directly at me and I obediently study his face. His eyes are large and frank, his nose slightly bulbous at the tip, his mouth generous.

'No one is ordinary when you look at them properly,' I answer, groping for a way out. 'Most people are ordinary when you only catch a glimpse of them.'

'I don't know whether to be flattered or insulted,' he says, joking. He is trying, I suspect, to set a neurotic woman at her ease, but it feels somehow inappropriate, as if he's overstepped the mark.

'What I mean is, I didn't get a chance to really look at him.'

'Well, perhaps Mrs Collins will be able to help us there.'

'Possibly, but unless he turned round she would only have seen his back.'

'Shame. Still, she might remember something.'

'I hope so.'

Tom's long legs are twitching and he's fidgeting with a pen on the table in front of him, turning it over and over between his fingers. He puts it down then picks it up again and clicks the ballpoint in and out. The last time I remember my husband this nervous we were sitting in the bathroom of his shared flat waiting for the result of my pregnancy test.

'I don't understand why he didn't slip out while you and Amber were talking in the kitchen,' he said. 'He must have heard you come in. He must have heard you putting Josh to bed. He had time to get away.'

'I don't know. I wasn't inside his head. For some reason he didn't. Maybe he didn't get what he wanted. Maybe he was scared and panicked.'

'Jesus. If I was a burglar, the last thing I'd do is go anywhere near someone's baby.'

Grayling follows this exchange, his eyes moving between us as if he's watching a tennis match. Then they attach themselves to mine and rest there. 'Mrs Seagrave, you probably remember more than you think. I'd like to try an E-FIT. See if we can piece together a picture from your memories. Say by the end of the week.'

'But what about Josh—'

'We can sort that,' Tom says. 'Talk to Magda.' He stops abruptly and then adds, 'Doesn't she come on Mondays? Wasn't she here?'

'She was ill.' I find the text on my phone and hand it to Tom.

He cracks a faint smile when he reads it. 'We can get her to look after him while you and Amber go. Between the two of you, you might be able to give them something to go on. The sooner they catch this guy, the better.'

Grayling holds up his hand to stop us. 'There's no need for any of that. I'll send someone to you.'

8

Monday, 11 January 2010

'YOU'RE A STAR. THANKS SO MUCH.' I USHER AMBER IN as Sophie, Rose Forsyth and my girls shuffle past us into the hall. Jenny Forsyth hovers behind Amber, holding her pram. She's relatively new to the area and hasn't been round before. She seems nice. Intelligent and sensible.

'Have you been out at all today?' Amber asks as they divest themselves of their coats and scarves and drape them over the banister.

'No. I couldn't face it.'

'I don't blame you,' Jenny says. 'After your horrible experience. What a nightmare.'

I look from her to Amber. 'Are people talking about it?'

Jenny nods. 'It's a hot topic in the playground.'

'This woman I showed a house to this morning,' Amber says. 'She'd heard about it through a friend and wanted to know if the area was safe.'

'Oh God. How did it get around so quickly?'

'I told a couple of people. It had to come out eventually

and I thought it might be easier for you this way. They'll be bored of the subject by the end of the week. And you should come to school, Vicky. Let them ask questions.'

'I came this morning,' I say defensively.

'You must think I'm really nosy,' Jenny says, and I sense the interruption is diplomatic. 'But I'd love to see what you've done to this place. We're trying to make decisions about our house.'

The hint of flattery lightens my mood and I help her manoeuvre Spike's bulky pram past Josh's. The girls, in the meantime, charge upstairs. Magda has been today so the house is positively gleaming.

'Wow,' Jenny says, following me into the kitchen. 'Darling, this place is amazing. Did you design it?'

'I drew it on the back of an envelope and managed the build, but we used an architect for the technical drawings.'

'Don't undersell yourself,' Amber says, turning to grin at Jenny. 'Vicky is a brilliant painter and decorator.'

She fills the kettle and switches it on. It's a curious thing to do. It's as if she's telling Jenny something; establishing a pecking order. I transfer Josh to his high chair and Jenny sits down with a gentle sigh with Spike on her knee and tightens the elastic at the base of her thick brown ponytail. I take three mugs out of the dishwasher and nudge Amber out of the way. She sits down.

'At the moment all we do is pay for the renovations,' Jenny says. 'Whenever I mention anything else, like holidays, for instance, Simon just says, "That'll be your granite worktop, then", or something equally irritating.'

I glance at Amber. She must hate listening to other

66

people bang on about their houses. But she doesn't appear to have noticed. Today's paper is still where Tom left it, in the middle of the table, and she's been turning the pages idly. I haven't had a chance to read it because Josh has been impossible to put down all day. Not his fault, I remind myself. It's mine.

'Awful, isn't it,' she says.

'What's happened?' I try to read the headline upside down and she swivels it towards me.

'Some poor woman left her two-year-old in the car for five minutes while she popped into her local shop for a pint of milk and a passer-by reported her. They took the child away.'

I reach for the paper and scan the article. There are three pictures; the largest is of a fraught-looking couple, desperation clear in their eyes. Overlapping that is an inset of a smiling toddler clutching a teddy bear, and a picture of the three of them snuggled up on their sofa. They look so ordinary and yet their lives have been picked up, shaken and dropped. The couple have been to court, which is why the case has finally hit the news, and have won the right to have their child back. But it's taken a year. A year. My God. My hands are shaking as I fold the paper and put it down.

Beside me Josh starts to whinge. I give him my keys and he flings them on the floor. Amber reaches over with a teaspoon and taps him on the nose, making him giggle.

'It's unbelievable,' she says. 'Big Brother is watching.'

Jenny removes her glasses, pulls the corner of her shirt out from under her jumper, uses it to clean them and puts them back on. 'I suppose social services would argue that it's evidence of a behaviour pattern in the family.'

'She was in a hurry,' Amber exclaims. 'God. I've parked on Tennyson Street and nipped into the Spar for a can of baked beans without taking Sophie with me. I lock the car, obviously, and always park where I can see her. We've all done that, surely?'

I wonder if she realizes how awkward this is for me. I watch her for a moment and feel uncertain. Have things changed between us or not? I know I've disappointed her, I've disappointed myself, but I thought we were strong enough to get over that.

'I agree,' Jenny says. 'But, speaking as a lawyer, it's a hard one to call. There are people who leave their children on their own for much longer than that poor woman did, and I'm talking across society, not one section. You'd be surprised. This case is extreme though, but at least it highlights what can happen. Parents find themselves caught in a Kafkaesque situation. A case like this might make someone else think again. To be honest,' she adds, 'I can't understand any woman who would leave her child alone. In my experience it usually means there's something else wrong in their situation. Either domestic abuse or a failing relationship. Either way, you're talking about unhappy women who are so completely engrossed in their own problems they lose sight of what's really important – their children.'

Amber sends me a quick, amused look over the rim of her mug. 'Right, well, don't hold back.'

Jenny laughs. 'Sorry. I didn't mean to start lecturing.'

'In fairness,' Amber says, 'sometimes there's no choice.

And anyway, is it really any worse than taking the baby monitor next door so you can get pissed with the neighbours? There are degrees . . .'

I remember something. I'm waking up in a pool of sweat, opening my curtains and pressing my head against the cold glass, feeling the condensation run on to my cheeks. I call for my mother but my throat is so sore it comes out as a croak. When she doesn't appear, I go into her bedroom but her bed is empty, although it has been slept in. The flat we lived in back then was tiny, consisting of two bedrooms, a small kitchen and a sitting room. There was nowhere she could have hidden.

I hear myself telling Amber and Jenny about this before I'd even made up my mind to say anything.

'Really?' Amber says.

I flush. 'Yes. But I wasn't a baby. I was ten.'

I can date it precisely. It was the week before we moved in with my grandparents.

'Ahh. Still, that's rotten,' Jenny says. 'Where did she go?'

'I don't know. I waited for her in the sitting room but when I heard her car pull up I went back to bed. She was crying when she came in.'

I pull at my ear, remembering how it felt, standing inside my door, opening it a crack. When you're a child a parent in tears is the worst thing in the world. It's far worse than their anger, worse even than their disappointment. I remember the ball of panic in my stomach, the confusion, the feeling that I had stepped on to quicksand. I wanted to comfort her but I thought she would be embarrassed if she knew I'd heard.

'I thought you had lodgers,' Amber says.

I'm confused by her tone. It sounded like a challenge.

'Not then. That was when we still lived in Streatham. It was right before we moved, actually.'

Amber knows my background already but I find myself telling Jenny about my upbringing, about the chaotic house by the sea and the guests.

'So how did you and Amber meet?' Jenny asks.

'At NCT,' Amber says. 'We were the youngest women there. Clueless.'

I listen to her tell the story with a smile on my face. Back then I didn't even know what NCT stood for. The reality of becoming a mother, what it really meant, hadn't penetrated as deeply as it perhaps should have done, considering I was six months in. I was still partying with my non-pregnant friends, full of energy and plans that didn't include babies. I knew not to drink alcohol or eat unpasteurized cheese, but even those things didn't come close to preparing me mentally. It wasn't that I was actively refusing to accept the situation – there wasn't a situation. Even the kicks felt surreal.

I remember standing outside a converted school in Brixton staring at the labels beside the buttons and wrinkling my brow. Someone came out, so I went in. There was no clue to where the class was, just a flight of concrete stairs. After two aborted attempts that had me backing apologetically out of a small advertising agency and an accountancy firm, I pushed open a door and found a group of women seated in a semicircle, gossiping amongst themselves while a midwife unpacked a wheelie suitcase. Several of them turned as I came in, and one of them was Amber. She smiled, and it was such a beautiful smile, like a blast of light and colour and warmth. Everything seemed better, heightened and more real. I remember she was wearing a stripy top, French style, the stripes curving over her neat bump; black leggings and trainers. Her hair was blonde, the dirty kind, and shaggy. I sat next to her.

I found out that Amber was half German – her father left when she was a baby, went back to Frankfurt to visit his family and never returned – and that her mother, an alcoholic, died when she was seventeen. She told me months later that she had never forgiven herself for not getting home in time to raise the alarm. I can only imagine what it must be like to carry that burden.

I smile and pick up the story. I tell Jenny about the irritating woman who kept interrupting the midwife with her opinions on natural labour, about struggling to contain our mirth when someone silently broke wind.

'And look at us now,' Amber says. 'Still kindred spirits.'

I don't tell Jenny how desperate I was not to lose sight of Amber, how worried I was that she wouldn't come back the following week, how I had racked my brains over how to ensure this without coming across as needy. I don't tell her because I've never told Amber. I had old school friends down in Sussex and I had my university friends who had started careers in London, but they couldn't get their heads around what was happening to me. In the end though I needn't have worried because

71

when we wandered out into the sunshine, it was Amber who suggested we go for a coffee.

We found a table at the back of Costa. Amber had a cappuccino and I had a hot chocolate. I used a spoon to eat the cream off the top and the sugar hit made my baby kick.

'Do you worry about this at all?' she asked.

I looked round. 'What? Loitering in coffee shops?'

'No,' she laughed. 'That you're going to be a good mother.'

I stirred my drink, watching the creamy swirls dissipate into the chocolate. 'I don't really think about that side of it. I suppose I sort of assume it'll happen and I'll do what I'm meant to do. Why? Are you worried?'

'No,' she said. 'I'm fine.'

'My mum was a disaster, but I'm all right. Not too traumatized by the experience. Children are very resilient.'

'Are they?'

I paused, unsure again. 'Yes. Well up to a point, obviously.'

She sat back and placed her hands on her bump, slim fingers splayed. Her engagement ring was a square-cut sapphire surrounded by diamonds. 'How long have you been married?'

'A month. I looked like a white van.'

I pulled out my phone and showed her the photograph of me and Tom outside the register office, beaming with happiness, my voluminous white dress flapping in the January wind.

'You do not look like a van,' Amber said, taking the phone from me. 'You look gorgeous.' She flicked through the pictures.

'Who's that?'

'That's Mum.'

'Your mum? That's your mum?'

'Yes.' I wasn't surprised by her reaction. I got it all the time.

'She looks too young.'

'She was only seventeen when she had me. She's thirty-nine now and totally underwhelmed by the idea of becoming a grandmother.'

Amber hung on to my phone, gazing at the picture. Then she handed it back with a grin. 'You will come next week, won't you?'

Jenny gets up to leave soon after that and I feel guilty. I should have explained that Mum is fiercely independent, kind, loving and the best of neighbours. When we moved down to Bognor, into the house on Waterloo Square that she had bought on impulse at auction, there was barely anything there; no heating, no electricity and no water, but by the end of the first day the house was buzzing, candles lit, buckets filled from neighbours' taps, broken windows blocked with plywood and resident pigeons and seagulls dispatched. And that was because of her personality; because, for all her moments of bad judgement, she has a genuine and generous interest in other people. She gives more than she gets. I wish I had got that across.

Amber waits in the kitchen with Josh while Vicky shows Jenny out. She could have left at the same time, probably should have, but two things made her hang around. One was that she liked to be seen by other friends as being completely at home in the Seagraves' house. She's

73

aware that this is pathetic, but it doesn't stop her from needing that feeling of being one of them. The other reason is that she sensed Vicky's puzzled uncertainty over the article and is already wondering if she went too far, if it wouldn't have been better to have changed the subject rather than allow Vicky to suspect she was needling her or deliberately trying to make her feel guilty. The last thing she wants is to drive a rift between them.

She hears Jenny hoot with laughter. They're still talking on the doorstep. Jenny is chatty and friendly, and sometimes difficult to dislodge. Amber finds it hard to imagine her in her other guise as a family lawyer. She's too big and jolly.

Josh plays with her fingers with his good hand, laughing as Amber waggles them up and down. He gets overexcited and forgets about his arm, knocking it against the side of the table. His eyes widen with surprise and then his face crumples, reddening in an instant.

'Little man,' Amber coos.

She pulls him out of his high chair before he starts wailing, not wanting his mother to come running just yet, enjoying having him to herself.

'There there.' She kisses it better then blows a raspberry on his cheek and licks the residual saltiness from her lips.

She moves across the room and picks up a photograph of Tom, in a silver frame. He's grinning at the camera, the wind in his hair, the sea behind him, his eyes crinkled. She feels a strange tightness in her chest and sets it down quickly, disconcerted.

'Look, Joshie,' she says, carrying him across to the

glass doors and pointing at the neighbour's elegant, blue-eyed Siamese cat. 'Isn't he posh?'

Josh's lower lip sticks out and his chin wobbles but she murmurs words of reassurance and strokes his soft head. He nuzzles into her neck.

She and Robert had planned to have more than one child, but six years after Sophie it still hasn't happened. Mostly she's OK with that but just sometimes she wishes things were different. When Vicky fell pregnant for the third time Amber had felt crushed. It was somehow worse that the pregnancy was unplanned and as much a shock to Vicky as it was to her. She had helped her friend through a bad patch then, so was it any wonder that she felt a certain amount of ownership towards Josh?

Vicky goes on about her so-called deprived childhood but she has no idea what she's talking about. If a child has a loving mother she doesn't need material possessions. Which is why Amber is so horrified by her behaviour. Mothers don't do that.

She adores this baby, feels an affinity with him. Like her he has moments of intense anger and emotion, like her he always wants more than he gets; and there is something else about him, some inner insecurity that Amber recognizes because it's in her too. It's as if he instinctively worries that life is precarious, that his next meal might not come, that his mother might go through a door and not come back. Which makes her wonder . . .

Vicky admitted to leaving him once or twice before; but what if it was more than that? What if she made a habit of it?

* * *

75

When I come back in, Amber is sitting on the kitchen floor with Josh. She's playing This Little Piggy with his toes and for the first time since the accident he is really laughing, his cheeks bunched up and pink, his eyes sparkling. Amber lies on her back and props him on her tummy. She's very relaxed, very natural with him. Her hair is fanned out over the stone, her skin pale in the light from the windows. Her arms gently pump him up and down. He waggles his feet and shrieks with delight.

'Why don't you and Tom come for supper on Saturday?' she says, smiling up at me. 'I'll see who else is around.'

'That's so nice of you, but do you mind if I say no? I don't think I can face the world yet.'

'Just me and Robert then. You need to get out. It's all a bit tense around here.'

'I don't know, Amber.'

'Saturday week then,' she presses. I agree, reluctantly.

'Good,' she says, as if that was that.

'I can't bear lying to everyone, Amber. This is awful.'

'I know. I hate it too. But it's the right thing to do.'

'If you're sure?'

'Of course I am. Anyway, the truth is more implausible than the lie. Women like you don't leave their babies alone while they go and look round houses.'

'Women like me?'

'You know what I mean. Yummy mummies.'

'Thanks a bunch.'

'Vicky,' she says. 'You do see, don't you? This will blow over a lot quicker if you don't say anything.'

'All right,' I mutter.

Later I wonder if she's right or if she's overreacting. Surely the authorities wouldn't take him away. I try to examine it from their point of view and, yes, I confess with a sick feeling, if I was teaching and discovered one of my parents was doing what I'd done, I would report them and I would expect Child Protection to act.

Can I trust Amber? The answer should be an unequivocal *Yes*, but there's something I can't put my finger on. Then I remember.

Women like you.

When she said that it created a distinction between us that had never existed before. We had always been partners in crime; sharing jokes, attitudes, disappointments and triumphs. There's a message lurking behind those three words, even if Amber is unaware of it.

She could destroy me.

But that doesn't make sense. Why on earth would she want to do that?

March 1992

THE HOUSE MAGGIE TOOK HER TO THE FOLLOWING
Monday turned out to be a bungalow. It squatted halfway
down a wide, tree-lined avenue on the border of Streatham
and Croydon. With its two bay windows sitting either side
of a bright-red door it reminded Katya of a fat-cheeked,
sleepy-eyed face, the half-nets only adding to the impression. White-painted lions crouched on the gateposts
guarding the stone path that divided a neatly trimmed
lawn with flower beds. The roses had been pruned severely
and new shoots pointed enthusiastically towards the light.
The place where Katya had lived before had a yard but
no one really played out there. It was for the bins.

The street was called Hillside Way and the room that
Katya was to have was in the front on the other side of
the corridor from a lounge and divided from the bathroom by stairs that led up to Sally and Luke's loft
bedroom and bathroom. At the back, the kitchen had a
conservatory that ran across the width of the house and
out into the garden. A pinewood table sat in the glazed

area and on the other side a beige sofa, glass-and-steel coffee table and widescreen television took up most of the space. Outside, because the road was on a steep hill and the houses behind were much lower and far away, there was a dramatic view over south London.

Sally Bryant was a stick insect, petite and shockingly thin with narrow hands and feet. Her hair was short and spiky and bleached almost white and she reminded Katya of a sprite or a pixie; like she could sprout wings. Her husband was extremely handsome; his face just how Katya imagined a fairy-tale prince's should be. Dark-brown hair swept back, a square jaw and thin lips. She stared at him until he winked at her.

Maggie stayed for a cup of tea and a chat while Katya watched *Rugrats* and only half listened to the adults. When Maggie came over to say goodbye, Katya dragged her eyes away from the screen.

She dropped her voice. 'Do they know about my mum?'

'They know everything about you, Katya. But they aren't going to judge you or Linda. They love children and they understand that sometimes life can be tough. Promise me you'll be good and go to school every day.'

Katya nodded. Her eyes filled with tears but she forced them back. Maggie saw and bent to her level. She took her small hands and held them in hers. 'You're going to be OK. Now smile.'

Katya smiled but it felt like she was stretching her mouth into position.

'Good girl. I have to go, or I'll be late picking Emily up, but I'll call tomorrow to see how you're getting on.'

* * *

79

Luke Bryant was tall and stood as straight as a soldier. Sally had already told her he used to be in the army, which was why she thought of it. He wasn't easy company like his wife and had a habit of talking at Katya, like a teacher, rather than treating her as a person, the way Sally did.

Before he left for work Luke kissed Sally on the lips. Katya glanced down, discomforted, and stared at her plate.

'Someone's looking perkier this morning.' He ruffled her hair.

'She slept well,' Sally said. 'Didn't you, Katya?'

Her mouth was full of toast so she couldn't answer.

'Still feeling a bit shy, are you?' Luke said. 'Well, you'll get used to us.' He gave her shoulder a quick squeeze and the pressure of his fingertips remained long afterwards, like little bruises. She was the sixth child they had fostered over the years.

She wanted to go home but home didn't exist any more. There might even be new people living there. She hoped someone had cleaned up the mess. At the thought of that she saw her mother again, lying curled round the syringe on the floor beside her bed, the lavender-coloured sheet pulled askew. She could hear the sounds she was making, the uneven rasp of her breath, the gurgle of vomit in the back of her throat. Katya jerked herself free of the images and got down from the table. She asked if she could go and clean her teeth, and Luke quirked his eyebrows at her polite formality.

That evening she unpacked and put her clothes in the chest of drawers, folding them neatly. She took her battered copy of *The Blue Fairy Book* and got into bed. It was the only possession apart from her clothes and toothbrush that she had brought with her from the flat.

She read *Snow-White and Rose-Red* before she went to sleep. It was her favourite now because it reminded her of her and Emily Parrish. *The two children loved each other so dearly that they always walked about hand in hand whenever they went out together, and when Snow-White said, 'We will never desert each other,' Rose-Red answered, 'No, not as long as we live.'* That was what it must be like to have a sister or a best friend, and that was what Katya wanted more than anything in the whole world. She felt that she knew Emily, even though they had never met. It was a very strong feeling, deep down inside her, as strong as hate and love, and it was what made her put up with all the horrible things she had to put up with: the knowledge that one day they would meet and they would be like two halves of a circle fitting together. It would be like a fairy tale.

9

Wednesday, 13 January 2010

GRAYLING SHAKES MY HAND AND GRUMBLES PLEASANTLY about the traffic. I make tea while he sets up his laptop on the kitchen table, running the wire across the floor like Tom does. He pulls a chair round so that we can sit next to each other.

'Lovely garden,' he says, looking over the top of his screen.

'Do you like gardening?'

'I love it. It's how I wind down after a week of thwarting criminal masterminds.'

He's funny. 'What's your success rate?'

'Oh, about ninety-three per cent.'

That silences me. I listen to his fingers tapping the keyboard.

'Do you usually do this?' I sound nervous even to myself; I only hope I don't sound guilty as well.

'Sometimes. Depends how busy I am.' He picks up his mug and puts it down again. 'This isn't something you pass or fail, Mrs Seagrave. I want you to be relaxed; try and remember what you saw, what kind of impression he gave you. Have you remembered anything since we last spoke?'

'Not really. Bits and pieces.'

On the screen are nine boxes, each containing a basic face shape. I don't have much imagination and the thought of conjuring someone up out of thin air is daunting. In my head I scroll through people I've met over the course of my life; old boyfriends of mum's, teachers from school and professors from university. I want someone they would never think to look for. My hand goes to my face but I bring it down to my lap and pin it between my thighs.

'That one,' I say as Grayling clicks through the images.

A face pops into my head, very different from the man who broke into my house, but it's one I can describe. I'm not even sure why I remember him, except that my mind connects him to unpleasantness and to that chaotic move. Maybe he was one of Mum's more fleeting liaisons.

Grayling guides me through a dizzying range of possibilities: noses, mouth, eyes, ears, chin and hair. 'How're we doing?'

'Hair a little thicker,' I say. 'And the mouth should be thinner, nose longer.'

'I'm impressed,' Grayling says, making the adjustments. 'How's he looking?'

I narrow my eyes. I remember his insinuating smile and the moment when his veneer slipped. I chew at my bottom lip, bringing back that feeling of second-hand fear, knowing I wasn't the one in trouble, that I was safe; that my mother would turn the car round and drive us home.

'I don't know,' I say, shaking my head. 'I can't remember.'

Grayling sits back and surveys his handiwork. 'Well, it's something, I suppose.'

He gets up and wanders over to the glass doors, stretching his arms behind his head. He's disappointed in me. He turns and catches me watching him.

'So, what happens next?' I ask.

'I'll put him on the system and we'll see if it jogs anyone's memory. With the baby angle, it might even be a good fit for *Crimewatch* and with a picture as detailed as that, I'll be extremely surprised if no one recognizes him.'

I imagine Grayling in his car, key poised in the ignition, scratching his head in confusion, like you do when you come out of the cinema after seeing an overcomplicated thriller in which plot holes abound. I know he'll think about what I've said and what I've shown him. He's trained to know when people are lying or hiding something, or merely being economical with the truth. It can't be as simple as me touching my ear or my lips. Everyone knows about that. There must be other things, more subtle signals.

'I hope so.'

He looks at me for a long moment and then takes his mug to the sink and starts to wash it out.

'You don't need to do that.'

'The wife has me well trained.'

My doorbell rings. I hover uncertainly, extremely

averse to anyone knowing who I have with me, but then I see how ridiculous that is and go and answer it. It's Amber.

'Do you have time for a coffee?' she asks, and then grimaces when Grayling comes out of the kitchen into the hall. 'Oops. Sorry, Vicky. I didn't know you had a visitor. I'll come back later.'

'I'm on my way out,' he says. 'Don't mind me.'

She cocks her head so that she can see him more clearly. 'Oh, DS Grayling. I thought it was you.'

He reaches past me and shakes her hand, and she moves aside to let him out.

He hesitates. 'Although, while I'm here, would it be a lot of trouble to ask you to have a look at the E-FIT Vicky's done? I know you only had a back view, but it might jog a memory.'

'Of course I will. Happy to help.'

Her tone is verging on flirtatious and I raise my eyebrows, inclined to giggle. As we all traipse back to the kitchen I nudge her hard.

'Well, he's very attractive,' she mutters into my ear as Grayling sets the laptop up beside my computer.

He leans over the chair, resting one hand on the table, one covering the mouse. The screen fills, and there he is. Amber, standing beside me, says nothing.

'Does it mean anything to you?' Grayling asks.

'No.' She walks away, opens a cupboard, gets down a glass and runs the tap. 'Sorry. I only saw a glimpse of his profile. Has there been any progress?'

He shrugs. 'Not really. We didn't find any prints that we couldn't rule out. We're hoping the E-FIT will help. You'd have thought somebody would have seen something. He needed to climb over the side gate into the garden, for a start.'

'People tend to live in their kitchens these days,' I say. 'Particularly round here. Everyone's got their extensions. Front rooms are mainly used in the evenings.'

'Is that so?'

I wonder if I've offended him. Maybe he thinks I'm spoiled and privileged.

I thought he was about to leave but he gestures at the kitchen table and pulls out a chair. We both sit down. Amber flicks her hair away from her face and leans back, crossing her legs. Grayling waits for what seems a very long time, watching our faces. Eventually he speaks.

'Is there anything you ladies would like to tell me? Off the record.'

'Like what?' Amber asks. She rests her elbows on the table and cradles her chin in her hands. 'We've told you everything.'

His expression is benign. 'Well, that's just it, Mrs Collins. I don't think you have.'

I want to tell him. I want to pile my troubles on to his broad shoulders, and Amber knows I do because she presses the side of her foot against mine.

'I don't know what you mean.' I return the pressure to let her know I get it. 'It's quite simple . . .'

'Simple enough for me? Come now, Mrs Seagrave, I'm not a fool. I know when someone's not telling me the whole truth.'

'But we're not lying,' Amber says.

'Did I say that?' He pauses for long enough to make

me feel like a schoolgirl sent to see the headmistress. 'If there's anything else you'd like to share with me, now's the time.'

'There isn't,' I say firmly. 'We've told you everything we know. I hope the E-FIT helps.'

I stand up and he follows suit, wedging the laptop case under his arm and fishing his keys out of his pocket. His face is no less friendly; there is no irritation in evidence, no sense of frustration, but I feel like I'm being dangled on the end of a line.

'I'd like to catch this man, Mrs Seagrave. It's frustrating that no one seems to know anything.'

'Isn't that the nature of criminals?'

'Someone always knows something.'

He walks down the steps and turns back and my heart stops. He's thought of something. In whodunnits they always do that. The detective strolls towards the exit, hesitates and gives the witness a friendly smile before saying, *Oh, and one last thing . . .*

'Fabulous magnolia.'

I let out the breath I've been holding. 'Won't last long, sadly.'

'No. Beautiful things often don't.'

I close the door. I don't want to get into an existential conversation with the detective sergeant in charge of my case.

Amber is standing at the end of the garden with her back to the house. I watch her and when she realizes I'm there she swivels round. I come out and join her.

'That was nerve-racking. I thought for one minute we were—'

'That face,' she interrupts. 'The E-FIT.'

'What about it?'

'Do you know who it is?'

I don't know why but the hairs stand up on the back of my neck. 'No. It's just some random person from my childhood. I wouldn't describe someone I actually know.'

'But he is real?'

For some reason the memory of the face is accompanied by a sense of shame, a sense that I've let myself down. Which I suppose I have. 'Does it matter?'

'Not particularly,' she says airily. 'I wanted to check you weren't about to land some poor innocent in the shit.' There's a pink ball in the grass and she manoeuvres it with the toe of her boot.

'Well, I'm not. So what's happening with Browning Street? I want Tom to have a look.'

'There've been a couple of ridiculously low offers which have been turned down, but they're opening gambits. They'll offer more. Have you talked to Tom about it?'

'No, not yet. There hasn't been a good time. I doubt his reaction will be positive, so I'll have to pick my moment carefully.'

The truth is, I know exactly what he'll say and I don't feel like fighting my corner at the moment. An odd gloom has settled over me in the last few days, a cloud that won't lift. It's to do with Josh, of course, and the plaster cast encasing his fractured arm; a bulky and glaringly white reminder of my mistake.

'I wouldn't hang around if you're serious about it. It's only a matter of time.' Amber wanders out over the lawn and turns to look back at my house. I have a feeling she's itching to be asked to sell it.

April 1992

KATYA WAITED IN THE PLAYGROUND, EXPECTATION making her jiggle from foot to foot. Then Maggie waved and she burst into smiles and waved back, her hand dropping when the gates opened and Maggie walked in alone. Perhaps Emily was in the car. There was no reason why she should have come into the school. She shook Mrs Burton's hand and ran to Maggie.

'Well, don't you look smart, Katya.'

Katya looked down at herself. Her gingham dress was brand new and so were her socks. Her shoes were old and getting tight, but they'd been polished and Sally Bryant had promised her new ones soon.

'She's not your mum,' Gabriella Brady said as she trailed past her in the wake of her father and big brother.

Gabriella was the only person at the school who Katya could call a friend, and even then the friendship wasn't exactly something she could count on. Some days Gabriella didn't even speak to her, or if she did, it was to say something mean. Katya hadn't been invited back to her house either, and she wasn't going to invite Gabriella to the Bryants'. Not in a billion years. Gabriella was friendly if she had fallen out with her other friends, which happened often enough for her to need Katya to fall back on, because she was very annoying and bossy, but Katya didn't particularly care about that. She just cared about not looking like a loser.

Katya pulled on Maggie's hand. They left the school and walked down the road, Katya expecting her to stop and get her keys out at every moment.

'Where's your car?' she said at last.

'Over there.'

She glanced to where Maggie was pointing and recognized the red Fiesta. There was no one in it. 'Are we picking Emily up from her school?'

She had already imagined how the afternoon would go. Sitting at the Parrishes' kitchen table and eating cake, talking and giggling while Maggie looked on indulgently. She imagined Emily to be a mini version of her mother, with thick brown hair and big soft eyes. She knew that Emily didn't have a dad either, because Maggie had told her. So they had something important in common.

'Oh, I'm sorry, Katya. You misunderstood. It's just you and me, I'm afraid. Is that all right? I was only able to come and get you today because Emily's at a birthday party. I'm taking you out for tea as a treat.'

Katya kicked at a fallen leaf, her shoulders slumping. She barely registered when Maggie took her hand to cross the road. She only knew that she wasn't going to her house and she wasn't going to meet Emily.

'You're disappointed, aren't you? I'm sorry. But I'll make it up to you one day, promise.'

Katya forced herself to smile. The misunderstanding left her feeling small and ugly.

'What did you do at school today?' Maggie asked.

Katya picked despondently at the icing on her bun. 'Maths and games. Geography.'

'Emily's good at maths. One of the best in the class. I had no idea until parents' evening. It came as a complete surprise when her teacher said she should be in the top stream.'

Katya wanted to say that she was good at maths too, but didn't like to show off. And anyway, she much preferred hearing about Emily, and Maggie was as eager to talk about her.

'She enjoys books as well, of course. She's reading *The Lion, the Witch and the Wardrobe* at the moment. She loves it. I'll lend it to you once she's finished.'

'I only like fairy tales.'

Maggie tilted her head to one side. 'Well, Emily likes those too. But there are other good stories, for when you grow out of them. Now, Katya, there's another reason I brought you here.'

Katya, looking at her face, realized that, whatever it was, that was the real reason. Under the table she crossed her fingers.

'Luke and Sally want to keep you. Isn't that wonderful? I know it's only been a couple of weeks, but they've asked if you can become their permanent foster child. If things work out, they might even adopt you.'

Her heart sank. 'Adopt me?'

It was as if all she was and all she had was nothing. No past, no future. How silly to have thought Maggie might want her. It would do no good to tell her that she was nervous around Luke, that even though he was kind to her something about him made her feel panicky, because she had already tried to explain. The trouble was Luke never shouted. When he was angry his voice stayed calm and reasonable, so that it was always Katya who saw red and slammed doors. She saw the effect he had on other people too; how he made them feel insignificant; made them lose their tempers. It was almost like he was playing games with their minds. There was this bloke two doors down who had three cars and he kept parking one of them outside the bungalow. He didn't do it again after Luke had a go at him. Katya had watched from the lounge window. One of them had been all wound up, gesticulating and swearing, purple in the face, and it hadn't been her foster father.

And then there was nice Luke; the Luke who talked to her and petted her when Sally was out and bought her the cakes and sweets she liked; who liked to watch television with her; who absently played with her hair or took her hand when something was funny.

Maggie had sat her down that one time and explained that Katya's problem was that she wasn't used to living with a man and that she associated men with her mother, in a bad way, but that most men weren't like that. Most men were perfectly ordinary, decent and reliable human beings, and she needed to learn to trust again.

'They've become very fond of you and they care about

what happens to you. They don't want you to have any more upheaval. And you're doing so well at school. What do you think about that?'

She didn't say anything. Maggie leant forward and tapped her hand.

'Katya?'

'You'd be better than Sally.'

Maggie laughed. 'I don't see how. I certainly can't cook as well as she can.'

'I don't care about food!' Katya exploded as the afternoon's disappointments finally became too much for her. 'I could cook for you and Emily. I could do anything.'

'Sweetheart, calm down. I am so sorry, but it isn't possible. I'm your social worker. That means my job is to see that you're well cared for, safe and happy. I'll still come and see you. And Sally has my office number, so you can always call if you need me.'

'It isn't the same.'

'Oh, don't cry. I know it's a lot to take in, but think about it. It's very hard to find a permanent adoptive family for older children and you'd be miserable in a home. You need a family, Katya, and they're offering to give you one.'

She handed her a paper napkin. Katya screwed it up and pressed it to her nose. Her tears ran down between her knuckles. Other customers were watching, but Katya didn't care. She wanted them to see how unhappy she was. Maggie got up and moved her chair round so that she was sitting next to her. She held her until she stopped crying.

'You're so young,' she said. 'Things will get better. You'll see.'

As they left the tea shop she wondered if people assumed she was Maggie's child, and looked up just as Maggie looked down at her. Her heart skipped. She imagined Maggie banging on the Bryants' door at the last moment, shouting, 'I made a mistake! I want her!'

10

Saturday, 23 January 2010

'YOU HAVE NICE TIME,' MAGDA SAYS.

She holds the door open, smiling reassuringly, desperate for us to leave. I know that I can trust her, but that makes no difference to the fear I feel. After what has happened, leaving the children for an evening out is extremely hard. I only agreed because it's Robert and Amber.

'OK, but if Josh cries . . .'

'I go up. Don't worry, Vicky. You go relax.'

'Don't have the TV on too loud, just in case. And keep his door open . . .'

Tom is backing out, wrapping his scarf around his long neck. 'Come on. Leave Magda to it.'

He takes my hand, tucks it into his coat pocket like he used to when we were students and breathes deeply. 'Admit that it's nice being out doing something.'

'I suppose so,' I smile. 'I do feel better now I've put some slap on.'

'You look stunning.'

'And you look very handsome.'

I feel proud walking down the street with him, our fingers entwined. Above us the night is clear and clean, the moon a thin crescent, the few stars bright dots. The crisp freshness of the winter evening stings my cheeks pleasantly.

'I mean it, Vicky. Sometimes I look at you and I feel so lucky.'

'Me too.'

More so than you realize, I add silently. I listen to our footsteps on the pavement, the heels of my shoes tapping the concrete. Then I stop and turn to face Tom, reach up and kiss him on the lips.

He arches his eyebrows. 'What was that for?'

'Nothing. Just felt like it.'

I want to have a light-hearted conversation, but the words I need are out of reach or loaded with an overwhelming desire to explain everything and plead for understanding and forgiveness, and I can't do that because it would mean the end of everything; the end of trust and the end of the life I love. I need him. When he smiled at me just now, I understood that. David North was an aberration. A seven-year itch.

'You're very quiet,' he says. 'What are you thinking about?'

I shrug. 'Nothing important. Can we take a quick detour?'

Tom complies willingly and we turn left and then right into Browning Street. When we get to number 17, I stop and hold my breath. Tom looks up at the house. Even in the dark its dilapidated state is apparent.

'This is where you went that morning?' he says.

I put my hand on the brick pillar and nod. 'It's beautiful, isn't it? Tom, what do you think? Could we put in an offer?'

'Hey, slow down. What's wrong with where we are? I love Coleridge Street.'

'I do too. But this house is better. It's bigger and it's just . . . well, I'd love it and it would be a fantastic investment. I'd do most of the work myself.'

He laughs out loud. 'I don't doubt you'd try, but, Vicky, you're going back to work in September and by then Josh will be on his feet and running you ragged. It isn't feasible.'

He starts to pull me away but I hang on.

'Could you at least look at it?' I wheedle. 'If you can get there by six thirty on Monday, Sarah Wilson does do evening viewings.'

He steps back and stares up at the windows, and when he sighs I know I've won the first battle. I grin and tuck my arm through his and we hurry on to Amber and Robert's.

'Perhaps we should talk to Amber about it,' he says as we turn into her street.

I'm about to say yes, but on reflection I shake my head. 'I'll talk to her before I make the appointment, but I don't want to get into it tonight. Not with Robert.'

'No, you're right. That wouldn't be tactful.'

I allow myself a secret smile. He's already getting his head around the idea.

At Amber's, music is coming from the flat downstairs and as we approach the door a couple of blokes turn up with bags of alcohol, clearly pissed.

Tom glances at me and mutters, 'No wonder they're so desperate to buy somewhere.'

Amber buzzes us in and holds the door open. She's wearing a simple dark-grey woollen dress with a V-neck and a tiny Tiffany heart on a chain; Robert's present to her on one of their anniversaries. Robert pulls the cork out of a bottle of white wine before kissing me and shaking Tom's hand.

Ten years Amber's senior, comfortably paunchy and balding, and obviously besotted with his wife, Robert Collins is kind, intelligent and well intentioned, but a hopeless businessman. He makes money, but it's never enough, or if it is it isn't put to good use. It's an uncharitable thought to have but, despite liking him very much, I can't shake the feeling that if he doesn't pull his socks up and give her what she needs, he might lose her. Someone better might come along. I cringe inwardly, thinking about David. He wasn't better than Tom; just different and new.

The flat is warm and tidy, scented candles burning in the alcoves and on the shelves, the curtains drawn. Tom's right; it feels great to be out and about. I wonder if Amber's said anything to Robert. I hope not.

Tom hugs her, hands her a bottle of wine and smiles goofily when she tells him he's looking very handsome. Oddly enough, when they first met he didn't like her at all. I had been talking about her for weeks and expected him to feel the same way I did. When she visited after I had Emily she gushed about the baby and said all the right things, so it confused me when Tom, after he had seen her out of the house, was less than enthusiastic.

'I thought she'd never go,' he said, settling down beside me and letting Emily wrap her tiny hand around his finger.

'What did you think of her?'

'Uh.' He scratched his head. 'Dunno. I felt like she expected me to admire her.'

I wrinkled my nose. I was facing him with my feet up on the sofa and he drew them on to his legs. His hands were warm.

'Maybe it's just that you expected her to expect you to admire her. I didn't get that from her at all. She's probably shy, meeting you for the first time.' I poked my toe into his thigh. 'You're such a stud.'

I can't pinpoint when that changed, but I do remember that their relationship relaxed into one of mickey-taking, and so it has continued.

Amber has switched the ceiling light off and our faces look young in the wavering candlelight. She's wearing her hair scooped up carelessly so that strands escape and caress her cheeks.

'You look lovely,' I say, and I mean it. It's easy to stop seeing someone you know really well, but occasionally the perfect light falls on her face at the perfect angle to highlight her bone structure, or I catch her unawares, smiling at some private joke or looking a million miles away, and I'm stunned all over again.

Tom, Robert and I lounge on the sofa and armchair, glasses of wine in our hands while Amber checks on the starters. She calls through. 'Did I tell you? Sarah's moving into Lettings. She's offered me more work. She wants me to head that department.'

'Wow,' I say. 'That's brilliant, Amber. Are you going to take it?' I get up to give her a hand transferring plates of carpaccio and rocket salad on to the table.

'I'm not sure,' she says with a nonchalant shrug. 'It would mean organizing extra childcare and it's not that well paid, so it's a question of whether it's worth it or not. Sit down, everyone. Tom, you sit opposite me and Robert opposite Vicky.'

'I can help,' I say, pulling out my chair. 'At least until September. When would she want you to start?'

'Not for a couple of months. She's negotiating the lease on the shop next door and it needs a complete refit. June at the earliest. So really it's a bit of a nightmare because it means starting at the end of term; and there's sports day and prize-giving. And then there's the ruddy holidays.'

I regard her over the candles. 'Do you want to do it?'

'Yes.'

'Then listen, Amber. Just do it. Take the job and we will muddle through. I'll look after Sophie until things are sorted out. And I really don't think Sarah is going to begrudge you a couple of school events. Once I go back to work I'll have an au pair, so we might be able to come to an arrangement.'

She beams at me. 'OK. Thanks.'

Tom leans back in his chair, watching us, a grin crinkling his eyes. He reaches behind him for their iPad and searches for something on the Internet.

'What do you think? Not bad, eh?' he says, handing it to Robert. 'We've got it for a fortnight.'

Oh great, I think. Tom and his big mouth. Why

does he have to show off? The villa he's rented for two weeks in the Easter holidays is a swooning hacienda, set in landscaped gardens with a pool that gleams azure against the surrounding paving. It's gorgeous, luxurious and expensive.

Amber wanders round and leans over Tom, her hand resting on his shoulder. 'Is that where you're staying? Very swanky. Bloody hell. You are doing well for yourself.'

'They upgraded us,' I say quickly. 'We couldn't have afforded it in normal circumstances, but they had to withdraw the house we originally booked. Something to do with the plumbing.'

'Well, lucky you.'

'Are you two going anywhere?'

'No. The timing isn't great at the moment,' Robert says. A look passes between him and Amber. Is she pregnant? No, surely not. She would have told me. 'Holidays are going to be off the agenda for the foreseeable. Amber and Sophie can always spend a week in Suffolk.'

'Yes, that's always great fun,' Amber says drily.

She catches my eye and I smile. I know exactly how she feels about staying with her in-laws.

The oven timer pings and Robert trails his wife into the kitchen. I turn to Tom and he sinks his head in his hands.

'I know. I'm sorry. Shit.'

There is something very endearing about Tom when he's feeling guilty. He's like a dog caught chewing a pilfered lamb chop.

Robert returns with a casserole, followed by Amber

carrying a pale-pink china bowl piled high with greens. They set them on the table and we breathe in the delicious aroma of Moroccan tagine.

'Do you want to hear the good news?' Amber says.

'Go on,' I answer. 'I'd love to.'

'We put in an offer on Browning Street and it's been accepted.'

Taken by surprise, I can't think of anything to say. I catch Tom's eye and he gives an almost imperceptible lift of his eyebrows.

'Browning Street?' he says, stalling for time.

'Yes. Didn't Vicky tell you she'd been to look at it?'

'The place you went to see that awful morning? Yeah, I knew about that.' He glances my way again and says, 'I don't know why you went to see it, Vicky. We don't need to move.'

I get the message. He thinks I should take a step back, not confront this head on; not turn it into an issue. He doesn't want to get into a property war with our best friends, and neither do I, but it doesn't stop me feeling as though I've been winded. Amber's timing is perfect. She's caught me off guard and made sure there are witnesses.

I take a deep breath. 'Tom's right. It isn't practical for either of us at the moment.'

Tom's smile of approval is all the recompense I get, but at least I've concealed my real feelings, behaved graciously. I can't believe it though.

'No, that's what I thought,' Amber says, directing her speech to Tom and not looking at me. 'I didn't think you'd mind. It makes sense. I can probably get their price down after the survey as well, because it has more problems than the executors are letting on. It's in an awful state, to be honest, but it's the only way we'll get our feet on the ladder.'

I muster a few words. 'It's still a lot of money.'

'Oh,' Amber says breezily. 'That's what mortgages are for. It'll go up in value.'

I try and feel excited for her but I can't. I love that house and if it hadn't been for what came next I would have put an offer in straight away, not waited until now. She knows that and yet she's stepped in. Why couldn't she just have told me?

'Vicky, you know how badly Robert and I need to move out of this place. I hate it here.' She stops speaking and in the silence we hear the boom boom boom of a bass and raucous laughter coming from downstairs. 'We're not students. We're a family.'

Tom is looking at me and I take a slug of wine and mentally step back from the edge. I force myself to see it from her point of view. Amber wants this as badly as I do and who am I to begrudge her the chance to change her life? Inwardly, I contain my bitter disappointment, aware that everyone is waiting for me, that Amber is particularly tense.

'I hope you get it. And if you do, I'll help you strip wallpaper.'

Her face relaxes. 'You don't have to.'

'I do. I want to. You know I love that sort of thing.' I am rewarded by the rare sight of Amber's eyes welling with tears. She wipes them away with a napkin and reaches across to briefly squeeze my hand.

'You can use me too,' Tom says.

'Er . . . perhaps not,' Amber says. 'Remember when you accidentally bought that disgusting, gritty non-slip paint and slapped it all over the bathroom floor? It took Vicky a week to put right.'

He pokes her arm. 'Let's wait and see what happens when you pick up a paint roller, shall we?'

'I wouldn't let him anywhere near the place, if I were you,' I laugh. 'He's a liability.'

'Don't listen to her, Amber. Point me in the direction of a wall and I'll strip the paper off. Or Robert and I can weed the garden. Anyway, let's drink a toast. To Amber and Robert, who are joining the ranks of the heavily mortgaged.'

'How's the investigation going?' Robert asks as he tucks into Amber's homemade lemon tart.

'Slowly,' Tom says. He moves his glass, swivelling it to and fro, and it catches my eye as candlelight glints against its surface. He explains about Grayling and the hospital, about the frustration of trying to get answers. 'They don't have a clue. That man, whoever he was, must have some serious balls, breaking into homes in broad daylight.'

'He's bound to be caught sooner or later with an M.O. like that,' Robert says.

'M.O.?' Amber laughs. 'Who do you think you are? Inspector Morse?'

Tom stops frowning and grins at her. 'I suppose, after last week, he won't be trying it again in a hurry. I should think Vicky scared the living daylights out of him.'

The Collinses are the only people we can joke about it with and I try to join in, but I feel sick. To my horror my heart starts racing, the room and the people in it blurring. They're still chatting away, the wine making them voluble, the men puffed up, describing how they would have reacted had it been either of them who had interrupted our burglar. I can't breathe and my limbs feel leaden. Why don't they change the subject? Can't they see I'm shaking? I drop my spoon and it clatters to the floor but I leave it, not trusting myself to move or speak.

At the sudden noise Amber drags her gaze from Tom's face and looks at me. Her smile is tentative, worried. 'Hey,' she says. 'Are you all right?'

'Vicky?' Tom finally notices. 'What's the matter?'

'We have to go home.' I push my chair back and nearly fall over. Robert grasps my elbow and steadies me, gently pressing me back down on to my seat. 'The children . . .'

'You mustn't worry so much, darling,' Tom says. 'Magda has it all under control.'

I stare into his eyes, willing him to take me seriously, trying not to cry, anxious not to make a scene in front of our hosts, but it's no good and I break apart.

'She's having a panic attack.' I hear Amber's voice through the muddle in my brain. She comes and crouches down beside me and pulls me round to face her. 'It's OK, Vicky. Breathe.'

I try. I pull air in and out of my lungs, my hands clasped in Amber's. I hold her gaze and she nods encouragement.

'That's right. Good girl. Everything's fine.'

Tom is on his mobile, having a brief, laughing conversation with Magda. 'I know, I know,' he says. 'It's just, after what happened, Vicky is understandably on edge.' He laughs again. 'Thanks, I knew you would understand.'

Slowly my pulse returns to normal and life flows back into my heavy limbs. I sit up straight, pull my hands from Amber's and attempt a smile.

'I'm so sorry.'

'Don't be. It's not your fault.' Tom pockets his phone and swaps places with Amber who goes into the kitchen to fetch me a glass of water. He puts his arms around me. 'I should have realized how deeply this has affected you. We can leave now if you like. I'm not going to force you to stay if you're really not comfortable.'

I shake my head. 'No. I'm fine now, honestly. It's passed.'

He smooths my hair back off my face. I can tell he's relieved.

Amber moves round the table collecting plates, her tiny waist flattered by the wrap-around dress. She notices Tom watching her and her skin prickles. She glances across at Robert, who has pastry crumbs down the front of his blue shirt, and feels a combination of irritation and tenderness. She chose him and tried to mould him into the man she needed him to be. The results have been mixed; and yet she does love him . . . in a way. She'll love him a lot more if he gets them out of this place. She shoots Tom a quick glance. He smiles at her

107

and she loses her chain of thought. Vicky says something and she has to ask her to repeat it. She's felt Tom's eyes on her more than once this evening and the almost covert nature of his scrutiny increases her sense of connection and makes her feel almost giddy. When did this happen? She can't remember a moment when her feelings towards him shifted, but that new feeling has cemented now, become something that she can no longer kid herself about. Her body seems to hum when he is close.

'Can I help?' Vicky is drunk, but in a good way, a way that makes her soft and malleable, which is a relief after that tricky moment earlier.

'No, I'm fine,' Amber says. 'You relax.'

She takes in the scene; candles and crumbs, flushed faces and sparkling eyes; twinkling glasses and laughter; fond jokes at each other's expense; shared memories; their children's foibles. This is her status quo, her safety. Or at least it was, before Vicky let the side down. Life doesn't feel stable any more; it feels like she's on ice, like the hands that are helping her stay upright could do more harm than a fall. She should let herself fall and take the risk. All the same, she can't help wondering how much she's prepared to lose. She doesn't have an answer to that question yet. Life is not that simple.

'Are you cold?' Tom says, and she realizes that she's shivering.

Robert leans back and smiles good-naturedly at his wife. 'Put the heating up a notch if you like, darling.'

'Lucky me,' she mutters, and he flushes.

She takes their dinner plates into the kitchen and sets them down on the counter, then stops, still holding the dirty cutlery, and closes her eyes in despair. She must be kinder to Robert – it's not his fault he doesn't bear comparison with Tom Seagrave, not his fault that she feels so trapped. Actually, she pities him. He works so hard and for what? So that they can pay an outrageous rent to a greedy landlord. Amber clenches her teeth as she scrapes wasted food into the bin. She's ready now. Things are going to change. Silently, she repeats, *I am good; I am strong; I matter.*

Behind her, Vicky walks in with the remains of the tart. 'You have to let me help. I need to move. Shall I make the coffee? I think the men could do with some.'

She means Robert, Amber's guessing. She nods and Vicky gives her an impulsive hug.

'I'm so grateful to you,' Vicky mutters thickly.

'You scared me back there,' Amber says. 'I thought you were going to start confessing.'

'I wouldn't do that. At least, not without discussing it with you first.'

Amber and I are stacking the dishwasher together; she is scrubbing the larger items while I dry up and put away. The kitchen is tiny and reminds me of the one Mum and I had when I was little, with two chairs and a table crammed against one side. My eyes stray to the digital clock on the oven which tells me it's almost eleven forty-five. I rinse a cloth under the hot tap, wring it out and use it to wipe the surfaces, scrubbing at dried-on spots of sauce with unnecessary vigour. Despite my moment of weakness and Amber's genuine solicitousness, there is still a hard knot of anger in my stomach.

'I'm sorry about Browning Street.' She wipes her hands on a tea towel. 'I know you're pissed off with me.'

'I'm not,' I lie. 'Really. Something else will come up.'

'But you would have enjoyed it and you're so good at all that stuff.'

I shrug depreciatingly. 'The money though, Amber? I thought the whole reason you were stuck here was because you couldn't raise enough for a deposit.'

Amber isn't facing me and I don't hear what she says. I wait until she turns round and repeats it, still whispering.

'I thought you could help with that.'

This is one of those moments, one of those awful, awkward moments that life doesn't prepare you for, when it's vital to answer a question with sensitivity but the chances of getting it right are virtually nil. I feel cornered and embarrassed, and my thoughts scurry in all directions in a frantic attempt to dredge up the least worst response.

'Amber.' I swallow but my mouth is dry. 'Look . . .'

Amber waits for me to go on. The noise pulsing from downstairs is getting worse. There's a shout of laughter and then the music stops. In the brief pause before it starts again, I keep my eyes on her face.

'I'd love to help, and I've already offered to give you a hand with the DIY, but I can't pay your deposit. You know that.'

Her lips turn down and for a moment I think she's going to cry, but those big blue eyes are unreadable. 'But you can get it. You've got so much, you two. You don't understand what it's like not to have a home. You—'

'Oh, Amber. I'm so sorry. I've been incredibly insensitive. You know I'll do all I can. I said I'd look after Sophie and I will. But the money . . . I'm really sorry, but we can't help you there.'

She winds her long hair round her hand and then pushes it behind her shoulder and a sigh shudders out of her. 'Forget I said anything. I didn't mean it.'

'Don't be silly.' I have a brainwave. A way I can make amends for Tom's tactlessness, and for my less than enthusiastic response to her news. 'Come with us to Spain. Please, please, please! It would be so much more fun with you lot. The house is all paid for. All you'd need is your flights.'

Her face brightens. 'Do you mean it?'

I wonder if the impulse wasn't a mistake, if I should have slept on it and at least checked with Tom, but her expression makes it all worthwhile. 'Of course I do. We'll be there for my birthday, so the more the merrier as far as I'm concerned.'

'What about Tom? Won't he mind?'

'He'll be delighted. He'll have Robert and I'll have you and the girls will have Sophie. Win win!'

Robert stands behind Amber as we leave, with his arms wrapped protectively round her waist. She gives me a smile that is at once complicit and affectionate and it confuses me. Poor thing. The idea of asking a friend for money appals me, as it must appal her. She must have been thinking about it for days, worrying about how to put it, and I probably made her feel so much worse. I won't tell Tom, I decide. She would be mortified if he knew. By the time we leave the flat I'm clear in my mind that the offer of a holiday was not only the right, but the only thing to do.

May 1992

JUST BEFORE HALF-TERM LUKE WAS MADE REDUNDANT. He said it was to do with government cuts and seemed unworried. Sally said they were fine for the time being because she was able to go back to work at King's, but it took Katya barely a second to realize that this meant Luke would be in charge of her in the evenings. She sat at the kitchen table while Sally explained all this. Luke was out. Sally said that he would have a new job in no time at all, but until then they would try and make sure nothing changed too much for Katya.

'I could come to the hospital after school and wait for you,' Katya said.

Sally ruffled her hair. 'That's sweet of you, but you'd only get bored. No, it's straight home every afternoon for your tea.'

Katya's mouth turned down at the corners.

'Hey.' Sally stroked her hair back, her eyes searching Katya's face. 'Are you all right, love?'

'I don't mind if you don't want to keep me. If I cost too much money.'

Sally gave her a hug, pressing Katya against her bony body. She smelt faintly of onions. 'I wouldn't give you back for all the tea in China. You deserve some stability in your life. You're not going anywhere.' She let her go, smiling now, and got the biscuit tin out of the cupboard.

Katya chose a chocolate-chip cookie. When her mum was alive she often didn't go straight home after school. She liked to give Linda plenty of time to get herself together and had had enough nasty surprises to know not to hurry or walk in without letting her know she was there. She would go to the library and do her homework, or in the summer she would hang around the park and the playground, hiding behind a book, avoiding people. She could do that again. It would be easier now she was nearly eleven.

'I thought I'd pop by and see how you were both doing,' Maggie said. It was four o'clock, and Katya had come in from school to find Maggie sitting at the kitchen table with Luke, mugs of tea in front of them. Sally was at work.

'We're getting along like a house on fire, aren't we, Katya?' Luke said.

Maggie stood up and went to the window. 'What beautiful tulips.' Her voice sounded funny, not natural. More like she was acting a part.

'That's Sal,' he said. 'She does the flowers; I do the heavy stuff.'

He held the glass door open for her and Katya watched as the two adults wandered across the lawn. She thought it was weird how they seemed to suit each other better than Luke and Sally did. They were both tall, both brown-haired and brown-eyed. When Luke was with Maggie it felt like he was wearing the right set of clothes.

The kettle clicked and she filled their mugs. They had pink rosebuds on them. At home none of the mugs matched so you could have your favourite. It seemed less personal somehow when they were all the same. But at least they got washed up. She hoped she would get a chance to talk to Maggie on her own this time. Luke was looking pleased with himself, like he'd told a good joke. He had his hands shoved in the pockets of his jeans and Maggie was rocking on her feet. She looked a bit mad, Katya decided.

Later Maggie went through things with Luke while Katya pretended to read. In reality, the book was a struggle and boring so she listened to what they were saying instead. How had it been? Was he under any pressure? How were finances? How was his relationship with Sally? She wonders whether, if Luke told her about the quarrels he and Sally had been having, she might get to leave and live with Maggie. But he left that bit out.

'You've done so well,' Maggie said. 'I wouldn't blame you if you decided that you couldn't carry on with the fostering.'

'I can't imagine not having Katya with us.' He added in a louder voice, 'You're happy, aren't you, Katya?'

She turned round slowly, as if her attention was on her book. 'I don't mind if you want me to go.' She tried to catch Maggie's eye, but the social worker was gazing at Luke's profile, her mouth twitching at the corners.

'Now you've hurt my feelings,' Luke said.

He made a face at her so that she knew she hadn't. He was teasing. She didn't like it when he did that; it made her feel as though he'd come too close, like he knew what was going on inside her. Something had changed. It was nothing she could explain; it was just a feeling like when something tiny gets stuck between your teeth and your tongue keeps worrying at it.

'I'd better get on,' Maggie said. 'Emily's round at a friend's. I should pick her up. Katya?'

'Yes.'

'Why don't you show me to my car?'

Maggie chuckled at something Luke said and touched his arm lightly. Katya scowled behind their backs. She was jealous. It was a horrible feeling, filling her head so that normal stuff was pushed out. She had felt it with Linda in the early days, before she realized there was safety in numbers, and at school with Gabriella.

'Now,' Maggie said, once they were out in the street. 'Is everything all right?'

'Why do I have to stay with them?'

'Because they know you and they like you. You don't want to have to start all over again with a new family, do you?'

She shrugged. 'I don't like it here. There's nothing to do.'

Her chin started to wobble and she tensed the muscles in her face. She couldn't put it in words because words would get her into trouble, so she stared at Maggie, but

Maggie wasn't looking at her, she was digging in her leather bag for her keys. By the time she'd found them, Katya had pulled herself together.

'Let's see how you get on for the next few weeks. We'll talk about it again.'

'Why can't I stay with you and Emily?' The words burst from her.

'I've explained that,' Maggie said. 'It wouldn't be appropriate.'

'But why not?'

'Katya.' She let out a breath. 'I'm extremely fond of you, but you have to understand, this is my job. If I adopted every child I looked after, my flat would be bursting at the seams. The only way I can do this is to keep a bit of distance. Do you understand what I mean?' She held her shoulders and, when Katya started to cry, drew her in so that her face was pressed against her generous bosom. She stroked her hair but managed to gently push her away at the same time. 'Cheer up, lovely. Things will get better. I promise I'll always be here for you.'

Luke was reading the paper, his feet up, when Katya came back in. 'Come and sit down then.'

She perched on the arm of the sofa.

'Here. Snuggle up.'

She dropped down reluctantly. He folded the paper and chucked it on to the coffee table before putting his arm around her. He ran his fingers through her hair then pressed a strand against his nose and breathed in.

'What did you say to her?' His voice was very quiet, very measured.

117

She pulled her hair out of his hand and pushed it behind her ear. This was how it always started, with the air twanging with tension. 'Nothing.'

'Then why do you look guilty? Did you say something about me?'

'No I didn't. I wouldn't.' She tried to extract herself but his arm was like steel.

'That's my girl.'

11

Wednesday, 27 January 2010

THERE IS SOMETHING ABOUT BOGNOR REGIS IN THE winter time, perhaps about any British seaside town, that reminds me of abandoned pets. Something forlorn and needy. Without the holidaymakers, it's a deserted and lonely place and the rain that drives in off the sea seeps into every nook and cranny. Yet, it has a certain rundown charm, a desperation to be of use, to please. People live here. My mum does. She still lives in the house she bought when I was eleven; a ramshackle late-eighteenth-century affair across the road from the seafront. It's white and has a wrought-iron balcony, which once would have been elegant but is now enclosed by salt-blurred glass. Despite living here for ten years I never really had my own space; where I slept depended on demand. In busy periods, that often meant a Z-bed in the front room and occasionally a mattress on the floor of my mother's bathroom.

Mum bought in Bognor because she had fond memories of holidays spent there with her grandmother. That was her excuse, anyway, but it helped that the house was dirt cheap at auction and had vacant possession. She was in a hurry and didn't care where we ended up so long as it gave us a roof and a living. The town never changes, has barely dipped a toe into the water of the twenty-first century, and mobile phone outlets are the only reminder that I haven't stepped back in time. Many of the shops that lined the high street when I was a child have survived. The arcade is drab, the pier uninviting, but there are positives. The model shop is still trading; the displays of Hornby train sets still drawing children and men. The cafés with their steamed-up windows thrive, providing a meeting place and a social scene for an elderly population. The smell of vinegary fish and chips pervades.

When I was a teenager we used to find our fun in Littlehampton, one stop down the train line. There was a semi-decent nightlife there. I had friends who lived out in Pagham, in pretty flint-stone houses with enormous gardens, but it was my house we descended on if we wanted to chill out, which says a lot for Mum. No matter how many of us rolled in past our curfew or what sort of state we were in, she never minded. She didn't care if the sofas were occupied by comatose teenagers either. She would start frying bacon, knowing the smell would get us up faster than any attempts at persuasion. The flip side was that my male friends all fancied her. That was embarrassing.

I often hated her and was frequently embarrassed by her. Other girls' mothers were perfectly happy to have one husband or partner, so why couldn't she? Why did she have to keep being dumped and then get all excited about the next one? It was only later that I came to understand her. My grandmother, her mother, had criticized her constantly. Her self-esteem plummeted, leading her to look for ways to make herself feel better, feel attractive, feel wanted. So she slept around. She was easy and she got herself a reputation. The poor kid who made her pregnant was only fifteen at the time, and she refused to name him. She only told me after I had Emily. I met him but I didn't feel anything; no connection, no skip of the heart as we shook hands. He is a perfectly good bloke who lives in Dorking with his family and works for a computer parts company. He was extremely relieved when I told him I wasn't interested in a relationship, but that it was nice to have met him at last.

When we had to leave Streatham we spent several weeks in my grandparents' 1930s semi. It wasn't the best time, what with Mum jobless at twenty-seven and still reeling from whatever had happened to her, and my grandmother making cutting remarks over the Sunday roast. 'I hope you're teaching Vicky to value herself. We don't want her going down the same road.' And my grandfather making unhelpful allusions to wasted potential. 'You were such a clever kid.'

As I carry Josh in, a man walks out, giving me a small bow as he stands politely to one side. He's tall and in his mid-fifties with leonine white hair and a prominent nose. I raise my eyebrows at Mum.

'Don't be silly, he's stupendously gay. He's in *Lady Windermere's Fan*.'

'Oh. Sorry.'

Max, her miniature Schnauzer, greets me with touching enthusiasm, jumping up and resting his paws on my knees. I give his bearded chin a friendly scratch.

'So,' Mum says, taking my coat and hanging it over the back of a chair. She tries not to overdo the physical affection when I give her a kiss, but she can't resist and practically smothers me. 'How are you?' She starts to smooth my windblown hair and I brush her off.

'Mum! I'm not ten years old.'

Her kitchen is small, chilly and impractical. There's enough room for a sixties Formica table and chairs and there is a Mickey Mouse clock on the wall above the fridge. She has a larder, and a door leads to an outside space that's more a corridor between this house and the one behind than a patio. Fortunately, she's never been interested in gardening. There's the green opposite, with a handy playground, and the beach twenty yards away; more than enough to cater for the needs of Max and her grandchildren.

I rub at a tea stain on the table while she drops two slices of bread into the toaster. The thing I used to love about the B & B was toast made from Mother's Pride, left to grow cold and rubbery, spread with butter and Robertson's marmalade and washed down with strong tea. The toast she gives me now has been cut from a fresh, wholegrain loaf.

'It's from the coffee shop on the corner,' she says as she sketches a new moon surrounded by stars on Josh's cast. 'We're very up to date here.' She picks him up and lets him play with her beaded necklace. 'I've taken three bookings for next week. They're all from the Chichester Touring Company. Oscar Wilde season. I'm going tomorrow night. You just met the leading man.'

I smile, trying to take all this information in. I'm going

to have to talk to her soon, but not yet; not till we've caught up with her news. 'Have you heard from Peter?'

She shrugs and pulls the other chair out. 'He rang last night, but it was only about picking up his things.'

'He'll be back within three months. You'll see.'

'Well, that's up to him.'

Mum tucks her hair behind her ears and her dangly earrings shimmer in the light from the window. These days her hair is dyed, and not particularly well. It has a metallic look about it. She's wearing a beaded wool dress, black woolly tights and high-heeled ankle boots. She is a very attractive woman. I find it extraordinary that there are mothers at the girls' school the same age as she is.

'Oh, Mum.'

'Don't you "Oh, Mum" me, Vicky. Are you going to tell me what's happened?'

I can't finish the toast. I push the plate to one side and concentrate on my tea. She watches me while I drink it, waiting for me to speak. Then she hands me my coat.

'Let's take that darling boy of yours for a walk. You can tell me all about it.'

We trudge along the promenade with the wind in our faces, a see-through rain-cover pulled down over Josh. I describe meeting David and feeling punch-drunk with the excitement of it. I tell her how, whenever I saw him, my brain scrambled, how in the space of half a term I went from sane to obsessed. A glance and a smile from him could empty my mind of my family and conscience and make anything seem possible.

I've borrowed one of her woolly hats and pulled it down over my ears. Max scampers ahead of us, investigating other dogs and bits of litter flung up by the sea. He comes back with a length of blue nylon rope in his jaw. Mum fights him for it, laughing as he whips his head from side to side, eyes popping. About as threatening as a guinea pig.

I remember when we first came here, thinking I was in paradise. I didn't care about the state of the house, all I cared about was that the sea was barely spitting distance away and I could see the pier and the crazy golf from the front windows. It was wonderful. In Streatham I'd had much less freedom.

I wipe the sea spray from my cheeks and push my damp hand back into my pocket.

'Tom doesn't know, that's the main thing,' Mum says.

'But that means I have to lie to him for the rest of my life. I don't think I can sustain that.'

'That's up to you, of course, but you need to think about what will happen. It won't be a question of getting it off your chest and it going away. Once he knows, he knows, and his first reaction, even if he calms down, is the one that will stay with him. You aren't in love with this man, are you, Vicky?'

I shake my head. 'No.'

'Well then.'

We walk on in silence, listening to the gulls. Over the sea the sky is blue, but as is so often the case, to the north it's cloudy. I love that about the coast; you can drive through depressing weather knowing that on the other side of the South Downs there's a good chance the sun will be out, making the sea shimmer. It works the other way round, of course.

'Do you ever wish you'd married?'

Beside me, Mum snorts. 'No, not at all.'

'But there must have been someone, once, who you loved more than any of the others.'

She counters smartly with, 'Yes, but he turned out to be worse than all the rest of them put together.'

'Which one was he?' There were several to choose from.

'Never you mind. We're talking about you, remember. Have you heard from David?'

I shake my head. 'No. And what with the break-in and Josh's injury, I haven't had a moment. If I stop to think I just feel sick with relief. I could have lost everything, and for what? What was the point?' I can't bring myself to tell her what actually happened on the morning of the break-in. For some reason, I'm far more ashamed of that than I am about David North.

Max comes trotting back to us, sniffs around the wheels of the pram and dashes off along the beach. He races to the shore and barks frantically at the waves.

'You'd never think he's lived by the sea all his life,' Mum says. 'Or maybe he has amnesia and every time's the first time. Can dogs get that?'

I laugh. 'I have no idea.'

We walk a short way before she says anything else. I'm happy in the silence.

'It's just life and human nature, Vicky. Chemistry.'

'Was that all it was for you?'

'Oh, I don't know. I went with it. I was weak. But you aren't weak. You looked at what you had to lose and made a decision. I never did that – and look at me now. I'm scraping the barrel with men like Peter Calder.'

'He wasn't that bad. Tom liked him.'

'Did he?' Mum turns to me and smiles. 'That was sweet of him to say so. I don't have many regrets, but I suppose I never had as much to lose as you do, and I've always been independent. I've never wanted to be tied irrevocably to anyone.'

I turn to face the sea and breathe deeply. A tanker breaks the line of the horizon, moving so slowly that it seems suspended. 'You know what I'm worried about?'

She moves beside me and tucks her arm into mine, bending to pat Max, who is evidently wondering why we've stopped. 'What?'

'That I'm fighting my true nature. That my whole life is going to be a struggle not to fall for other men; that I'm going to end up alone.'

'I think you're getting the whole thing wildly out of proportion.'

'Wildly?' I smile, pulling strands of windblown, salty hair from my lips and cheeks, stuffing them back under the hat.

'For goodness' sake, everyone fancies other people; it's just that most do nothing about it. You've had a wake-up call, Vicky, nothing more. You're the only one who knows, so don't worry about it. David is hardly likely to tell his wife. And you won't tell Tom, because Tom is the love of your life.' She stops and looks at me, her full skirt flapping around her legs. 'You won't, will you?'

'No. But I did tell Amber.'

'Well, I'm sure you can trust her. She is your best friend, after all.'

'Yup.'

Josh pushes himself forward and I lift the rain-cover and unbuckle him. We leave the pushchair behind us on the path and walk down to the sea. I hold him upright on the sand and kiss his pink cheeks as he points at the gulls. Small waves crash and froth at our feet.

'I haven't been a great role model, have I?' Mum says, her voice almost lost in the gusting wind.

I turn to her. 'Yes, you have. You taught me how to stand on my own two feet. You made sure I was equipped for that. And you taught me to be generous in my dealings with others. I don't want you to think I'm blaming you for my shortcomings.'

After lunch I spend a contented hour and a half regrouting the tiles in the yellow bathroom. Josh, refusing to allow his plaster cast to impede his progress, plays with Mum's supply of plastic toys in the empty bath. Mum touches up the woodwork. The radio is tuned to a local channel and the music perks me up. I used to love doing this sort of thing with my mother, in the same way that most children love baking cupcakes with theirs. There's the easy intimacy, the rest of the world shut out so that it's only us. I smile to myself and glance at her. We get things done, me and my mum.

Once I've sponged off the tiles, I perch on the side of the bath picking the grout off my fingers and admiring my handiwork. Mum wipes her forehead with the back of her hand, leaving a smear of paint in her hair.

'Why don't you come with us to Spain?' I say.

'That's very kind, but I don't think so. I'll be busy here.'

'Couldn't Maureen take over?'

Maureen has been my mother's neighbour right from the beginning and has covered Mum's holidays for as long as I can remember. She's prone to small disasters but has never burnt the place down. Breaking crockery and putting the chain on the door at night so that guests can't get in is more in her line.

'I'm sure she could, but you need to concentrate on your family.'

'It'll be fine. I think we're having Amber's lot for the first week. You could do with a change of scene, and the house is big enough. There's a pool and Barcelona isn't far away. The children would love it.'

She thinks about it and shakes her head. 'I'm sorry, Vicky. It's a busy time of year for me.'

'I nearly forgot – before you go . . .' She hurries to the dresser and picks up a shoebox. 'I found this in the attic at the bottom of a box of old junk I was throwing out. It belongs to you.'

'To me?' I hold out my hands and take it. It's heavy, the objects inside shifting as I set it down on the table. 'What is it?'

'Open it and see.'

I lift the lid. Nestling in tissue paper and cotton wool is a collection of memories. I take them out one by one. There's a porcelain shoe decorated with tiny forget-me-nots that bite into my fingers, a miniature Venus de

Milo, the white paint flaking off the lead. Mum watches me, a smile playing on her lips.

I look up at her. 'I'd forgotten all about these.'

I take more of the things out: a small framed photo of me and Mum eating lollipops on the beach. I wonder which lover took it. There's also an ivory elephant, about two inches high, missing one of its tusks, and a porcelain frog. A dozen or more objects. I lay them all out on the table. I can remember their positions on the shelf above my bed and I start to move them, switching them round to find their companions.

'We left in such a rush,' Mum says. 'I remember putting them in the box, but we lost such a lot between there and my parents'.'

I nod, but my mind is elsewhere. There is an anomaly. The elephant wasn't beside the Venus. There was something in between them. I edge them apart with my finger and gaze at the gap. It feels like when you get to the end of a puzzle and there's a piece missing.

'The amber,' I say with a smile of satisfaction. 'It isn't here.'

'I'm sure I took everything. I wouldn't have left anything out – not deliberately, at least. Maybe it got knocked down behind your bed.'

'It doesn't matter. It's nice to have these. The girls will be thrilled. Anyway, I have an alternative Amber now.' An unwelcome image intrudes; my friend crouched inside the block of sap, a black silhouette. It melts away from her and she unravels her body and steps out of the sticky mess. 'I'll save them for Christmas.'

12

AMBER WATCHES VICKY PUSH JOSH'S PRAM AT A BRISK trot up the street to the school gates, weaving through families already on their way home.

'Thank goodness you're here!' she says, falling into step as Vicky races breathlessly into the playground. 'Could you have Sophie for tea? I need to go and see our financial advisor. I'm so sorry about the short notice, but he's free at four and Robert's got time, so . . .'

Vicky doesn't hesitate. 'Of course I will.'

Amber relaxes. She hasn't been sure how welcome the request would be, whether there would be awkwardness between them after Saturday night. It's likely that Vicky assumes Amber was drunk and didn't really mean it. But she did. Very much so.

Sophie zips up her dark-blue Puffa, smiling her gap-toothed smile. 'Am I coming to your house?' she asks Vicky.

'Yes, you are. Aren't I lucky?'

'You're late, Mummy,' Emily says.

Not for the first time either, Amber thinks, as they head out, Polly clutching the handle of the pram and skipping beside them. Her god-daughter is such a sweet, undemanding child. Vicky doesn't deserve her.

'I know, Emily,' Vicky says. 'I'm sorry. I've been to see Granny and the traffic was bad.'

The kids vie for the adults' attention, wanting to talk about their day, so it's impossible to discuss anything important. To Amber, it feels as though the subject of Vicky's disastrous lapse in judgement has become taboo. And there's the other issue: Vicky's affair. She's done some calculations, looked back and remembered certain things; hints her friend has dropped over the last few months, things she's avoided saying, and she's made an educated guess. She understands her only too well, knows that she's desperate to share her secrets but can't in all conscience do so.

She gives her a friendly nudge, saying in a sing-song whisper, 'I know who he is.'

Vicky is visibly startled. 'Who?'

'Him. The man you were seeing.'

'You don't!' Vicky says. But she isn't as outraged as she sounds. Her eyes are laughing.

'Oh yes I do. It was a process of elimination. It's Astrid North's father. I'm right, aren't I?'

'So now you think I'm a complete idiot.'

'Why would I think that?'

'Because he's married, old and flabby.'

'So? That didn't stop Anne Boleyn.'

Vicky concedes the point with a wide smile. 'I don't understand why you're so interested.'

'You'd be just as curious if the tables were turned.'

'True. It's a good thing Astrid will have left before I

131

start work again. I don't think I could stand it otherwise. It was a moment of madness, Amber. I honestly don't understand what got into me.'

'When did it start?'

'When Hellie went back to Sweden for two weeks. He had to come in and talk about Astrid's problems. I cannot believe I was so unprofessional!' Vicky groans. 'Can you imagine the fuss if it got round? When I think about it – teacher having an affair with a pupil's father – it is so tacky. Not that I did have the affair,' she adds quickly.

'Of course not. And he's very attractive. Sexy eyes.'

'Stop it!'

She laughs. 'OK. I'll let you off. Wish me luck this afternoon. We've been stalling the vendors like mad.' She watches Vicky's face redden with a certain amount of satisfaction. Let her feel awkward.

'You haven't managed to raise the deposit?'

'No, and obviously there are other buyers sniffing around. I'm terrified we'll be gazumped. That's why this meeting's so important.'

'But you work for the estate agent. Surely that gives you an edge?'

'Not when it comes to money, it doesn't. Vicky, I honestly hate to do this to you but I am desperate. Is there no way you and Tom could lend us the deposit, just for a few months?'

Vicky wraps her pashmina around her neck and pulls it close, hiding inside its soft folds. 'You know we can't.'

The weather has turned bitter again. Amber shouts at the girls to wait at the crossing and they stand obediently, Polly with her finger poised near the button. They catch up and wait for the green man and then Vicky steps off the kerb and is nearly knocked down by a cyclist. Amber grabs her in time and yanks her back.

'It's not like I haven't put myself out for you recently,' she says.

'Amber! I don't know what you think, but Tom and I haven't got pots of money floating around. What we have is invested in our house. We can't just go to the bank and ask for it; we'd have to remortgage to get anything like what you need. Surely it's better to do that through a proper loan, rather than involve us?'

'You're right. Sorry.' Amber's smile is thin. 'Let's talk about it another time.'

13

THE BOLOGNESE SAUCE IS BUBBLING MERRILY ON THE hob when Sophie comes downstairs. She's dressed in Emily's precious Belle costume, the yellow gauze billowing out from her rotund little body, the poppers at the back left open so that her vest shows. She stands in the doorway, holding an old evening bag of mine, and contemplates me. Even though she looks like Robert, she has the same steady, sometimes disconcerting, gaze as her mother.

'What's for dinner?' she asks.

I grab a handful of spaghetti and push it down into a pan of boiling water. 'Spag bol. Are you hungry?'

'Yes.'

'Well, it'll be ten minutes, so why don't you go upstairs and tell Emily you have to get changed.'

'Can I wear this?'

'No, Sophie. Not with spaghetti. It's too messy. Go and put your clothes back on.'

She goes up, her little feet heavy on the stairs. Thumper, I think, giving the Bolognese a stir. I'm still bothered by the conversation with Amber. Should we be helping them? Could we, if we really wanted to? Am I being mean? God, I don't know. I hate being put in this position, made to examine my conscience and my personality.

Minutes later there are more feet, Emily's this time. She's dressed as a ballet dancer and Sophie is still in costume, so clearly this is an attempt at a coup. I concede defeat with dignity.

'You look beautiful,' I say. 'Very elegant.'

'Can I wear it at Emily's birthday party?'

'You'll have to ask her, but I'm sure she'll say yes if she doesn't want it herself. And in that case you'd better keep it clean, hadn't you?'

The girls skate around the floor in their socks and Polly pootles in and starts telling her imaginary friend which cakes she likes best. Fondant Fancies. And which she thinks is disgusting. Jamaican Ginger.

I pour a glass of wine and drink it leaning against the counter while the children eat. I've begun leaving Josh to his own devices with food, on the basis that he's more likely to get on with it that way. Mum's suggestion. I cover his plaster cast with a special plastic sleeve and hope for the best, but it is getting revolting. His latest trick is to tip his plastic bowl on to his head. Our previous battles have been entirely fruitless and it is such a relief to let him do things his own way. He grins at me, his face smeared with food, and I make a face at him.

At six thirty when Amber still hasn't arrived, I begin to get twitchy. I need to get Josh cleaned up and the girls into their bath. I check my phone to see if she's texted, but there are no messages. At six forty-five Tom's motorbike roars on to the forecourt and the girls rush to the door to greet him, Emily clacking in her heels. He picks her up and plants a kiss on her nose, does the same for Polly and chucks Sophie under her chin. I glance meaningfully at my watch.

'Amber should have been here three-quarters of an hour ago.'

'That's all right, isn't it?' he says. 'It isn't as if we haven't taken advantage of her plenty of times.'

He deposits Polly on the floor, wraps his arms around me and nuzzles my neck. I turn into him and press my head against his shoulder.

'Hey, what is it?'

'Nothing.' I lift my face and kiss him.

'Umm,' he says, kissing me back then pulling away and raising his eyebrows. 'The sea air obviously agrees with you.'

His face makes me smile, and if I'm so used to it that I barely notice any more, I only have to remind myself of the first time we met; how, despite the other very good-looking students with him, it was Tom Seagrave I noticed. I am so glad I came to my senses about David. I know what I want my life to be and who I want to spend it with.

The doorbell rings. I let Amber in and she breezes past me, spots Tom's leather jacket hanging over the banister and calls out a greeting.

'Hi, Amber,' he calls back.

She takes that as an invitation and goes through. 'Sorry I'm late. Someone jumped in front of a train. We were stuck between stations for half a ruddy hour.

Honestly! If they're going to do it, I wish they'd pick a better time.'

'Yes,' Tom says. 'I can't think why they failed to consider your convenience. So selfish.'

She laughs. 'Get you.'

'Drink?' he asks.

'Please.'

She wanders over to the window, turning to take the glass from his hand, and he remains standing at her side, looking out, away from me. Amber is shorter than I am, and narrower in build, and she's dwarfed by Tom. The light from the window creates a kind of halo around them. She is part of the furniture here, always has been.

'It'll soon be warm enough to play outside,' she says, turning to me with a happy smile and catching me staring at her. 'I can't wait. I really hope we've completed on Browning Street by then.'

'You will, won't you?' Tom says. 'There's no chain?'

'No. Thank God. But the money situation is a tad complicated.' She shrugs and looks at me. 'But I won't bore you with all that.'

'So, have you thought about Spain?' Tom says. 'The offer's still open, you know. Unless, of course, Suffolk is a more tempting prospect.'

Amber rolls her eyes. 'Yeah, right. I love listening to Angie carping about Sophie's weight and Philip hinting about us moving up there.' Her voice lowers as she imitates her father-in-law. ' "Because the dear boy will be more comfortable." God forbid. But I shouldn't complain. They're generous. It's just not my idea of a holiday.'

I reach for the wine bottle and refill our glasses. 'You have to come with us, Amber. The girls will be much happier if they have a friend with them.'

'You are sweet. But Robert . . .' She shrugs eloquently.

'Robert what?' Tom says.

'Robert thinks he'll feel like the poor relation.'

'Ah.'

'So you see my problem.'

'Why don't I talk to him?'

'Be my guest.' She takes her glass to the sink, tips the residue down the drain and puts it in the dishwasher. 'Obviously, I'd love it. I . . . well, you know. I have to be sensitive to his feelings.'

While Vicky is bathing Josh, Tom and Amber search for Sophie's reading book. At least he sits on Emily's bed watching Amber while she looks. There is a pensive nature to his scrutiny. Vicky is singing, 'The wheels on the bus go round and round . . .'

Tom picks a half-dressed doll up off the floor, does up the Velcro strip at the back of its wedding gown and smooths the waves of bright-yellow hair. Why is he up here? He's making her nervous. She gets down on to her hands and knees and checks beneath the bed.

'Found it!' She brandishes the book.

'I haven't had a chance to talk to you about that morning,' Tom says.

That's all it is then. She hides her disappointment. 'I have talked to you, haven't I?'

'Not properly.' He lowers his voice. 'Not without Vicky there.'

She hesitates. 'There's no secret, Tom. Nothing I wouldn't say in front of her.'

'I just get this feeling that there's something she isn't telling me.'

'Well, there isn't.' It feels odd, protecting Vicky, when she could use what she knows to her advantage. Old alliances die hard, she supposes. Confusion too; not knowing whether she loves or hates her friend, bothered by how much she cares.

Tom contemplates her patiently. She avoids his gaze and sits down beside him on the bed, trapping her hands between her thighs.

'Honestly, there's nothing to tell. I expect she's shocked. After all, Josh had a very lucky escape. When you think what might have happened . . .' She lets him think, sees the shadow behind his eyes as he winces.

'Thank God you were there.'

He touches her lightly on the arm; it's nothing and yet it's electric. She turns her head and finds he's already looking at her. Something passes between them, a flicker, a stifled breath, a missed heartbeat.

'Tom,' Vicky calls. 'Can you give the girls a shout?'

He gets up abruptly and goes to the door. 'Polly! Emily! Bath time!' And then goes downstairs at a run.

Amber stays where she is, the palm of her left hand resting on the warm patch of duvet he left behind him. If she was to be bad and weak she would take him.

Enough. She's better than that. She jumps up. It's time to go.

In the bathroom, Vicky is struggling to keep Josh's cast out of the water. By now the gleaming whiteness has gone and it's covered in dirty marks, felt-tip and stickers. Food stains too. If truth be told, it smells.

'I'm off,' she says. 'Thanks for having Sophie.'

'*De nada*.' Vicky smiles up at her.

Amber picks up a cluster of bubbles with her finger and deposits it on Josh's nose. 'See you tomorrow, little man.'

May 1992

'WHAT HAVE YOU TWO GOT PLANNED FOR THE DAY?' Sally passed Luke a mug of coffee.

It was the middle of half-term. The longest half-term holiday Katya could remember. She had managed to get herself invited round to Gabriella's once and had even asked her back. Luke had said she could have a friend round if she wanted and she reasoned that he was hardly likely to do anything if someone else was there. But Gabriella refused the invitation. It was almost as though she sensed something not quite right, something invisible and ugly. Or maybe she just had better things to do.

Sally leant against the counter, looking unlike herself in her blue uniform. She reminded Katya of a bell. If she swung her legs, the stiff dress would rock in the opposite direction, side to side.

'We'll go swimming,' Luke said.

Katya glanced out of the window in panic. 'I don't have a swimming costume.'

Sally smiled at her. 'That's no problem. I'll borrow one off the neighbours.'

Four doors down there was a family with two daughters and a son. So far they hadn't been introduced. Katya couldn't help feeling that their mum disapproved of her. If they happened to be out front at the same time, she always had an excuse for taking her kids away. Katya doubted she would lend anything belonging to her precious girls.

'I don't like swimming, actually,' she said. 'I'd rather stay here and watch TV.'

'You don't want to be sat here all day glued to the box,' Luke said. 'I think swimming is a great idea, and I could do with the exercise.'

A piece of toast went down the wrong way, providing a distraction as she started to cough. Luke slapped her between the shoulder blades, making her eyes prick.

'I don't feel well.'

'You look fine to me.' Luke covered her forehead with his large cool hand. She went very still, his touch almost taking the breath out of her. 'Feel fine too.'

Sally glanced at Katya's face and frowned. 'Katya, love, can't you swim?'

Katya hung her head. 'No.'

'You don't have to be ashamed. It's not your fault you haven't had the same advantages as other kids your age.'

'Well, that settles it,' Luke said. 'We're going swimming and I'm going to teach you. If we go right now, the place won't have filled up. Sally can run round to Annie's and borrow one of the girls' suits.'

'But I don't want to,' Katya said, horrified.

She hated the water. When she was four years old her

mother's so-called boyfriend became so irritated with her that he put her in the bath that Linda had vacated, shoved her head down under the water and held it there. She had never forgotten the feeling of his hand pressing down or the pain in her lungs or the terror.

'Don't be silly,' Sally said. 'You have to learn to swim, it's a basic skill. It could save your life one day. Go and find a towel and tie your hair back.'

The swimming costume, lent so grudgingly that Sally was visibly ruffled when she came back with it, was pale pink with white piping around the neck and a spangly mermaid on the front. Katya thought it was hideous and, apart from that, it was too big and sagged when it was wet. She sat on the edge of the pool for a full ten minutes, breathing in chlorine fumes and getting cold, before she was finally persuaded to get in with the promise that she wouldn't have to put her face in the water, as leverage. A promise Luke broke within five minutes.

Her foster father was wearing a pair of navy swimming shorts. In the water his skin was shockingly white and his dark hairs floated out from his ribcage and stomach. He told her to hold on to the side and kick her legs and she did so, relieved that she wasn't expected to move.

Luke's hand slid under her stomach, the splay of his fingers reaching across her. The shock of his touch made her tighten every muscle.

'Kick, Katya. That's right,' he said. 'Keep your tummy up.'

The pressure increased and she kicked harder, making her arms rigid so that she could hold her body higher.

Being touched, her body moved and manipulated, her legs pulled into position, was horrible. It was as if the water gave him permission to ignore her personal space and her feelings. There was a clock high above the pool and she kept her eyes fixed on it.

'Can I get out now?' she asked after fifteen minutes in which she still hadn't managed to let go of the side despite Luke's repeated urging.

'Ten more minutes.'

He turned from her, threw himself forward and started to swim, his arms rising and slicing cleanly into the water. She watched as he twisted his head from side to side, his wet hair flicking. When he came back he rose from the water like a seal.

'We're not leaving until you've let go, so come on. Time to be brave.'

She shook her head. 'No. I'm not going to. I don't like it.'

'Don't be silly. Swimming's natural. Here.'

He started to peel her fingers away, one by one, standing behind her while she struggled. His chest hairs tickled her shoulders. When she fell back against him it was almost a surprise. He laughed, turned round with his hands under her arms and dropped her into the water beyond where her feet could reach. She shrieked, half in dismay, half in excitement, and sank, flapping her hands and feet, gasping and spluttering. She could see his feet, his legs, the undulating fabric of his shorts – and in her panic reached out and grabbed his waistband. He clamped his hand over hers and for a terrifying moment she thought he was going to hold her down there, but he pulled her against him and lifted her out of the water. Her knees rubbed against his chest.

'Once more without holding on to the side,' he said. 'I won't let you go.'

He made her float on her stomach and supported her with the flat of his hands again, but this time one of them slid lower. At first she thought it was a mistake and that he didn't realize and then she knew he must do. There were other people in the pool now and she was too embarrassed to protest or fight him. Tears streamed from her eyes, mingling with the pool water, unnoticed by the other swimmers. It happened so quickly, barely a second passing before he set her down in the shallow end and grabbed the stainless-steel arms of the ladder.

'Perhaps that's enough for one day,' he said abruptly. 'How would you like some hot chocolate?'

She didn't answer. She got out of the pool, still coughing up chemicals, her eyes stinging. She wanted to hurt him. She imagined digging her fingers into his eyes and gouging them. She imagined kicking him hard in the bollocks and making him double over in agony.

'You're trembling like a leaf,' he said. 'Go and have a shower. I'll meet you in the foyer.'

She dried herself off and dressed; picked up the offending swimming costume and rolled it into her towel. Once ready, she stood behind the door, not wanting to come out. The noise of the pool had increased since they arrived, but the voices sounded far away, lost in the echoing space. On the back of the door, under the fire exit instructions, someone had scrawled *Luke is a wanker* next to a crude drawing of a penis.

14

Half-term ❧ Saturday, 20 February 2010

I AM FINE ALL DAY, ACTUALLY LOOKING FORWARD TO Jenny's drinks party, and then at seven o'clock, after I've settled the children, had a bath and decided what to wear, it all goes wrong. It's Polly who reminds me that all is not well in this house. She potters into my bedroom while I'm getting changed.

'I don't want a burglar to come,' she says.

I lean closer to the mirror and run eyeliner above my lashes. 'He won't come, Polly. I promise.'

She looks at me in the mirror, big-eyed and trusting. 'Has the policeman catched him?'

What do I say? That they haven't caught him because I've lied about what he looks like? Do I now have to lie to my child? Yes, I do. I take a deep breath.

'He can't come back because he's too scared and he isn't in London any more. They know he's hundreds of miles away because they talk to other police in other places and they've heard he's in Scotland now.' Poor Scotland.

'I don't want to go to Scotland.'

'Well, you don't have to. Back to bed, sweetie. I'll come and tuck you in in a minute.'

It gets worse when the babysitter arrives. Magda is looking after Sophie Collins, so we've had to use someone else. She's sixteen, or so I've been assured, but she doesn't look more than fifteen, with her plaits and tatty jeans, sweatshirt and tired Converses.

The Forsyths live in a narrow Victorian mid-terraced house on Keats Avenue. Tom heads straight into the sitting room while I take our contribution, two excellent bottles of wine, into the kitchen where a girl who can't be more than twelve is arranging canapés on a tray. I get caught by Jenny, who thinks I'm an expert on paint colours and wants my opinion, and by the time I get into the crowded sitting room Tom has found a home with Simon and Robert.

The noise is overwhelming, exacerbated by the lack of carpets and curtains. The floorboards show where they've been hacked about to make way for plumbing and electrics. At the back of the room, another pre-teen is serving drinks from a trestle table covered with a sheet. I make my way over and take a glass of white wine. To the right of the makeshift bar French windows look out on to a long garden where fairy lights have been trailed across overgrown shrubs and woven in and out of the trellis. On the ground tea lights glow from inside jam jars dropped into brown paper bags. No one has braved the cold yet, but it's only a matter of time before the smokers discover its charm.

Amber has joined the men. She's wearing a wine-red

dress that makes her look more curvaceous than she actually is, hugging her body, enhancing her waist and pushing up her breasts. The hem falls barely halfway down her thighs. Her hair has been blow-dried and bounces off her shoulders. Amongst the unthreateningly soignée mothers she looks miraculously sexy. Millie taps me on the shoulder and I join a group of mothers. We talk about the usual things: children and schools. Even those of us without older children are already obsessed with the next stage. They expect me to know all the answers because I'm a teacher, but I'm only a fraction less neurotic about it than them. After that, conversation moves to my break-in. They want all the details: how he gained access; what burglar-alarm system we use; why we were so blissfully unaware that there was anyone in the house.

'So you came in and made coffee and put Josh down for his nap, and all the while, that man was hiding somewhere! Oh my God. I would freak if it was me.' This from Imogen Parker, who openly boasts that she never puts her burglar alarm on.

I escape politely after a few minutes and head for the drinks table where the nice twelve-year-old refills my glass.

'We were talking about dreams,' Tom says.

'I was pole-vaulting last night. It was fantastic.' Simon's whole body shakes when he laughs.

'Vicky dreams about murdering babies,' Amber says, winking at me.

I laugh uneasily. 'Amber! I'm never going to tell you anything.'

148

She leans into my husband and smiles at him and he takes his cue and puts his arm around her waist. Tom has always been physically affectionate and I've never minded before. I try to analyse why it's jarring now, and I think it's because Amber is tense when normally she's so natural with him. And perhaps it's because I'm no longer sure I know her as well as I thought I did.

'All it was,' I say, turning to look beseechingly at the others, 'was that when I was pregnant with Josh I had violent dreams. It was hormones. I never said anything about killing babies. It was about murdering my friends.'

'Oh, Vicky,' Amber says, pulling me into her side so that she's sandwiched between the two of us. 'I was only teasing.'

Later, I find myself on my own and overly self-conscious. I don't feel up to the task of forcing my way into a conversation so I push open the French windows and step outside into the chill. The garden is so beautiful and calm. The candles light the cherry tree from below, making a ghostly web of its branches and picking out the tiny green buds.

At the far end, the shed is in darkness and I wander over, hoping to hide until I feel better or get hypothermia; whichever comes first. Behind me, other guests take my cue and follow me out of the house. I walk away but my heels keep sinking into the lawn. Someone laughs and I turn abruptly, but it has nothing to do with me. Tiny lights flare as cigarettes are lit. A man's figure detaches itself from the group and starts moving towards me. It's Robert.

'Having a shifty fag?' I laugh. There's a tremor in my voice. I swallow and try again. 'Amber won't be pleased.' I don't want a conversation so I turn to go back in, but he blocks me.

'Stay a minute. It isn't often that I get a chance to speak to you on your own. How are you?'

'I'm fine.'

'Poor old Vicky. You've had a shit time of it, haven't you?'

I cross my arms against the chilly air and turn to him, scrutinizing his face.

'What's Amber told you?'

I have a horrible feeling that I feature heavily in their pillow talk.

'Don't worry. She hasn't been divulging your deepest secrets. I meant the last few months, since you had Josh. I get a sense that it's been more of a shock than you're letting on.'

'I have nothing to complain about,' I say. 'I'm really lucky.'

'But . . .'

'Well, you know . . .' I shrug and he smiles at me. It's nice that he understands. He is a lovely man.

'I wanted to ask you something,' he says.

'Fire away.'

He pauses. Robert has never been a great one for talking about himself. He's the kind of man who will always tell you everything is all right.

'Have you noticed anything different about Amber lately?'

150

'In what way different? I suppose she's happy about buying the house. That's bound to affect her mood.'

'It isn't that.' He grunts and starts again, and this time the words burst out. 'Being happy is fine. Euphoric is fine. But she's . . . I don't know. Just different. I can't do anything right . . . I'm sorry. I shouldn't be saying this to you.'

Do I tell Robert that I know exactly what he's talking about? But what good would that do? He's not expecting me to agree. He wants reassurance that he's wrong.

'To be honest, all I've noticed is that she's over-excited about the move. And I don't blame her. I would be too.'

His face falls. 'I've done my best.'

'I know you have, Robert.'

'Only, what I don't understand is where the money for the deposit is going to come from, and Amber doesn't get that. Or if she does, she's refusing to accept it. I've never seen her like this. It's as if she's possessed with the idea of owning that place and God help anyone who stands in her way. Including,' he adds ruefully, 'me.'

I need to tread carefully. 'I think she feels that if she perseveres and refuses to take no for an answer, it will happen. It's the way people tend to think these days. Is there no way you can raise the cash?'

'Short of murdering my parents, no. I work on a knife edge as it is, and it wouldn't take much to bring the company to its knees. When I was on my own it didn't matter. It's very different now. The pressure is enormous.'

'I know what you mean.'

'And even if I did manage to beg, steal or borrow

enough to secure it, how the hell am I supposed to pay for the renovations? She's living in cloud cuckoo land.' He stops and flushes deeply. 'I'm sorry. I shouldn't have said that.'

'Don't worry. I won't repeat it.'

He drags hard on his cigarette and lets the smoke filter out slowly. 'I suppose what I'm really worried about is that if I can't provide her with what she wants, she'll find someone who can.'

That is honest. It takes me a moment to process what he's said, even though it's crossed my own mind.

'She isn't like that. She loves you.'

'She's my life.' He pinches the bridge of his nose, his forehead bunching. 'I'm petrified of losing her.'

In the darkness, in his despair, he is attractive. It's a surprise. His eyes, though small, have a remarkable intensity.

'Why would you lose her?' I find I've dropped my voice to a whisper.

'Because I don't think I've ever really had her. I'm under no illusion, Vicky. I love Amber more than she loves me, and I don't resent that, because she deserves to be loved. But I wish . . . well, I wish we'd had another child and I wish I'd made more money. I feel such a failure. And now it looks like we're piggybacking on to your holiday.'

Those last words smack of despair and I hesitate before I answer. I understand his pride. Mum didn't accept financial help, even from boyfriends. We managed by finding all sorts of ways around our problems.

'I do know how you feel. I grew up in a difficult financial situation myself, but you really mustn't talk about piggybacking. You and Amber are practically family. Please come.'

'All right. Thank you.' He takes my hand and to my surprise, kisses it, still holding the remains of his cigarette between two fingers. It's a side of Robert Collins I haven't seen before, and it charms me. 'Do you know something, Vicky? You are a really sweet person.'

'I'm not sweet. I just care about my friends. It will be OK. You'll see. You'll move into the house and everything will settle down. Come on, let's go in. They'll be wondering what we're talking about.'

He tightens his hands round mine, keeping me from moving away. 'I'll understand if you feel you have to tell Tom about this conversation, but please don't tell Amber.'

'I won't tell either of them.'

Tom is in a good mood when we get in around eleven. He pays the babysitter and waits for her to unlock her bicycle and ride off, then pulls me into a hug. I wriggle out of his embrace and collapse on to the bottom stair, pull off my high heels and rub my feet.

'Why don't we drive down to the coast tomorrow?' he says, suppressing a yawn. 'I could do with some fresh air.'

I tilt my head, thinking about it, and then shrug. 'Yeah, why not. The kids will be happy. I'll call Mum in the morning and let her know.'

He looks down at me as he hangs his coat over the banister. 'Why don't you see if Robert and Amber want to come too?'

I pause. 'We could,' I say carefully. 'But let me try

Jenny and Simon first. I want to get to know them better.

He gives me an appraising look and I smile up at him blandly, as if it's nothing. He doesn't know that I've begun to question my reliance on my closest friend. I love Amber to bits, but sometimes I feel owned by her, as if I have to ask permission to do anything and include her in absolutely everything.

'They'll still be clearing up,' he said. 'They won't want to come.'

But he's reckoned without Jenny, who, by the time I call at eight, has already been up for two hours and is only too happy to round up her family and jump in the car and escape.

June 1992

To avoid going home Katya went to the library after school and did her homework there. It was maths so it didn't take long. She wondered whether Luke was worried about her and decided she didn't care if he was. She didn't think he would tell because that would make Sally curious about why she was avoiding him. She wandered round the children's section, taking out books, flicking through them and rejecting them. Sally said her reading was coming on, but not compared to Gabriella, who was on quite grown-up books now. She found something with pictures and tried to ignore her hunger. She was hungry all the time these days, and thought she must be growing at last. She read a few pages and then rested her head on her arms and dozed off, waking with the side of the book imprinted on her cheek.

She wandered out into the early evening and walked all the way down to McDonald's, where she knew she would be left alone, and managed to kill an hour learning her spellings. *Friend, lorry, cinema, lioness, parsley, exercise, castle, tablet.* It upset her that her spellings were different from the ones Gabriella got given. She had words like *excellent, accommodation, alienate* and *catastrophe.* Katya didn't like to be made to feel inferior, particularly to Gabriella, who never passed up an opportunity to show off at her expense.

Luke and Maggie were approaching on the other side of the road. Spotting them, she hastily repacked her rucksack. What were those two doing together? Luke must have phoned Maggie and told her some story; pretending to be a good foster parent, worried sick about Katya. Maggie was gesturing, her arm bumping Luke's, and he had his hands in his pockets, his shoulders slightly rounded as he leant in to catch what she was saying. Katya pretended to be surprised when Maggie rapped on the glass. Maggie and Luke exchanged a few words, and Luke shrugged and pulled a packet of cigarettes out of his pocket. She left him outside and slid into the seat beside Katya.

'So, are you going to tell me what's up?'

Katya glanced out of the window in time to see Luke release an unhurried plume of smoke. 'I didn't feel like going home.'

'You can't go scaring people like this. Luke and I have been at our wits' end. If we hadn't found you in a few minutes we would have had to call Sally.'

'I don't like him.'

'But he's such a nice man. He cares about you; they both do. You can't repay their kindness by disappearing. It's not fair on them.'

Katya shrank from describing how he made her feel.

'They quarrel,' she said at last. 'It's my fault. Now he's not got a job I'm just a nuisance. I want to live somewhere else.'

Maggie took hold of her hands. Her brown eyes seemed to change colour, to darken. 'What kind of quarrels?'

'Stupid ones. I hate it there. I don't . . .'

She made a face. She couldn't tell Maggie what was happening, about the touching. Luke had warned her about the consequences. He would say she was just like her mother. But he also said he loved her and she thought she might love him when she didn't hate his guts. He treated her like an adult, telling her things about him and Sally that she really shouldn't know, congratulating her on being so mature even though she was only a kid. She was so confused that when she started to think of him at night, the only way to stop was to jab herself with a compass. She ran her fingers over the constellation of little scabs on the back of her hand, over and over, knowing their position by heart.

Luke leant over her to shut the front door. She tried to make herself small. She had looked at the clock in Maggie's car before she got out, so she knew it was gone twenty past seven. Only one hour and forty minutes until Sally got in. Too long for her peace of mind.

'You're not scared of me, are you?'

'No,' she mumbled.

He cupped her face in his hands, the pads of his thumbs against her lips. They smelled of cigarettes. She held her breath.

'Because you know I've got your best interests at heart, don't you?'

She nodded as she imagined sinking her teeth into his flesh, his roar of surprise and anger. She desperately needed a wee. Luke let her go and she darted for the bathroom, hearing him laugh as she slammed the door. Ten minutes later she found him spooning baked beans out of a saucepan on to a slice of buttered toast. She ate slowly, making the meal last as long as possible even though she wanted to wolf it down.

'I'm not going to tell Sal what you did today, so don't you go telling her I was smoking,' Luke said. 'There's a good girl.'

Later she sat on the edge of the sofa with her hands underneath her bottom, watching *Coronation Street*, a programme she had become addicted to ever since Sally started her on it. She was used to the oppression of Luke's presence in the house when he had nothing to amuse him, used to being expected to entertain him, but she hoped he would at least allow her to watch the episode till the end.

'Why did you stay out?' He had snuck up behind her and was leaning on the back of the sofa.

She shifted so that she couldn't smell the alcohol on his breath. Lately he'd begun to smell like some of the men who had visited Linda.

She stared at the television set. 'I don't know.'

He massaged her shoulders and she tensed, holding her breath as his fingers kneaded and pummelled her muscles, getting right in deep between her bones. From his angle above her he couldn't see that her face was all scrunched up, that she was mouthing, 'Stop it,' under her breath.

'Feeling better now, Princess? Sally loves that when she's stressed.'

He moved into the kitchen area and Katya pulled her feet up, contorting herself into a tight ball. She chewed the hem of her dress where it stretched over her knees.

15

Sunday, 21 February 2010

'HAVE WE LOST ALL SENSE OF PROPORTION? WHAT parent hasn't left a child asleep in their car while they've dashed into the shops?'

We are listening to Paddy O'Connell's Sunday-morning programme on the way to the coast and one of the celebrity guests has picked this particular case as their news item.

'The problem is where to draw the line.'

'Surely you must agree there's a wealth of difference between leaving a child locked in his bedroom while you go clubbing and picking up a bottle of milk from the corner shop.'

I reach to turn the radio off, but Tom stops me, pushing my hand away from the knob.

'Leave it on. I'm interested in this.'

I fold my hands on my lap. What is Tom thinking? Is he connecting what they're saying to Josh? To me? I twist round and glance at the children. Josh is asleep, Emily is staring out of the window and Polly is eating the remains of the toast and Marmite I couldn't get her to finish at breakfast.

'You know that most accidents happen at home or close to home? It only takes a second.'

'So what are you saying? We never leave a child even for one moment, in case lightning strikes?'

'The point is small children are extremely vulnerable. Animals don't leave their young in case a predator comes along. It's survival instinct.'

'Did the baby die?'

'What?' I shake myself, rattled.

'Did the baby die?' Emily repeats.

Tom switches off the radio. 'No, the baby did not die. The baby was fine. Nothing happened.'

'Then why are they talking about it?'

'I don't know, sweetie.'

'You won't leave me alone, will you, Mummy?'

'No, of course I won't.'

I bend down and reach for the box of CDs at my feet. 'Why don't we put on some music?'

By eleven, after a stopover at Mum's to soothe our mild hangovers with a full English breakfast washed down with strong tea, we are on the beach, accompanied by an over-excited Schnauzer. The sun is shining, wind gusting off the sea, and it's nippy, but we make a happy troupe in our padded coats, hats, scarves and walking boots. Jenny, in a ski jacket, a fur hat with flaps and sheepskin boots, looks as though she's come prepared for a trek across the Arctic. I'm used to the seaside and the way the sun can shine while the wind replaces its heat with chill. I feel the cold, but it doesn't bother me here like it does in London. It's part of the package and has a quality that reminds me of childhood; of feet smacking on seawater, of seagulls and the impenetrable mists that regularly enveloped our house in swirling clouds of grey so that we felt as though we were in the clouds.

The tide is as far out as it can go and the girls rush down to the shore in their brightly coloured fleeces and crouch in the shimmering sand, water pooling round the dips made by the weight of their booted feet. Max scampers after them, sniffing at the hole they are digging, occasionally looking back at us and barking. Rose picks up a worm on the end of her spade and she and Emily charge across the beach screaming, Polly in hot pursuit, her fine blonde hair flying out behind her, Max at her heels. They spread their arms and move in formation, like a flock of starlings turning in flight, and veer towards the shore, shrieking as they splash through the shallows.

'Oh, look at Emily!' Jenny cries. 'Isn't she fabulous?'

My daughter has thrown herself into a series of cart-wheels, her legs flying, her landings perfect. Rose emulates her and Polly tries, flinging down her arms and doing a little skip with her legs.

Tom and Simon, who have Josh and Spike in child carriers on their backs, walk ahead, occasionally turning to check on the girls. I'm glad they're getting on so well. And I like Jenny. I feel relaxed in her company the way I used to with Amber. The thought pulls me up. Am I really not relaxed with her any more? How odd and sad that it should be so. Is it about money or is it about what I did? I'm not sure, but I'm beginning to think the two things are connected. I shocked her when I left Josh on his own and hurt her when I failed to tell her about David. I was wrong on both counts, but it's too late now. I just have to hope she forgives me.

Jenny takes a big breath and lets it go slowly. 'This is so much fun. Thanks for inviting us.'

She digs in her capacious shoulder bag for a bottle of water as the girls run over, unscrews the top and hands it to Rose, who tips her head back and glugs, squeezing the bottle until it cracks, earning a reprimand from her mother. Tom and Simon wait for us to catch up. They are wearing similar coats, oilskin in a muddy shade of green, but that's where the resemblance ends. Tom is in black skinny trousers and Simon is wearing mustard-coloured corduroys. Simon is short and stout, Tom tall, lean and apt to stoop when he's with a smaller companion.

'This is fantastic,' Tom says. 'It's so great to be out of town. Whose brilliant idea was it?'

'Yours, darling.' I plant a kiss on his cheek.

We find a reasonably dry patch and sit down on our coats so that the boys can crawl around. Josh is in a good mood, having slept for the best part of two hours. He pushes himself forward by concertinaing his legs, like a frog sitting on its bottom, and tries to scoop up the sand. I cover his cast with the protective sleeve and he tugs it down. I tweak it into place and he shouts at me, pushing his fingers into the plastic, his frustration with it rapidly turning into anger.

'He doesn't like it,' Polly says.

'Sorry, Joshie. But you have to wear it. I haven't really thought this through,' I say to Jenny. 'He's not allowed to get the plaster wet.'

'When does it come off?'

'Next week. Can't wait. It's ridiculous how hard it makes life. And it's really held up his crawling.'

Jenny lets Josh wrap his fingers round hers. 'You're a brave boy, aren't you?' She earns a winning smile.

'Amber looked amazing at the party,' she says a few minutes later. 'Really gorgeous.'

'Yes, she did look lovely.'

I mean it sincerely, but I can feel the conversation leading somewhere. Maybe it's to do with the fact that Jenny's a lawyer; she picks up on nuances others might miss.

'I know this is none of my business, but have you two had a row?'

'No. Why do you ask?'

She brushes sand off her fingertips. 'Well, you seem on edge with each other, that's all. Sorry, maybe I'm imagining it. Forget I said anything.' She holds her hair away from her face and squints into the winter sun. Twenty yards away Simon and Tom take turns with the three girls, holding them by their wrists and whirling them around above the breaking waves. Max is going mad.

I smile and look back at Jenny. 'There's nothing wrong.'

I can't tell if she's fishing for gossip or if her concern is genuine. I don't know her well enough yet. I didn't think my relationship with Amber had visibly changed – I thought it was only me. How awful that it shows.

She scrabbles around in her bag and I have a feeling she's playing for time and I'm right because when she does speak she chooses her words with care. 'It's just . . . she flirts with Simon. She had him eating out of the palm of her hand at the party.'

'Ah.' I try not to laugh as I glance at her portly, ruddy-faced husband. 'Amber flirts with all the men. Simon was probably flattered. He's a bloke and she's very attractive. You have nothing to worry about. She's the same with Tom. It's harmless.'

A text pings into my phone. 'Talk of the devil.'

Have you got time for a coffee? Ax

I stare at the message and start to type:

Sorry, I'm out all day. Vx

Why didn't I say we were down in Bognor, or that we had the Forsyths with us? It feels weird not to have made that clear. Instinct, I suppose. But instinct is often my Achilles' heel.

'I love this house,' Jenny says when we're back inside at Mum's, our cheeks pink and burning from the wind, the children changed into dry clothes.

Mum makes them hot chocolate with marshmallows and coffee for us. She coos over the babies, opening the sea chest full of toys and encouraging the boys to strew them all over the dining-room floor. Spike and Josh fall into the pile, burbling ecstatically. In the kitchen I lay the table while Mum makes soup. Jenny sips her coffee and asks her all about the B & B and how it works and whether she still enjoys it.

'Yes and no. I sometimes think I should move on, do something different. I've been here for seventeen years and the town doesn't get any better. I was thinking I might like a change.'

'You never mentioned that to me,' I say. 'I can't imagine you not being here.'

'I know. But I am only forty-six and I'm beginning to feel like it's time for a change; I could start over, reinvent myself.'

'What made you come here?' Jenny asks.

'Oh, circumstances beyond my control.' Mum's smile closes the subject.

'I'm going to get the papers,' Amber shouts up at Robert.

'Do you want me to come with you?'

'No, that's all right. You finish what you're doing. Sophie's happy with *The Princess Bride*. I'll only be twenty minutes.'

She flings on her black jacket, wraps a baby-pink scarf round her neck and runs downstairs. She glares at the door to the ground-floor flat. They've been away since Friday. From time to time the lads get tired of slumming it and go back to Mummy and Daddy in the countryside, no doubt taking their festering washing with them. She picks up their post and sorts through it, drops anything boring back on the floor and keeps a couple of important-looking envelopes. She rips them up and drops the pieces into her bag.

It's one thing to take the Forsyths out for the day, but to try and keep it from her when the lie could be, and was, so easily detected, is downright cruel. Amber knows all about it because Robert bumped into Simon on Tennyson Street when he went for the Sunday papers and Simon told him they were going. Amber had struggled to maintain her cool, not to lose it in front of Sophie but she's angry and hurt. She gave Vicky a chance to come clean but she blew it. She's a coward.

Amber lets herself into Vicky's house, switches off the alarm, closes the door quietly behind her, puts her bag down on the floor and slips off her boots. The Seagraves and the Collinses have been keyholders for each other for years. She's used to going in and out when they're away, checking things for them, twitching curtains, picking the mail up off the floor and making it look as though the house is occupied. It's no big deal.

There's a basket of blue hyacinths on the kitchen table and their scent mingles with that of toast and coffee, but the place feels different without the family in it; hollow and lacking in warmth. She finds that even with the mood she's currently in she can make a dispassionate assessment of its current value. She reckons on twice what they paid for it, if not more.

But that's not what she's here for. She runs up to the children's floor, goes into their bathroom, turns on the basin tap and pushes in the plug. Done. It could have been either of the children, though Amber guesses the blame will most likely fall on Polly because Polly does do some odd things and is allowed to get away with far too much. The scribbled-on walls are testament to that.

Before she leaves she goes into Tom's study. His desk is cluttered but tidy. He's not a slovenly person but he does like his stuff. There's a navy-blue fleece hanging over the back of the chair and she picks it up and presses her nose into it. It smells of washing powder, not of him, so she puts it back and turns her attention to the shelves. A quick perusal of their bank statements proves that they do have money. She remembers Tom's grandfather dying last year. He had said he'd been left a useful chunk of cash. Not a fortune, granted, but enough for her needs.

She replaces the file and goes upstairs for a quick peek into the bathroom where water is already pooling on to the floor around the pedestal. She's made allowances, she's been forgiving, but now as far as she's concerned she's no longer under any obligation. Whatever loyalty she still feels for Vicky Seagrave is rapidly dissipating. She needs to know that actions produce consequences.

As an afterthought she edges round the puddle and pushes the white plastic stepping stool in front of the basin.

Then she leaves.

16

THE CHILDREN ARE OUT FOR THE COUNT WHEN WE GET home just after six, Polly's head lolling on Josh's lap, rusk crumbs sticking to her cheeks and hair. Josh's water bottle has tipped, the water dripping from the rubber teat into his trousers. Emily is sound asleep. My hair is a mess, whipped up by the wind and sticky with salt, but I feel the right sort of tired. We've had a lovely time and I have the satisfaction of knowing that Jenny and Simon enjoyed themselves too. Amber's text is bothering me, but I can't do anything about it to-night. Tomorrow I'll drop it into conversation and try not to look as though I deliberately tried to hide anything from her. It was a bad move and I regret it.

Tom turns into Coleridge Street with a sigh but his relief turns to dismay at the sight of a squad car parked a few yards from our house. The policewoman sitting in the driver's seat looks up as we turn on to our forecourt. Grayling is with her.

'What do you think they want?' Tom says.

'God knows.' My heart is pounding.

Grayling gets out and comes to lend a hand as we

struggle with sleepy children, coats and bags. Polly looks amazed. Emily stares but is thankfully too drowsy to initiate an interrogation. I put the bags down at my feet and transfer a slumped and damp Josh into the crook of my left arm, but my nerves make me clumsy and I drop the keys.

'Move your foot.'

I shift and Grayling retrieves them, opening the door for me and I walk into the dim hall. Josh stares at the detective over my shoulder while I deal with the alarm. He grabs at my hair, tangles his hands in it and starts to scream. Grayling is silhouetted by the street light.

'It's all right, son,' Grayling says, flicking the light switch. 'He must have thought I was the burglar.' He smiles sheepishly. 'Sorry about that.'

'Don't be. It wasn't your fault.' I actually like this man. He's sensible and intelligent and seems sympathetic. The girls cling to my legs, gazing at him. 'So, what's happening? Why are you here?'

'We've brought someone in. He's helping with our inquiries at this stage, but if you wouldn't mind, we'd like to put you and Mrs Collins in front of an identity parade.'

'When? I mean, we've only just got in and we've been out all day. Couldn't it wait until tomorrow?'

Tom takes the baby from me, detaching his fingers one at a time. 'I'll make them their supper,' he says. 'You do what you have to do.'

I turn to Grayling, raising my eyebrows.

'Now would be ideal, if you can bear it. We can't keep him in much longer. I'll take you. One of my officers is picking up Mrs Collins.'

'Oh fuck,' Tom roars from the kitchen. 'I don't believe this.' The kitchen door bursts open and Emily runs out.

'There's water,' she says, wide-eyed. 'Everywhere!'

I turn away from Grayling and hurry after her. She wasn't exaggerating. I look up at the ceiling. There's a large round wet patch from which water is dripping rapidly, splashing into a small lake on the stone at my feet. Tom bangs a saucepan down underneath it, hands me Josh and runs upstairs. Moments later I hear him shout for the girls. I glance at Grayling, who nods and smiles, as if to say, Take your time.

'Can you give me a minute?' I ask.

'Sure. No problem. I'll be in the car.'

Tom is standing in the bathroom doorway, with Polly and Emily. The floor is flooded, the blue and white lino tiles ruined. Even the landing carpet squelches underfoot.

'Da,' Josh says, pointing at his father.

Polly puts her thumb in her mouth and gazes at me with wide, anxious eyes.

'Which one of you was it?' Tom asks.

On cue, both girls shake their heads, but Polly's bottom lip trembles whilst Emily remains firm in her defiance.

'It wasn't me,' she says.

'Polly?' I crouch down and stare into her eyes. 'Did you do this, darling? Tell me the truth.'

'I didn't,' she says.

I keep looking at her. Tom puts his hand on her head and strokes her hair.

171

'Are you sure you didn't? It could have been an accident. You can tell me.'

Tears run down her cheeks and I glance up at him and frown. I don't know what to do. I've got Grayling waiting downstairs, but we need to deal with this. It's already too late to be cross with her, but we can't just ignore it. Josh wriggles so I set him down. He needs a bath anyway. He crawls straight over to his sister and gazes up at her in mute concern and soon they're both howling. I can't get a word of sense out of Polly and Tom has already hurried downstairs with Emily hard on his heels to fetch the mop. I pick up Josh and take them both into the girls' bedroom.

'It doesn't matter,' I say, wiping her tragic face with one of Josh's muslins, Josh under the other arm, clinging to me. Tom clumps back upstairs with the bucket and mop.

'You'd better get off,' he says.

'Will you try and find out what happened?'

'There's no point. It's far too late.'

'OK. There's no need to snap at me, Tom.'

'Sorry. But I refuse to ruin a lovely day.'

'And you think I want to?'

The whole business has upset me more than I thought possible. Polly has never been devious. Yes, she can be destructive, but she always confesses and always says that she's sorry. I've never known her to tell lies. Maybe, I've wronged her. Maybe it was Emily. But even that's out of character. Emily can be a little madam, but she's never deliberately got her sister into trouble. And now

Tom and I are getting at each other. All I want is a glass of wine and a takeaway, but I have a police car waiting for me, and I'm going to be seeing Amber sooner than I expected.

17

THE POLICEWOMAN EXECUTES A NEAT U-TURN AND heads towards the London Road. Traffic is backed up at the lights and there's a problem with a double-decker bus way ahead of us, so we're stuck for a while. I explained what had happened as I hurried out of the house with Grayling, but since then I've been silent. The damage is considerable, passing through the house from the top floor all the way to the kitchen. The tap must have been on full flow, twisted hard round, for it to have achieved that. It was no accident. I wonder what I've done wrong, or what Tom's done, to have made Polly or Emily do it. It's so out of character. The stool had been placed at the bottom of the pedestal and that smacks of Polly. Emily doesn't need it any more. Polly has always been the uncomplicated child, the child who wears her emotions on her sleeve.

Grayling twists round and says conversationally, 'I hear you've been to the coast for the day.'

I gather my thoughts. 'Yes.'

'Whereabouts?'

'Bognor Regis.'

He catches my eye in the mirror and crow's feet fan out as he smiles.

'My mum lives there,' I say, defensive of poor maligned Bognor. 'And it's where I grew up. There's loads for the children to do.'

'Good to get away from London.'

I catch him looking at me. His expression is benign, almost avuncular, as if he wants me to think his interest is friendly and unthreatening, but since he's made it clear that he's sceptical, that cuts no ice.

The traffic moves and we make it halfway to the crossroads. The bus is surrounded by orange cones, its engine door open. As we edge slowly past, a teenage girl waiting at the bus stop looks up from her phone and straight into my eyes. I recognize the waitress from Jenny's party.

You'll never guess who I saw in the back of a police car. Vicky Seagrave.

I twist round and peer through the rear window. Her eyes are glued to her phone again. I lean back against the leather seats and close my eyes. I have to get a grip. I'm on my way to help with inquiries, not under suspicion. One day I'll be relating this as an anecdote. People will laugh at my consternation.

Grayling breaks my thoughts. 'You and Mrs Collins are very good friends.'

Does he have any inkling how loaded that question is? He must do, as Jenny must have done when she brought the subject up. He's an intuitive and thoughtful man. This isn't merely an exercise in polite conversation.

'I've known her since before Emily was born.'

'My wife has a best mate but they're always falling out. Drives me nuts.' He flicks his eyes at the mirror and catches mine momentarily. 'I don't understand it myself. Male friendships are much simpler.'

'Like Jesus and Judas,' I reply.

He laughs like I've said something genuinely funny. 'Touché.'

'What does your wife do?'

'She doesn't. She used to be a social worker but had to stop when she had children.'

'That's a difficult job,' I reply carefully.

'You're telling me.'

'Does she miss it?' Is there a subtext here? Am I being probed, delicately, for fault lines?

'A little. She wanted to make a difference but there were times when a case kept her awake at night, shook her so badly that she could barely even talk to me. It got easier as she became more experienced and better at detaching herself emotionally, but you know, that wasn't ideal either. She's a lovely person and what she saw . . . well, it can be hard to wash out. It's like a stain on your psyche.'

'Poor woman. She's lucky to have you.'

'No, I'm lucky to have her.' He opens his mouth to say something else and apparently changes his mind.

I fill the gap. 'So who is this guy I'm going to look at?'

'He was caught last night breaking and entering a house about two miles from yours and the earlier burglary. Similar kind of set-up and same point of entry. Broad daylight.' He looks up at the mirror again, straight

176

into my eyes. 'He doesn't match your description, to be honest, but I thought it was worth a shot.'

I don't blink. 'Of course it is.'

We're finally through the traffic lights and the road ahead gives us a clear run to the police station. The WPC swings the car into a narrow lane that leads to a car park at the back, and slots us between an unmarked car and a motorbike. We get out and Grayling leads me through the back door, along a corridor with grey walls and a squeaky lino floor, and into an empty waiting room.

'Where's Amber?' I ask, turning to confront him. 'I thought she'd be here.'

'She'll have gone in already, I expect. Can I get someone to bring you a cup of tea?'

'No thank you.'

Rows of blue chairs line three of the walls and above them posters warn helpfully of the perils we might come across in our daily lives. I mentally sort them into alphabetical order: Abuse. Burglary. Car theft. Drugs.

I had fully expected to go in with Amber and I can't help wondering if he's done this on purpose, if it suits him better this way. I had imagined us scrutinizing the suspects together. I check my emails and texts but, apart from the earlier one, there's nothing from her. Why didn't she call me?

A copy of the *Mail on Sunday* lies folded on the seat beside me and I pick it up. My stomach clenches when I read the headline: 'The Price of a Pint of Milk'.

It's a rant from a female journalist about the family who had their child removed; outraged and acerbically amusing. The words blur. I shove it away, as if it's something alive and disgusting. After what feels like hours, a policewoman pushes the door open and I start guiltily.

'We're ready for you, Mrs Seagrave.'

Down the corridor, Amber is being escorted out by a young policewoman. She smiles and raises her hand in greeting and I raise mine. It feels as though time slows and stretches, and then we pass with a brief snagging of our eyes and it speeds up again. I learn nothing from the encounter, am able to read nothing in her glance. If anything, it makes me more nervous.

On the other side of the mirror in the viewing room there are eight men dressed in T-shirts and jeans. They stand with feet apart, right hand gripping the left wrist. Grayling leans against the wall a few feet away from me, his arms folded across his chest.

'Take your time, Mrs Seagrave.'

I take him literally and give at least ten seconds to each man. The intruder who broke into my house is second from the left. I recognize everything about him, including things I didn't even realize I'd noticed, from the shape of his forehead, to his hairline, to the way his left shoulder is lower than the right. I recognize his thin, pale mouth and the broad shape of his face. His head is dipped and he's gazing straight at the mirror from under lowered lids. His expression is absolutely blank but I can easily guess what he's thinking. I can't accuse him and he can't accuse me. *Impasse*. I debate whether it matters if my responses don't match Amber's and decide it doesn't. Maybe they made them turn their backs towards her because that's how she says she saw him.

I shake my head.

'No one even faintly familiar?' Grayling says.

'They're not the right type. Sorry.'

He moves away from the wall and comes to stand beside me. I feel his presence intensely and it makes my heart jump about. The seconds tick by and he doesn't say anything, and I start to sweat. It prickles beneath my arms and heat rises uncomfortably up the back of my neck. Finally, he moves to the door and holds it open for me. I don't breathe until I'm out of the building and in the back of the police car. A WPC drives me home, for which I'm thankful. I don't think I could have stood another tête-à-tête with Grayling. When we are nearly there I have a thought and ask her to pull over outside the Spar on Tennyson Street. I tell her I need to get some milk and will walk the rest of the way. She doesn't question it. I go in and hover close to the door until she's done a U-turn and driven off, then I leave the shop and head towards Amber's.

Amber presses the buzzer to let Vicky in and opens the door to the flat. She hums as she transfers the leftovers of Robert's roast chicken into a smaller dish, covers it with cling film and pops it in the fridge. Should be plenty for lunch tomorrow if she makes a salad out of it. She turns as Vicky drops her bag on to one of the chairs.

'Where's Robert?' she asks as she kisses Amber's cheek.

'Nice to see you too.'

'Sorry. Start again.' She takes off her jacket and hangs it on the hook where Amber keeps her apron. Her hands are cold and she holds them against the radiator for a moment. 'It's freezing out there.'

'Robert's reading to Sophie. Glass of wine?'

'Oh, no. I can't stay long. We've had a bit of a disaster at home. I just wanted a quick chat about tonight.'

Amber nods and closes the kitchen door. 'So how was it for you?' She twitches her eyebrows, making Vicky laugh.

'I don't know. OK, I suppose. It was difficult, trying to pretend not to recognize him without hamming it up like a bad actor. I was convinced Grayling could tell. It's the way he looks at you, like he's got a degree in body language.'

'I know what you mean. Wasn't it weird, seeing that man again? Gave me the shivers.'

'What did you tell Grayling?'

She regards Vicky over her glass. 'Nothing. You needn't worry. You've got away with it.'

'That's not how it feels. I should have told them the truth straight away and I shouldn't have involved you. I am so sorry.'

'Don't be silly.' She pauses. 'So how was Jenny? Did you have a nice day beside the sea?'

She allows the silence to stretch. They contemplate each other and it's Vicky who looks away first. Downstairs are back, judging by the music. Amber looks out of the window. One of them is out there, sitting in the dark on the bricked edge of the flower bed, smoking a cigarette. Graham, she thinks. Or is it Paul? It might be

180

Paul. She's never taken the trouble to learn who's who. He taps ash into a beer bottle at his feet, looks up and catches her eye. She stares him out. She hates the lot of them.

She turns. 'You didn't have to hide it, you know.'

Vicky gazes at her and tears well up. 'I meant to tell you. I am sorry.'

'No,' Amber says hurriedly. 'Listen. It's as much my fault as yours. Things have been a little strange recently. And I know you've been under a lot of pressure. I was only teasing.'

'I should have mentioned it but I was fighting Josh over his protective sleeve when your text came in. I wasn't thinking.'

'Vicky, I'm not going to go into a jealous frenzy because you and Tom have taken some other family to the seaside. I just want to know, does it have anything to do with what I asked you? Have I spoilt things between us?'

'No! No, of course not. Amber, you are my best friend.'

And you are so transparent. She can see where Polly gets it from. The mere hint that she might be in trouble and she dissolves. Poor Vicky. All Amber has to do is pet her and stroke her ego and all will be well.

But then why does she feel so sad? So lost? Where has this sudden welling of emotion come from? She bites down on her lip and turns her back on Vicky, wrings a cloth out under the hot tap and starts to clean the surfaces. Robert is an incurably messy cook. Maybe it's just that she's finding it hard to contemplate the end of a friendship. Because, when all this is over, what will she do without Vicky? Is it worth it even? Maybe she should go back to where they were before, ignore all the provocations, the reminders.

'Amber, what's wrong?' Vicky's hand is on her shoulder.

She turns round and allows herself to be hugged. 'Sorry,' she sniffs. 'It's not your fault. I've had a shitty weekend.'

'Browning Street?'

She nods. 'I can't help myself. I took the keys home on Friday and I keep going back, even though it's torture. I want it so much. It's eating away at me. That's why I needed to see you this afternoon. To get some perspective.'

'I don't think me telling you it's just a house is going to help.' Vicky is joking and Amber manages a small smile.

'No. You won't say anything to Robert, will you? He doesn't know I've been round and I don't want him to.' She extricates herself from Vicky's embrace and blows her nose. 'So what's the disaster?'

Vicky is already putting her coat back on, doing up the buttons, turning up the collar. She groans.

'You won't believe it, but one of the girls left the tap running in their basin upstairs. It's gone right through the house.'

'Oh my God, how awful. Which one of them did it? Not Polly, surely.'

'They're both denying it.'

Amber gives a little shrug. 'It might have been an accident.'

'I don't think so. The plug was in. That's what's so upsetting.'

'Goodness. I've never had either of your girls pegged as malicious.'

A hint of defensiveness passes across Vicky's face. 'They aren't.'

That was poorly judged. 'No, of course not. Maybe you or Tom said or did something inadvertently. Something that made one of them feel demeaned? I don't know, but these things don't come out of nowhere and it's easy to forget how deeply children can feel.'

'Oh, I'm in no doubt it's my fault,' Vicky sighs. 'But I don't think there was anything wrong this morning. And we had a really happy day.'

So you did, Amber thinks. Good for you.

June 1992

MAGGIE'S GREEN LINEN COAT WAS HANGING OVER THE banister. Katya frowned at it. The school must have noticed her absence already and raised the alarm. It was the first time since she'd been at the Bryants' that she'd gone missing during the day, but Gabriella said Linda had died because she was a junkie and a prostitute and refused to let Katya join in her game. She left right at the beginning of lunch break, so it would be a surprise if they had noticed that she was gone yet, but not impossible. Luke wasn't even supposed to be here or she never would have come back. He'd told them he had an interview in the city and would be gone all day. He must have lied. Maybe he always lied. But how was he going to get a job if he didn't go to interviews? This was a problem.

She found Maggie in the kitchen wearing a colourful cotton summer dress that flowed out from an elasticated waist under her boobs and her hair was loose and wild. The radio was on. Katya watched as she spread butter on two slices of bread, swaying her large bum to the music.

'Maggie.'

Maggie jerked, dropped the knife and pressed her hand to her throat. 'Katya! You scared the life out of me! Why aren't you at school?'

Katya took in the scene and answered with a question of her own. 'Why are you here?'

Maggie retrieved the knife and put it in the dishwasher. When she faced Katya again her skin was flushed. 'I was passing so I dropped in to have a quick chat with Luke about your transition to senior school.'

Katya glanced down at Maggie's bare feet and back up at her eyes. Maggie turned away abruptly, cut the sandwiches into triangles and took them to the table.

'Where's Luke?'

'In the shower. When I got here he wasn't even out of bed.'

She spoke too fast, like she was making up excuses. Their eyes met and held and Katya felt a dawning horror. She backed out of the room, shaking her head slowly. Maggie rushed over and caught her by the arm.

'Let go of me! I know what you're doing.'

She struggled, but Maggie's grip tightened. Katya had always thought of her as soft, when she was in fact very strong. It was the fear in Maggie's eyes that told Katya she was right. They had been doing it while the house was empty. She'd seen that expression and smelt that particular scent on her mother.

'He said he had an interview!' she yelled, squirming to free herself. 'Why are you telling lies?'

'Shh. Don't be silly. No one's lying. Luke is unhappy about the job situation, and he's been trying so hard to pretend everything's all right. When I saw the state he was in I told him to get a wash and I'd make him something to eat. I felt sorry for him, darling. That's all.'

'What are you doing back here?'

Luke appeared in the doorway roughly towelling his hair. He didn't look particularly upset. Maggie let her go and Katya shrank from her, rubbing her bruised arms.

'She's going back to school now,' Maggie said. 'She forgot her games kit. Perhaps I'd better go too.'

A look passed between her and Luke. He leaned over and said something under his breath and then they both went out front. Katya ran into the lounge and watched from the window. She saw how close they stood, how Maggie placed her hand on his chest, quickly, as if she'd been trying not to smile. She looked sappy. Katya's breath misted the window. She wanted to crash her fists against it. Instead she gripped the curtain so tightly she left nail marks in the fabric.

She expected Luke to take her to school but after that he seemed to assume that she'd stay, that they'd be together for the afternoon. That made up her mind. There were twenty minutes before her science class started and with any luck, if she ran, no one would notice she'd been gone.

18

Saturday, 6 March 2010

THE ENTERTAINMENT FOR EMILY'S BIRTHDAY PARTY arrives: Princess Daisy-Petal and her box of face paints, sequins and feathers, ridiculously bubbly and smiley and ready to transform fifteen little girls into fairies and princesses. She prances into the house in character before she's even changed, exclaiming at how lovely everything is, how gorgeous the children are, how she can feel the magic in the air. I wouldn't have been surprised if she had sprouted wings. Slightly overwhelmed, I settle her and then the bell rings again and I find Amber at the door with Sophie. Emily greets her friend and drags her into the kitchen to show off the table she's helped decorate.

Despite our best efforts, chaos rapidly descends. The doorbell keeps ringing. Parents issue instructions I'll immediately forget, about not giving one child chocolate and another needing reminding to go to the loo. I make myself react with pleasure and understanding when handed a plastic tub of gluten-, egg- and sugar-free treats, and I say that, yes, I am trained in the use of an EpiPen. Then, just as someone else is explaining that their child shouldn't take their socks off because they have a verruca, I get a text.

I check it, thinking it might be a last-minute cancellation or someone mislaying our address, but it's from David. I swear silently.

I can't stop thinking about you. I understand how you feel about this but I need to see you.

The noise of the party grows louder but I feel out of it, pulled away from my family. Despite my annoyance I can feel David's arms around me and the rasp of his stubble against my cheek. Why is he doing this?

'What is it?' Amber says, making me jump. 'Vicky? What's the matter?'

I turn to her and smile brightly. 'Nothing. I zoned out for a moment.'

I'm still holding my phone. She takes it out of my hand, looks at it and rolls her eyes. Someone bangs the door knocker and rings the bell at the same time. Amber doesn't let me answer; she shouts for Magda and pushes me up the stairs. I walk into my bedroom and sit down on the edge of the bed.

'What a bastard,' she says. 'Why can't he leave you alone?'

I shrug.

'I thought you were over him.'

'I am,' I insist. 'I don't know what else I'm supposed to do. I've tried ignoring him, but evidently that's not working. I thought he took it so well at the time. He was so sweet about it and said he totally understood and respected my decision. Obviously, that's not the case. I must have hurt his pride.'

Amber wanders across the room to the dressing table. There are photographs on the marble surface; a wedding picture and one of our two families together when it was just the girls and Josh wasn't even a twinkle in his father's eye. She picks it up, scrutinizes it and sets it back down.

'I think you ought to see him. It wasn't exactly fair, the way you left it, was it? Flouncing off and leaving him standing in his birthday suit. The poor guy deserves a proper explanation.'

'I didn't flounce.' I manage a smile. 'And he can't be a bastard and a poor guy at the same time. Make up your mind.'

'Which do you think he is?'

'I have no idea. And it's all very well saying go and see him, but it's not that easy. There's Josh, remember.'

'It might be a good idea to have him along.' She raises her eyebrows. 'Stop you doing anything you'll regret.'

My expression tells her exactly what I think of that suggestion.

'So hire Magda for the morning. Tell her you've got an appointment in Harley Street. That usually stops people asking questions.'

'I'll think about it.'

I go to the mirror, brush my hair and smooth the creases out of my white shirt. I do feel calmer.

'I'm sorry about the other day,' I say. 'You were right to be pissed off.'

'No, I completely overreacted. And anyway, who needs Bognor when we have Spain to look forward to?'

She rests her head against my shoulder affectionately. We make an odd couple, Amber with her almost brittle beauty and my more comfortable, less threatening attractions. It still surprises me that I'm the one who contemplated an affair.

Downstairs, the doorbell rings again. She snaps out of it and briskly twists her hair away from her face.

'OK, that's enough moping. We'd better get back before we're missed.'

Jenny, wearing ill-fitting chinos and a jumper capacious enough to cover her bottom and much of her thighs, is in the kitchen helping divest children of coats and shoes. She turns her head and smiles as I come in. 'Hectic morning?'

I must look hassled. 'Non-stop.'

'Rose has been so looking forward to this. Do you want any help? I can stay if you like.'

'It's all right. I'll manage. I've got Magda, and Tom's about somewhere.'

She studies me through her glasses and frowns. 'Are you sure you're OK?'

Why do people keep asking me that? 'Fine. It's been a full-on morning. I should have done more prepping yesterday. My fault.'

Once the party gets going there's no time to worry about David's text because we are all too busy organizing games and herding any child seen trying to leave the kitchen back inside or into the garden. Fifteen is a large number in terms of crowd control. They slip through our fingers in their shimmery satin and lace, evade our outstretched hands with squeals as they scuttle into the banned zones, namely our bedroom and Tom's study. They are like a pretty virus, getting everywhere and bringing chaos and giggles with them.

I watch Tom charging around outside, pursued by a dozen little girls in Disney finery, all of them oblivious to the cold. He turns back on himself and roars, arms outstretched, and they scatter screaming to the four corners of the garden. He is hyper-energetic, limbs all over the place, face contorting, eyebrows leaping, eyes widening and mouth gurning; not caring that he is going ridiculously, superbly over-the-top. The children love being frightened by him, adore being chased by this whooping monster. Our poor neighbours. Amber joins in, squealing as loud as any of the kids; high-fiving Emily when they both evade capture. I stand with my hands on my hips watching her, thinking how incredible she is, how vibrant and charismatic. And then I notice Tom. He's bending to catch his breath, hands on his knees, his head raised, and he's watching her too.

Princess Daisy-Petal vanishes in a puff of sparkly smoke dead on five, by which time the fairies and princesses are running wild, rampaging around the house and garden and I've long since given up trying to bar the stairs. It's pick-up time and the first parents begin to trickle in and I go down to the cellar to bring up more bottles of wine. It's the one area of the house we didn't throw money at and is used as a depository for various items: suitcases and holdalls, Tom's skis, the guitars he no longer plays and my tools. I take a couple of bottles of white out of the fridge and am halfway back up the stairs when the doorbell rings. I assume it's someone's mother or father and I'm smiling, words of greeting at the ready, a chilled bottle in one hand, the other tucked under my arm, when I open the door, but the man and woman standing on the step do not look like parents. Their clothes are wrong and their demeanour is wrong and the fact that they are both carrying official-looking files is wrong. For a moment I think they might be Jehovah's Witnesses and am about to politely refuse them entry when the woman speaks and I remember that we've met before.

'Mrs Seagrave?'

'Yes. I'm sorry. I don't remember your name.'

'Don't worry. You were having a stressful morning when we last met. I'm Miriam Cornwall and this is my colleague Ian Banner. We're from the Lambeth Child Protection Team. May we come in?'

19

MIRIAM IS ALREADY LOOKING OVER MY SHOULDER. Beside her, Ian, in a brown V-neck sweater and blue cords, waits patiently. He has a beard; not a neat goatee, but a modest Hagrid. He appears junior to Miriam, following her lead. Weirdly, they both have blue eyes. Miriam has thick, wiry black hair that sits in a stiff cloud around an oval face.

'You'd better come in,' I say.

They step past me and wait politely while I close the door with my shoulder. I'm still holding the bottles, my hands getting colder, at a loss to know what to say. Ian looks around inquisitively and I feel judged for having too much. I want to tell him that my blood, sweat and tears have gone into this place; that I scraped, filled, sanded and painted every inch of it. But what's the point? I'm sure he's already pegged us as middle-class and entitled.

It's funny how having the wrong people in your house can change the atmosphere. What was a riot of children's laughter and jolly, gossiping parents, now sounds like the mad chatter of geese. If I could wave a wand or point a remote control and conjure instant silence I would do so. There's a shrill cry as a child with an elf's green face races out of the kitchen and stops in her tracks, her eyes widening. She's holding a magic wand in one hand and a crushed pink Fondant Fancy in the other.

'What are you after, Isabel?'

I see myself from outside; a woman who wants to come across as caring and hopes that by raising her voice to an unnatural pitch, no one will miss the point.

'I want my mummy.'

Isabel transfers the cake to her mouth and with her free hand picks her nose, wiping the result of her excavations on the sparkly net skirt of her dress. Beside me Ian can't resist a tiny wrinkle of his smooth brow. I guess he doesn't have kids of his own yet.

'Mummy should be here in a minute. Go back and find the others, sweetie. I'll come in.'

Isabel chews at her thumbnail but she pushes open the kitchen door on a blast of 'I Wan'na Be Like You'. I must have given my visitors a wild-eyed stare because I finally get what I interpret as an apologetic smile.

'Birthday party?' Miriam asks.

'Yes. My oldest daughter. I'm sorry, but you can see this is a really bad time. Perhaps we could reschedule? I don't like to be uncooperative but I've got fifteen little girls running amok in my house.' I make an effort to temper the note of panic in my voice. 'I need to be with them.'

'I'm afraid not,' Miriam says. 'It's the nature of surprise visits, Mrs Seagrave.'

So few people address me this way. Even at school I'm Miss Vicky. On Grayling's lips it sounds respectful, but coming from these two, it feels like an attempt to establish authority.

'How long will it take?'

'That depends.'

We gaze steadily at each other.

'Could you at least give me five minutes to get our guests out of the house. I'm not having this conversation in front of my children's school friends and their parents. It isn't fair on them, or me and Tom for that matter.'

'Take your time,' Ian Banner says. 'We aren't in any hurry.'

Tom is lounging against the counter talking to Amber, a tousle-haired Polly wrapped around his legs, a bottle of lager in his hand. I stand there, watching them, then the doorbell rings again.

'Magda, get that will you,' I say.

She looks at me, noting the strain in my voice, frowns and nods.

Three more sets of parents jostle into my kitchen. The very fact that most of the women have brought their husbands makes it clear that they see this as a social event and expect to be offered a drink. And of course they would be if I didn't have two vultures waiting for me in the front room.

Their offspring groan with disappointment. No one wants to go. They are having way too much fun. And it has been fun, I tell myself. I've laid on a great party.

'Tom, could I have a word? In private.'

He unpicks Polly's fingers from his legs, scoops her up and plants her down next to Amber. We go out into the garden and I slide the doors closed behind us.

'We've got to get everyone out.'

He makes a big thing of looking round. 'So where's the fire?'

'Tom, I'm serious.'

He registers that I'm not smiling. 'What on earth's the matter?'

I lower my voice even though no one can possibly hear us through the triple-glazing. 'There are two social workers in our sitting room and they're refusing to go away until they've spoken to us.'

He doesn't get it, so I'm more explicit. 'Child Protection.'

'You have to be kidding me.'

I shake my head.

'Shit. What the hell are we going to do about this lot?' He gestures at the guests.

Behind us, above the houses in the next street, the clouds are tinged with pink and orange. The sun is setting. On the other side of the glass doors, Amber tilts her head, a question in her eyes. I stretch my mouth into a smile.

'We have to go back in,' I hiss. 'People are looking.'

In the kitchen I clap my hands and the room falls silent. There is an air of confused expectation, as if they think I'm about to suggest a toast, but I am the only one not holding a glass or a mug. Before people can reprise their conversations I speak, instinctively modulating my tone as if I'm talking to a class of children, getting them to line up at the door.

'I'm so sorry, everyone, but I'm going to have to call time. Thank you all so much for coming. We've had a lovely afternoon.' There is a chorus of disappointed cries, but I ignore it and keep smiling even though my facial muscles ache from the effort. 'I've had some bad news that I have to deal with.'

I catch Amber's eye. Is there a touch of pleasure in the smile that greets me or am I imagining it? I drag my gaze away.

'It's my mother. She's been rushed into hospital,' I improvise. 'I am so sorry, but I do need you to go. Thank you.'

Once I've done the hard bit, Tom throws himself into finding coats and shoes and children misplaced in the upper reaches of the house. I hear his voice bellowing and the sound of squeals as he chases them down. I answer questions politely, and try to accept the sympathy and goodwill without betraying myself. For someone who's had to lie a lot recently, I'm remarkably bad at it.

'Let me help,' Jenny says, appearing at my side. Her expression is uncertain but I'm only grateful that someone cares.

I'm trembling but I tell myself to keep it together for appearances' sake. For the children. 'Would you mind handing out party bags? They're over by the television.'

Amber is being wonderful. She's talking to the parents as she sorts out shoes and hands over coats, even remembering to return the plastic tub of revolting health food – barely touched, I notice.

Sophie is at the table picking Smarties off the half-eaten cake. She assumes the dismissal doesn't apply to her and in the past that would have been the case. Her face has been painted to look like a water nymph, a line of ice-blue sequins tracing a swooping pattern from the bridge of her nose to her temples. It is exquisitely done.

I get a cloth and wipe her fingers and then lead her over to her mother.

'Why can't I stay?' she asks.

'Because Vicky needs us to go,' Amber says. 'Sorry about your mum,' she adds, raising her voice and winking at me. 'I hope she improves.'

Slowly everyone departs. Children are urged to thank Emily's mummy and I smile at all of them and tell them how gorgeous they look. Emily stands still at the bottom of the stairs. I recognize the look on her face. She's storing this up for later.

Nothing I can do about that now.

Tom touches my shoulder. 'Everyone's gone,' he says.

Together, we walk to the sitting room. Every step I take feels as though it's bringing me closer to exposure.

20

EVENING HAS ARRIVED WHILE WE WERE RUNNING around and either Miriam or Ian has switched on the light without closing the curtains so the room is like a theatre. Anyone walking up to the house could have seen them. I yank them shut angrily as they rise to their feet.

'This is my husband Tom.'

He shakes their hands, towering above both of them. Only I can tell he's been drinking, he conceals it so well, but the knowledge still makes me nervous. He tends to talk too much when he's had a few beers.

I sit deep in the corner of the sofa so that Josh can fall asleep on my lap. Tom sits next to me and takes my hand. His black trouser legs ride up to reveal kingfisher-blue socks.

'So,' he asks, leaning towards Miriam and smiling at her. 'What's this all about?'

Miriam sits up straighter and touches her hair. 'We've had a call from a neighbour concerned about your children's well-being.'

Tom doesn't lose his rag. He speaks calmly and the

only clue to how he's feeling is the tension in his jaw. 'May I ask who contacted you?'

There's only one person I can think of who might wish me ill, and that's Hellie North. But I can't believe she knows anything. David won't have told her, he isn't the type to have a crisis of conscience. All the same, maybe I should have a conversation with him. But that's something to think about later. Not now.

'I'm afraid we can't tell you that, Mr Seagrave. Now please don't worry too much, often neighbours' fears turn out to be unfounded. They've heard a child crying in the night, or screaming at their parents, that kind of thing. But in view of Josh's accident, we need to make sure we've ticked all the boxes.'

Tom maintains an interested but not convinced expression. 'Right. Well, I appreciate that you need to do your job, but frankly, your timing couldn't be worse. Ask your questions so we can all go back to normal. It's the weekend. I'm sure you both have better things to do. I know I have.'

'There is nothing more important than a child's well-being,' Ian says. 'I can assure you. We'd like to take a look round now and we'll need to ask the children a few questions.'

'You're not dragging them into this, surely?'

'Tom.' I shoot him a quelling glance. 'That's fine. Why don't I show you round the house. Tom can have a chat with the girls.'

'I'm sorry, Mrs Seagrave, but we can't allow that. We wouldn't want any suspicion that the children have been schooled in what to say.'

'No,' I say quickly. 'I understand. Why don't you follow me?'

Tom takes Josh and I lead Miriam and Ian up to the master bedroom. We station ourselves to one side while they sniff around. They push their noses and fingers between the clothes in the wardrobe, open the drawers in the bedside tables, check the titles of the books we are reading and slide their hands under the mattress.

In the ensuite Miriam opens the mirrored cupboards above our basins and checks them for poisonous substances left within reach. Ian tests the locks on the windows while I stand with my arms folded, my shaking hands stuffed under my armpits.

'Any potential deathtraps?' Tom asks drily.

Ian doesn't respond. He makes notes and we move on. Tom points things out and makes conversation. Ian Banner remains poker-faced; immune to my husband's slightly desperate charm.

They're more interested in the children's bedrooms. Evidence that the party overflowed up here is everywhere. The beds have been bounced on and there are toys strewn across the floor. Polly has a tendency to scrawl on walls and at least one child has joined in. I'm not cross. I'm pleased because it proves to Miriam and Ian that I'm not a dictator.

They have a look at the bathroom and I explain we've had a leak. That's why the lino has been pulled up and the boards are bare, and a bit rough and splintery. It's when we get to Josh's room that I become really uneasy. Magda has worked her magic since the forensics team was here and the black smudges on the door and cot

201

have vanished, but it's all still in the air. Even after three weeks I still don't feel the room is completely back to normal and I no longer close the blackout blinds when I put Josh to bed. I put my hand on the rocking chair, pull it back and let it go. Miriam inspects the fitted wardrobes that flank the little white-painted fireplace. She won't find anything in there except linen, towels, spare duvets and pillows.

'So this is where it happened?' Ian says, walking over to the cot. His eyes scan the room as if he's measuring it. 'It must have been a shock for you.'

My lips are dry but I don't lick them in case he spots how tense I am. 'It was awful,' I agree.

'It's odd that you had no idea there was someone in your house.'

'Yes, I know. But it's a big place and he was upstairs.'

Ian frowns and picks up the baby monitor from the mantelpiece. 'Was this switched on?'

'No. Yes . . . I mean, this one was. The one in the kitchen wasn't.'

'Is that normal? A house like this, I would have thought a monitor would be essential.'

My knees are feeling weak and I long to sit down. 'I've been so tired lately, what with Josh not sleeping through the night . . .' Tom sends me a look. 'I usually put it on, but I had my friend with me and I couldn't think straight. Josh always makes a huge fuss when I put him down for his morning nap, so I occasionally turn it off. It's perfectly normal. I don't have to listen to him all the time.'

He sets it down again, adjusts its position and writes a note. 'You really ought to use it regularly.'

'Of course we will,' Tom says. 'It's one of those things. Unfortunate, but in the end not too much harm done.'

'When a baby fractures his arm,' Miriam points out, 'I'd call that a great deal of harm.'

'Well, yes of course,' Tom says stiffly. 'I only meant . . . well, he's all right.'

'Have the police charged anyone?'

I shake my head. 'As far as I know, there hasn't been any progress.'

'That's a shame.' He hesitates. 'But there was a man?'

'What do you mean? Of course there was a man.'

Ian tips his head back and surveys me through lowered eyelids. It's a weird, predatory look that sets my nerves on edge.

'It's all right, Vicky,' Tom says. 'We all know you were telling the truth.'

Do they? I turn back to Ian. 'You can speak to DS Grayling if you don't believe me. Why would I make something like that up?'

Miriam glances down at her notes. 'There's a packet of Amitriptyline in your bathroom cupboard. They're antidepressants, aren't they?'

'What?' I frown and remember. 'Oh them. It's a really low dose. I was prescribed it to help me sleep through Josh . . .' I realize that makes me sound callous and add hastily, 'He doesn't need to wake up at night, but he does anyway. The doctor thought that if I slept through it would help him kick the habit. I didn't use them until after I'd stopped breastfeeding and I didn't take them for long because of the way I felt in the morning.' I pause. 'I don't need to lie to get attention.'

'Thank you for sharing that with us,' Miriam says.

When they hear that I am the only child of a single mother, Ian and Miriam perk up, thinking they've unearthed something interesting. Ian asks about my relationship with my father. We've obviously moved on from Munchausen to Freud.

'I don't have one,' I reply tersely. 'A relationship, I mean. I have a father but he's never been part of my life. I've only met him once. He lives in Dorking with his family. You'd have to ask my mum about him.'

'What about father figures?' he persists. 'I assume your mother has had other relationships since.'

'Why would you assume that? You don't know her.'

'Vicky,' Tom says. 'Answer the questions. It's getting late.'

I glance at my watch. It's half past six. High time the girls were in the bath and I had a stiff drink in my hand. This cannot be happening to me. I am not the sort of person who gets visited by Child Protection. This family is ordinary.

Tom puts Josh in his cot and I pray that he'll behave. Thankfully, he's too exhausted to put up his usual fight. A hush falls on the room. All I can hear is my heart beating and a car driving past the house. A second passes; two. Then we breathe again. He's asleep.

'There have been three or four.' *Or eight or nine.* 'They've been nice, overall. My mother has never married but her relationships have been reasonably long term, and there haven't been many tensions.'

Ian looks sceptical and I suppose it is unlikely that things would have been perfect. Daughters don't

204

tend to warm to their mother's lovers, at least not if their mother is an ever-hopeful serial monogamist and they change with the regularity of the seasons. He's right, of course. I didn't think much of any of them. I assume he's hoping I'll tell him one of her boyfriends interfered with me; Mum may not be the best judge of character but she isn't a fool and nothing like that ever happened.

I lead them out of the room and close the door. Miriam asks about the break-in, about the way Josh got his fracture; whether or not he's been hurt before while in my care, and I answer all their questions. It's basically a rehash of everything she asked me at the hospital. As we troop back down to the kitchen to talk to the girls I ricochet from one anxiety to the next; what if Miriam and Ian know something they're not telling us; what if they've already judged and sentenced me in their minds and are merely looking for a halfway decent excuse to take my children away; what if the girls tell them something incriminating about me?

I attempt to explain Miriam and Ian's presence. Polly rubs her eyes. Emily's expression is shuttered but she climbs on to my knee. Polly sits on Tom's with her father's arm locked protectively round her.

Miriam chats about families, school and friends and eventually gets to the point. 'Sometimes grown-ups get cross and shout, don't they?'

Emily wrinkles her brow. 'Yes . . .' I hold my breath and try not to stare too hard at her. This isn't her fault. 'Sometimes Sophie's mum shouts at Sophie.'

I could kiss her.

But she hasn't finished. 'And once she told me I was spoilt. I'm not, am I, Mummy?'

I'm surprised to hear that, and frankly, shocked. What was Amber thinking? 'Of course you aren't.'

'And when Polly . . .'

I stroke her hair. 'It's OK, sweetie. We don't want to talk about Sophie's mummy now.'

They ask the girls if they ever get bruised at home. Emily shows them a scrape on her elbow and the gap where her molar was.

'What about you, Polly?' Miriam says.

Polly's brow furrows and she starts to suck her thumb. Tom draws it gently out of her mouth.

'Polly,' he says. 'Do you get bruises?'

'At playtime Oliver sometimes is rough. I falled over.'

Tom shrugs, lets go of her hand and the thumb goes back in.

Miriam gathers her papers, closes her briefcase with a click and that appears to be that.

'Sometimes calls are made with malicious intent. I can see that's probably the case here.'

I search her face for signs of disappointment or distrust but she's too professional to let me know what she really thinks.

'Will we be on file?' Tom asks.

'A note will be made. But don't worry. We can see your children are loved and well looked after.'

At the door Tom moves behind me and encircles me with his arms, pulling me back against him, resting his jaw on my head. They leave the house, turning to look back at us standing there with our fixed smiles, and walk up the road. I close the door quietly behind me.

Tom is slumped, exhausted, at the kitchen table. He puts his arm around my thighs, pulls me against him and presses his head into my abdomen.

'Are they all right?' he asks.

'Polly's out for the count. Emily wanted to know if Mum was going to die. I told her it was a false alarm. She's fine. I thought she might be cross with me for breaking up the party, but I have a feeling she was secretly relieved when everyone left. She was overwhelmed.'

'What about you? Are you OK?'

'A bit shaky.' I hold out my hand to prove it. 'I feel violated. Is that too strong a word?'

'No.'

I pull up a chair and sit down, my knees against his legs, rest my elbows on the table and yawn.

'Malicious intent,' Tom says. 'Why? What have we done to deserve it? I keep trying to think who I've upset. We know most of our neighbours, and the others we're at least on nodding terms with. Do you think it's someone from the flats behind us? What about that guy who I asked to turn down his music? Or the old dear who lives next door to the Boxers. She hates my motorbike.'

'Tom, don't. You can't go around suspecting everyone.'

'Don't tell me you're not doing exactly the same, because I won't believe you.'

'I'm doing my best not to. Look, I'm as upset and

shocked as you are, but the main thing is, we were cleared. They won't be back.'

'I wish I felt as confident.'

I don't feel confident either. I've been considering and dismissing people as well but it's Hellie North with her ice-blonde Scandinavian looks who dominates my thoughts. If she's discovered her husband's little affair with their daughter's teacher, she'll be out for revenge and I can imagine her going down the subtle route to get it. My mobile is lying on the worktop beside the two unopened bottles of white wine. I try not to keep looking at it, itching to text David, to warn him that she might know, but in the end the urge is too strong and I pick it up.

'I'll go and sort out their bedroom, then we can put them to bed.'

He nods and stands up, picks up the broom and starts sweeping. He's haphazard about it, but I forbear to point out places he misses. I leave the room and text David, then don't send because if it wasn't Hellie, I could be doing an extraordinary amount of damage. I decide instead to wait until Monday when he and his phone will be at work.

June 1992

'KATYA?'

She realized that Luke was trying to grab her attention. She'd been daydreaming. Yesterday, she and Luke took the bus to the Arndale Centre and when she looked out of the window she had seen Maggie with Emily. They were holding hands and Emily was practically dancing to keep up with her mother. Emily was wearing home clothes; a pair of flared jeans, trainers and a purple bomber jacket. As the bus turned the corner Katya craned her neck to see Emily's face, but they were on the top deck so it was hard to get a good look. She wasn't as pretty as Maggie had described her. Just ordinary. But in Katya's opinion that was a good thing. Gabriella was very pretty but she could be so mean. Emily Parrish looked kind. Katya turned away with a sigh of satisfaction.

Before Luke broke into her thoughts she had been imagining that she got off and followed them home, and then perhaps fainted on the doorstep, through hunger, and had to be carried in and laid on their sofa. And Emily had asked who this strange, pale child was and Maggie had said, 'This is Katya. She has no one.' And then Luke called her name and the images disappeared.

'Come and tell me what you think,' he said.

Katya got up reluctantly and padded in her socked feet to where Luke was standing over a saucepan of stew. He blew on a spoonful and offered it to her. She tried to take it with her hand but he guided the spoon to her mouth, waiting until she parted her lips.

'It's nice,' she conceded, stepping back to make sure he knew not to try again.

'Just nice? Is that all you can say? I've been to a lot of trouble. Hold still. You've got some tomato stuck to your lip.'

He picked it off with his fingernail, his other hand cupping her head so that she couldn't move and she fixed her gaze on the wall, anywhere but on his face. She hated the way his eyes tugged at her, making her feel angry, scared and guilty all at once. He dropped his hand but she could still remember how it felt hours afterwards.

Sally was on nights this week, leaving after Katya got home from school and returning at dawn. The not knowing what mood he was in, whether he'd want a cuddle or whether he'd ignore her, made her so anxious she kept having to go to the toilet. He had suggested another swimming lesson as well, pretending to be concerned about her. So far she'd managed to put him off, but the offending swimming suit hadn't been returned. It was still rolled up in the towel at the bottom of the wash basket. She hoped it would get mildew.

'Can I do my homework now?'

He let her go, added a generous pinch of salt to the stew, replaced the lid and slid the casserole dish into the oven.

That night Katya listened to his movements from her bedroom. He switched off the lights and paused outside her door. She held her breath until she heard his tread on the stairs. Above her, in the intense quiet, the stream of his pee hit the water.

21

Wednesday, 10 March 2010

'JESUS NO. DO YOU THINK I'M MAD?' DAVID SEES MY face and softens his tone. 'Vicky, I am sorry about what happened, it must have been awful, but you have to believe me. Hellie doesn't have the slightest idea. And besides that, darling, she wouldn't do anything so crass.'

'Don't call me darling. And I don't think it was crass. I think it was Machiavellian.'

We're in Hyde Park, walking beside the Serpentine – his office is in Lancaster Gate where there's little chance of bumping into an acquaintance – and I'm paying Magda to look after Josh for the morning. David is wearing a dark wool overcoat but still manages to look shambolic. I'm in jeans, scuffed boots, navy-blue winter jacket, gloves and scarf. Defiantly unmistressy. There are a couple of boats out on the lake and a group of swans stalk us, hoping to be fed.

I find it interesting that I'm married to Tom, who has a couple of ounces of spare flesh at the most and exercises regularly, and yet I was attracted to scruffy, overweight David, who I doubt has seen the inside of a gym in twenty years. To be honest, I still am attracted to him. The difference is that I don't want him now. That irrational need has gone.

We met at the Italian Gardens. He was there first, which surprised me, holding a takeaway coffee in each hand, breaking into a smile as I waved and hurried towards him. The coffees precluded us hugging, which was probably a good thing in the circumstances, but he did lean in for a kiss. I proffered my cheek awkwardly and we clashed noses.

The thrill of being in his company is unchanged; the expectation and anxiety are still there, but as for the illusion that our actions were justified because it was true love, that has entirely gone. Even so, it is hard. His smile and his voice and his wicked sense of mischief still make me go weak at the knees.

'Fuck it. I wish I'd gone to bed with you,' David says out of the blue.

I can't help laughing. 'Sorry. It wasn't to be.'

It's not as if we even spent that much time together. Up until that awful day, our clandestine meetings only ever consisted of a coffee in town once every three weeks if we were lucky. Sometimes I saw him out and about with his family, and he'd acknowledge me as Hellie did, as their child's teacher. The consummation of our relationship was doomed from the start. The mere fact that it had been planned down to the smallest detail drained it of romance. Hellie had taken Astrid to Sweden to see her grandparents and I used Mum's broken heart as an excuse. If Peter hadn't conveniently walked out, I would have thought of something else.

There was no spontaneity. I'll never forget the dawning awkwardness of getting undressed in daylight for sex; catching sight of myself in the mirror and seeing my untoned baby belly, scarred with silvery stretch marks. The contrast to the first time Tom and I fell into bed was so marked it almost makes me laugh.

We had come back to his grotty shared house with a bunch of fellow students after a party and carried on drinking. Tom went up to bed earlier than the others because he had a football match in the morning and about an hour later I knocked on his door, thinking I might be pissed enough to seduce him. I'd been after him for weeks but he'd entirely missed the clues. He was having too much fun, I think. I walked in, he opened his eyes and saw me and before I could draw a breath, let alone ask if he was awake, he threw back the covers, sprang out of bed and dragged me back in with him. The memory still gives me the shivers.

David leans forward and tries to kiss me on the lips. I avoid him neatly.

'You are far too sensible, Victoria. Misbehave for once.'

'No. Be good or I'm going straight home. Seriously, you wanted to meet and say goodbye properly, so let's do that. Let's talk like friends and part like friends. I have enough problems at the moment without you making it difficult.'

He is immediately concerned. 'What kind of problems?'

I tell him about the break-in and Josh's injury. I am sorely tempted to be honest, but I mustn't because if he's not my lover, then he has no right to my secrets.

'I heard about that,' he says.

'You did?'

'Yes. Hellie told me. Poor you. You must have been terrified.'

Two roller-bladers race towards us and scoot by, one on either side. I used to roller-skate along the Esplanade with my friends when I was a child, propelled by the wind and then fighting our way back.

'I miss you,' David says. 'I am so sorry about what happened. It was the wrong thing to do. I pushed you before you were ready. I'm not surprised you ran a mile.'

I pinch my lips together, feeling let down by vanity – because I am flattered. But the brutal truth is, if I had slept with David North it would have opened a door that I might not have been able to close. I'd have ended up like Mum, addicted to romance, to that first kiss; those moments that you give up when you get married. It's not what I want, or what I will ever want. Life will never be perfect but I prefer the imperfections of marriage to a life searching for the Holy Grail. I want Tom, my children and stability. Excitement, I'm prepared to find elsewhere; in the buying and developing of property, for instance. I'll happily get my kicks that way.

'Do you love Hellie?'

'Yes. I've never hidden that from you. And you love Tom. This was only ever meant to be fun.'

'But you seem to think that makes it all right. David, you are wonderful and sexy and you make me laugh,

215

but here's my problem – you are not Tom. I don't want to play your games.' I can't believe I'm crying. I wipe my eyes angrily. 'I'm saying goodbye now.'

'No you aren't.' He stops smiling and takes my hand but I wriggle it out of his grip. 'Don't do this, Vicky. Walking away won't achieve anything. You can't just go.'

'Watch me.'

I don't look back; I keep walking, not back up to Lancaster Gate, but in the direction of Hyde Park Corner. I've done it. It's properly over now. Thank God. I can claw back some self-esteem.

Amber hurries across the Common, grasping her phone. She should have looked at it earlier but the morning's viewings had been going so well. She'd been on a roll, extolling the virtues of a beautifully renovated house on Graves Avenue, and hadn't thought to check when it vibrated in her bag. She assumed it was Robert but it turned out to be the school wanting her to pick up poor little Polly Seagrave who had thrown up and was running a temperature. By the time she rang back, Tom had already dashed across London to collect her.

She rings the doorbell, brushes back her hair and smooths down her skirt.

Tom pounds downstairs and opens the door. 'Amber!' He looks flatteringly pleased to see her. 'Come in.'

She bustles inside, trying to behave like an efficient and concerned friend, rather than a grown woman who's recently developed an inappropriate crush on her best friend's husband.

'Do you need to go?' she asks, hoping he won't rush

out immediately. Much as she wants to help, she doesn't particularly relish hanging around Vicky's house until she gets back from her tryst. It makes her feel like a second-class citizen.

He glances at his wristwatch. 'I can stay a few minutes. I'll make you a cup of tea.'

'Thanks.' She pulls off her coat and hangs it over the end of the banister. 'So where's Vicky?'

'I haven't got a clue. Her mobile's switched off.'

'That's odd,' she says to his back. 'I'm really sorry I didn't get the message.'

Tom switches the kettle on and turns round. 'It's not your fault. You were working, weren't you? You wouldn't have been able to come anyway.'

She has always been nervous on her own with Tom but until now she's never analysed it. But, she muses, there's always been an undercurrent. She puts her hands on the table in front of her and clasps them.

'Didn't she tell you where she was going today?' The kettle clicks and he pours boiling water over the tea-bags, adds milk and stirs.

What is she supposed to say? She and Vicky never discussed this scenario. 'No, but I was in such a rush to get to work this morning we didn't have a chance to chat. How mysterious though.' She adds. 'Perhaps she's got a lover.' It's pure mischief, she knows that, but no more than Vicky deserves.

'Yeah, right.'

'What? You don't think she's attractive enough?'

She's teasing but he doesn't pick her up on it. He's obviously not in the mood. He puts the tea in front of her. She doesn't really want it but at least it's something to do with her hands. She steals a glance at his face and tries to ignore her bolting pulse.

'I expect she'll be back soon. She's—'

'Has she told you about the social workers?' he interrupts.

The sense of possibility evaporates and she answers smoothly, disappointed. 'Yes, she has. It must have been horrible.'

'I don't understand it. Do you think people heard what had happened to Josh and wanted to make trouble?'

'I don't know. I expect it was motivated by jealousy. These things usually are.' She gives a small sigh. 'I just worry . . .'

He glances at her. 'About what?'

'Well, about what it might do to Vicky's state of mind. I'm worried she might have a breakdown if she goes on like this.'

'A breakdown?' He looks horrified.

'Sorry, I'm probably going way over the top. But she is fragile at the moment.'

He buries his fingers in his hair and groans. 'I'm feeling pretty fucking fragile myself.'

Tennyson Road at one o'clock is a busy hub of mothers, prams and small dogs. There's a café called Boiled Eggs and Soldiers about halfway down and when I walk past its windows I see Jenny inside with two other women. They are engrossed in their conversation but as I hesitate Jenny catches sight of me and gestures at me to join them. I smile and shake my head.

The first thing I see when I unlock the front door is Polly's school bag and coat in a heap at the bottom of the stairs and, next to them, Tom's motorbike helmet. I freeze, confused, my mind trying to put two and two together and finally, painfully, realizing that I have a problem. In the kitchen my husband and best friend are sitting at the table, Josh on the floor, playing at Amber's feet. He crawls over, stretching his arms towards me and bouncing on his bottom.

'You're back,' Amber says.

'What's happened?' I pick Josh up and shush him. 'Where's Polly? And Magda? She should be here.'

'Polly's in bed,' Tom says. He picks up his keys, jangling them between his fingers.

'Well, is she all right?' I start to go upstairs but he grabs my hand.

'Magda had to leave an hour ago. Where have you been?'

I ignore the question. 'She said she could do until one thirty. What do you mean, she had to leave?'

'She isn't well either,' Amber says. 'She hasn't completely kicked that bug and it looks like she may have given it to Polly. I'm so sorry I didn't get the message in time to stop them calling Tom, but I had my phone on silent. I came as soon as I could. I was going to take over so Tom can get back to work, but you're here now.'

I listen to all this with bemusement. Tom is anxious to leave and obviously irritated. I pick his helmet up and come to the door with him.

'I'm so sorry.'

'I was in a meeting, Vicky. You didn't tell me you were going out.'

'It was a spur-of-the-moment thing.' I cannot think of an excuse. I pass him the helmet and hope he won't press the point.

He does. 'So where were you?'

'I went to Southbank to see the Barbara Hepworth exhibition. Then I went for a walk along the river. I needed to get out of the house.'

He looks puzzled. 'Right. I'll see you later.'

I go back in to find Amber pulling on her jacket.

'You don't have to go straight away, do you? Stay and have some lunch.'

I run up to Polly but she's sound asleep. I lay the back of my hand against her forehead. Her teddy has fallen off the bed so I tuck him under her arm and kiss her hot cheeks, then leave the door open in case she wakes.

I heat up some shop-bought carrot-and-parsnip soup and pour it into bowls. Amber saws a couple of slices of bread from the loaf, butters them and arranges them on plates. We sit opposite each other with the salt and pepper pots between us.

I pick up my spoon and set it down again. I've lost my appetite. 'I've made a mess of things, haven't I?'

'That's your perception. You inconvenienced Tom, but he doesn't know anything. You must hold it together, Vicky. He's starting to worry about you.'

'What do you mean?'

'He's worried you're too fragile.'

'He said that?' I look her straight in the eye and she recoils. I didn't mean to sound combative, but I absolutely hate the idea of the two of them discussing my sanity over a cosy cup of tea in my kitchen. 'Does he mean mentally or physically?'

She doesn't respond at first so I snap at her. 'Amber!'

'Oh God, Vicky, I don't know. It wasn't exactly a conversation I was comfortable having with him.'

'Was that what you were talking about when I came in?'

'No. He was telling me about the visit from Child Protection. He's really cut up about it, isn't he? And I'm not surprised. I couldn't bear to have someone come into my house and make those ugly insinuations.'

When I flinch she reaches over and pats my hand. 'Come on. Cheer up. No one knows about it. Tell me how it went with Mr Lover-man.'

'Fine. We said goodbye and it was all very civilized. He's a lovely guy.'

'And what about you?'

I lean my head back and stare up through the windows as a crow flies over the house. 'I don't know. I'm glad I did it; it would have been like leaving an open sore if I hadn't seen him, but it was rough. The right decision though. Thank you for persuading me.'

22

Easter Holidays ❧ Saturday, 27 March 2010

NO ONE ELSE SUCCUMBS TO POLLY'S BUG, AND TWO
and a half blessedly uneventful weeks later term ends.
We fly to Spain, leaving in drizzle and touching down
at Barcelona Airport in full sunshine. Everything goes
remarkably well; our baggage is amongst the first on the
carousel, our hire car is ready and waiting with a tank full
of petrol. The satnav has been set to English and works a
treat, and in the back of the car peace reigns as the children, who have zero interest in beautiful scenery, doze.

Our rented villa is about thirty-five minutes' drive
from the airport, surrounded by vineyards that spread
across miles of flat farmland and sweep up and over the
distant hillsides. Wisps of cloud barely move in a sea of
bright blue. We turn in through extravagantly wrought
iron gates and draw up outside what looks like a small
Mediterranean palace. Emily presses her face against
the window and gasps.

Amber found a dirt-cheap flight from Luton, but it
meant that they arrived the morning before us and as

we get out of the car Sophie comes running round the side of the house. She's wearing a pink bikini and flip-flops, chattering as she reaches us, describing the pool and the two televisions and the beds. She throws herself at Tom, wrapping her arms around his legs.

'Easy, Tiger,' he says, tugging her wet ponytail.

'We got here first! We're the winners!'

'It doesn't matter,' Emily says. She shows it does by adding, 'We would have been first except Daddy had a meeting.'

'I got to choose my bed first and it's the best one.'

I catch Tom's eye and wrinkle my nose. 'Never mind all that. It's our fault Emily is late, so we'll make it up to her with something nice.'

'What will she get?' Sophie asks.

'It's a surprise,' Tom says, turning them all round and giving them a gentle shove. 'Off you go. We'll catch you up.'

Sophie charges off, making sure we all know how familiar she is with the geography of the place. My heart bleeds for Emily. Polly, I don't worry about. She couldn't care less who arrived first. She's just happy to be freed from the car. I extract Josh and cuddle him as he wakes from a sweaty sleep. His back is drenched. He looks around, wide-eyed, then abruptly buries his head in the crook of my shoulder.

'Quite something, isn't it?' Tom elbows me affectionately in the ribcage.

The villa is two storeys high and about forty foot wide, sparkling white with hot-pink bougainvillea sprawling exuberantly across the lower walls and white muslin curtains spilling out of open windows. Pine trees and palms stand like guards to either side. I hear a splash and a joyful shriek and my mood gets even better. We stroll across the drive and round the side of the house, following the noise, the hardy grass stiff beneath our shoes. The house wraps around a large terrace dominated by a modern L-shaped wicker sofa with olive-green cushions and a vast wooden table that would comfortably seat twenty, sheltered under a giant parasol. The pool lies beyond that, enclosed on three sides by another bougainvillea-clad wall. It ripples and glitters in the sunshine.

I wander over and look down, squinting against the brightness thrown up by the water. Robert is swimming with Sophie and Polly while Emily sits on the side, dipping her toes in. Polly has flung off her clothes and is doggy-paddling in her knickers, but Emily wouldn't be seen dead in anything except the correct attire. Amber is lying on a sunlounger in an electric-blue bikini and a baseball cap which she tips up as we approach. She's had time for a spray tan and leg wax, which is more than I can say for myself. Even though she isn't wearing make-up, her eyes look less shadowed.

'You're here! Fantastic.' She swings her ankles elegantly off the lounger, sits up and stretches her arms behind her, pulling her shoulders back. 'I'll show you the house.'

I bend to kiss her cheek. She smells of coconut oil. 'No, don't get up. We can find our own way round. Emily, come back to the car with us. I'll dig your swimming suit out for you.'

'OK,' Amber says. 'Leave Josh with me then. We've

taken one of the bedrooms at the back. I wasn't sure which you'd want, but they're all really lovely, so I don't suppose it makes any difference.'

Tom and I carry our cases into a spacious hall. The floor is dark wood and above us wooden beams support the ceiling. We slip our shoes off and climb the oak staircase to a landing that leads to a warren of rooms where we soon locate the one Robert and Amber have chosen. It is unmistakably the master bedroom with the vaulted ceiling that Tom had earmarked for us. The shutters have been thrown wide and the curtains billow in front of French windows. I wander over, part them and look out on to a terrace with a picture-postcard view of the gardens and surrounding land. Beside the pool, Amber's feet are visible, poking out from under the parasol. Her diamanté-studded flip-flops twinkle in the sunlight. There are two comfortable wicker armchairs on the terrace and an English newspaper, caught by a breeze, has distributed itself across the terracotta-tiled floor.

Tom joins me wordlessly, and we turn to face the room and stare at the vast bed. The sheets have been flung aside and the pillows are still squashed from last night; two dressing gowns lie draped over the end. An open suitcase squats on the stand and in the corner there's a small pile of dirty clothes. We wander silently to the ensuite where damp towels are bunched over radiators and toothbrushes lean against each other in one of the glasses. Two toiletry bags and a bottle of suntan lotion stand on a glass shelf.

'She must have known we expected to have this one.'

'Do you want me to say something?' Tom asks.

'No. I will.'

I sit on the end of the bed, plant my toes deep in the lush cream carpet. On the last night of our penny-pinching holiday in India, Tom and I blew what was left of our funds on a room very like this one. We were used to student bedrooms with damp patches and musty carpets, sneaked trysts on single beds at our family homes in the holidays and nights spent in bug-infested youth hostels, on beaches and under the stars. We couldn't believe our eyes. I remember lying on the bed watching him walk naked across the room, a strip of leather wrapped around his wrist and a necklace of brown beads. It bridged the dip of his clavicle in a way that made my knees turn to water. I was so happy.

'Did you notice there's no other car?'

He screws up his face. 'I did, as it happens. But, Vicky, we did say it wouldn't cost them anything apart from the flights. And please don't mention it. They're about to buy a house and I know for a fact that Robert's not doing well at the moment. Have some compassion and understanding. Don't embarrass them.'

I am immediately riled. 'Give me credit for some sensitivity,' I say and stomp off.

Sophie's suitcase is in the twin where a camp bed has already been set up and made comfortable, so there's nothing to complain about there. Tom goes for the rest of our things while I check out the kitchen to see what our guests have managed in the way of food shopping. There's very little and what there is looks as though they

226

brought it with them. A couple of Sainsbury's bags lie scrunched up on the side. The kitchen isn't tidy; there are crumbs on the table and a saucepan and two mugs left to soak in the sink. A buttery knife lies on the edge. Children's voices, piping and merry, float in through the window. I decide to ignore the mess and join them. To clean up would be to make a point and I'm not going to begin our holiday on a sour note. I leave Tom getting changed and go back outside.

Robert is still in the pool, three little girls attached to him like baby monkeys. He throws them off one at a time and they explode out of the water, screaming for more. Polly is easily as proficient as Emily. Sophie, though, is a fish. But then Amber, who can't swim, has always taken her daughter's swimming extremely seriously. She was having lessons at six months.

'Aren't you hot?' Amber asks, glancing at me.

She has Josh on her lap. He's been smeared with suntan lotion and is wearing nothing except his nappy and his body is deliciously chubby, his tummy as round as a Buddha's. I roll my jeans up to my knees, choose the shadiest lounger and lean back into the cushions. Even under the parasol the sun penetrates through the fabric of my clothes and heats my skin. It feels amazing and slowly the tension slides from my shoulders.

'Bliss, isn't it?' Amber says.

'Mm. Amber . . .' I pause. This is awkward. She glances at me but her attention is really on Josh who is at his most giggly. 'It's just, that bedroom . . .'

'What about it?' She blows an impressive raspberry against Josh's stomach. He thinks it's hilarious.

'Well, that's the master bedroom. I wouldn't say anything, except, this is Tom's holiday too and he is paying, after all.'

Instead of answering Amber bounces Josh on his toes against her thighs. She puts on a baby voice that sends a trickle of unease down my spine.

'This little boy thinks Mummy's being mean.'

'Amber . . .'

'This little boy hasn't forgotten he was all by himself.'

'Stop it.' Despite myself, I become tearful. I reach for Josh but she holds him away from me.

'This little boy says the least Mummy can do is make sure Auntie Amber is happy.'

At that point I leap up and practically snatch him from her. Shaking with fury, I'm about to counter with something equally pointed when Tom appears. He's wearing shorts, a pale-blue linen shirt with the sleeves rolled up and leather flip-flops.

'Hey.' He bends over Amber and kisses her cheek. 'Nice to see you've made yourself at home. I'm going to go and do some shopping. Any requests?'

'The nearest shops are in the village you came through,' she says. 'There's nothing within walking distance. We would have hired a car, only it just seemed like a waste of money when all we want is a week vegging by the pool.'

I've been watching her as she speaks, noticing that she's fidgeting, scratching lightly at the tiny scars on the back of her hand. Tom comes to her rescue, telling her she's absolutely right. Why waste good money that could be spent on important things like paint stripper and a pair of overalls.

'I'll come to the village with you,' Amber says, holding out her hand so that he can pull her up. 'I need a change of scene. You and Robert can keep an eye on the girls. I'll nip inside and get dressed.'

'But I . . .'

'We won't be long,' Tom says.

Before I can protest or even think of a way of doing so without appearing to be jealous, they vanish round the side of the house. A few minutes later the car door slams, the engine starts and they drive away with a jaunty toot of the horn.

Tom says, next time we're alone, 'So you didn't mention the bedroom to her?'

I don't look at him when I shrug. I continue unpacking the shopping. 'No, it didn't seem worth it in the end.' I close the fridge door and turn to him with a smile. 'It's a First World problem.' I came up with that earlier, while they were out.

Tom leans back in his chair and reaches for my hand. 'It's only you I was worried about. I'm a bloke. I don't care where I sleep.'

He pulls me on to his knee and I curl my arms round his neck. 'Prince Charming.'

'Remember India? Sleeping on the beach.'

'How could I forget?'

'It was fucking uncomfortable!' He grins. 'Didn't get a wink.'

June 1992

MAGGIE SAID SHE'D COME TO SPORTS DAY AND CHEER Katya on if she managed to get away, but she couldn't promise anything because she had a busy morning. Katya hated thinking about her with other children and when they filed out of the school and down to the playing fields, she deliberately didn't look out for her. Sally had to sleep, but Luke was there, looking handsome in chinos and a white shirt, the sleeves pushed up his forearms. He was surrounded by pretty young mothers in summer dresses hanging on his every word like he was some sort of god. He waved and she annoyed herself by waving back.

Katya was roped to Gabriella Brady in the three-legged race when she spotted Maggie and mis-stepped, bringing the two of them to the ground.

'Katya!' Gabriella yelled. 'Now look what you've done!'

They disentangled themselves and started again and Maggie, who had clapped her hand across her mouth in dismay, shouted encouragement.

'Well done you!' she said as the girls flopped down on the grass to catch their breath. Katya undid the knot and Gabriella, freed, ran off without a backwards glance. Katya thought she probably hated her after that.

'We didn't win,' she said.

'It doesn't matter. I am so proud of you.'

Maggie hugged her like the other mothers were hugging their kids. She was wearing more make-up than usual and looked better, almost beautiful. Like she had that day she caught her in the house with Luke. It made Katya watchful. She tried to keep herself apart, concerned that people were wondering about their relationship, embarrassed by the way Maggie acted around Luke. She reminded Katya of Gabriella, who turned into an idiot whenever any of the boys were nearby.

After the long jump, which she came third in, Katya hung out with a group of girls while their parents organized picnic lunches, flapping out rugs and spreading them on the dry, patchy grass. It hadn't rained in weeks. Maggie and Luke were sitting side by side, an unpacked basket at their feet, but she didn't approach them. She watched Maggie fiddling with the hem of her skirt where her toes peeked out. Her toenails were varnished dark red.

'She doesn't really think that, does she?' Luke said.

Maggie leant her head back and her hair fell between her shoulder blades, soft chestnut waves lustrous beneath the afternoon sun, too engrossed in Luke to notice Katya sulking nearby.

'I have a horrible feeling she does. I don't want to hurt her feelings but she knows things no child should. Her mother – honestly, Luke, you wouldn't believe how appalling she was. Not only the prostitution and drug-taking, but her failure to shield Katya from them. It's not the child's fault that she's damaged, but I can't risk it.'

'You're too nice, that's your trouble.'

She laughed softly. 'Poor little thing. Perhaps she'll forget about it. I don't need to say anything really, just make sure they don't run into each other. I feel such a bitch saying that, but it's true.'

'You're only protecting your child.'

He reached over and took a lock of hair between his fingers, and to Katya's disgust Maggie let him do it, even appeared to like it. Katya came and sat down as if she'd heard nothing, smoothing out the ribbons of her yellow rosette and humming to herself. Luke glanced at her. He knew she'd been listening. She could tell. And anyway she had long suspected he could read her mind.

'Ham or Marmite sandwich?' Maggie asked. She nudged the basket towards Katya. 'Take your pick. There's jam doughnuts for pudding; the ones you like.'

Katya stripped off her trainers and socks, set them neatly on the grass, toe to toe, the socks folded and tucked into the shoes. When she looked up, Luke was staring at her naked feet.

'Water?' Maggie handed her a bottle.

She drank half of it then took her sandwich and walked off. Maggie called after her, but she didn't turn round.

23

Thursday, 1 April 2010

ROBERT PUTS HIS HAND ON HER BOTTOM, ROUSING Amber from a dream about Tom. She turns to him grumpily and he smiles. It's a hopeful smile. She pushes his hand away and sits up, dragging the sheet round her. To her relief, she can hear the kids downstairs.

'Everyone's awake,' she says.

She drinks some water and leans back. She feels guilty about taking this room, but not that guilty. She loves the shutters and muslins and can imagine the master bedroom in Browning Street done out in a similar white and breezy style. She's going to try and copy the ensuite as well.

'They won't hear,' Robert says. He rolls over and rests his head on her thigh. His hair is greasy and the bald patch is growing. She doesn't want to look at him.

'I don't care. I won't be able to relax. Move, will you? I need the loo.'

Robert sighs and gets up, pulls on his shorts and a polo shirt and leaves the room. They are losing each

233

other. In the bathroom she stares at the mirror. She's pushing him away. She doesn't want to, but she can't help it. Everything he does irritates her now, even the way he breathes.

'I am good,' she murmurs. 'I am strong. I matter.' The face in the mirror gazes impassively back her. *Yes, you tell yourself that*, she seems to say. *If it makes you feel better.*

Later on, she and Vicky sit in the shade of a canvas parasol, building plastic towers for Josh to knock down while the men do their duty as lifeguards and the girls play like dolphins around them. There has been a touch of frost between them but nothing she can't handle. Vicky hates a quarrel. When they get too hot, Vicky takes the baby for a dip in the pool. He loves the water, battering his hands on the surface and laughing with delight, but most of all he loves watching the girls; particularly Sophie, who he idolizes. Vicky moans about having three, but she doesn't know how lucky she is. It feels to Amber like life has stacked the cards in her friend's favour, giving her Tom, three children, money and even a lover, though what on earth those two saw in each other she can't imagine. Vicky is so ordinary and David North, well, he might be attractive in a louche sort of way, but it's his wife Hellie who, apart from looking like a model, earns the money and wears the trousers.

'Emily!'

Amber hears the hint of exasperation in her daughter's voice. Sophie has been teaching Emily to dive. She's a good teacher, but inclined to be impatient, throwing up her hands and rolling her eyes when Emily gets it wrong.

'I'm trying!' Emily splutters.

'Keep your feet together. Pretend you're an arrow.'

Emily swims to the side, pulls herself out and does it again, this time joined by Sophie, who executes a perfect swallow dive. Emily's feet are all over the place, but she keeps her hands together above her head and enters the water cleanly. Vicky whoops in support and Robert lifts a squealing Polly, roars like an ogre and chucks her in.

Tom ducks down and comes up again, flicking his head and spraying water like a dog. 'Why don't you come in, Amber?' he says. 'You're missing half the fun.'

She shades her eyes and squints at him, taking her time before answering. Pool water drizzles down his face. He sweeps his dark hair out of his eyes and grins. His tanned shoulders glisten, provoking a memory that makes her flinch. A voice barges in, more insistent than Amber's own thoughts. *Take him from her.*

'You're among friends. No one's going to laugh at you.'

Josh starts to nag. Vicky stacks more plastic cups for him; red on yellow on blue on red. He pushes them over and they roll away. One drops into the pool and Emily swims after it.

'Come on,' Tom wheedles. 'Dip your toe in at least.'

She shakes her head. 'I can't go near water. Aquaphobia. Sorry.' She drawls the apology.

'Ah.' Tom swims to the side, looks up at her through

235

his wet fringe and starts to pull himself up out of the water. 'Have you tried aversion therapy?'

He has a wicked, mocking smile. Amber leaps off the lounger and darts behind it, warding him off.

'I mean it, Tom. I'm not going in and you can't make me.'

He starts to walk towards her and she runs away screaming and hides behind the wall, and the children, sensing a good game, charge after her.

She sets off across the garden, but he comes after her, catches her round the waist and snatches her into his arms. Her sarong comes away, snags between them and then falls on to the grass. He can't tell, and she can't make him understand, that the laughing is to do with fear and hysteria and nothing to do with enjoyment, that her kicking feet and flailing arms are genuine re-actions. He holds her and even though there is intense pleasure in his arms locked round her semi-naked body, she can't stop the waves of terror that engulf her. She screams and slams her fist into his shoulder.

'Ouch.' He sets her down on her feet and rubs the bruise. He looks embarrassed.

'I'm scared of water,' she mutters.

She's trembling from head to foot and he's not laughing any more. Her bikini strap has slipped down her shoulder and she pulls it up. She feels broken and upset.

'I'm sorry. I had no idea it was so bad.'

They stare at each other, both of them breathless. Then the girls run over and grab her hands and attempt to pull her towards the pool. She tries to shake them off, close to tears.

'OK. That's enough,' Tom says sharply. 'Leave Amber alone. Off you go.'

'That's not fair,' Sophie says. 'You throw us in.'

'You enjoy it.'

Vicky has come up behind her, Josh in one arm, Amber's sarong in her free hand.

'It's a phobia,' Amber says, taking it and tying it round her hips. 'I should have explained properly before, but I've always been embarrassed about it.' She sits down on the side of the lounger and hugs her body. 'I'm sorry, Tom. Did I hurt you?'

'No more than I deserved.'

24

Friday, 2 April 2010

ON THEIR FINAL EVENING ROBERT INSISTS ON COOKING.
After a blokey outing to the market with Tom, he's
doing a Catalan stew with pork and aubergine and
the mouth-watering aroma of frying meat, onions and
garlic fills the entire house. At seven Tom disappears off
to have a soak in the bath and Amber goes up to read
with the kids, leaving me alone with Robert. He hands
me a glass of wine and pours another one. He seems
tense.

'For the wife,' he says. 'Could you take it up?'

I leave mine sitting on the table and carry hers
upstairs, grateful for an excuse to go. The master-
bedroom door is wide open; the room that ought to
have been mine tinged a pinkish orange by the setting
sun. I pause, chewing my bottom lip. The moment she
leaves I'm going to strip the bed and put on fresh linen,
hoover and dust, clean the bathroom and then put my
feet up and sink into the pillows. Perhaps it's mean-
spirited, but then perhaps I'm also imagining that the

flirting between Amber and Tom is threatening to cross a line.

I shrug and go to say goodnight to the girls, stopping outside their door at the sound of Amber's voice. She's telling them a story. Three little princesses called Emily, Sophie and Polly run through woods populated with fairies and goblins, chased by a wicked queen and helped on their way by a fairy and the fairy, of course, is called Amber. The wicked queen is called Tor and she has their kind father held prisoner in her dungeon and won't let him go unless she is allowed to keep one of the princesses as her own little daughter.

Tor is short for Victoria. It hurts, but I shrug it off. Amber is merely telling them a story they can engage with, by adding our names. It's fun and it's working because they love it. I look round the door and a movement to the right of the room snags my attention. It's a bare foot. A man's foot. Tom's foot, in fact. He must be leaning against the bedroom wall, listening to the story and watching Amber's delicately carved, animated profile, dwelling on her ruby lips and sun-bleached hair. I'm beginning to experience a growing sense of alienation when the two of them are together. I back away and go silently downstairs, only realizing when I enter the kitchen that I'm still holding the warmed stem of her glass. Robert glances at it as he stirs the stew.

'She's telling them a story. I didn't like to disturb her.'

'Amber's good at those,' he replies. 'I keep telling her she should write them down. She has a wonderful imagination.'

He pauses and I sense that he has more to say. I don't

want him to think I'm avoiding being on my own with him after our heart-to-heart in Jenny's garden, so I wait. He smiles at me and I smile back and sip my drink.

'Amber told me,' he says.

My stomach flips. 'Told you what?'

'That she asked you to consider lending us money towards the deposit. I'm so sorry, Vicky. I'm very angry with her and embarrassed. Please forget she ever said it.'

'Of course I will, but you mustn't be embarrassed. I'm only sorry we can't help. I know it's tough.' I hesitate, trying to find the most tactful way of putting this. 'Sometimes I do things that I regret too. I get all worked up about something and for a moment nothing else matters. And I make mistakes. Amber is only human.'

Tom appears, his hair still damp. The sun-caught redness of his skin has mellowed into a healthy tan. When Amber comes in I get the distinct feeling she knew all along that I was up there listening. I look at her and wonder: is this friendship worth fighting for?

'Very retro,' Tom comments on her floaty green dress.

'Camden Lock,' she explains. 'It's seventies.'

Her hair has been messily screwed away from her face and clasped in a tortoiseshell claw. She looks like she's escaped from one of her fairy tales.

I'm wearing cropped trousers and a pink linen shirt that looked great when I put it on a couple of hours ago but is now crumpled so that the part around my middle is ridged like a paper fan. I pull my tummy in and instinctively run my fingers through my hair. They snag.

While I clean up after Robert, washing the pans and cutting boards, Amber makes a salad, halving an avocado and running the knife in parallel lines through the flesh before scooping it out of the skin with a spoon. She arranges the pale-green crescents on a bed of leaves and adds the tomatoes while Tom mixes up a dressing. Now that I'm consciously looking for signs, they are everywhere. The way she sucks a smear of avocado off her finger, the way she turns her head or lifts her chin, elongating her elegant neck, the way she looks at him and then casts her eyes down. Has it always been like this or am I being paranoid? Not so long ago I was laughing off Jenny's anxiety, telling her that it's just the way Amber is. Why aren't I laughing now?

'I was thinking,' Robert says, as we wipe morsels of bread around our plates to scoop up the last of his stew. 'I know I've got to get back because I'm off to Singapore, but there's no reason Amber and Sophie couldn't stay on.'

The table goes quiet. I put my glass down carefully and glance at Tom. He doesn't react.

'Robert,' Amber says.

She sounds as though she's chiding him, but I suspect it's for show.

'Don't you have to be back at work?' I say.

Robert turns to me with a pained smile, and I get the message loud and clear. This was not his idea. Odd. It isn't like Robert to be disloyal.

'No,' he says. 'She has next week off as well, don't you, Amber?'

She nods but doesn't say a word, leaving her husband floundering.

'It would help me because I wouldn't feel so bad about

leaving them during the holidays. And Sophie has been so happy this week, hanging out with your girls. It would be a shame to split them up. Anyway, it's up to you two. This is your holiday and we certainly don't want to encroach where we're not wanted.' His voice peters out.

'Oh God, no,' Amber says. 'Forget he even said it, please. We're having such a lovely time and you've been brilliant to include us at all. The last thing I want is to outstay my welcome.' She swiftly changes tack. 'So, Vicky. Birthday girl tomorrow. How do you want to celebrate?'

I hadn't realized it until this moment, but what with the bedroom fiasco and all the flirting, I've been longing for her to go. It's hardly a surprise. It's only natural that I should want Tom to myself. I raise my eyes to Amber's and she smiles at me, a warm generous smile, full of fondness. It's impossible not to return it.

'We can drive to the beach, if you like,' Tom says when I remain quiet. 'Make a day of it.'

After that, although Amber and I contribute, the conversation and energy is disproportionately supplied and sustained by our husbands. The possible prolonging of their stay isn't mentioned for a while but I sense it in the gaps in the conversation and the pauses; the air of expectation. I sit back, fingering the stem of my glass. I don't have to wait long.

'About what I said earlier.' Robert looks round the table and his gaze lingers on me.

Tom is contorting himself in order to scratch his back. Amber reaches over and does it for him, over his shirt thankfully. I catch his eye and he has the grace to adjust his posture so that he's less easily accessible.

'This week has been great fun,' I say. 'But . . .'

'Hasn't it?' Amber interrupts. 'It's so relaxed here and so wonderful having the children occupied.' She beams. 'If I have to get on the plane tomorrow, I won't mind at all, but if you could bear to have us with you for another week, it would be amazing. I'd have your company and the girls would have each other for a few more days.'

To my horror she wipes a tear from her eye and Tom is thrown into knightly confusion.

'Why are you so upset?' he asks, and I can see he genuinely wants to know.

'Sorry. It's only that these last few days I've felt like I really belong. You and Vicky, you're like a brother and sister to me.' Apologizing again, she wipes her eyes on a paper napkin. 'Ignore me, I'm being ridiculous.'

'You're not,' Tom says. 'Listen, it's no trouble at all. In fact, it would be a pleasure to have you stay until the end.'

Oh, Tom.

'Thank you, Tom,' she breathes and then looks at me. 'I'll swap rooms with you, Vicky. There's no point me rattling around in that enormous bed without my husband.'

I get up and begin clearing the plates. It's a fait accompli and I have to admire their skill in managing it. Ah well, the children will be happy at least. Maybe she could babysit them while Tom and I go out for a romantic meal. The thought cheers me.

'So,' Tom says. 'That's settled. Anyway, I've arranged a birthday surprise for Vicky tomorrow, so it would be lovely if Amber and Sophie are still here.'

June 1992

THEY SAT AT THE KITCHEN TABLE; MAGGIE PARRISH
and Sally Bryant opposite Luke and Katya. Maggie had
a file open in front of her and was leafing through it.
Luke looked thoughtful and Sally concerned and tired.
For once Maggie was wearing a suit.

'Katya, what do you have to say?' she asked gently.

Before she could respond Sally said, 'It's not that we're
not very fond of you, love, but I've got a lot on my plate
right now and I can't be worrying about where you are all
hours of the day. I have a duty of care.'

'Katya?' Maggie repeats.

But Katya didn't want to speak. Not with Sally and
Luke there. She shook her head and looked down.

'You were doing so well. Why have you started skipping school again? Are you being bullied?'

'No.'

Sally shrugged. 'She's like this all the time now. I can't
get a sensible word out of her.'

'OK,' Maggie sighed. 'Perhaps we'd better start looking

for an alternative. What a shame.' She tapped her pen on a sheet of paper, making it bounce up and down. 'I'll make some calls. But in the meantime, are you happy to keep Katya? I don't want to put her into a children's home unless it's absolutely necessary.'

'How long do you think?' Sally leant forward and took Katya's hand, preventing her from picking at her scabs. 'I'm so sorry, love. Please don't think it's your fault.'

She turned back to Maggie, pleading to be understood. It felt to Katya like she was trying to get rid of an obligation without looking bad.

'And there's my sister too. She has terminal cancer and I should be seeing more of her.'

Sally started to weep quietly and Katya was horrified by the mess it made of her face.

'Sorry. Sorry. I feel such a failure. We did so much want it to work.'

Luke turned to his wife. 'You tried, love. Don't beat yourself up.'

Katya glanced at Maggie to see how she was taking this but her face was impassive as she closed the file.

'So we'll leave it like that. I'll give you a ring in a week or so and let you know what I come up with. Katya, I expect you to behave. Go to school and come back home at the right time. It's not fair to give these kind people so much worry when they only want to look after you and make you happy.'

Katya stared at her so hard that Maggie blinked and looked away. She wanted her to understand, but it was obvious that Maggie didn't see or hear what she didn't want to see or hear. She thought Katya was bad, not good enough to breathe the same air as her daughter, and not only that, she also thought the sun shone out of Luke Bryant's bum, so it was only to be expected. Katya wondered what would happen if she said something now. She could. She could look up and say, *Luke won't leave me alone. He touches me where he shouldn't and he had sex with her.* And let the shit hit the fan. She was too much of a coward though.

Overwhelmed by resentment, she scraped her chair back, stormed out of the room and slammed into her bedroom, flinging herself down on the bed. She raged against Sally for being so thick and blind, against Linda for failing her, against Maggie for showing her what it was she should have had in a mother, and then letting her down. Why did no one care about her enough to understand? The injustice of it made her feel sick.

From behind the door she heard Maggie getting ready to go. When she knocked, Katya turned her face to the wall. Maggie came in and sat down beside her and placed her hand on her shoulder.

'Don't worry, lovely. Everything will be fine.'

'Go away!'

Katya waited until she'd left the house before peeking out of the window. Luke was outside, watching Maggie's car drive off, but he turned away well before the car was out of sight. On his way back up the path he saw her in the window and winked.

25

Saturday, 3 April 2010

THE EVENTS OF LAST NIGHT ELBOW THEIR WAY through my sleep-fogged mind and an image of Amber solidifies. She is scratching Tom's back. Such an easy, familiar gesture, like monkeys grooming each other, born of kinship and trust. Amber has always been physical, Sophie too. I fling the sheet aside and sit up, drawing my knees to my chest.

Last night I had one of my dreams. This time I was back at university and Amber had come to stay. I was trying to explain her to my housemates, particularly trying to explain why she and Tom had shared a bed and why I was on the sofa. But as I sat up and pushed the sleeping bag off I felt damp and brought my hand away and it was covered in blood. It had seeped into the cushions and I started to worry about the landlord and our deposit. Then Tom came down, in his boxers, unshaven and hungover, and I said, 'Where's Amber?' He looked at me like I was mad. 'She's right there.' He pointed to the corner of the room where she was sitting, her arms wrapped around her abdomen, her chin dropped on to her chest, blood puddling on the floor beside her. I can feel the horror coming back as the memory returns. Normal dreams leave nothing but a tiny, frustrating residue; these ones stick.

It was hard to go back to sleep after that. I kept trying to blank my mind, but Ian Banner and Miriam Cornwall kept barging in. In the depths of the night I convinced myself that I'd be found out. I went through the scenario over and over again; what I would say; what I would do; how I would persuade the authorities that I could be trusted with my own children.

Polly charges in and throws herself on to the bed. Tom, carrying Josh and a mug of steaming coffee, lets Josh roll out of the crook of his arm and on to my stomach. Emily has her hands hidden behind her back.

'We brought you a present, Mummy,' Polly says, throwing her arms around me.

Polly's arms are a miracle. The instant they coil round me my mood lifts. I close my eyes and hug her, breathe in her morning smell and pray this never changes, that she will always want to hug me, even when she's thirty.

'Well, where is it?' I ask. I pretend to look, tipping up the pillows, leaning over the edge of the bed and peering underneath. 'Are you sure I've got a present?'

'Yes!' Emily shows her hands and reveals a book-shaped object wrapped in glittery paper and climbs up beside me. 'Open it,' she commands.

'Cards first,' Tom says, handing me three envelopes and kissing my cheek.

He hasn't shaved since we arrived and the texture of his stubble has transitioned nicely from sandpaper to small, rough-furred animal. The last time he stopped shaving was on paternity leave. He became rumpled. I remember wanting to weep the morning he came in with my cup of tea, smooth-cheeked and shiny.

He sits beside me and I budge over for him, but Polly crams herself between us and then Emily wants to join in so I have to move even further over. I open Tom's card. It's a copy of a Pre-Raphaelite painting, *The Lady of Shallot*. Inside he's written, *Happy Birthday to my gorgeous wife, Love Tom*, and a poem that makes me cringe and giggle at the same time. I am so happy, I could pop. My smile is as wide as the bed and he's looking pretty sheepish and pleased with himself too.

'Read it!' Polly insists and I do as I'm told. The girls think it's the best thing ever written.

> *There are not many words that rhyme with Vicky*
> *And this is no time to be choosy or picky.*
> *So Victoria, I adore-yer,*
> *Irritations I ignore-yer,*
> *With my love I won't bore-yer,*
> *Happy birthday, Victor-yer!*

'You are a very talented man.'

The kids shove their cards under my nose. Josh has done a bright-yellow handprint. Both Polly and Emily have drawn a family holding hands under a huge yellow sun.

I trace the figures with my finger. 'Is that me? I'm not that beautiful!'

'Yes you are,' Polly insists and kisses my cheek. 'You are the most beautiful mummy in the world.'

'Thank you, darling.'

I unwrap the present and hold it, a lump in my throat. It's a photograph in a plain black frame.

'We got it done while you were in Bognor, cheering your mum up.'

David's face instantly intrudes. It's not Tom's fault – he isn't to know that it was taken on the day I nearly destroyed us – but I wish he hadn't told me, not today at least.

The photograph is of Tom and the children. They are sitting on the bench in the playground and all of them, even Josh, are sporting woolly hats and huge cheesy grins. It's a daft picture and they all look geeky, but it makes me smile. Behind them a black dog races across the Common.

'Look at you all.'

'The hats were Amber's idea.'

'Oh really? Did she take it?' Of course she did. I'd forgotten she was with them.

'Yeah.' He holds out his hand and I pass it to him. 'Maybe I shouldn't have worn the hat. I look nerdy.'

'You look like you.' I lean over and kiss him. 'Thank you.'

'You're getting something else later.'

'What?'

'Never you mind. It's just something I wanted to do. To let you know how much I love you.'

'A hot-air balloon trip?'

'No. Stop trying to guess.'

'We're going to make a cake,' Polly says, interrupting the moment as children will when they feel the attention has shifted too far from them. 'It's going to be chocolate.'

A taxi picks Robert up at ten and we say our goodbyes. The girls, tired from too much sun the day before, play happily in the den. We sit round the table on the terrace eating brunch and Amber hands me a card and starts to reminisce about how we met and what she thought when she first saw me and how wonderful the last few years have been because of our friendship. She hasn't bought me a present, for which she apologizes.

'I've had too much on my mind, what with the house and everything. Sorry, Vicky. I feel really guilty now.'

'Don't be daft. I don't need presents.'

I can't bear to admit to myself that things are changing; it may be because of Browning Street or there may be another reason entirely, but our relationship is not the same and I don't know what I'm supposed to do to put it right or if I even want to. I resolve to make an extra effort with her. I'm sure she still likes me – she wouldn't be here otherwise – but something precious has been lost.

Tom reads his emails and casually swats at a persistent wasp and the children play until Amber and I deem they've had enough time between eating and swimming. Tom hasn't bothered Amber about getting in the water again and nobody comments when she takes up her book and flops back on a lounger with a groan of pleasure.

Tom dives in. He's a strong swimmer but a big splasher, his feet kicking up a tsunami. The girls, clinging to a green-and-blue striped lilo, bob up and down in the swell.

Josh nods off in my arms and I lie him down on a folded rug and make sure he's properly shaded. I thought he would be miserable in the heat, but it's the opposite. He positively embraces the sun. His skin has tanned gently under the Factor 50, his hair has bleached almost white and he's sleeping through the night. And what's good for Josh Seagrave is good for all of us.

I dive in, swim under water and tickle Emily's toes. She kicks out at me, grabs me as I surface and climbs on to my shoulders. Not to be outdone, Sophie joins her, wrapping her arms around my neck and practically choking me. I duck down, slip out of their grasp and swim away laughing.

At some point in the morning I go in to fetch a handful of loose change for the girls to dive after. My phone pings as I'm shaking the contents of my purse into my hand. My heart sinks. A text from David. I thought I had made it perfectly clear that we were over.

I never saw you naked.

I go bright red. That's splitting hairs. I did get down to my bra and knickers before I bottled out. This is becoming intrusive. I text him back then wish I hadn't as soon as I've sent it. It would have been far more sensible to have ignored it.

Please do not contact me again.

* * *

252

Back outside I fling the coins into the water and sit down beside Amber. She pulls her sunglasses down her nose and looks at me over the frames.

'What is it?'

I show her the text silently.

She giggles. 'Oh dear.'

'It's not funny, Amber. I really don't need this right now.'

'No. You're right. I shouldn't laugh. What are you going to do about it?'

'Fuck knows. Nothing, I expect. He's an intelligent man, he'll get the hint. Either that or someone else will take his fancy.'

'Mummy,' Emily shouts. 'We found them all. Now you come in.'

She slaps the wet coins down on the stone where they gleam like salvaged bullion. I grimace at Amber, fling them in and dive-bomb after them, splashing the girls and making them squeal. We dive over and over again and most of the time I let them win, but not always, and it's because I'm underwater, searching for an elusive euro, that I don't hear the car pulling up around the front of the villa, or its door thunking shut before it drives away. And because I've turned my back on the sun, I only realize that something's happened when Emily screams, 'Granny!' and swims to the side of the pool.

When I see my mother standing with her arms out as my children race towards her, I want to shout for joy. Tom grins from ear to ear.

'Surprise!' he says.

I don't stop to thank him. I get out and grab the towel that's draped over the end of Amber's lounger, and as I do, I catch her expression. She looks dismayed. I pull the towel around my shoulders like a cloak and run, leaving wet footsteps on the paving.

'Mum! I don't believe it. When did you plan this?'

'Tom twisted my arm. What a beautiful house.' She hugs me and I wriggle, laughing, out of her embrace. She's dressed absurdly in a black gypsy skirt, a peacock-blue beaded top, straw hat and earrings made out of blue and green feathers.

Amber puts her book aside, strolls over and kisses her on both cheeks. Mum makes Amber look tiny.

'Maggie. How are you? It's been ages.'

I get the feeling that she's not altogether pleased at this turn of events. My mother and my best friend don't harmonize. I noticed it at the christenings.

'The last time was Josh's christening, wasn't it? And this must be Sophie,' Mum says. 'I remember you very well. You liked my chocolate cake.'

She tells Tom how handsome he's looking and then the girls claim her for a guided tour and they wander off, Emily demanding to know who's looking after Max, Sophie informing her that she's been teaching Emily to dive.

Amber goes back to her lounger and picks up her book. She doesn't trust herself yet. Why didn't Tom warn her? It was one thing keeping it a secret from Vicky, but she should have been part of it. She's been made to feel the outsider, as per usual. Maggie looks good; healthy and young. She ought not to. She ought to look beaten down by guilt. Does she have no conscience? Why should Amber be the one to feel self-hatred and disgust, and Maggie just breeze through life as though it had never happened?

She can hear her voice, calling to the girls, laughing at them, admiring the house. Amber leans forward and peers round her parasol. Maggie is on Amber's terrace, Vicky standing behind her. Tom shouts, asking if anyone wants a coffee and Maggie calls back. Polly giggles. Happy families. Sophie is more a part of it than she is.

What should she do? It was one thing merging into the background at parties, Maggie too busy with her grandchildren and her own guests to notice Vicky and Tom's friends, especially since she was one of many. Even when she became Polly's godmother, Maggie seemed insensible. But then Maggie had been in charge of Emily, who was barely two at the time and a handful. Now they would be together for a week, moving in the same spaces, having conversations, making eye contact. Amber fingers her hair. When she was young it had been much blonder and cut to just below her shoulders, parted in the middle. Now it was longer, darker, shaggier, with a soft fringe. As a child, she had been elfin and undernourished. She's still slim and petite, but she has a healthy glow and adult features. It's conceivable Maggie might take a couple of days, but she'll get there in the end. At any rate, Amber needs to be ready. Or perhaps even intercept her? She doesn't want her telling tales to Vicky. She thinks she'll be too scared to do that though, because Amber has a tale or two of her own up her sleeve.

* * *

255

'Thank you. That was a really lovely surprise, Tom. I'm touched.'

'Good. I'm glad.'

We walk along companionably, talking mostly about the children. Then I go and spoil the moment.

'I get the feeling Amber isn't very pleased about Mum.'

'Why wouldn't she be?'

'Oh, I don't know. Perhaps she doesn't like not being the centre of attention.'

His eyebrows connect. 'Vicky, sometimes you have the sensitivity of a rhino. She's embarrassed. I should have warned her. She wangled an invitation to stay longer when all the time your mum was coming and it was going to be a family thing. She thinks she's in the way and there's absolutely nothing she can do about it.' Josh has started whining. Tom tilts his head and talks to him, his mouth against his hair.

'I suppose it could be that.'

'Well, what else could it be?'

'I don't know,' I say irritably.

He kisses my temple, pulling me against him. Josh doesn't like this and grabs a handful of my hair.

Tom disentangles Josh's fingers and takes him away, his furious yells disrupting the serenity of the scene. I don't go with him. Instead I watch him stride back to the pool, back to Amber and her lovely brown legs and blonde hair. He speaks to her then laughs and walks towards the house. She sinks into the lounger and crosses one ankle over the other.

With Josh inside now, probably being appeased with

a bread stick, the garden goes strangely quiet. Even the birds aren't singing. From across the garden I catch Amber staring at me. She waves me over, smiling. To be fair to my husband, he's probably right about why she reacted so badly to the arrival of my mother. In her position, I would have felt exactly the same. And I should feel sorry for her, not resent her, if I'm right and she does have a crush on Tom. Glass houses and all that. I decide I owe it to her to be more understanding so I wander over and sit down beside her.

'Budge up.'

She shuffles over. Neither of us say anything at first but then, unexpectedly, she leans against me and for a moment we are perfectly still, watching insects alight on the water.

'How are you doing, birthday girl?'

'I'm fine. I'm glad you stayed.'

26

FROM TIME TO TIME TOM GLANCES AT ME, WONDERING, but I don't catch his eye. Mum over-compensates for my dullness, wittering away about her actors and their foibles. She's funny and her anecdotes help the meal pass. I'd planned an early night, but now I can't leave, not until Amber has gone to bed. Eventually, Mum goes up, leaving the three of us to drink our coffee in the living room. We sit on the huge sofa, Amber with her legs tucked up underneath her, me leaning back and constantly yawning, Tom on the other side of her, his long, hairy legs out in front of him, his hands clasped behind his head.

The grander of the two sitting rooms is vast, with beams that stretch the length of it and dark wooden chandeliers. The rugs spread across the polished floorboards are deep and soft. Terracotta lamps with pale-cream shades soften everything and induce an atmosphere of relaxed luxury. I desperately want to stay awake but conversation is desultory, sleepy and intermittent and at some point I fall into a light doze. Their voices filter through as though muffled under a thick blanket; a comforting murmur that reminds me of childhood, of falling asleep to the sound of my mother reading me a story.

I don't know how many minutes go by. It could be five. It could be half an hour, but I surface when Amber laughs. I keep my eyes closed.

'You hated me when we first met,' she whispers. 'Admit it.'

'I didn't,' Tom protests.

'Don't deny it. It was totally obvious. I don't mind. I would kind of like to know why though.'

I feel the cushions shift as he sits up and picture him leaning forward, bringing his feet in, his arms going round his knees.

'Since I don't remember feeling that way, I can hardly be expected to explain it.'

I listen to the silence until I think I can distinguish Tom's breath from hers. The hairs on the back of my neck rise.

'Did you feel threatened by my relationship with Vicky?'

'What a load of crap. Typical female, over-thinking things.'

'You're evading the question.'

He laughs softly. 'Remind me what it was again.'

Their cotton-wool voices float around me. I stop breathing when I sense a change in tone.

'What did I do wrong?' Amber asks. 'What did I say or do that set you against me?'

'You didn't do anything. It was one of those things. We were so young and had made this huge decision,

259

had had to sacrifice dreams – both of us I mean, not just me – and I suppose I was touchy. I wanted everyone to think I was cool with it, able to cope. I was twenty-two.'

'Do you and Vicky ever talk about it?'

'Not really. There's no point. We made a commitment and we've worked at it.'

'You make it sound like a chore.'

'Do I? It isn't. And I don't regret it or feel any need to rake it up. It is what it is.' He hesitates. 'And I love her.'

'I know you do.'

There's a telling silence. How can he allow himself to be manipulated like this?

'Well,' Amber murmurs. 'Maybe that explains why . . .'

'Why what?'

'What I said to you a few weeks ago, that I think she might be on the verge of a breakdown. Maybe I'm wrong.'

'I hope you are.'

What the hell? I can feel him thinking this over, wondering if she's right, if he has actually noticed odd things about me, if I've been withdrawn. I have been; not for any reason he would think of, but because for a few short months I was infatuated with someone else. It could have felt like detachment. I know that now. I want them to stop but at the same time I'm thirsty for more. I want to know what they both think of me. The curse of the eavesdropper.

'If I'm right,' Amber says, 'she needs to be encouraged to seek help. There's the children's well-being to consider. I care about you two and she's vulnerable at the moment. I think having Josh came as a big shock. I've noticed a tendency for her to fixate on him as the source of any problems. I wouldn't want . . . no, I'm sorry. Don't listen to me.'

'Wouldn't want what?'

'Nothing.'

He sighs. 'Maybe I haven't been as aware as I should have been, but work . . . well, you know what it's like. You get so caught up in life you let small inconveniences slide. Thank you, Amber. I don't know what we would do without you.'

I can't bear any more of this. I grunt, pretend to be waking up, open my eyes sleepily and rub at an imaginary crick in my neck. They both sit back, turn to me and smile.

'What time is it?'

Tom glances at his watch. 'Half eleven. Past your bedtime.'

He stands and holds out his hands and pulls us both up. I brush against Amber's bare arm by mistake and her skin is warm and silky soft. Her hair-grip has gone and her hair falls behind her shoulders, a shaggy honey-toned mass that suits the new brown of her skin. The dim light softens her angles.

I snuggle into bed, fitting my knees in behind Tom's. He turns his head and kisses me.

'Are you OK?'

'Mm,' I murmur. 'Tired.'

'But not completely wiped out?' he says hopefully.

'Not quite.' I put my hand on his hip and let it rest there a moment and then I kiss his shoulder and run my fingers down his thigh. He rolls over and our lips meet, our bodies responding quickly to familiar cues.

I do something I haven't done in years. I give him a love bite, deliberately, on the side of his neck, out of sight, where he won't notice it when he looks in the mirror.

Afterwards he falls straight into a heavy sleep but the ten-minute doze I had on the sofa has ruined my chances of dropping off and I lie awake long into the night reviewing what I heard, wondering if they were right to worry about me. Something must be wrong with me or I would never have left Josh like I did and I would never have considered having an affair.

At breakfast Vicky is so tired and clumsy she knocks over a glass of fresh orange juice and it spreads across the table and drips on to the floor. Amber leaps up to grab the kitchen towel while they move the plates and cups.

Maggie examines Vicky's face. 'Headache?'

Vicky nods and Maggie hands Josh to Tom, opens her bag and flourishes a packet of painkillers with an air of triumph. 'Why don't you go back to bed for an hour or so? We can look after the girls.'

'You do look a bit seedy,' Amber says. She pours her a glass of water and watches while Vicky swallows back the pills. She's not surprised her friend is having sleepless nights. So would she, in her shoes.

'Thanks. Do you mind if I go and lie down? I feel shit.'

'Too much sun yesterday, I expect,' Tom says. 'Go on. You won't be missed.'

Vicky manages a snarky smile and gets up. Amber follows her out of the room and looks up at her as she tramps heavily upstairs. 'What's the matter?' she says.

'Nothing.' Vicky holds her gaze for a moment and then continues on her way.

Amber walks into the sitting room where the girls are lounging on the floor in their pyjamas playing card games. They barely acknowledge her as she tidies up around them. Shoes and socks, books and comics and plastic toys. She doesn't feel great herself, but she's a guest and sees it as her duty to remain upbeat. She plumps up the cushions and sits down with her book. It's a quiet morning, everyone subdued. Even Josh is less rumbustious than normal.

Two chapters later her eyes begin to grow heavy. She doesn't want to fall asleep so she stretches, gets up and wanders out into the hall. The kitchen door is ajar, Maggie and Tom's voices audible. She stops for a moment, her hand against the door panel, and listens, even though she knows that eavesdropping never made anyone happy.

'But do you like her?' Maggie is saying.

'I am extremely fond of her.'

There's a long pause. Amber holds her breath. Her nerves tingle.

'Is there a *but* there?' Maggie asks.

'It's not as simple as that. Amber is a complicated character; she makes you feel like you have to be constantly on her side, or you're not her friend.' He laughs. 'I'm tying myself in knots here, but it's hard to explain. She's always been there for Vicky, and vice versa. I'm grateful to her and Robert for their friendship and support.'

'I just think they make an odd pair. Amber isn't like the girls Vicky hung out with at school and university. It's a pity she's let those friendships slide.'

'Well, you know what it's like when you have children. You get so involved in your local area there isn't always time for people who aren't at the same stage in life as you are. We still see them from time to time. And she and Amber might be very different, but they give each other something. Vicky has a tendency to worry and over-think things, and Amber keeps her grounded. Vicky gives Amber a sense of belonging.'

'That's interesting,' Maggie says.

'Amber is rootless and lonely. Vicky is her shield against that.'

'If you ask me, Amber is a dog in the manger.'

'I'm not asking you. Sorry, I don't mean to sound rude but it's none of my business either. I would never judge or interfere.'

'Of course not. I never said you should. All I was thinking was that maybe you should see more of other friends. I did like Jenny and Simon.'

'Yes.' The defensive tone has gone. 'I will admit they're a breath of fresh air.'

No, no no no. Amber runs outside, round the side of the house, and hides behind the white wall. She rips at the bougainvillea, petals scattering at her feet, pink staining her fingertips.

Noises rise up to me: the clink of cutlery; a peal of

laughter from Josh; the constant clickety chatter of crickets. My eyes won't stay closed. My mind keeps forcing me back to that moment when I opened the door to Josh's bedroom; to the intruder staring at me, Josh in his arms. I understand now that the man was horrified to have been caught like that. I doubt he meant to hurt Josh; all he wanted was for him to be quiet so that he could get out of the house without being seen. I feel less anger towards him than I do towards myself. What possessed me to do it?

On impulse, I get up and wander into Amber's empty bedroom. She never did swap with us. The room is reasonably tidy, the bed properly made, the clothes picked up and folded. I wonder what it means when her environment is less in control. I'm not the only one with problems. There's a book beside her bed; not the one she's been reading by the pool, but a well-thumbed paperback. I sit down and take it in my hands. *The Blue Fairy Book*. Inside the flyleaf its previous owner has written, *This book belongs to Linda Field. 1970*. Amber must have found it in a charity shop. I read some of these when I was young and they don't hold back on the brutality and violence. Blue Beard and his blood-drenched brides gave me nightmares. I make a mental note to ask her not to read them to my girls.

I'm about to leave the room when a breeze catches the muslins and as they float away from the window I see Amber at the edge of the pool, at the deep end, looking down into the water. She pulls her hair into a twist and lets it fall in front of her shoulder. I wonder what she's thinking as she stares into the blue depths.

At the corner of my vision, a stealthy movement alerts

me to the presence of the children. I squint into the sunlight. They are hiding behind the shrubs. I try to work out what they're up to and something, perhaps the light catching my eternity ring, makes Amber look straight at me. A strange thing happens. As if in slow motion, she starts to lean over the edge, to lean until her leg comes forward and her arms fly out and she floats downwards. Time speeds up as the water surges up around her, embraces her and sucks her down. For a few brief seconds I am so transfixed by the scene that I don't act.

She surfaces and starts turning circles, thrashing her arms, screaming for help, and I do nothing. I'm in a trance, my feet glued to the floor, my legs useless. Polly, Sophie and Emily must have been watching because all of a sudden they are there and Sophie starts screaming. She jumps in and my girls race towards the house and still I don't move. I merely watch fascinated as Amber sinks and rises, sinks and rises until she goes still and her hair spreads like crow's wings in the blue . . .

What the hell is wrong with me? I spin away from the window and start to run, taking the stairs two at a time, yelling for Tom. But he's there already and as I burst out of the house he sprints across the terrace, dives into the pool and brings both of them spluttering to the surface. I jump in, relieve him of Sophie and get her over to the side. She's all right, only shocked.

Polly is wailing but I can't deal with her now. I watch Tom with Amber. She is draped in his arms, her head back, her hair everywhere, in her face, across his lips, tangled in his fingers. Her clothes cling to her body and it's that that kills me, the way her small breasts, her flat stomach and slender thighs are moulded by the wet fabric. Tom gets her to the steps, picks her up and lifts her out of the water. He lies her down on her back, bends over her and gives her the kiss of life. She splutters immediately and cries out. I turn my head away and concentrate on towelling a sobbing Sophie dry and telling her how brave she's been.

27

Sunday, 4 April 2010

'I MUST HAVE FAINTED,' AMBER SAYS WEAKLY.

We've brought her into the smaller of the two sitting rooms. In the other one, the girls have started rehearsing their play with Mum who, with unusual restraint and lack of melodrama, rounded them up, dried their tears, gave them each a chocolate Easter egg and suggested they think about where their stage is going to be.

'It must have had something to do with the light flickering on the water. I'm so sorry to give everyone such a fright. Lucky the girls heard me screaming or that would have been it.' She hesitates. 'Where were you, Vicky?'

'On the loo.' It's the best excuse I can manage.

She frowns. 'Oh . . . I thought I saw . . . well, never mind. Thank God the girls were there.'

'I haven't seen Tom run that fast since he played football for his university team.'

Tom smiles. 'I've still got it.'

'I thought that was it. Everything went foggy and I

even stopped panicking. I had this soft, drifting feeling. And then there you were. Like Superman.'

'The real hero is Sophie,' Mum says, coming back in. 'She was incredibly brave. She could have drowned too.'

'Oh God, absolutely! In fact, I'm grateful to you all.'

She's crying. Her tears begin quietly and become great whooping sobs, and she flaps her hand in front of her face in an effort to stop them.

'Try and drink some of that tea,' Tom says. 'You've had a nasty shock.'

He pulls his chair closer to hers and puts his arm around her. I love men's arms. Tom's are dusted with dark hair, the muscles and sinews well defined. Amber collapses against him, her face pressed into his armpit, shivering even though she has changed out of her wet things. The blue cashmere sweater Tom was wearing last night is hanging over the back of a chair and he passes it to her. She pulls it on and is swamped by it, her hands almost vanishing into the sleeves.

There is no denying it; Amber – the vulnerable version – is alluring; even to me. I want to put my arms around her and shield her from the world. And if I can feel that way, how much more must Tom feel, how hard would it be for him to resist her? I think she knows how adorable she looks, drowning in his jumper.

'When will the grown-ups come and see our show?' Emily asks.

'After lunch, poppet,' I say.

'When's lunch?'

'About an hour? When everyone's hungry. How are the rehearsals going?'

She makes a face. 'Not good.'

'Oh dear. Why's that?'

'Because Sophie's mummy nearly drowned and Sophie's too sad for shows.'

'Ah, well. I think that's understandable, don't you?'

But Amber sits up and brushes her hair back. 'Don't worry. Tell Sophie I'll be very disappointed if I don't get to see it. I'm sure once I've had something to eat I'll feel much better.'

Josh sits on the tiled floor surrounded by wooden spoons and saucepans; a noisy combination. Amber is slumped like a teenager, her hair bedraggled, her arms crossed loosely over her abdomen. She sniffs at Tom's jumper then frowns, remembering the mark on his neck. How childish Vicky can be.

She's keeping an eye on the baby while Maggie advises the girls on their big production. As part-time landlady to a regular stream of actors, actresses, wardrobe ladies and make-up artists, she is the voice of authority on all things theatrical.

The door opens. Amber lifts her head and catches the older woman's eye, and there it is: that shock of connection and recognition.

What took you so long, Maggie?

'Tom and Vicky not back yet?' Maggie says.

'I'm sure they won't be long.'

Maggie stoops to talk to Josh, who drops his spoon and crows at her, delighted to get some attention. Amber isn't much fun at the moment. On the other side of the hall, Sophie's voice rises. She's inclined to become strident if unchecked.

'No, Polly,' she squawks. 'Like this. You have to concentrate. Do you know what concentrate means?'

Amber pictures her with her hands on her hips, lips pursed. She is as bossy as Robert's mother. She isn't keen on that aspect of her daughter's personality.

'Katya,' Maggie says, in a voice so quiet Amber nearly misses it.

'I don't use that name and you mustn't either.' She smiles at her. 'I don't suppose you thought you'd ever see me again.'

'No, I didn't.'

'But here I am.'

'Have you known it was me all along?'

'Of course I have. You haven't changed. I can't believe you didn't recognize me.'

'I didn't. You've grown up. Your hair's so different.' Maggie peers at her, as if trying to fathom the riddle. 'The fringe changes the shape of your face. But it isn't just that. You used to be such a scared little thing. It's your confidence. That's why I missed it.'

'I wasn't looking for you either, you know. It was pure chance.'

It's perfectly true. She hadn't realized, not until she worked it out from Vicky's wedding photo, that she was Emily Parrish. What had hurt was that Maggie hadn't recognized in her daughter's new friend the broken child she had walked away from eleven years previously. Emily Seagrave's christening had passed off without any dramatic unveiling. It was only at the christening that she discovered Vicky's middle name was Emily. It was an obvious choice when she thought about it. Maggie had had to think quickly.

'Do you honestly expect me to believe that?' Maggie says.

'Why not? I wasn't interested in you. I'd moved on. You say I seem confident to you, but if I do, it's because I've worked at it. It hasn't been easy.'

'No, I can imagine it hasn't.' Maggie's tone is conciliatory and she's leaning towards Amber, her body language accessible. She doesn't realize, she thinks that she's forgiven. 'I'm glad things have gone well for you, Amber.'

Amber shrugs. 'I met some wonderful people at Fairhaven who helped me turn my life around. Then I met Robert. Now, if you have some idea of wrecking things for me by talking to Vicky, you need to think carefully, because I can do as much damage to you as you could ever do to me.' She dips her head until her hair falls forward and then raises her eyes and looks directly into Maggie's face. 'So. What are you going to do?'

'I was fond of you, you know,' she says, as if that was answer enough.

'But you were fonder of him.'

Maggie ignores the provocation. 'Whatever it is you're up to, Amber, please don't hurt Vicky. It was my fault and my weakness. If you're looking for an apology, I'll gladly give you one, but leave my family alone.'

'I don't know what you're talking about.'

Maggie sighs, waits for a moment and then tucks her hair behind her ears and leans forward until she's as close to Amber as she can get. She speaks quietly, aware of the children in the other room. 'You are flirting with Tom. It's a waste of time. He's not interested in you. He loves my daughter. You won't succeed in breaking them up.'

'Who says I want to?'

'Anyone with eyes. You're jealous of Vicky. It's written all over your face. That's what that display was all about – attention seeking. Leave them alone, Katya.'

'It's Amber!'

Her cry takes Maggie by surprise. She lurches into the back of her chair, her hand splayed protectively across the region of her heart. Amber is half standing, her hands pressed on to the table, her face twisted.

'Why did you leave me, Maggie? I was a child. How can you live with yourself?'

'I . . .'

'You knew things weren't right. Don't deny it. I don't forgive you and I don't accept your apology. You said so many things that weren't true. You made promises you never intended to keep. You are pathetic and a coward, and I'm going to hit you where it'll hurt you most. I can do what I like with Vicky's life. Try and stop me. I don't care. I'll enjoy it.'

The door opens and she spins round. Sophie looks from one woman to the other, a worried frown buckling her forehead.

'Will you come and watch us now?'

Amber sniffs and wipes her eyes. 'Of course we will. We just need to wait for Vicky and Tom to get back from their walk.'

'Why are you crying, Mummy?'

Maggie leaps up and walks out of the room. Amber listens to her footsteps fade before she replies.

'Give Mummy a hug.'

Sophie climbs on to her knee, puts her arms around her and presses her cheek to Amber's. 'Are you sad?'

'It's the shock of falling in the pool, darling. I'll be all right. Your play will cheer me up.'

28

TOM AND I STROLL ALONG THE TRACK IN SILENCE, vineyards to either side of us, the grapes still small and hard as bullets. Our feet disturb the yellow dust and scatter loose pebbles. I turn and glance at the big white villa and rub the back of my neck. I have horrible butterflies. I can't be expected to keep everything screwed down so tightly.

'Tom, I need to ask you something.'

He takes my hand and the gesture is so reassuring that I nearly change my mind. But then I think about Amber last night. That conversation with Tom was instigated by her. She could have stuck to talking about children and houses. She didn't need to get personal.

'I should have told Amber Maggie was coming. That was my fault. I shouldn't have snapped at you about it.'

'It's not that.' I watch a bird of prey hovering in the distance. This is the hardest thing to do and surprisingly humiliating.

'What is it then?'

'Is there anything going on between you two?'

That stops him. He turns and looks at me, shading his eyes. 'What on earth are you talking about?'

I walk faster but he grabs hold of my hand. 'Vicky?'

'It's nothing.'

'Well, obviously it isn't. Talk to me.'

'All right.' I stoop and pick up a stone, fling it ahead of us and wait to see where it finishes up. It bounces and settles on the dry verge. 'It feels like the two of you are getting a little too close.'

He groans. 'You daft cow. There is absolutely nothing going on between us. She would be as horrified as me if she knew you thought that.'

'You won't tell her, will you?'

He smirks. 'Are you jealous?'

'I might be.'

'Come here.'

He puts his arm around me and we stand locked together, a warm breeze encircling us. An aeroplane sings high overhead, cutting a white trail through small puffs of cloud. Out of the house and away from Amber's presence I feel more confident and lighter; willing to believe him and disbelieve my own eyes.

'Victoria, I adore-yer.'

I punch his stomach playfully. 'You are so pleased with that, aren't you?'

We have gathered in the smaller of the two sitting rooms, each of us clutching a ticket. Each ticket has a drawing on it that has some connection to us. Mine has a ruler because I'm a teacher. Mum's has a portrait of Max, Tom's has a motorbike that looks like a stag beetle on wheels and Amber's has a picture of a house. Tom has moved the furniture so that the white leather sofa and matching armchairs are in a row. For the set, the three girls have built the walls of a castle using cushions stolen from the two sofas in the other room.

Mum and I sit side by side. Amber and Tom take the chairs. I lean forward and look beyond my mother and see that Amber is still wearing Tom's sweater. She seems to have recovered from her ordeal. I glance at Tom and he sends me a rueful smile. When I frown at him, his smile widens.

'Ladies and gentlemen,' Sophie says with aplomb. 'We welcome you to our show, which is called *The Princess and the Witch*.'

We all clap madly and settle down to twenty minutes of chaos, bossiness, tears and suppressed hysteria. Sophie Collins is clearly the star, a born performer. She owns the stage, swirling around in a pink sparkly vest and one of her mother's skirts. Emily wants everyone to stick rigidly to the plan, even if, like Polly, they can't remember what it is. Polly can't take her huge eyes off me and every so often wanders over for a hug. I haven't laughed so much in ages. I take pictures and film short bursts for posterity on my phone. At the end, we give them a standing ovation. Emily bows, Sophie curtseys and Polly stands there with a daft grin on her face and the tracks of dried tears on her cheeks.

After that, it seems only fair to let them watch a DVD. Mum wants to get out of the house, so I suggest going to Sant Cugat to see the ancient Benedictine monastery. She seems odd – on edge and nervy – so even though I'd have preferred to get stuck into my book, I agree. Unfortunately, Tom doesn't want to come.

'But why not? I thought you wanted to see it.'

'I think it's a bit much to ask Amber to look after the children, especially after what she's been through today,' he says. 'And I need to answer emails.'

I stare at him and he stares back, the corners of his mouth lifting. He thinks it's funny that I'm bothered.

'I wasn't intending to leave Josh.'

It's a pathetic effort and is ignored by everyone. Mum isn't averse to spending an afternoon without the children and points out that I barely ever see her without at least one of them in tow these days.

'I'm not sure I like your friend very much.'

We've taken refuge from the heat in the monastery cloisters, and found a shaded wall to sit on. We stretch our legs into the sun and drink from our water bottles. The place is busy with tourists, mainly Americans.

'Well, you're in a minority because everyone else thinks she's the cat's pyjamas.'

'Perhaps she doesn't flirt with everyone else's husbands.'

'Mum! That's a dreadful thing to say.'

'Sorry. It's none of my business.'

'Actually, you're right. She does flirt with him. But I've spoken to Tom about it and he's reassured me. I think it's just Amber wanting to be the centre of attention.'

Mum raises her eyebrows.

'Don't look at me like that. 'Even if she did fancy

278

him – which I'm not saying I think she does – he knows her far too well. And apart from that she and her husband are about to buy a house together and she's hardly likely to do that if she's trying to steal Tom from me.'

'I think she's trouble. I mean, where did she come from? How much do you actually know about her?'

'I know enough. You're stirring, Mum. Stop it.'

She laughs at me but I don't laugh back. She's hit a raw nerve.

'What about that business in the swimming pool?'

'What about it?'

'Well, don't you think it was odd? Falling in and then doing the damsel-in-distress bit with Tom. She strikes me as the sort of woman who takes pleasure in small acts of malice.'

She sets her bottle down at her feet and lifts the rim of her big floppy hat so that she can see her surroundings properly. She looks like a character out of a Merchant Ivory film. I watch her for a moment, still feeling defensive, then let it go. I don't want to talk about Amber. I know that Mum is right, up to a point, but that's annoying in itself. Amber is my problem and I'll deal with her in my own way.

'Don't move, Mum. I want to take a picture.' I open my bag and push aside my purse, glasses case and bottle of water and scrabble amongst the loose receipts and Josh's teething rings. 'Damn. I must have left my phone back at the house. Do you have your camera on you?'

She hands me her Instamatic and I capture the moment.

'So if it isn't Tom,' she says, 'then what is upsetting you? Is it that man?'

'No. That's well and truly over.' I'm about to cry. My eyes are hot and my throat aches. I look away from her and swallow hard, thankful for my sunglasses.

Mum waits. She drinks some water and looks around her. Two Chinese girls walk past us, stop and take formal pictures of each other framed by the ancient arches.

'Is there something you want to tell me?' she asks. She searches my face. It's like we've gone back twenty years and it's just the two of us again. Maggie and Vicky.

'I've made a horrible mistake.' My voice trembles. 'And I don't know what to do.'

She strokes my cheek. 'I doubt it's as bad as some of the mistakes I've made.'

'I've broken the law.' I stare down at my lap and rub at a speck of food on my linen trousers. Polly's handiwork.

'Tell me what happened, Vicky. Maybe I can help.'

'I doubt it. I lied to the police about the morning Josh had the accident. I wanted to see a house that Amber was marketing and I'd had a really bad night with him, and he was asleep and, to cut a long story short, I left him at home on his own while I went to the viewing. When I came back that man was in his room. Amber saw him leave. I'd lied to her as well and told her that Magda was looking after him.'

'Does anyone know?'

'Only Amber. She helped me cover it up.'

'Ah.'

'What does *ah* mean?'

'Nothing. I'm being silly. She's your friend and you've known her for years. I've only spent a few days with her. Ignore me.'

I hesitate. 'OK. Social services came round in the middle of Emily's birthday party and completely ruined the day. I lied again. God, Mum, I wish I'd confessed right at the beginning.'

'You mustn't do that. Please believe me; it's a bad idea.'

This is not the reaction I expected. 'Amber said the same thing. But it's the right thing to do, surely?'

'I was a social worker for two years, remember. I know how those decisions are taken. Don't underestimate them, Vicky. For your sake and your family's.'

'I went out without him, Mum. I feel sick when I think about it. It was a purely selfish act that could have ended in tragedy. At the very least I should have told Tom the truth.'

'That would have been a good idea, but what's done is done. There's no point working yourself up into a state.'

I fish in my bag for a hanky and wipe my eyes.

'So why did you invite Amber on holiday with you?'

Not Amber again. Why was she so obsessed with her?

'I felt sorry for her. She was meant to go home with Robert.' I stand up and brush the dust off my trousers and look at my watch. 'Come on, time to go.'

She catches at my arm and I look down at her. 'Wait.'

'We should get back.'

'In a minute. I know that you're way past taking advice from your mother, but I'm going to say this anyway. When you get back to London, I think you should distance yourself from Amber Collins.'

'Mum—'

'Just listen a minute, will you? She's jealous of you. She's like that child you were friends with at school. I've forgotten her name. The one who tried to alienate you from your other friends.'

I wrinkle my nose. 'Laura Griffin.'

'That's the one. Amber reminds me of her. I'm not saying drop her entirely, but maybe dilute her a little. Jenny was very nice. Why not see more of her?'

Old loyalties kick in and I feel the stirrings of an almost adolescent irritation with my parent. 'Amber might be slightly screwed up, but she's still my friend. She'd never do anything to hurt me. If I'm feeling insecure at the moment it's entirely my own fault. I'm the one who nearly wrecked my marriage and I'm the one who put my child at risk.'

She squints at me, the sun in her eyes. 'All right. I'm sorry. It's none of my business.'

'You're my mum. You're entitled. And I'll be fine. You worry far too much.'

June 1992

THE PHONE RANG AT FIVE IN THE MORNING. KATYA woke blinking in the darkness, her body slow to catch up. Above her, the low vibration of Luke's voice was closely followed by the sound of feet crossing the floor. The toilet flushed, the feet padded back and the wardrobe doors slid open on their runners. When someone left the house, Katya was awake enough to kneel up on her bed and open the curtains a crack. A salmon-pink dawn reflected against Sally's shiny white hatchback as she drove away.

When she woke again two hours later and emerged from her bedroom, Luke was already up and about, wearing a suit, smelling of aftershave.

'Where's Sally gone?' she asked.

'She's at the hospice with her sister.'

Katya felt a chill run down her spine. 'How long for?'

'How long is a piece of string?' He fetched a box of cereal down from the cupboard and handed it to her. 'She'll be back when it's over. A week at the most, I would have thought. But don't worry; we'll manage fine.' He chucked her under her chin. 'I don't know what I'd do without you, Princess.'

Katya turned away, making a face. 'I'm not your princess. I'm just me.'

She put on her summer uniform: red-and-white checked dress, white socks and red cardigan, and left at the same time as Luke, who had another interview. She almost reached the school gates but then Gabriella Brady gave her that wrinkled-nose look, like she was repulsive, that put ice in her veins, and she turned away at the last moment, pushing against the tide of children coming in the opposite direction. If she was in that mood, there was no point in Katya being at school. The weather was strange for a summer morning, not fresh but thick and humid. She pulled off her cardigan, tied it round her waist and stood on the corner of the street wondering where to go, then decided to take the bus into Clapham.

Clapham Junction was where Linda used to take her for a treat, usually on her birthday but once or twice when things were tough. She remembered they went after that time Linda's boyfriend held her under water. They would visit the toy department in Arding & Hobbs and spend at least half an hour choosing something and then go to the café on the top floor where they would have a pot of tea and a slice of cake each – Katya loved having a pot all to herself. She always chose the coffee and walnut; Linda had the carrot cake. She would get her present out of the bag and take it out of its packaging. She remembered a particular Barbie doll, dressed in a suede miniskirt, checked shirt, cowboy hat and boots. Linda loved that one. She said it reminded her of a song called 'Harper Valley PTA'. She promised to find it sometime and play it for Katya but she never did, so Katya still didn't know what the doll had to do with it.

Standing opposite the shelves of dolls Katya was saddened to find that she didn't feel like she had expected to feel, like she used to feel. It was completely different on her own; the sound, the smell, the lighting, all seemed harsher, intruding on her thoughts and blocking the magic, if it ever existed. Without money and without her mother to discuss each choice, the brightly boxed toys had lost their power to transport her.

People were looking, thinking she ought to be at school. She ran down the escalators and out into the street. The energy had gone, leaving her despondent. On the upper deck of the bus she turned her face to the window and wept silently as she passed her nursery school and the boundaries of the estate where she lived before Linda died. She was filled with longing, not for happier times, because there weren't many, but for a place that at least felt like it belonged to her. There were bad men in those days but they had no interest in her; all they needed was alcohol, drugs and sex with her mother. She watched the sky darken and litter scud along the pavement. One day, when they were grown up, she was going to share a flat with Emily Parrish, somewhere north of the river, somewhere where bad things hadn't happened. She tried to imagine that Emily was sitting beside her now and it worked so well that she almost turned to speak to her. But the seat was empty. A crash of thunder announced the onset of rain and within seconds the skies opened.

As they rumbled through Streatham she saw Maggie walk out of Boots and open a small purple umbrella, the sort that fitted in a handbag. The wind buffeted it but miraculously it kept its shape. Katya darted down the stairs and got off at the next stop. She followed Maggie along the busy high road, turning left into a residential street. Maggie walked almost to the end before she stopped outside a tall, red-brick Victorian house, dropped the umbrella at her feet and rummaged in her pocket for her keys. Katya waited, hidden in the alleyway between two blocks of flats. Then she went up to Maggie's front door and pressed her finger against the bell marked *Parrish*.

29

Sunday, 4 April 2010

THE HOUSE IS SO BRIGHT, THE BOUGAINVILLEA BLAZING against its walls, that I'm forced to shield my eyes when I get out of the car. We walk round the side – nobody uses the front door – and find the garden empty, the poolside deserted.

'Hello!' Mum calls. 'Anyone in?'

'In the kitchen,' Amber shouts back.

We follow her voice. Josh is on the floor playing with a heavy-bottomed casserole dish and two wooden spoons. The girls are sitting at the table with their colouring-in books and felt-tip pens. Tom's there too but he doesn't look at me at first, and when he does I know something is wrong.

'How was Sant Cugat?' Amber asks.

She washes her hands and dries them on a tea towel, then scrapes the garlic she's been crushing into a pan of frying onions. The smell that rises from it is redolent of the Mediterranean.

'Very interesting,' Mum says. 'The monastery is named

after a martyred saint. Apparently he was covered in vinegar and pepper and roasted alive.'

'Ugh,' Amber says.

'Why was he?' Polly says, looking dismayed.

'Mum! I don't think that's very appropriate. She wasn't talking about a person, Polly. She was talking about an animal. It's called a martyr. They only eat them in this part of Spain.'

'Wow,' Tom says. 'That's going to make an interesting subject for show and tell.'

I glance at him and tilt my head slightly. He holds my gaze but doesn't say anything.

'Right,' I say, bothered by his tone and determined to sound cheerful. 'Well, if there's nothing I can do, I'll put the furniture back.'

'We've already done that,' Emily says.

'Oh, OK. Did you see my phone? I think I left it on the sofa.'

Tom slips his hand into the pocket of his shorts and brings it out. He holds it out to me then puts it down on the side so that I can't take it from him. I'm puzzled but I don't want to question him in front of an audience. I swipe and glance at the screen automatically, and feel the blood drain from my face.

I look up at Tom, but he's talking to Mum, asking her questions about the afternoon.

'Can we talk?' I say. My hands are shaking and there's a huge lump in my throat. I've been unforgivably, catastrophically careless.

'Not now.'

* * *

There's a heaviness building in the air. At first I think it's me, but the atmosphere has a sultry quality that reflects the mood of the house. It's partly the weather, partly Tom's clouded brow. I don't think he wants me anywhere near him and it breaks my heart. I never loved David and I never fell out of love with Tom; the affair was a temporary blip.

I put olives and wine on the table and light the candles. A breeze touches my face and I look up.

'There's going to be a storm later,' Mum says. There's a question in her eyes. She feels it too.

'Hope so,' Amber replies.

Conversation is stilted. Oddly enough, I miss Robert. I hadn't understood until he'd gone, but his presence provided a sponge that drew the tension out of the atmosphere. Without him I can almost hear the uncomfortable fizz in the air.

'So, Amber, where did you grow up?' Mum asks, after a silence that lasts so long even Tom looks like he's going to crack.

'South London.'

'And what about your family? Are they still there?'

There is an edge to Mum's tone that makes me look from one to the other. Even Tom looks puzzled.

'Mum died twelve years ago,' Amber says. She seems oblivious to Mum's mood. 'I don't have any contact with my father. He's Norwegian.'

I'd swear she told me he was German.

'But let's not talk about depressing things.' She smiles. 'Let's talk about nice things. Weren't the children fantastic this afternoon? We should have filmed it.'

'I filmed some of it on my phone,' I say, glancing at Tom. He doesn't react.

'Oh good. Could you email it to Robert?'

I say I will and rack my brains for something else to talk about, but Amber gets there first.

'You're very quiet, Tom. You've barely touched your food.'

He looks down at his plate, rubs his fingers through his hair and smiles in a way that shows it's an effort. 'I'm not hungry.' He pauses, remembering his manners. 'How's Robert doing?'

'Oh, he's all right. He flies to Singapore tomorrow, so he's very busy. Fingers crossed this deal works out. I'm trying not to think about it too much, but it'll make all the difference if it does.'

Tom takes a mouthful, chews it and swallows without showing any sign of enjoying the food. He holds the fork as he speaks. 'What's happening with the house? Have you exchanged yet?'

'No. Probate's taking forever. But that's to our advantage because we're still getting the deposit together. Robert's trying to negotiate them down to seven per cent. It'll happen though. I'm determined.'

'I'm sure you are.'

'I expect Vicky was the same when you were going for Coleridge Street.'

He looks at me then and I hold his gaze. Under the table my fingers pull at a paper napkin. He doesn't smile. I see a flash of lightning, followed about twenty seconds later by thunder booming in the distance.

'Did you see that?' Mum says.

'Yes,' Tom says. 'Vicky tends to get what she wants when she puts her mind to it.'

Amber raises her eyebrows. 'Is that how she got you?'

'You could say that.'

'Uh, Amber dear,' Mum interrupts. 'Perhaps we should clean up now, before we all get too tired.'

We finish at half past ten, at which point I go to bed. Even though I know I'm relying on them too heavily, I pop a sleeping pill out of its blister and swallow it. I half expect Tom to stay in one of the two unused bedrooms but he joins me. He gets undressed in the bathroom. I listen to him drop his clothes on the floor and clean his teeth. He takes ages and when he gets in beside me he's careful not to touch me.

'Is now a good time to talk?' I ask. I lean up on my elbow. He doesn't turn round.

'I'm tired.'

'But we can't go to sleep without saying anything. You have to at least let me explain.'

'What is there to explain? You had an affair. It's pretty simple, isn't it?'

'No, it isn't. It's complicated. And I didn't have an affair. We never did anything.'

Frustrated by his obstructiveness I switch on the bed-side light and he screws up his eyes. There is such a distance between us now that I'm scared I'm not going to be able to bridge it. This has never happened before. Even when we've rowed I've still felt close to him, known that he's my friend and that the anger will pass. Now I'm not so sure. His profile is unreadable, the set of his mouth implacable. It's completely my fault, but I'm still hoping for something, a soft area, his Achilles' tendon, something that might give if pressed hard enough.

I touch his shoulder and he turns his head with an impatient snarl. He looks so angry, so unlike himself, that I pull my hand away.

'I made a mistake and I'm sorry. I love you.'

He sits up and shuffles back against the cushioned headboard. 'Tell me what that means to you. Because you know something, Vicky, I don't think you've ever genuinely loved anyone. You're like your mum. Never content. Always wanting the next thing, whether it's a house or a man. Nothing is ever going to be enough for you.'

'That's unfair.'

'Why is it unfair? You were thinking about moving when you went to look round that house, weren't you? And you must have considered leaving me when you had your little fling with David.' He sneers the name. 'Don't tell me you didn't imagine what it would be like, because I won't believe you.'

'I didn't. I never would have left you!'

'Well, that makes me feel so much better.'

There is a long pause. Both of us are staring at anything but each other.

Eventually I speak, but quietly, hoping to pull his anger back a notch. 'I don't know why I did it. I have no excuse.'

'Well, you obviously aren't happy with me.'

'I am happy with you. It's just, since I got pregnant with Josh, I think I must have gone a little mad.' I start to cry and wipe my eyes on the edge of the duvet. I despise myself for using this tactic, even though the tears are real. I could have stopped them if I really wanted to.

'So you're blaming it on your hormones now? That's convenient.'

'I'm not. I know it's down to me. I'm trying to explain that I haven't really been myself lately.'

'Or perhaps you have. Perhaps all this time you've been acting a part and this is the real you.'

'I promise you I've asked myself that. I've looked at Mum's behaviour over the years and wondered if I'm fighting against my true nature, but you know, even if I am, that's my choice. You are the only man I want.'

'Oh great. That's hardly reassuring. And why should I want to be with a woman who needs to fight her attraction to other men?'

'Am I supposed to believe you've never been attracted to anyone else?'

He doesn't respond. I sit up. 'I'll take that as a no then. I don't give a monkey's if you fancy other women from time to time. It's normal human behaviour. I want to be with you. We love each other.'

'Do we? Are you sure about that? Or is it another thing you've forced yourself to believe, because it means security?'

'It's not like that.' I am digging myself such a big hole. I blurt out, 'I wish we were at home. It's hard to think straight with Amber around.'

He laughs grimly. 'You mean the woman I'm supposed to be shagging on the side. Christ, I never had you down as a hypocrite.'

'I did not sleep with him. You have to believe me.'

I slide down in the bed and we lie with our backs to each other and what feels like an acre of space between us.

'Infidelity is not just about sex,' Tom says into the darkness. 'It's about loyalty as well. You know that as well as I do.'

The tension in my chest increases, as if my ribcage has tightened around my lungs. Rain patters on the terraces and the pool, splashing off the long spear-like leaves of the palm trees. It acts like a lullaby, comforting me as the drug takes hold and I fall asleep.

30

Easter Monday ❧ The small hours

AMBER WAKES. THE CRICKETS HAVE LONG SINCE GONE silent but it's still raining. She gets up and goes to close the French windows but the breeze on her face is exquisitely seductive and instead she reaches for her wrap and walks outside. The scent of wet grass and soaked dust from the vineyards hangs in the night air and the pool water is as black as the sky, rippling with ever-expanding circles. It's the first night she hasn't been able to see the stars. The tiles are wet and cool underfoot and her hair and shoulders are quickly soaked.

A faint glow falls across the stone flags outside the kitchen. Someone else is up. She goes back in and towels herself off in the bathroom. She's curious to know who's downstairs at this hour. It may be Maggie, suffering from insomnia, in which case they could finish their conversation. There are things she still needs to say, and to hear.

Maggie won't tell Vicky. How can she? The moment she tries to undermine Amber, Vicky will discover what her mother was up to all those years ago.

295

Her wrap is damp but the house is so hot it hardly matters. She tiptoes out on to the landing and goes down-stairs. The kitchen door is closed. Whoever is in there doesn't want to risk disturbing the rest of the household. She pushes it open and walks in. It isn't Maggie.

Tom has lit the candles and is sitting at the table in semi-darkness, staring out at the rain, a bottle of red wine and a glass at his elbow. He doesn't realize she's there at first and she's able to study him. The candlelight is flattering to the angles of his face. His nose looks even more patrician than usual, his eyes deeper.

He starts, as if roused from sleep.

'Sorry,' she says. 'I didn't know anyone else was up. I was hungry.'

She opens the fridge and takes out a plate of cold meats covered in cling film. She isn't hungry at all, but she can pick at it. She puts it on the table and fetches another glass. Tom doesn't speak but he acknowledges her by pouring her some wine.

'Penny for them?' She rests her chin on her linked hands and waits.

'You don't want to know.'

'Try me. I'm a good listener.'

'OK. I didn't think this would ever happen to us. I thought we were rock solid.'

'Life is full of surprises.'

He stares into his glass then finishes his drink quickly and pours some more. 'Did you know?'

'I knew something had happened, but not the details.'

He rakes his fingers through his hair and groans. 'What the hell am I going to do?'

She holds out her hand and lets it rest on his forearm and he immediately covers it with his. Thunder rumbles but it's faint now. The rain smells sweet and the air is still hot and sultry, though not as heavy as earlier in the evening before the storm broke. She twists a damp strand of hair around her finger and lets it go.

'I can't understand it,' she says. 'I've always thought Vicky was so blessed. She has you and her mother, love and security. I've never . . .' She hesitates. 'I've never felt secure. I've never felt able to take anyone for granted. I wish I could.'

Tom's eyes drift to the damp patch on her wrap then back to her face. 'You have Robert and Sophie.'

She smiles faintly. 'Yes, I know I do. You probably think I'm self-obsessed, but I've always thought that I don't deserve to be happy. I've never told anyone about my childhood and I'm not going to start banging on about it now. It was horrible, but it's over. But there's a legacy, a price to pay for survival. I have to work extra hard to maintain my relationships because part of me is expecting them to break down.' She bites her lip and wipes away a tear with the edge of her hand. This isn't an act, it's the truth. She wants him to see her as she really is. 'Maybe even wanting them to.'

Tom puts his arm around her and she leans into him. His body is warm and firm, and he smells of toothpaste and Factor 20.

'What happened to you?' he murmurs. 'Tell me.'

She turns her head so that her hair brushes his chin and he touches her forehead briefly with his lips. She goes very still, and waits, her whole body tingling. It's a long, exquisitely painful moment before he kisses her, their breath audible above the rain and the hum of the fridge. She holds him, twisting in her chair, shaping her body to his as the kiss deepens, and lets his hands explore where they want, digs her fingers into the muscles of his back. He kisses her neck and she moves his hand to her breast. The storm retreats, the rain settling into a softer rhythm. In the muggy heat of the night, in the candlelight, they grasp at each other, sweaty and rough, not stopping to think, Amber lifted easily by Tom on to the table. The edge cuts into her thighs but she doesn't care. His hands are under her wrap, his lips mapping her sun-kissed skin. When he at last sets her down, the wrap slips from her body and pools at her feet. He bends to pick it up and drape it round her. He does the sash up himself.

She gazes at him, her lips parted. She feels animal, wild and abandoned.

'I am so sorry, Amber.'

'Don't be. We needed . . . I needed to be held.' She smiles shyly at him. 'It was exciting.'

His smile is awkward and apologetic. He picks up his glass and takes it to the sink then rubs the back of his neck. 'You won't . . .'

She moves between him and the candles so that he can see the silhouette of her body. 'No, of course not, Tom. It's our secret.'

His expression clouds for a moment and she moves towards the door. It suddenly feels vital that she should be the first to go, not be left alone with the empty glasses and the shadows. She runs silently upstairs and into her bedroom, then stands behind the door with her hands on the panels, her body humming, his semen dribbling down the inside of her legs. She smiles to herself as she gets back into bed and pulls the sheet over her naked body. There is no point even trying to sleep.

'Tom.'

She whispers his name, savouring it on her tongue, smiling to herself. Then her smile vanishes and she sits up. Her mind has shed the euphoria and replaced it with foreboding.

I am good, I am strong; I matter.

31

Monday, 12 April 2010

TOM WANTS A DIVORCE. HE TOLD ME SO ON THE NIGHT
we came home. It is such a stark thing that I can't think
about it without it seeming to be about someone else. I
don't understand how this can be the end when I still love
him. I am bemused by how fast things have moved, how
quickly our life has been dismantled. I can't help thinking
that some of it is Amber's fault. I'm not making excuses
for myself. I know I've behaved badly. But I could
have come through this without catastrophe if Amber
hadn't known. I still want to give her the benefit of the
doubt – she's not herself, she's under pressure, she's
unhappy, maybe even depressed – but I'm not blind and
I can't hide from the bald truth: that lately where she goes
calamity follows. As long as she doesn't tell Tom about
Josh. I have to be cautious now that there's custody to
consider. At least Miriam and the dreaded Ian haven't
been in touch again. With any luck, I'm off their radar.

Ideally, Tom would have moved into the spare bedroom
on his own but because it's directly under the children's

bathroom and needs redecorating and a new carpet we have to put up with each other's company at night for the time being. The house smells damp. I've put dehumidifiers in all three damaged rooms but our decorator reckons he won't be able to start for a couple more weeks.

Because Tom's asked me to, I make some calls and three sets of estate agents turn up to value the house. I can't help dwelling on the fact that my desire for a new project – to make money – was what started it all. This is not what I had in mind and, leading the agents from room to room, seeing the lovely, lived-in house through their eyes, I remember Tom and me working on this place together in the time before Josh was born, when everything was easier and we were so hopeful and enthusiastic. Tom stripping varnish off the banisters with the radio blasting rock music and Emily corralled in a playpen on a dusty floor, asking endless questions.

'What dat?'

'It's a screwdriver, Emily.'

'What dat?'

I remember picking her up and standing her beside me while I undid the bottom screw of a door hinge and showing her the result.

'Me!' she shouted, grabbing at it.

I laughed and set her back amongst her toys. 'When you're bigger, I'll get you one of your own.'

I have lunch with the children and watch an animated film and slowly, section by section, the day fills up with blocks of killed time. I give the kids an early supper, read them a story, and then kiss them goodnight and pour myself a glass of wine. This is not the motherhood of magazine articles. I should have baked with them, painted, made models out of lavatory rolls and cereal packets. Instead, I've spent the whole day outside myself, not engaging, doing the bare minimum; longing for them to be asleep. Their voices have barely registered, like bells in a faraway village.

Tom phones to say he's meeting colleagues for an after-work drink and that I shouldn't worry about supper for him. He also tells me that he's found a rental flat that he can move into in a week's time. I don't get a chance to think about it until the children go to bed, and when I do, I can't even cry.

'Oh, Vicky,' Mum says when I tell her the news.

I'm in our bedroom, sitting on the edge of the bed, bent over with one elbow resting on my knee, the other supporting a head that feels too heavy. I've been drinking alone, which is not like me. I choke up at the thought that I've disappointed her.

'Tell me what to do.'

'I'm not exactly an expert, lovely.' She hesitates. 'I could have the children for a day or two, if that would help.'

I close my eyes and take a deep breath. 'It would. It really would. Just for a couple of nights, so we can talk things over properly. I'll bring them down.'

'No, don't be silly. I'll come and get them.'

'Don't you have guests?'

'Yes, a full house.'

'Then don't. It's too much. Or at least, don't have Josh.'

'It isn't too much, and I will have Josh. Maureen can help. She's always round here anyway, and Emily is old enough to give me a hand with the other two. She can do the breakfasts. We'll be fine.'

'Well, I am truly grateful. You are a saint.'

'No,' she says. 'I've never been that.'

Mum is as good as her word and drives up to London the next morning to pick up the children. Tom has taken the day off work and he and I hug Polly and Emily, kiss Josh's fat cheeks and wave them off. Then I take a damp cloth to the kitchen table and wipe spirals on it; taking my tension out on ancient stains.

'You're going to rub a hole in it if you carry on like that.'

Tom says it without anger, which is worse somehow. It feels like he's moving on already. I read real concern in his eyes. For my sanity maybe, or for my unhappiness. He can't help being kind even when he isn't.

That evening we order a takeaway curry and supper arrives, hot and fragrant, twenty minutes later. I've warmed the plates in the oven and laid the table. We don't say much at first but I can't stand silences, so I put down my knife and fork and wait for him to notice I'm not eating.

It doesn't take long. He raises his eyebrows.

I launch into a speech, the words sounding rehearsed, because they are. 'I know you don't think there's anything left to say, but I do. I've agreed to a divorce but I want you to know that it is the last thing I want. I love you very much, and I love my family and I think you're overreacting. We need time to let this settle and see how we both really feel. I know you're angry and hurt and that I'm entirely to blame, but why does it have to be so final?'

He waits, eats a mouthful then says, 'Are you finished?'

I nod, my eyes glued to his face.

He drinks some wine and puts down his glass, twists it with his long fingers. 'We've known each other a long time.'

'Yes, we have. I—'

He holds up his fork and I shut my mouth. 'We were barely out of school when we met. You were my first really serious relationship. I always assumed I'd have lots of girlfriends. My dad even joked about me sowing my wild oats. That was the expectation. My expectation. I never expected to meet someone at twenty-one and spend the rest of my life with her.'

I pull my mouth into a semblance of a smile. The reaction from friends when we announced my pregnancy was not one of unmitigated joy. They split pretty much into two camps: those who genuinely did wish the best for us and crossed their fingers, and those who thought that I had ruined Tom's life, scuppered his future, put a spanner in his works. I did think at the time: well, what about me?

Before it happened I would have said *no way*. If I thought about it at all, I assumed I would have a termination. But once the baby was a fact, the *no way* became something else entirely. *No way* would I get rid of it. None of the friends who disapproved had been in my situation, so I didn't care what they thought.

But Tom? I know it's there, at the back of his mind. I know some of his friends, the girls particularly, encouraged him to do the wrong thing. But he didn't, and I didn't, and for better or worse, here we are. And he's talking about not sowing oats. That hurts.

'Vicky. Try and understand. I had plans. I was going to travel the world and have adventures but I gave up that dream because I loved you and I thought you loved me. Now I wonder if I've ever been enough. Perhaps I'm the one who stifled your spirit, not the other way round.'

This is so patently unfair that I am almost lost for words. 'I'm sorry it's been such a disappointment,' I mutter.

'No. You don't understand. It's been the best thing. Christ.' He shoves back his chair violently and walks over to the window.

'I've let you down,' I say to his back. 'I am so sorry.'

I wait for him and eventually he comes back and refills my glass. We drink in silence and when I stand up, I sway. I start to clear the table and he tells me to leave it till morning but I can't because it'll smell, so we work together and he even ties up the bin bag and takes it out. When he comes back I'm sitting at the bottom of the stairs, my chin resting on my linked fingers. He looms over me, then takes my hands and hauls me up.

'Are you pissed?' he says.

'Mm.'

'Me too. Do you want to watch a film?'

This seems like a good idea and we collapse on to the sofa companionably. I draw my legs up under me as he reaches for the TV controls.

'So what do you want to watch?'

I shrug. 'You choose.'

I lean my head back into the cushions while Tom checks what we've recorded. I study his profile. I like his big nose. I've never tired of Tom's face and have always thought he'd make a fantastic character actor. He catches me watching him and raises his eyebrows.

'What about this?' he asks. 'Not too violent for you?'

'No.'

It's still light when he starts the film and leans back into the sofa cushions. There's a gap of about a foot between us and my feet are pointing in his direction, so there's no way, unless I change my position, that we're going to get any closer. The curtains are open and I leave them that way because closing them would send an odd message. I try hard to concentrate my mind on the plot, but Tom is always there, at the edge of my vision, a constant distraction. When the ads come on, instead of whizzing through them, he gets up and goes for a pee. I turn round so that I'm sitting closer and drape the rug from the back of the sofa over my knees. When he comes back in, he slips his feet under it.

'Cold?'

'A little,' he says and jumps up to close the curtains.

Normally, we would have cuddled up and kept each other warm. I shift my feet so that they're touching his and he doesn't move away. It feels nice, the balls of our feet pressing against each other, but I'm careful not to wiggle my toes. It's hard to sit like this, without communicating or even commenting on the film, like I normally would, complaining that the violence is gratuitous, or giggling at some crass piece of dialogue. I fight the onset of misery. I think, inappropriately, about sex.

'Are you falling asleep?' Tom asks.

'No. I'm fine.' I stretch my arms above my head and yawn. I'm tingling all over. 'This is so weird.'

Tom pauses the film. On screen, two middle-aged men face up to each other, their noses practically touching. 'Weird how?'

I focus my mind. I'm not going to leap on my husband because I don't think I could handle the rejection. 'Unnatural. We haven't rowed properly, have we? I mean, we've argued, but we haven't yelled at each other or thrown stuff. It's just been miserable and painful.'

He looks at me and a memory returns with such force I blink. Tom lying in bed beside me while I feed Emily, his head propped by his hand, gazing at us. Trying to understand what he was seeing, trying to put it into the context of our lives.

'Can I tell you how I feel?' I say.

I stare at his mouth and under the rug my hands clench into fists. I channel my need into forcing myself to confront him, to make him listen even though any discussion of emotions makes him uncomfortable.

'You've already done that, Vicky.'

I let the pause speak for me and he lifts his hands in surrender. 'Say something then.'

I shake my head and rest my hand against his jaw. He pushes it away but he does it gently, without conviction, and I let the tears fall. Finally, he leans forward and our foreheads touch. He wraps his arms around me and I feel a shift in him. This is what I've been waiting for. I

307

let him hold me and my arms go round him, and I rest my hand against the nape of his neck. The position isn't exactly comfortable, but that doesn't matter. I tilt my head and let him feel my tears on his cheek.

'Vicky,' he says. 'Don't. I need to tell you something.'

'No you don't.'

My voice cracks and he wraps me in his arms and crushes his face into my neck. I want him and even though I've engineered this, the way I'm trembling is entirely involuntary. I love the smell of him, even with the overtones of curry. Without thinking, I kneel and his hands slide to my waist and our lips touch. The light from the television is a warm glow and enough for us to see each other. I pull my shirt over my head and he groans and pushes his hands down the back of my jeans and we lie like that, touching and kissing until we are both frantic. Afterwards, I lie in his arms, giddy with happiness.

By the time I've finished brushing my teeth, he is sound asleep.

I lie awake looking at him. His shoulders are bony, hunched over like a baby bird, his shoulder blades protruding. His ears are set close against his skull, the lobes and tips turning out a touch. They are neat. He has stubble. I enjoyed the rasp of it as we made love. I reach to touch him, my fingers hovering so close to his skin I can almost feel his pulse and then I change my mind. The thread between us is too delicate. If he wakes, it will be over.

He sleeps the same way he always has; away from me, hand and forearm flat under the pillow, the other arm bent over and under it, as if the pillow is afloat and the bed a calm sea. We've always slept facing away from each other. Tom because he likes to sleep in his own personal bubble, me because I don't like that feeling of being about to pitch forward into the dip the weight of his body makes. When it's particularly cold, I turn and fit my body into his, tucking my knees behind his knees, my stomach, ribs and breasts moulded against his back. But only if he's asleep, and sometime during the night he'll twitch and I'll roll away.

I think of all the things this man has been to me; a figure in the distance, tall and thin with broad coat-hanger shoulders and bandy legs; a boyfriend, fiancé and husband. Soon to be ex-husband. I smile softly in the darkness. Or maybe not.

Maybe I should tell him the truth about Josh's accident now, while we're feeling so close to each other. The thought chills me and I push it away. I don't want to risk it. Maybe when it's all blown over, then I can tell him. My deception is a real, three-dimensional thing, not an idea. It's on record with Children's Services and with the police. I've perverted the course of justice, deflected attention both from me and the man who broke into our house. I've allowed him to be free to hurt someone else in order to save my own skin. I am complicit in whatever he chooses to do next. Sometime in the future, someone will say something and Tom will know.

But not yet. Not during this fragile truce.

June 1992

'IT'S KATYA,' KATYA SAID.

There was a small hesitation before Maggie responded. 'What are you doing here, lovely? You should be at school.'

'Can I come in? Please.'

'Oh . . . yes, of course.'

The hallway was so dark that Katya had to feel for the light switch. She pressed the round button with the base of her palm and a yellowy light came on. A door opened somewhere upstairs and she followed the sound.

Maggie winced. 'You poor thing; you look like a drowned rat. Come in.'

She was surprised by the place, had expected something grander, and compared to the Bryants' neat and shiny house, Maggie's flat was tired-looking. Her eyes darted around, taking it all in. She got an impression of light and colour, of mismatched furniture, much of it painted, and pictures, lots of them, filling the walls. Maggie helped her off with her wet cardigan and shoes, disappeared into a bedroom and came back with a warm jumper and a pair of dry socks.

'Here, put these on and sit down. I'll make you some lunch and then we'll think about getting you back to school. I'll call Luke now and let him know you're safe.'

'He's at an interview today,' Katya said.

'Ah. OK. Never mind. I'll call the school and tell them I picked you up from the playground but forgot to sign you out. So I'll be the one in trouble, not you.'

The kitchen was minuscule with a row of white units to one side and a Formica table with two matching chairs. There was a Mickey Mouse clock above the fridge and a window that looked out on to a long and narrow garden. The rain was finally letting up, the sun thrusting through narrow breaks in the clouds, brightening the herbs in their pots along the windowsill. The oven was the same as the one Katya and Linda had in their house, white with a grill above it so you could watch the cheese melt and brown on your toast. The Bryants' grill was inside the dark-windowed oven and she wasn't allowed to use it on her own.

She turned to Maggie. 'Can I have cheese on toast?'

'Of course you can.' Maggie glanced at her and frowned. 'What have you done to your hand?'

Katya hid it behind her back but Maggie waited, looking at her in that gentle way she couldn't resist. Slowly she held it out, palm up and then turned it over. Maggie stroked the half-formed scabs with the pad of her thumb.

'Did you do this?'

Katya shrugged.

311

'Do you want to tell me why?'

Katya picked up a Jacqueline Wilson book that had been left on the table and flicked through it until Maggie reached over and closed it. She kept her hand on the front cover.

'Why are you hurting yourself?'

'I'm not.' She sounded sulky. 'I was bored.'

'Katya, it isn't normal to hurt yourself out of boredom. I think you need to talk to someone about this.'

'I don't want to. I'm fine. I won't do it again.'

Maggie looked at her for a long time, long enough for Katya to start feeling uncomfortable. She resisted the urge to wriggle and fidget, and sat very still, waiting for Maggie to insist, hoping she would.

'Are you making friends at school?'

Katya thought about Gabriella Brady, who sometimes was her friend and sometimes wasn't.

'I'm trying to.'

'Then couldn't you invite them round, darling? The Bryants wouldn't mind. You need a distraction to stop you dwelling on what happened to your mum. You're good at stories, aren't you? I know you like fairy tales. Next time you have nothing to do, why don't you write them down? I'm sure Sally could get you a notebook if you ask her nicely.'

That seemed to be the end of the conversation. Maggie went back to making lunch and Katya examined the illustrations in Emily's book. She felt as though she'd escaped something that she didn't exactly want to escape. And she felt disappointed too.

Maggie set the plate down in front of her with a glass

of orange squash, but despite a gnawing hunger she couldn't eat it. It made her anxious. She stared at the slowly cooling cheese, picked it up, nibbled the edge and put it down.

'What is it, Katya? Don't you like it?'

'I don't want to go home. Please can I stay here? I'll be good, I promise. I won't tell Emily about Mum or anything.'

Maggie hesitated, scrutinizing her face. 'Did you hear me talking to Luke at sports day?'

Katya nodded.

'Well, I'm sorry. It was unforgivable and unprofessional to talk about you like that, and I can only apologize.'

A tear dropped on to the glistening cheese and spread. Katya wiped her nose on the back of her hand.

She wanted to tell Maggie that she loved her. Instead she said, 'I hate him.' It felt the same.

'That's a bit strong, isn't it? I have a feeling you won't like anyone I send you to. But I am trying. You have to be patient. These things take time to organize.'

'But I like you. Why can't I stay here with you and Emily?' She was desperate, her forehead bunched as though her worried frown had become permanently imprinted on her brow. Her right knee bounced up and down.

'I've explained this to you. You know it isn't possible.'

'But you said. You promised you would look after me.'

'Well, of course I did, and I am looking after you. But I'm not in a position to adopt you.' Maggie glanced up at the clock and started tidying up, wrapping the cheese and putting it in the fridge, the bread in the breadbin. 'Come on, eat up and I'll get you back to school.'

Katya shoved her plate away and sobbed wildly, tears and snot smearing her face. However hard she tried to be good, it made no difference, because of Linda. Why was it her fault? Why did her mother being useless mean that Katya's life had to be ruined? One day she was going to change her name and then Katya wouldn't exist any more. Someone better would take her place.

Maggie came and sat down and brushed Katya's hair away from her face. She took her in her arms and Katya leant into the warmth of her body and closed her eyes, let herself be stroked and petted.

'Love, I know you've been lonely, and I understand that you've become attached to me, but I can't be your mother and Emily cannot be your sister. Please try and understand—'

The telephone ringing interrupted Maggie's speech. She gently pushed Katya away and reached for the receiver.

'Hello?'

Katya stared out of the window, pretending not to listen while Maggie spoke to Emily's school. The windows weren't clean. She ran her finger on the glass, drawing a line in the dust.

'Emily isn't well. I have to fetch her.'

Maggie looked torn, like she didn't know what to do with her uninvited guest now that Emily was coming home early. A bit like Gabriella really, Katya thought. Darting off when someone better comes along.

'Can I come too?'

They both glanced out of the window at the same time. The wind was punishing, the rain almost horizontal as it lashed against the glass.

'Best not. You've already been soaked once. I'll run. I'll only be ten minutes.' She switched on the television, put in a video and pressed play, then guided Katya on to the sofa and arranged a rug over her. 'There you are. All lovely and cosy. I'll work out what to do when I get back.' Maggie glanced at Katya's blotched face and smiled ruefully. 'It'll be OK. You'll see.'

It didn't take a big brain to work out that she didn't want Katya to know where Emily went to school.

As soon as the door closed behind her, Katya threw off the rug and jumped up. She looked around. The sitting room was square with most of the space taken up by the sofa with its exuberant ethnic scatter cushions. On the windowsill a plant with bright-red flowers and rubbery leaves sat squashed into one corner with a sprinkling of spilt earth beside it. There was a small dresser with photographs arranged along it, mostly of Emily at different ages.

In Emily's room there was a white bed with a Snow White duvet cover and a painted chest of drawers with little silver hearts dangling from the handles. A row of dolls and soft toys, bunched shoulder to shoulder, filled the entire length of the windowsill, their glass eyes staring at her. On the bedside table there was a light, a book and a glass half-full of water and fogged with fingerprints. She was enticed by a shelf filled with little objects: a chunk of fool's gold, a piece of amber, a pottery cottage, a couple of glass-blown animals, some rubber cartoon characters and an ivory elephant with one tusk missing. Katya picked up the amber and held it so that the light shone through it. Deep inside was an insect, a mosquito. She stared at it, fascinated. As she rocked it from side to side the raindrops rolling down the window made it look as though it was struggling to get out. On impulse she popped it into her pocket and rearranged the shelf so that the theft wasn't immediately obvious.

She was on the lookout, watching from the sitting-room window, when they appeared squashed together under Maggie's brolly. Emily looked miserable. Maggie spotted Katya and raised her hand in a little wave.

'Are you sick?' Katya asked.

Maggie replied for her daughter. 'She's running a temperature and she's got a horrid sore throat, haven't you, Emily? There's no point taking you back to school now, Katya. Let's see if Luke's home, shall we?'

Katya held her breath and prayed but it didn't do any good, because he was there. She listened with disgust as Maggie punctuated the conversation with chuckles that sounded false and made comments about silly girls and said he was a saint to be so patient. Katya glanced at Emily, catching her eye, but Emily didn't react, didn't seem to see anything strange in her mother's flirting.

'Oh, shush,' Maggie said. 'I'm hanging up now.'

'A fortnight, Katya. Then I promise you, if you still want to move, you can move, even if I haven't found you a family.'

316

Maggie was rapidly losing patience. She had sent Emily to her bedroom while they talked and they were sitting on the sofa together, Maggie twisting round, Katya with her arms wrapped tightly round her shins and her chin pressed into her knees.

Katya snuffled and looked up. 'I won't cry any more.' Her chest felt rock hard and her stomach ached.

'Good girl. You can come here if there's nowhere else. But only as a last resort and only if you stop making such a fuss.'

'I'm not making a fuss.' She paused, then took a deep breath and forced the words out. 'I don't like Luke. He's a bad man. He touches me.'

Maggie's face darkened. 'You mustn't say things like that, even to get something you want. I know that when you were with your mum you saw things and learnt things that no little girl should. But you mustn't let that colour your view of the whole world. Most people can be trusted. Most people are good and have your best interests at heart. I know that it's hard for you to see men as anything but a threat, but for your own sake, you have to try. Luke is a lovely person. He's honourable and generous and he takes things to heart.' She sighed and tears welled up in her eyes. 'If you knew what that man is going through . . . but you're far too young and I won't burden you with it. He's had to make difficult choices and he's done the right thing.'

Katya pulled her hand out of Maggie's clasp and dropped her head.

'This is very, very important, Katya. You must not repeat false accusations about respectable men. You could do an incredible amount of damage. Look at me.'

317

She lifted her eyes to her face and looked. Maggie was as white as a sheet. 'Promise me you won't go spreading lies about Luke Bryant.'

Katya nodded listlessly.

'Good girl. I am very fond of you, but if you hurt Luke you do understand that we won't be able to be friends any more, don't you? And I'd hate that. I would miss you.'

32

Wednesday, 14 April 2010

'ARE YOU SURE THIS IS ALL RIGHT?'

'It's fine.' Amber checks her watch. 'I don't have to be back at the office for an hour.'

She turns the key and I enter the house on Browning Street for the second time. I don't have to pick up the kids from Mum until tomorrow, so I can look round it with an easy conscience, if not joy. I'm not sure why I've come; whether it's genuinely to support Amber, or out of curiosity, to see how far she will go. She's lost my trust.

The sun shines through the large front bay, the air alive with dust motes. Amber throws open the French windows with a flourish and I join her on the wrought-iron balcony.

The grass is overgrown, the trees covered in new leaves, rosebuds suspended on long, arching stems that shiver in the breeze. The flower beds are carpeted in delicate, purplish-blue forget-me-nots and at the far end the foxgloves are starting to bloom. A squirrel dashes across the grass, stops to look at us, then scoots up the craggy bark of an elderly fruit tree. It's an English cottage garden, neglected in the best possible way. I swallow my envy and try to resign myself to reality. If the worst comes to the worst and I have to move I'll be buying something modest and manageable. What a depressing thought. Over the fence, two little girls shriek and there must be a baby as well, the one I heard that morning. The one that brought me to my senses.

Amber breathes in deeply and lets it go, like a smoker inhaling the first cigarette of the day, a mixture of profound bliss and relief. She turns and walks back inside, pulling a notebook, pen and tape measure from her bag.

'Shall we start upstairs?'

She wants to measure the windows even though she and Robert haven't exchanged contracts yet. It feels to me like she's setting herself up for disappointment, but I don't say anything. I'm here to provide moral support, not undermine her. And perhaps to prove to myself that we can salvage something from the friendship.

As we explore I try not to get emotional. The house is as incredible as I remember it. It's impossible to tell when it was last redecorated but I doubt in the last thirty years, and even then it was obviously more a case of patching up than modernizing. Everything from the light fittings to the lavatories are antique. The wallpaper in the old lady's bedroom is original Arts and Crafts; pink peonies winding in and out of pale-green leaves.

'Isn't it amazing?' Amber says. 'I can't wait to get my hands on it.'

'Amber . . .'

'Yeah, I know. You don't have to tell me. I'm counting chickens.'

We leave the bedroom and go up to the top floor. From the front room we look down on to the tree-lined street.

'So what are you going to do?' Amber asks.

'About what?'

'Well, selling the house for a start. I can't tell you how sorry we are. Robert is devastated. It's so sad when your friends break up.'

I turn away from the window and wander out of the room, a smile playing on my lips.

'January is the best time,' she says, following close behind me. 'But even if you market it now, you'll still do really well. I can help you find somewhere new.'

'Will you put Sophie up here then?'

She glances at me. 'Yes. And there's room for an au pair, so if we get in quickly I won't have to impose on you. I might even be able to help you out.' She hands me one end of the tape measure and pulls it across the width of the window, writes down the measurement and reaches on tiptoe for the top of the frame. 'You won't move away, will you?'

I am not entirely sure her concern is genuine. 'No. I'm not going anywhere. The thing is . . . Tom and I, well, we . . . what I mean to say is, we may not be divorcing.'

The tape measure and notebook go limp in Amber's hands. 'What do you mean?'

I smirk. 'Do I have to spell it out? We had a few drinks and one thing led to another.'

'Oh . . . so that's good. Wonderful. I'm really pleased for you.'

She embraces me and leaves the room. I follow her into the next one, trying to gauge her reaction. It's pathetic to use playground tactics – he fancies me, not you – but I can't help myself. She has her back to me and she thinks I can't see, but from the movement of her arm I know she's scratching the back of her hand. Then she turns round.

'I wanted to talk to you about the deposit.'

'I thought we already talked about that. I thought you understood. We can't lend you the money.'

'I'm not asking you to lend me anything.'

'Oh.' I smile, relieved. 'I'm really sorry. I didn't mean anything—'

'I'm asking you to give it to me.'

'I beg your pardon?'

'Let's clear this up once and for all, shall we?'

Her expression has changed, become bitter and hard, as if something I've done has so disgusted her that she can't look at me without curling her lip in distaste.

'Perhaps you'd better.' I glance behind me, looking for a means of escape, trying to concoct an excuse, but I have none. I've already told her I have the morning to myself.

'You left your baby alone while you went to look at a house. How many times have you done that and got away with it?' She waves at me when I start to interrupt. Her voice is a hiss. 'You put him at risk and, if that got out, if the police or social services were to get an

322

anonymous tip . . . you know as well as I do what happens next. They're already suspicious. Grayling definitely is.'

The change in her is extraordinary and all I can do is stare. I turn to leave, but she grabs my wrist, wrapping her fingers around it and pulling me so close that I can feel her breath on my cheek. She speaks directly into my ear.

'You also lied about what the burglar looked like. That's called perverting the course of justice.'

There is a long silence while I digest her words.

'I need it next week,' she says. She turns away, fumbles with her phone, checks it and puts it back in her bag then faces me with a sigh. 'Don't be like this, Vicky. It isn't such a big deal. We're doing each other a favour. I help you, you help me.'

'I'm afraid I don't follow your logic.'

'You are funny.'

'I didn't mean to be. I don't know what you think, Amber, but I don't have that kind of money. Tom deals with our finances and I'm certainly not dragging him into this.'

'No, I wouldn't do that if I were you. You're already in enough trouble there.'

'Don't you dare use my relationship with Tom against me.'

'Of course I won't.' She pauses. Eventually she says, 'Ask your mother.'

'Forget it. You can't really do anything. You wouldn't dare.'

'Are you sure about that? Who do you think made sure darling Tom read that text?'

I gasp but she doesn't let me interrupt.

'And who do you think called Child Protection on Emily's birthday? I can do a very good "concerned neighbour".'

I lurch towards the door, my hand to my mouth, run downstairs and slam out of the house. I stride along the road, my fist clenched round the strap of my handbag, almost running. A couple with a pram look affronted as I push past them. My mobile starts to ring as I turn into Coleridge Street.

'Vicky, you can't run away from this.'

'Who said anything about running away? I don't want to deal with you any more, Amber. You need help.'

'No, you need help. Let me put it simply, so that you know where you stand. I expect that money to be transferred by next Thursday. If not, I will contact the police and Child Protection and your world will collapse so fast you won't have time to make excuses or wind Tom round your little finger. Your children will go.'

'Is there anything else?' I say between clenched teeth.

'Nope. That's it.'

I put my head in my hands. There is no doubt in my mind that she is serious. What have I ever done to her?

Tom hunches over, his hands clasped. He looks at me and my heart fills with dread. 'I should apologize.'

'You don't need to. It takes two.' I hesitate then rush on. 'I'm glad it happened. I don't want to split up.'

He lifts his clasped hands to his mouth and chews at

the corner of his thumb. 'Nothing's changed, Vicky. Last night was—'

'Don't say it meant nothing because I won't believe you.'

'I'm not saying that. Christ, this is so complicated. Look, what happened happened, and it was lovely, but it doesn't change anything at all. I don't regret it, but it doesn't mean I can rewind the last few days. I never thought this would happen to us but it has, and we need to think about the children. I know it may seem hard but it's better now, don't you think, while they're still little. They'll get used to the idea.'

I try to keep the stammer out of my voice but I'm collapsing inside. Whatever I say, he has an answer. It's as if he's asked himself every single question I could possibly come up with, every excuse, every piece of emotional coercion, and he's prepared for it. He is destroying us. I should desist, because I know I'm beaten, but the words tumble out, unstoppable, distorted by my sobs.

'But why should they have to get used to it? Why can't we try again? David means nothing to me. I've apologized and I know I've been an idiot. But why do you have to be so extreme? Can't you just not speak to me for a couple of days?'

'David was a symptom. You aren't happy. Not really. You take me for granted because I've always been there for you. I've never looked at another woman, not since I met you. But it's all gone to hell now.'

I stare at him. 'Is it really about that, Tom?'

'What do you mean?'

I sniff and look around for a hanky, tear a sheet of kitchen towel from the roll, rub the scratchy paper across my eyes and blow my nose. 'Amber's been talking about me, hasn't she?'

'What's that got to do with anything?'

'I don't know. But I think she's manipulated you. I think she has an agenda.'

'This is between me and you. How could you think I'd make important decisions based on anything Amber said?'

He's angry suddenly. And defensive. I look at him, suspicion and jealousy crowding in.

'OK,' I say carefully. 'But I was awake that night in Spain when you two were having a cosy chat on the sofa. I heard everything.'

'Then you would have heard me tell her that I love you.' His eyes are filled with pity. 'You know what? I look at you and I feel this weird sense of detachment, when I used to feel like you were part of me, under my skin. I have no sense of what is real and what isn't.' He sees me struggling to control my facial muscles and adds, 'This isn't all your fault, Vicky. I'm not whiter than white either. It's over, that's all.'

I swallow. 'I'm sorry. I wish to God it never happened, but it did, and I have to live with it.'

'Well, so do I.' His eyes meet mine and then he looks away. He seems to withdraw.

'Everyone does stupid things.'

He nods and then he walks out and I let him go and sit staring at the wall. There's a lovely black-and-white photograph taken, ironically, by Amber, before Josh was born, before I was even pregnant. We are in the garden and it's a summer's day and we're all bunched up together, smiling into the lens. We look free of care, in a bubble of love.

I wonder if she hated me even then.

33

Monday, 19 April 2010

I GET DOWN ON MY HANDS AND KNEES AND PRESS A section of skirting. Hidden behind it is a shallow wooden box. I turn it upside down and its precious contents roll out and settle into the palm of my hand.

Two days have passed since Amber made her blackmail threat and I've given in. The girls are at school, having had a wonderful weekend being spoilt rotten by my mother, her guests and Maureen. When I picked them up Emily actually cried, she was so devastated at having to leave. She wants us all to move down there, preferably next door to her grandmother. Even Josh seems better tempered.

I push the rings apart with the tip of my finger. There's the solitaire that Tom bought me after I had Emily. It's an antique, a future heirloom, he said, for Polly or Emily to inherit and pass down to their daughters and on through the generations.

Can I pawn it? I fold it into my palm and hold it so tight that it leaves a mark. Yes, if it comes down to a choice between a piece of jewellery and my children, of course I can. I love jewellery; I love the way it sparkles, the little spikes of adrenaline the sight of it produces. Pawning isn't selling; I will get them back.

There's an eternity ring as well, and the ruby-and-diamond engagement ring that I'd been wearing on the day of the break-in. I have no idea of the rings' values, but the three of them together might possibly come close to the amount Amber is demanding. I try each on in turn and then together, rocking my hand from side to side to catch the light. When you put diamond rings next to each other, their sparkle increases tenfold. The effect is mesmerizing. I tug them off, drop them into a jewellery pouch and close it quickly before I can change my mind.

There is a pawnbroker's reasonably close to where we live but I choose to drive to Elephant and Castle, where there is no chance of being recognized. The street is uninspiring; a low, sixties-built parade with only ano-nymity to recommend it, cluttered with betting shops and fast-food outlets, choked by traffic. When I looked it up on Street View I expected something discreet and Dickensian, maybe cloaked in shame and dust, but the double-frontage is an unmissable bright blue and yellow.

Josh has fallen asleep in the car and the pneumatic drill going in the street right outside the shop wakes him up. Once inside with the door closed, the sound is some-what muted. The room is brightly lit and there are long, glass-topped cabinets arranged on three sides. Behind them, shelving displays all manner of objects; evidence of someone else's desperation.

'Good afternoon, madam. Can I help you?'

The man's voice is old-school working class. Overly respectful. I imagine him training his assistants. Tact, he would tell them. Tact and discretion is everything in this business. I dig in my bag for the pouch and shake its contents on to the glass counter. He puts his hand out and stops them rolling away.

'A beautiful piece,' he says of Tom's heirloom.

Josh pulls at his harness and protests loudly. I find a well-loved fabric book at the bottom of my handbag and give it to him. He throws it on the floor and then reaches for it, nearly tipping the pram over.

'It's turn of the century,' I say, my eyes on the top of his balding head as he bends over it with his magnifying glass.

He's mildly interested in the eternity ring and more excited by my engagement ring. 'Art Deco. Lovely.' He names a price for all three which is so far off what Amber is asking, it's laughable.

The incessant drilling and Josh's whinging make me incredibly stressed. Deep in my bag, my phone rings. 'You can't do better than that?'

'Sorry, madam. It's the going rate. Would you like me to take them?'

They're worth a quarter of what I need. I have nothing that I can raise the rest with, so there is really no point. I am furious with myself, with Tom, with Amber. I should not be in this situation.

'No thank you.'

330

He moves them back to me with nicotine-stained fingers and scratches the side of his nose. I can't get out of there fast enough. My mobile starts to ring again and I nearly drop it, my hands are so shaky.

'Where are you?' Tom asks.

I look round. Away in the distance the Shard pierces the sky. 'Out shopping.'

I shout above the noise of the drill as I dig in my pocket for the car keys. I point them at the door and press the fob, then try to extricate Josh one-handed from his pram.

'Well, check your messages, will you? I've had Amber on the phone, looking for you.'

I go still. What has she said to him? 'Why?'

'I don't know. Something about a parents' tea.'

'Oh no.'

'Vicky? What have you done?'

'I'm supposed to be at the school this afternoon.' I can't believe this.

'And you forgot?' His voice is hard.

'I . . . I've had a lot on my mind.'

'We all have a lot on our minds. For once, Vicky, could you put the children first?'

'I'm sorry.'

'Don't tell me that. Tell your daughters.' He disconnects without giving me a chance to explain. But what is there to explain? It would only mean another lie.

As I race across London I torture myself with the image of Polly watching the door for me, bewildered, forgotten and tearful, and in desperation I put our differences to one side and phone Amber. It galls me to do it, but no one else can help and Polly will only care that her god-mother has come especially for her.

'It's OK, Vicky,' she whispers. 'I'm in the classroom now. Miss Samantha called me so I dashed over and I'm playing mum for Polly. She is so sweet. She brought me a plate of biscuits and insisted on dunking them in my tea. And she's reading really well. I told Miss Samantha you'd had an emergency with Josh, so don't worry, she was very understanding.'

I doubt that. I've blotted my copybook. But I don't care what they think about me; it's Polly's hurt that breaks my heart. I swallow my pride and thank Amber and mean it. She's done something for my little girl and rescued what could have been a much worse situation.

'So where are you?' Amber asks.

'Somewhere off the Old Kent Road.'

'Really? What on earth are you doing there?'

'I'm outside a pawn shop.'

There's a tiny pause. 'Oh. Right, well, that's great. Will you be back in time for pick-up?'

I glance at my watch. 'Yes, if I get a move on. There's no money, by the way. My jewellery isn't worth anything like what you're asking for.'

'Well, at least you tried,' she says cheerfully. 'I'm sure you'll think of something.'

'I do understand you've had a bad week,' Polly's teacher says when I arrive flushed and ashamed at going-home time. The other adults in the room turn to look at me as I rush in. I force a rueful smile.

Miss Samantha only started in September, but even

332

though she's never known me as a fellow teacher, she knows I am one. I don't like her manner but I play the game and apologize abjectly. I don't want to alienate her.

'I am so sorry. Josh was running a temperature and I was worried there was an infection, you know, due to the fracture. So I've been back to the hospital with him.'

Polly's bottom lip wobbles. I kneel down and she wraps her arms around my neck and hugs me so hard I can barely breathe. If it had been Emily she would have reacted differently, she would have treated me to a stern reproof or a studied silence; Polly's sweet, unconditional forgiveness is hard to bear.

'It's important to come to these things.'

Her response implies that she doesn't believe my excuse; that she thinks, rightly, that I forgot about Polly; that Polly doesn't matter as much as everything else going on in my life. I hate her for thinking this.

Miss Samantha has a perfect, heart-shaped face, blonde hair, tanned skin, a curvaceous figure and wears kooky summer dresses in winter with cardigans and brown leather boots. The dads all fancy her. It's a local running joke and a safe crush because we all know she's besotted with her rich lawyer fiancé. Even so, when your husband is leaving it's impossible not to look at the women you both know and wonder who's going to share his bed next.

Polly extricates herself from my embrace and I stand up. 'Wait for me outside the door, sweetie.' I feel rotten and ashamed.

'Are we going home?'

'Two seconds. I need a quick word with Miss Samantha.'

I wait, watching her as she skips out of the room to the bookshelves that line the corridor.

'I do know.' I speak quietly so that Polly can't hear. 'I do understand. Obviously, if I could have helped it, I would have done.'

'Is there anything else going on?' she murmurs. 'Anything we need to know about? It's only that she's been unusually quiet since she came back from her holidays and sometimes, in my experience, it can be a sign that there are tensions at home.'

I glance round to make sure nobody is listening. I'd rather not tell her, but it's important that she knows the circumstances so that she can keep an eye on Polly.

Imogen Parker is bending over Alannah, doing up the buttons of her cardigan. I'm sure she's stalling so that she can listen in, and to my horror I feel myself blushing. I am the mother who failed to turn up; the selfish and neglectful Vicky Seagrave who doesn't deserve her beautiful family. I wonder if Chinese whispers about my marriage are doing the rounds yet. It never ceases to amaze me how quickly news spreads in this community.

Miss Samantha ushers me into the book corner and we crouch on two little chairs like co-conspirators. Josh squirms to be put down so I let him crawl over to the beanbags. I tell her the bald facts, that my marriage is in difficulties and that we may be separating. I can't say divorcing. The confession elicits sympathy, but also some patronizing advice about taking care that the children don't start worrying about their parents and an entirely gratuitous warning that they might think it's their fault. I resist a strong temptation to retort sarcastically *thanks for the tip* and force myself to be humble instead. When I get up to leave she gives me a sad smile and tells me to take care of myself.

Out in the playground the older children have lined up and Emily waves at us from the middle of her line. Beside her, Amber is doing up Sophie's shoe buckle. I can't see her face, but from the set of her shoulders I know she is as aware of me as I am of her. She stands up and turns. I nod curtly and she wanders over.

'Sorry you had a wasted afternoon,' she says. 'Why don't you come back to mine now and we'll brainstorm, see if we can't think of an alternative plan.'

Presumably still involving my money. I baulk and respond tersely. 'I can't, Amber. I've got things to do at home.'

'I think this is more important, don't you?'

'Excuse the mess, I'm having a chuck-out,' Amber says.

There's a box and two bin bags on the floor in front of the sofa and a pile of what looks like jumble beside them. I hover in the middle of the room, holding Josh. The girls have already deserted us and run up to Sophie's bedroom. It's sad that their friendship is probably as doomed as mine and Amber's.

'Sit down, you're making me nervous.' She smiles and gives an odd little laugh. 'For God's sake, relax, Vicky. I'll make some tea.'

She leaves us and Josh twists in my arms. I set him down and he immediately makes a beeline for the box, pulling himself up on it. It tips over, spilling its contents on to the floor. I pick up a one-eyed teddy bear and hold it out, but he's on a voyage of discovery and it doesn't merit more than a passing glance so I hug the bear to my chest. There was a time when Sophie was never without it and I'm surprised Amber is getting rid of it. New house new start, I presume. I set the box back on its base and start to pile the things back in. Josh thinks it's a great game and pulls the box back on to its side and this time I leave him to it.

Something catches my eye. I pick it up and hold it in the palm of my hand, stroking it with my thumb. I used to have one of these. It sat on the shelf above my bed. Sometimes, when the sun shone, I would take it down and hold it up to the light, rotate it and make the tiny mosquito dance.

The world is full of pieces of amber. Still I stroke the sharp edges and close my eyes, thinking that my sense of touch might be more reliable. And it kind of is; its fractured shape recalls my childhood and the flat. And mine has been missing for a very long time.

I hear the chink of a spoon stirring a teabag and swiftly pocket it. There is something very wrong here.

'You'll have to ask your bank for a loan,' Amber says, handing me a mug.

I set it down on the table. 'I'll think about it.'

'There's no time to think. Don't you understand? If I don't put down the deposit within the next few days, I'll lose that house, and I'm not going to let that happen.'

I stare at her face, frowning. Where have our lives intersected before? There's nothing about her that I recognize. I have no sense that we've ever meant anything to each other beyond our current friendship. I put my hand in my pocket and feel the warmth of the amber. I very nearly produce it. I even imagine holding it out on the palm of my hand and studying her reaction. But I don't. Experience has taught me that it's best to sleep on decisions.

'I don't want to have to ruin your life, Vicky. I really don't. You must believe me. You're my friend and I love you. But I need that money and you owe it to me.'

'I've got to go.'

I scoop Josh up and shout for Emily and Polly, who don't respond. Amber looks at me steadily. I leave the room hastily and yell up the stairs for my daughters. This time they come, their little faces wary, frightened by my tone.

June 1992

EMILY PARRISH IS HUDDLED IN THE FRONT PASSENGER seat, her arms crossed, her head tucked against the seat belt. Sitting behind Maggie, a sobbing Katya wiped her nose on the damp cardigan Maggie had lent her earlier. She was still wearing Emily's socks.

'Katya, stop that, for heaven's sake,' Maggie said.

Katya could feel her losing patience and quietened down, but her juddering breaths were still audible. She stared out of the window. The storm had finally blown itself out, leaving the roads and pavements wet and shiny. People were outside again, umbrellas down. As they came closer to Hillside Way her stomach started to ache. Emily took a painful sip from her water bottle and turned in her seat. For the first time Katya noticed how big and brown and long-lashed her eyes were. Maggie's eyes.

'Why don't you want to go home?'

'Emily,' Maggie said. 'Turn round.'

Emily did as she was told and slumped back again. 'Are we nearly there yet?'

'Almost.'

They turned the corner, drove up the hill and parked outside the bungalow.

'I like the lions,' Emily croaked.

'Wait here.'

Maggie got out and walked up the garden path. Watching her waiting outside the red door Katya started weeping in earnest again, only quietly this time, the tears rolling down her cheeks and dropping on to her chest.

'Why are they making you stay if you don't like it?' Emily asked. She shifted so that she could see Katya properly. 'Can't you go somewhere else?'

Katya shook her head. She had imagined this moment, how she would be eloquent, how she would convince Emily to come to her rescue, to insist they take Katya in like a stray kitten. Now she knew that it was nothing but a silly dream. As the front door opened and Luke looked beyond Maggie, she only managed two words and they seemed over-the-top, even in the state she was in, filling the space of the car like a drumbeat.

'Help me.'

Emily's big eyes widened. 'What with?'

But Katya didn't know and Luke was coming towards her, smiling, charming, concerned. She shrank back against the leather seats as he opened the door and poked his head in.

'Hello, Katya.'

She scrambled away from him. 'I'm not coming. I'm not. I want to stay with Emily.'

Emily turned away abruptly, but not from Luke or her mother; from Katya, who had crossed a line, embarrassed herself by asking for something that no one here could give her. Maggie came round to the other door so that Katya was trapped in a pincer movement. She clung to the handle, falling into the road when Maggie yanked it open.

'What a fuss over nothing,' she said. 'Be sensible, Katya. This isn't helping.'

She picked her up and held on to her, her fingers like claws.

'Katya,' Luke said gently. He crouched so that he could look directly into her eyes. 'Sally's sister is very sick so I don't want to have to call her about this. It would upset her desperately. Come inside. You can watch what you like on telly.'

'There, Katya,' Maggie said. She had stepped back, ceding her authority to Luke, her arms folded across her ribcage.

'I'll never forgive you,' Katya shouted. 'You're not being fair!'

Maggie's face fell. She looked puzzled and guilty as she hurried round to the driver's side, pausing as if she wanted to say something, to excuse herself, before getting into the car. But the moment passed and nothing was said.

Luke took Katya's hand and, as he led her towards that house with the windows that looked like sleepy eyes, she turned and stared back at Emily. The other girl pretended not to have seen. Luke's hand was like a cage round Katya's, his fingers crushing hers. They exchanged a look, he and Maggie. Then Maggie drove away.

34

Wednesday, 21 April 2010

WHILE I WAIT FOR JENNY TO GET OFF THE PHONE I glance around her sitting room, taking in the wedding photos, the domestic jumble, the folded-up newspapers in the basket beside the fireplace; the air of homely contentment that pervades, of being too busy to worry about the little things. Simon is making a chilli con carne and the smell of frying meat and onions makes my mouth water. I have a glass of red wine in my hand and a sense that I've yielded to fate. It's taken me two days to work up to this.

I've told Jenny what happened that morning, only keeping back Amber's demand for money. It's hard to explain why, since it's in my interest to portray someone else as the bad guy. There is an element of shame that inhibits me but also old loyalties come into play. She's not all bad. No one is. Something has happened to make her like this and I'm not ready to turn my back on her or accept that the situation is irreversible. Not yet. On the other hand, I can't go on as I have been. I need advice, and even though I don't know Jenny terribly well, I trust her.

'Hey.' She plonks herself down next to me. 'Sorry about that. My sister's having a crisis with her fourteen-year-old.'

'Oh dear.'

'They'll be fine. So,' she says. 'You've certainly given me a lot to think about.'

'Sorry.'

'Don't be. I'm glad you came to me. Honestly, Vicky, it's fine. And don't look so petrified. Tell me what it is you want out of this conversation.'

I didn't expect to be asked that and have to think. 'I suppose I want to be steered in the right direction. I feel like I'm blindly grabbing at answers. Basically, what I want is for someone to tell me what to do, however hard it is to swallow.'

'Fair enough.'

She turns when the door opens and smiles at her husband. 'Thanks, love.'

Simon is wearing a flowery apron, the tie barely reaching round his middle. He tops up our glasses and potters back to the kitchen.

Jenny takes a sip then puts her glass down, precariously, on the rug beside her feet. I keep hold of mine.

'I can't wave a magic wand, I'm afraid, but I can at least make sure you know what the consequences of your options will be. Then you can decide what you do. But it's very important you understand that you don't really matter in this. The only thing that does is the welfare of your children, and if it comes to court, that's what they'll want to see. That your kids are in safe hands. That's where you have to concentrate your efforts – not in justifying your actions.'

She glances at me, waiting to see if I want to add anything or even protest. I don't.

'Whatever you decide to do, I can assure you that anything you say won't go any further.'

Her kindness, mixed with an air of brisk authority, is so reassuring that for the first time in days I feel positive. Outside in the street a baby starts wailing. The sound electrifies me. Instinctively I draw my shoulders in. A front door closes and it goes quiet. I stop holding my breath. Jenny studies me, a smile of sympathy turning up the corners of her lips.

'Are you OK?'

I nod.

'Good girl. My advice to you would be to find yourself a criminal defence lawyer, preferably a barrister, and have an informal chat with them. Legal advice privilege means it would be confidential.'

She's not going to tell me to keep quiet then, like Amber and Mum did. I don't know whether to be relieved or afraid.

'If I was you, I'd come clean. It's your first offence, you could plead extenuating circumstances.'

'What are they?'

'Same as mitigating really. Things that could be used by the defence. It could be ill health, bereavement, or other personal issues which were unexpected, out of your control and may have affected your judgement.' She looks at me over the rim of her glasses. 'Vicky, please don't take this the wrong way, but you could plead momentary insanity.'

'I'm not telling any more lies.'

'That's fine. Let's leave it for the time being. It's only a suggestion. You know, everyone is different. We all react in our own way to motherhood. It can be wonderful, but it can go wrong, and we shouldn't feel ashamed when it doesn't turn out to be this blissful fantasy. It's hard. There's so much pressure to be the perfect mother. There have been days when I've thought I'd go completely round the bend. Especially since Spike was born.'

I can't help smiling. 'You're the calmest person I know.'

'Huh! I just have one of those faces. And also, I react to other people flapping by becoming catatonically calm. Very helpful for a lawyer.' She winks at me. 'No one knows that inside I am screaming, Get me out of here! I'm on your side, Vicky. I remember how overwhelmed I was when I became a mother; there was that enormous emotional kick, the shock at how deeply rooted my feelings were for someone I'd only just met. But that doesn't mean I've forgotten the tough bits; I remember how it felt to have my personal space invaded by this greedy, demanding little thing, and the fatigue and the mess. We become entirely for and about the baby, so it's no wonder that we occasionally pop.'

There's a moth-eaten cashmere throw bundled up in the corner of the sofa. I pick at the fringe. 'But most people don't put their babies at risk.'

'You made a split-second decision that wasn't based on sound judgement. Think back to that morning, Vicky. That week even. How were you feeling?'

'All of that. All of what you said.'

'You weren't in your right mind. There is nothing to be ashamed of. And since you asked for my advice, I would say use that. Be honest, but do anything it takes to keep your children.'

She pauses to let this sink in and I chew my bottom lip.

'OK,' I say. 'I will think about it.'

'Good. Now, as for your other lapses of judgement, creating a false E-FIT and lying at the identity parade, any lawyer, including me as your friend, would advise you to take a plea. That is, own up. You're less likely to be sent down and more likely to be given a suspended sentence and community service.'

I take a deep breath and release it. 'I could handle that, but what about Josh? The criminal neglect?'

Not to mention the public shame. My mind is groaning under the burden of decisions to be taken.

Jenny sits forward and turns to look at me. 'Vicky, you mustn't think of the law as some big bad machine trying to trip you up and make your life a misery. It's based on common sense and above all it is humane. I have absolute trust in the fairness of the British legal system and so should you. Judges are human beings. The children come first and the last thing they want to do is break up families. You might get supervision visits from social services – in fact it's more than likely, if you follow this route – but I doubt they'll be taken away from you. Not if you're completely honest from now on.'

'That's not the impression I get from the papers.'

'Like that baby? They write up the bonkers cases,

345

unsurprisingly. Do you know how many of these things go through the courts every week? Thankfully, most of them don't have such extreme results. Bottom line, Vicky, you're going to have to make a choice. I can't make it for you. If you choose not to say anything though, I won't take it any further. You don't have to worry about that.'

'Don't forget Amber knows,' I mutter.

'Of course she does. Then, darling, the only thing you can do is come clean.'

I nod. I can do this. I will do this. I'm going to go and see Grayling tomorrow and tell him everything. But the first thing I'm going to do is talk to my mother. There's a piece of amber in my pocket, crying out for an explanation.

'Will you be my lawyer?' The request is not spontaneous. It's a decision I made overnight, the decision that finally allowed me to fall asleep.

'I don't think that's a good idea. But I can give you the name of an excellent colleague. You'll be in safe hands. I'll just be your friend, if that's all right with you.'

June 1992

MAGGIE DIDN'T TURN THE CAR ROUND AND COME BACK for her. Katya had never felt lonelier. Even sitting on the cold concrete floor of a passageway that reeked of bleach, waiting for Linda's client to leave, hadn't been as bad as this.

'Let's go ice-skating,' Luke said. 'I don't want to be stuck inside all afternoon with Little Miss Misery.'

Katya hadn't spoken to him since they brought her home, not that he had noticed. She got up, moving like a robot. She was all cried out now, her eyes reddened and her nose blown so often that the skin round her nostrils felt rough and sore. At least ice-skating meant other people. She had only been once, with Sally, and it hadn't been a great success because Sally was as hopeless at it as she was, her long thin limbs as unsteady as Bambi's.

She had to run to keep up with his stride. When they crossed on to Streatham High Road and hit the busy shopping area Katya began to feel like she was in a

347

bubble, a cold world that other people didn't bother entering. She watched strangers and wondered what they thought when they saw her, if they saw her. She wanted to tell them he wasn't her dad. To shout it at their blank faces and wake them up.

'Right,' Luke said, as they pushed open the doors. 'Here we are.'

She regarded the rink with some trepidation but Luke didn't give her a chance to change her mind. He helped her do up her skates, crouching on the wet rubber floor to hook and tie the laces. He was excited about this; happier than she had seen him in weeks. Perhaps he liked it here. They hobbled to the rink and he was on first, skating a few yards, testing the ice, then coming back to her.

'Are you ready?'

When she didn't reply he merely smiled. She stepped on without releasing her grip on the rail. The ground almost slid from under her feet but she kept upright. She watched other children race by, some elegantly, some clumsily, grabbing the coats of their friends, righting themselves and zipping off again. There were plenty of children like her, timidly keeping to the edge, and she was determined not to be a coward like them. She let go and Luke grabbed her hand. At first all she could think of was that, the feeling of being both connected to him and trapped. It made her intensely self-conscious. And then because she was so focused on their hands she forgot about what her feet were doing and was surprised to find that she was moving.

'Good girl. Slide forward and out on one foot and

then the one behind. Your feet hardly need to leave the ice. No hurry. That's right. And again. One. Two. One. Two. You're skating.'

She felt a sort of rhythm develop but then slipped, her legs splaying. He caught her round her waist.

'Try again.'

They took a lap together before he released her. She wobbled, swivelled and stamped clumsily to the edge.

Luke laughed. 'Practise on your own for a minute.'

And he was off, weaving through the skaters, not leaning forward with his bum out like some of them, but standing tall and confident, as if it was second nature. She watched him cross his feet, switch direction and skate backwards, then switch back and shoot off. She wanted to be able to do that. He waved as he passed her and she looked away angrily. She wasn't going to be friendly whatever he tried, and anyway she was more than happy to be left alone to practise. She took an experimental step then glided, one foot after the other, keeping her balance, trying not to be distracted by anyone else, determined not to be useless. She made it all the way round without falling and when she got back to where she started Luke was waiting, his hand held up for a high five.

'Well done,' he said.

She set off again, this time trying to ape his posture, his air of ease. It didn't work and she fell but he was beside her in a flash, picking her up and brushing crushed ice from her trousers. He held her hand and they floated around and it was as if it wasn't him, but the prince of her dreams. She felt a surge of euphoria as they increased their speed.

'You OK?' he shouted.

'Yes!'

The word slipped out before she could stop it and she clamped her mouth shut. She hated herself for enjoying it so much but the cold air on her face and the music pulsing through her body were exhilarating. Despite herself, she caught the beat and then it was just her, her skates, the ice and the music. They came back to the side, Luke with an expert swivel and slice, Katya with a thump that almost bounced her off her feet.

'Well, look at you,' Luke said. 'Who would have thought it?'

She watched two girls skate past, their hands locked round each other's waists. One was a blonde, the other a brunette, and from the back they could have been her and Emily. They were talking, so relaxed and in harmony, they reminded her of ballroom dancers. She kept tabs on them as they wove between the other skaters. She wanted to catch them up, listen to their conversation.

'I'll teach you to skate backwards next time.'

Luke's voice made her jerk her head round and she lost sight of them. Were they going home then? She flushed and moved away from him, set off on her own. Maybe if she kept going round and round, nothing would happen. The girls were at the side now, gloved hands on small hips, pink noses and bright eyes, watching the crowd revolve, turning to comment and roll their eyes as a group of show-off boys dashed by. The clock above the rink read nearly half past six. The crowd was thinning.

She watched the younger families leave and wondered

why she had to be the unlucky one. No father and no mother meant having to fit in places that would never really want you in them, not without becoming a person who wasn't you at all. It meant not being listened to. Linda once said, 'There's none so deaf as will not hear.' Katya had been too young to understand, but their rhythm had ensured that the words remained with her until she did.

'Time to go,' Luke said.

She floundered and fell and the shock was much greater than before. It was more of an affront to her dignity. He took her elbow and set her back on her feet. She clumped back to the boot room, angry with herself, unlaced her skates and carried them over to the counter. Luke stood beside her as the assistant retrieved their shoes, still and straight, his hand on her shoulder. Her feet felt heavy as they wandered out into the summer evening. Luke was silent, his tread purposeful and ominous. She looked around for a means of escape but she wouldn't run or scream. Not now. It was too late for that.

The whole time they'd been there he hadn't commented once on her silence. Perhaps he hadn't noticed. Perhaps he would just give her supper and let her go to bed, not insist she keep him company.

35

Thursday, 22 April 2010

AMBER SLAMS THE CUTLERY DRAWER SHUT WITH
malice. The units are shabby and she loathes the flat
with a vengeance now.

She hasn't heard from Tom, hasn't seen him since
they got back from Spain. Usually the two families get
together at least once a week, but there's been nothing.
He's in shock, she reasons. But still, she needs some kind
of sign, an acknowledgement of what happened between
them. They spent the last day in Spain barely exchang-
ing a word that didn't have to do with the children,
their travel arrangements, or work. Granted, Maggie had
been transparently obvious in her efforts to make sure
Amber and Tom never found themselves alone, but still,
if he'd wanted to, he could have found a way to com-
municate with her. Men are such cowards.

She runs her fingers along the kitchen counter. Cheap
melamine. Browning Street is going to have granite;
black granite – the kind with sparkles. She can see the
kitchen in her mind's eye; light-filled with hand-painted

units and a limestone floor. She wants a big Welsh dresser and maybe an Aga. A conservatory the width of the house will bring the garden inside. Last time she was there she discovered an apple tree struggling for oxygen under a huge cloak of ivy. She'll rescue it. Sophie will love picking her own apples.

Everyone deserves a consolation prize.

She can still smell his skin. If she closes her eyes she can make herself shiver with the recollection of his mouth on hers. She reimagines the moment when Tom stopped fighting his baser instincts and kissed her, and shudders with pleasure.

Vicky's coy confession was a blow. It must have been a combination of alcohol and habit; that and perhaps pity on his part, desperation on hers. Tom is committed to the divorce – otherwise, why would their house be on the market? Unsurprisingly, they haven't gone with Johnson Lane. Sarah is pissed off, of course, but it can't be helped.

She makes herself a sandwich from the sliced white that Robert disapproves of, helping herself to generous wedges of Camembert and the homemade apple chutney she bought at a school summer fete, then takes it to the sitting room and idly flicks through an interiors magazine while she munches, lingering over the photographs. There's a fabulous blue-green bathroom with black and white flooring and dirty-white shutters. Gorgeous.

She'll miss Vicky. There was Gabriella at school, and one or two kids at Fairhaven that she got along with, but Vicky is the closest thing to a real friend she's ever had. She turns the page. That slubby-grey chaise longue would look amazing in the master bedroom. It's too late to be sentimental. Events have outstripped her conscience. It's time to finish this. There are others, maybe not so congenial, but equally worthy. Not Millie maybe, but Jenny.

Her phone vibrates and she glances at the caller display. For a second she's too thrown to answer.

'Tom,' she breathes. 'I knew you'd call.'

He misses a beat, loses track of what he wants to say, takes a moment too long to figure out how to pick up the thread.

'Listen,' he says. 'There's something I need to ask you. And I want the truth, not some version of it that you and Vicky have cobbled together.'

She's never known Tom take that tone. 'What are you talking about?'

Has Vicky told him about the money? She can't have. Even she wouldn't be that stupid.

'I want to know exactly what happened the morning Josh fractured his arm. And don't mess me around, because I know both of you are in on this. The whole thing was a pack of lies.'

She thinks quickly, resentment rising. This is no way to speak to her, not after what they've done. 'Not over the phone, OK. I'll meet you for a coffee. If I set off now, I can be in Soho in an hour.'

He hesitates. 'I don't think that's a good idea.'

'Sorry, Tom. You do deserve an explanation, but I am doing this face-to-face or not at all.'

'Victoria Station would be better. I'll meet you in Costa.'

This might not be a disaster, she thinks as she hurries out of the flat. Vicky has been rumbled and Amber won't get the blame. Vicky deserves this. She and her mother have outstayed their welcome in Katya's life. Amber, she reminds herself. In Amber's life. She no longer feels fettered by loyalty and it's such a relief. The air smells sweeter, her feet feel lighter, her shoulders relieved of the burden of trying to be what others want her to be: the good wife; the good mother; the good friend. Revenge tastes very sweet today.

Tom is there before her, which she takes as a good sign. He jumps up as soon as he sees her across the busy concourse. Her trek into central London was driven by adrenaline, anxiety and the delirium of hope, and at the sight of him she can't stop herself smiling, even though he isn't. Her whole body is aglow with excitement and love.

He touches her on the upper arm and there's an awkward shuffle when he goes to kiss her cheek but she aims for his lips, hitting the corner. His breath smells of coffee.

'What do you want to drink?'

'Skinny latte. Thanks.'

She smiles at his back as he crosses the floor to the counter, thinking how assured he is, how comfortable in his body, then she pulls her mobile out of her bag and texts Jenny:

Am in town. May run late. Are you able to pick Sophie up and keep her? Won't be long.

The reply comes back immediately:

No probs. Don't hurry.

Jenny Forsyth is a star and will make a good friend in the event that Vicky refuses to speak to her ever again. Life goes on.

'Tell me exactly what happened,' Tom says as he sets down her drink.

She holds his eyes for a moment, trying to read him. Her mouth is dry and she's scared. This isn't how she imagined it playing out. Maybe he hasn't come to terms with it yet. Maybe he's trying to kid himself that it meant nothing.

She reminds herself to be patient. To insist would be a bad idea. She doesn't want to scare him off.

'I begged her to call you, Tom. But she was so upset, so horrified, that she wasn't thinking straight.'

She doesn't bother asking why he isn't having this conversation with his wife. She assumes he's too angry with her. But he'll have to sooner or later, so this is her chance to tell it her way, to make sure she comes across the way she wants to: an honest and supportive friend inadvertently caught up in his wife's crime. She watches Tom's face and he doesn't take his eyes off hers. Every so often he groans in exasperation.

'Why the hell didn't you call me?'

'Don't be angry. I can't interfere in someone else's marriage. It was up to Vicky to tell you the truth. All I could do was advise her. And things happened so fast. By the time

I'd parked the car and found her again, she had already concocted this story. I couldn't then go to the authorities and tell them she'd lied, could I? There was nothing I could do except support her and look after the girls.'

She searches for some warmth in his eyes and thinks she sees a glimmer. A slim wedge of light that she can prise further open. A few metres away a couple are hugging and kissing. The young man is carrying a huge rucksack, almost big enough to tip him over. She guesses he's a soldier. She turns back to Tom.

'It wasn't my secret, but I'm glad you know now. I've hated lying to you. I've even hated Vicky for what she did and for involving me. But in my heart I know, if I hadn't confirmed her story, you would have lost your children and I . . . I couldn't do that to you.' The tears that come are genuine and she grabs a brown paper napkin and blows her nose. 'I'm sorry. I didn't mean to cry.'

He reaches over and takes her hand. 'It isn't your fault, Amber.'

'Please don't hate me.'

'I don't hate you. Far from it. I understand that you did what you did for the best reasons. I'll have to talk to Vicky now. I wanted to make sure I got the truth out of you first.'

'How did you find out?'

'Something Millie Boxer said when I bumped into her this morning.'

Oh fuck. Bloody Millie. She frowns and is about to ask more when he pockets his wallet and phone.

'I should get back to work.'

'Right now?'

'Sorry.' He touches her cheek lightly, almost absently. 'I've got a conference call in twenty minutes. We'll speak though. Soon.'

She wants to leave him with a lingering memory so she reaches up to kiss his cheek, her hand resting on his shoulder, and detaches herself with a smile that manages to be both mocking and rueful. He catches it and responds with a grin.

'Amber,' he chides.

She raises her eyebrows and he laughs, but he's quickly serious again.

'Please don't warn Vicky. Let me deal with this my way.'

For a moment she thinks he means their affair, then she realizes he's talking about Josh. Well, she never expected it to be easy; not with Tom, a man of principle who adores his children. This love affair wasn't part of the plan, but it's happened and, now that it has, it's worth fighting for. And the best thing is, Maggie will know exactly what it means. She'll understand the message. Katya is coming.

She looks up at Tom and smiles. 'OK.'

The tube rushes her back home almost too quickly. She needs more time to think. Now that Tom is aware of the circumstances, ought she to withdraw the demand for money? She chews at her fingernail. It depends how Vicky reacts. Would she tell him? Her insides flutter with anxiety. Probably. She doesn't want to become the bad guy in this. Tom has to understand that Vicky is the

358

one at fault; the criminally negligent mother and unfaithful wife. Not Amber. She can't let that happen, even if it means crawling to Vicky, getting back into her good books, at least until the dust has settled. She's going to have to back off and convince her to keep quiet. It'll be galling, but, when it comes down to it, although having both would be the aim, she would rather take Tom away from her than get the keys to that house. Hold on to the positive, she thinks. Forget the rest.

June 1992

LUKE HAD A BEER IN HIS HAND, HIS FEET UP ON THE coffee table, watching a James Bond film. Katya listened to the sound of gunfire as she undressed and got into her bath. She sat in the hot water hugging her knees and staring at her white toes and skinny ankles.

I am only a child.

She washed slowly, soaping her face and rinsing it, then pressed the wet flannel into her eyes and mouth, like a mask. The heat made her forehead bead with sweat. She slid down into the water, combed her fingers through her hair so that it floated out around her head, took the biggest breath she could and slid down further until it closed over her face. The ceiling rippled and her lungs felt like they would burst. She made fists of her hands and thumped the side, animal noises coming from the back of her throat. It hurt to drown, more than she expected it would. She let the air out in an explosion of bubbles and burst through the surface gasping for air.

She climbed out, reached for the towel and wrapped

it round her thin shoulders. The mirror had misted over. She wiped it and stuck out her tongue at her reflection. The yellow candlewick bathmat looked soft enough to sleep on and she was tempted to keep the door bolted against him and spend the night in there.

The television was still on when she came out, James Bond's voice, smooth and seductive, teasing some woman who Katya guessed was going to die. The door was partly closed and she peeked through the gap at the back of Luke's head. He sensed her and turned, so she scuttled into the bedroom, pulled the duvet over her head and started worrying at her scabs, making them bleed again.

36

Thursday, 22 April 2010

'HER NAME WAS KATYA AND SHE WAS TEN WHEN I inherited her case. Her mother had died of a drug overdose – she was a prostitute. I placed her with a foster family but it was a failure. She ended up in a Young Offenders' Institute and that was the last I heard of her.'

I slide down the door, gripping the phone. I'm hiding from the girls in Tom's study. 'You didn't recognize her?'

'Not until Spain, no. I've only ever met her fleetingly since you two became friends and she's changed so much. She was tiny then, underfed. And she's lost her south London accent; she sounds posher.'

'So what made you realize it was her?'

'I was watching the way she behaved around Tom, and I suppose things started to ring bells. It was the tiny scars on the back of her left hand that convinced me. When she was upset she used to stab herself with her compass.'

'She self-harmed? Poor little thing.' I know those marks. I asked Amber about them once and she said she was accidentally splashed by hot fat when she was a child. 'Why has she come after me? I haven't done anything to her.'

'The thing is, Vicky, I used to talk about you a lot. She was reserved and it seemed a good way to get her to talk to me. I didn't see that she was storing it all up, that you had become some sort of aspiration for her, a fantasy she could hold on to when things got rough. She got it into her head that I would eventually adopt her and she would be your sister. She was always going to be disappointed.'

'So that's all she was to you? A case. A cardboard folder?'

I try to picture my own daughters caught up in a similar situation and my heart bleeds for the child Amber was. No wonder she's screwed up. I wish she had talked to me. I should have realized something was badly wrong. I could have helped. I could have stopped things getting out of hand.

'I cared a lot,' Mum says tartly. 'But I had to maintain a distance. It's part of the job, like it is in teaching. It would have been unprofessional of me to get emotionally involved with one of my cases. You know that perfectly well.'

'OK, but are you telling me you ran out on her, left London and didn't even say goodbye, or sorry? Why would you do that?'

'Because I was scared. And I had you to consider. The truth is, Vicky, I should never have been in that job. It was a disaster.' She hesitates and I can feel her fighting her instinct to keep the worst back; to make herself look better. It makes me dread what she's going to say next.

'Katya told me that her foster father, Luke Bryant,

was abusing her and I refused to believe her. When it all exploded in my face, I decided to go. It was for the best.'

I am truly horrified and my voice rises. 'Why didn't you check? Why did you trust him?'

'The climate was very different then. People had no idea what was going on or they simply refused to see it or believe it. Luke was a very persuasive man and he was very clever.'

'But you're not dense,' I blurt out. The doorbell rings and I groan. 'Oh hell. That's the decorator coming to take a look. I have to go. I'll call you back.'

In the end, I don't get a chance to do that.

His name is Steve. I show him the bathroom first, then take him down to the spare room and, lastly, into the kitchen where the girls are sitting at the table; Emily doing her homework, Polly drawing a picture for my mum. She tells me it's a fish and I tell her it's the best fish I've ever seen.

Steve gazes up at the ceiling and nods wisely. 'That it then?'

'Yup, that's the lot. How soon can you start?'

He hums and haws then offers to come in two weeks, once he's finished a project down the road. 'Take me a week to do a good job. What happened? Pipe burst, was it?'

'One of the kids left the tap running and the plug in when we went out for the day. We came back to a flood.'

'Kids, eh? Little rascals. My two are always up to no good. And they're in their twenties now.'

'Yes, well, I don't know what I did to upset them.'

He laughs. 'Sounds like the green-eyed monster. Bit like the ex cutting the sleeves off your suits.'

There a commotion behind me and I turn as Polly's chair falls over.

'I didn't do it, Mama!' She's literally shaking with anger, her face wet and red.

'Oh, Polly. Darling, don't cry. We were only joking.'

Tears stream down her face, but it's more frustration than upset this time. She's furious and Polly furious is both heartbreaking and frightening. She is so desperate to be understood. I try to pick her up, wanting to comfort her, but she avoids me and charges upstairs sobbing.

'Sorry,' I say. 'I'd better go after her. Could you text me when you have a date?'

'You shouldn't have said that, Mummy,' Emily says when he's gone. She stops working out her sums and looks me in the eye. 'We didn't do it. I didn't and Polly never would.'

'Then who did?'

She shrugs. 'I don't know. Maybe another man got in the house.'

I open my mouth to speak, then just look at her, horrified, as realization dawns. Someone certainly did get in but it wasn't a man. Not a jealous lover but a jealous friend. I can't prove anything, but my gut knows it's true. Shit. I owe my daughters an apology. I go after Polly and find her curled up in a ball under her duvet.

She moves when she feels my hand on her shoulder, pokes her face out and wipes her eyes.

'I know you didn't do it, Polly. Or Emily. And I am very, very sorry I said you did. I should have believed you.' I lean over and she puts her arms round me and I hold her close as I carry her downstairs. Amber knew I'd blame the children: she knew it would damage my relationship with them. Even if I apologize, the sense of injustice will remain.

'I think it was Amber who flooded the house.'

I hover near Tom as he divests himself of his leathers, takes his helmet out of his hands and puts it on the side table. 'Tom, are you listening?'

'What are you talking about? Why on earth would Amber do something like that?' His glance is distracted, his mind elsewhere.

'Because she's angry. It makes sense. She has a key. She's used to letting herself in when we're away. She was pissed off because we'd invited the Forsyths down to Mum's and not her.'

He looks at me like I'm out of my mind. 'Oh my God. Will you listen to yourself!'

My mouth opens in surprise. It never occurred to me that he might have trouble believing it. It makes perfect sense to me. 'You have to admit it was out of character for either of the girls.'

'It was an accident. They're children. Shit like that happens. I can't believe you'd accuse Amber. She would never do something like that.'

I cross my arms and purse my lips, ready to do battle. It was her. I know it was. Tom gets himself a beer, prises off the top and drinks it straight from the bottle. He looks tired.

'Are the children asleep?' he asks.

'I think so.'

'Shut the door then. We need to talk.'

I do as he says and then move over to the worktop where I have supper semi-prepared: chicken breasts slathered in butter and sprinkled with salt, pepper and paprika; purple-sprouting broccoli in the steamer and sweet potato chips arranged on a baking tray and ready to go into the oven.

'You need to believe me. Amber isn't the person you think she is. I've found stuff out about her. Mum says—'

'All right. Enough.'

'But you're not listening to me. This is important, Tom. Why do you take her side all the time?' I'm becoming tearful. 'She's being a bitch.'

'What is wrong with you? I'm not interested in talking about Amber or what she may or may not have done to upset you this time; I want to talk about why you lied about the break-in.'

I stare at him. 'I didn't. What do you mean? What's she been saying?'

'Amber, more fool her, has been loyal to you.'

'You've spoken to her then? When was this?'

'It wasn't her, Vicky.'

'Then Mum?'

'Your mother?' He sounds genuinely surprised. 'No, of course not. I bumped into Millie this morning. We were talking about Josh and she said she never apologized for nearly running you over in the rain and spraying you with water that morning. She said she forgot because of all the excitement over the burglary.'

I'm still not there. 'When? I don't understand. What did she mean she nearly ran me over?'

'Apparently you crossed the road? She was distracted because she saw Amber standing in the doorway of one of the houses and the next thing she knew you came out of nowhere. Visibility was terrible, her wipers were going like the clappers and she didn't realize it was you until afterwards. And you know what else she said?'

My stomach drops. I remember now. Not seeing that car until it was almost too late, the water spraying up in a wide grey arc from under its tyres. It happened so quickly and the weather was so awful that I didn't see the driver, didn't even notice what the car looked like.

'Are you going to tell me?'

'She said that it was lucky you weren't pushing the pram because she might easily have hit it.'

'I know what you're thinking.'

'Do you?'

'I can explain everything, if you would just give me a chance.'

'What? That you lied to me and the authorities? That you concocted that frankly unbelievable story to cover up the fact that you left Josh on his own and then you dragged your friend into it? I knew something was off. I should have trusted my instincts.'

I tense my face and neck trying to delay the onset of tears. The effort distorts my voice so that it sounds jerky and choked. 'What would you have done if you had?'

'I don't know. But I would have talked to you about it.'

I nod sadly, acknowledging my mistake. I should

never have attempted to hide this from him. It has made everything so much worse.

'I'm sorry,' I say. 'But, honestly, Tom, it wasn't going to be for more than a few minutes and I couldn't have predicted we'd have a break-in.'

'No, and nor could you have predicted if there was a fire, or if Josh somehow managed to climb out of his cot and fall, or if someone had rung the doorbell and heard him crying up there on his own. There are a thousand things you couldn't have predicted, so why the hell did you take the risk?'

'I don't know. It was stupid.'

He slams the flat of his hand against the wall and I jump out of my skin.

'Stupid is how children get hurt!' he shouts. 'Stupid is how kids get abducted, have accidents, get killed!'

'Tom, keep your voice down.'

He breathes hard and drops his head, tearing his fingers through his hair. When he looks up his expression is cold and determined. 'I want you to go.'

'What do you mean, go?' I say, frantic by now. 'I can't just go.'

'Yes you can. Pack a bag and get out of my sight. You can stay a couple of nights with Maggie. We'll talk when we've both had a chance to calm down.'

'But I don't want to go to Mum's. And the children can't miss school.'

'Are you mad? You're not taking them with you. I can't trust you to look after them properly. They stay here, with me.'

I shake my head. 'No. No, Tom, you can't do this. They need me.'

'Like Josh needed you when that man was in the house? Like Polly needed you to listen to her reading at school and you forgot? Yeah, right.'

'Who's going to look after them while you're working? You won't . . . you won't ask Amber, will you?'

'No, I won't ask Amber. I've already rung my sister. She'll be here in time to do the afternoon pick-up.'

My eyes widen. 'You told Hannah?'

'I had to, Vicky.'

I finally lose it. The thought of my sister-in-law coming to take over; her smug face, the way she likes to contrast her life as a stay-at-home mum to mine, her sensible clothes and studied lack of personal vanity, are enough to tip the balance. Of course Hannah isn't that bad – she can be very sweet – but honestly the best thing about her is that she lives in Northumberland.

'You have no right to do that without consulting me. They are my children too. I don't want her in my house.' I pick up the phone and shove it at him. 'Call her now and tell her not to come.' I'm breathing hard, glaring at him. 'You can do what you like, but I am not leaving.'

He takes the phone and puts it carefully down on the side. He speaks slowly and patiently. 'I am not going to do that. I am asking you to give me a break for a couple of days, not leave this house for ever. Hannah won't be here for long, so you don't have to worry about her taking over. You need to do some thinking as well.'

'This is not fair, Tom. You have to give me another

chance. Let me stay tonight. We can talk about it in the morning when we're both less tired.'

'Please, Vicky. Be reasonable.'

Reasonable? 'I am not going anywhere.'

He grips my shoulders. 'Yes you are, because if you don't I will apply to the courts for custody and, after what you've done, I reckon I have a fair chance of succeeding. If you want to keep them, you'll do as I tell you.'

He is so calm and cold. I stare at him, searching for the man I thought I knew. I can't find him and I turn away, resigned, and pick up my keys and phone. I wander round the house collecting the few bits I need: a holdall with a change of clothes, my toothpaste, my phone charger, my book. I take a squishy penguin that I don't think Polly will miss, Josh's panda and Emily's cardigan.

'You can put your dinner in the oven,' I tell him. 'It's all ready to go. You don't need to do anything.'

'Why don't you take it?'

I glare at him. 'Take it where precisely?'

'I don't know. Your mum's? I don't want it.'

'Fine.' I pick up the baking dish and take it to the bin, flip the lid and dump its contents, along with the rest of the food. Then I march out of the house.

I have never in my life felt pain like this. I feel it deep in my chest, tearing at me. I have my bag; my bare necessities; my phone; the essential box of hankies. I have almost a full tank of petrol, but that's all I have.

37

I AM STARVING. THERE ARE TWO RESTAURANTS ON Tennyson Street but they're popular with locals and not the sort of place you can eat alone without looking odd. I speed up as the lights change and head for the sanctuary of McDonald's.

The rich aromas of grilled meat and fried onions hit me as I walk in. The only time I ever come here is when I'm with the children, and without them it's a lonely business; the bright colours and jolly paintings jar. I buy a burger, fries and a Coke, find a table away from the window and sit down with my back to the room.

I occasionally bring the children for their supper when I'm feeling lazy, but I haven't been in months. I don't have anything generally; just a cup of tea and the slices of mustard-smeared gherkin I've peeled off their hamburgers. I look around and I see us as we were: me and Tom with our polystyrene mugs; Josh in his high chair smearing ketchup on the table; Emily and Polly engrossed in the contents of their Happy Meal boxes. The woman that is me steals one of Emily's chips and earns a telling off and Polly offers one of hers and insists on putting it in my mouth herself, like she's posting a letter. Josh bangs the table with his fists, demanding attention. The image fades and I turn back to face the wall. We were happy once upon a time.

Where am I going to go?

I eat the last few cooling French fries, finish my Coke and contemplate spending the night in the car. It's easily big enough, but I reject the idea as too horrible and decide, with misgivings, to try Jenny. I don't know what else to do. I put my rubbish on the tray and take it to the bin and as I turn the doors open and David North walks in. He has his daughter with him. Not Hellie though, thank God.

David breaks into a smile but it leaves me cold. Beside him, Astrid clutches his hand and gazes up at me.

'It's Miss Vicky,' Astrid says, as if I'm an interesting freak, which, out of the context she knows, I suppose I am.

'Hello, Astrid. Have you had a lovely holiday?' I avoid David's scrutiny but I can feel his eyes burning my face.

'How are you?' he says.

'I'm good. I was just leaving.' I edge past him but he leans forward so that only I can hear what he says. His warm breath touches my cheek.

'You look gorgeous.'

I frown at him. Not only is it highly inappropriate, but I have never felt less gorgeous. Under my jacket sweat prickles between my shoulder blades. I don't want to talk to him at all, and certainly not with his daughter staring at us. He is oblivious to my discomfort, eager only for a flirtation. I mean nothing to him. I broke my marriage for a man to whom I was merely one in a million females to take his fancy.

I smile at Astrid, ask her which school she's going on to, and say goodbye.

'I can't meet you, darling,' Amber says. 'I'm working. Can you get a taxi?'

She holds the phone between her shoulder and her jaw while she pulls open a drawer and searches for her prettiest underwear. Her body is still warm from the bath and fragrant with scented moisturizer.

'Of course I can.'

Robert is disappointed but she's beyond caring. 'OK then.'

'I just thought it might be nice. I've got some good news. I won the contract.'

'Really?' She pushes the drawer in and holds the phone properly, standing naked in front of the mirror. 'That's fantastic. Is there much money in it?'

He laughs. 'Yes. I drove a hard bargain.'

'How much?'

'Let's just say, getting a deposit together is no longer a concern. The upfront money will be in my bank account by Monday morning.' He names a figure so wildly far from what she was expecting that she sits down, stunned. After all that, he's done it. Working quietly and patiently in his cramped home office, he's pulled it off. She feels bad that she never had faith in him. But it's too little, too late. Things have moved on, decisions have been made.

'Amber? Love? Are you still there?'

'Yes.' She feels a sudden urge to giggle.

'I thought I lost you.' He laughs and she cringes.

'Look, Robert, I have to go. I'll see you tomorrow. And well done. You deserve a break.' She's genuinely delighted for him. It'll help soften the blow.

'We both do,' he says. 'It's for us.'

'Yes, of course.'

She kisses him down the phone and hangs up. She looks around at the shoddy room with its magnolia wallpaper and oatmeal carpet. This flat has been home for six years but she feels no emotion towards it; not even hate any more. The trouble is, she can imagine herself moving, but not with Robert. She's fond of him and grateful. He saved her but he can't expect to keep her for ever, and in her heart she knows he never has.

She chooses a perfume and sprays it into the air then walks through the mist. Her life is about to change. She stares at herself, at her delicate shoulders and collarbones, at her toned arms and flat stomach, her long legs. Even good men have a limit to the amount of provocation they can resist. This is the endgame. After tonight, Vicky's perfect life will be gone and Maggie will see the devastation she's caused. It isn't Katya's fault this has happened. None of it is. Katya is just a child in search of protection and love. Katya wouldn't have to take it if it had been given to her honestly. Katya will steal what she wants through the back door, through Tom and his weakness. His lust. And Amber will make him love her because that's what she does best.

* * *

'Darling, you're shivering,' Jenny says. 'Come into the kitchen. I'll make you a hot drink. You can tell me what's happened.'

I explain as best I can, following her inside and taking off my coat. I hang it over the back of a chair and stand behind it, not sure whether or not to sit. She switches on the kettle then asks if I'd prefer something alcoholic.

My overenthusiastic, 'Yes please!' earns a raised eyebrow.

'Jenny, I am so sorry to do this to you, but could I stay with you tonight? I wouldn't ask unless I was really desperate.'

She doesn't answer immediately. This is a different Jenny, not the chatty mum, but the professional who knows how effective silence can be in eliciting confidences. It feels as though she's tunnelling inside my psyche, winkling things out of me that I never thought I would divulge. It would be unnerving if she wasn't such a kind person. She pours me a generous glass of wine.

'Listen, don't worry. I know it's asking too much. I'll go to a hotel.'

She must have read the despair on my face because she takes my bag out of my hand and puts it back down at my feet. 'Don't be silly. Of course you can stay. Goodness, it's eight o'clock. I'd better say goodnight to the girls.'

'The girls?'

'Yes, Sophie Collins is sleeping over. I'll be down in a sec. Go and talk to Simon.'

* * *

I don't because, at that moment, Amber rings. I wait before I pick up, then jam my finger on the accept icon.

'I don't know what came over me,' she says. 'I am so sorry, Vicky. Please forgive me.'

'What are you talking about?'

My mind is full of what my mother has told me. It changes everything. All this, all the manipulating and the lying, has nothing to do with Tom or that house, it's to do with Mum and the past. Amber is punishing me for something that I had no part in. And now she's scared because she knows she's gone too far and is about to lose me and the life she and Robert have built up around my family. I don't know what I should do, whether to tell her I know or let her have enough rope to hang herself. I break out in a cold sweat just thinking about it.

'I don't want your money. Your friendship is so important to me. I got carried away by that house. I forgot who I was.'

I don't find this in the least bit reassuring. 'Then tell me why . . .' I hesitate. I'm tired and I need to think before I go wading into a situation I am very far from understanding.

'What?'

'It doesn't matter.'

'Do you want to come round? I'm on my own tonight. Sophie and Rose are having a sleepover. We could have a glass of wine and put the world to rights.'

'Amber, I'm sorry. I can't. I'm over at Jenny's now. I . . . well, Tom asked me to leave.'

'Shit. Vicky. I am so sorry.'

And she sounds it. I'm drawn in, her sympathy playing

like the strings of a lute. And then I remember that the only reason we are friends is because she orchestrated it. She must have been following me for years to have kept up with my life, to have known that I was married and pregnant.

'I have to go,' I say. 'Jenny and Simon are waiting for me.'

'So you're staying the night there? I suppose it's for the best. It'll give Tom a chance to cool off. Oh, and Vicky, Robert's home tomorrow. You won't tell him about any of this, will you?'

'Of course I won't. I think you should do that yourself.'

Silence.

'Amber?'

'I know. You're right. Vicky, please give me another chance. You're my best friend. I've been weak and thoughtless but if you only knew ... well, I'll tell you sometime. But it hasn't been easy.'

I sigh. 'OK, Amber. I forgive you.' If she really has been through everything Mum described, then what else can I do?

38

I YAWN AS A PRECURSOR TO GOING UP TO BED. WE
finished supper half an hour ago and have been discussing Jenny's decision to go back to work. They are a
lovely couple and perfectly suited; Simon enormously
proud of his wife and Jenny, the more matter-of-fact
spouse, humouring him and laughing at his jokes. They
are hospitable and generous and have made me feel welcome. I don't want to encroach on their space.

'I'm bushed,' I say. 'I think I'll go up.'

Neither of them argues but they both smile at me and
Jenny holds out her hand and takes mine.

'You get a good night's sleep, Vicky.'

I have my doubts about that. My head is far too full.
I go upstairs and run myself a bath in the children's
bathroom and lie in it until my skin wrinkles. Rose's
toothbrush is in a dinosaur-shaped plastic mug, Sophie
Collins's Cath Kidston washbag on the glass shelf. A
string bag full of Spike's toys hangs from a dolphin hook
and the door, with its cracked panels and grubby finger-
marks, has stickers all over it: glittery butterflies, pirates,
exotic birds and Disney characters. Ranged along the

side of the bath is a family of bright-yellow, red-beaked rubber ducks. I miss my children, and when I think of them waking up in the morning and finding me gone, my heart breaks. I get out and sit on the side of the bath with my towel wrapped around me, in someone else's bathroom in someone else's house. Try as I might, I can't kid myself that things are going to get better. I fold my body over, suddenly nauseous, and weep silently.

Tom opens the door and looks at Amber as though she's the last person he expects to see. It seems to her that he's swiftly rethinking what he was about to say. Presumably he thought it was Vicky. He's as polite as ever but as tense and wired as a guitar string. Well, she's nervous too.

'Sorry about the mess,' he says, ushering her into the kitchen. 'Vicky's had to go away. My sister's coming to help but she can't get here till tomorrow. Do you want a drink?'

'Thanks, that would be great. I won't stay long. I just wanted to see how you both were.'

'I'm fine. Have you spoken to Vicky?'

'Not since yesterday.' A lie won't hurt at this stage. The words rush out. 'Tom, look, I feel partly to blame for what's happened.' She takes the glass from his hand. It's cold and she touches it to her wrist to help cool her down. 'It's such a mess.'

'You're telling me.'

He drinks his beer straight from the bottle, tipping it to his lips in a way she finds intensely erotic. Amber goes outside where the evening is warm and scented with recently cut grass. Their flower beds are full of bluebells.

She lowers herself on to the edge of the decking and slips off her shoes. Her toenails are mother-of-pearl. A goldfinch pecks at the feeder while the last of the sun shimmers above the rooftops. Amber waits for it to dip behind them with a sense of dreamy anticipation. A soft breeze plays in her hair and the alcohol insulates her nerves.

Tom joins her and leans on his bony knees, the bottle between his hands, his thumb rubbing lightly up and down the glass. She turns to him, meaning to start the conversation about Spain, but he speaks first, almost as if he's scared of even touching on the subject.

'When's Robert back?'

'Late morning.'

'You must miss him.'

She looks at him, tilting her head slightly and studying his profile. Why is he doing this? Her stomach rumbles incongruously and Tom laughs.

'I'm starving,' she says with a mock-petulant smile.

'So am I. I forget to eat when Vicky isn't here.' He looks around as if expecting food to miraculously appear. 'Actually she chucked my dinner away.'

Amber laughs. 'Did you deserve it?'

'Oh totally. I provoked her.' He brightens and jumps up. 'There's a pizza in the fridge. I'll put it in the oven. Where's Sophie?'

'She's staying the night at Rose Forsyth's.' Surely he doesn't need a clearer message than that. 'You don't mind me landing on you, do you? It's just that normally I'd have Vicky to talk to.' She readjusts her neckline downwards. 'We're not exactly on speaking terms, as you can imagine. She's convinced I ratted on her.'

He doesn't respond. Perhaps he hasn't heard. After a moment she wanders in after him and hovers while he takes the pizza out of its packaging and slides it into the oven. He tops up her wine.

'Cheers.' He smiles as he clinks his bottle against her glass.

'Cheers.'

He turns to fetch plates, knives and forks. Amber sips her wine and watches him.

'This bloke, David North. He's a father at the school, isn't he?'

'His daughter's in Year Six,' she says. She goes over to the cupboards and takes out two of the white china plates, standing close to him. He moves away and sets the table, making her feel as though she's chased him across the room. That's not nice.

'So Vicky taught her last year. Classy.'

'To be fair,' she says, pulling a chair out and sitting down, 'I think it was more to do with him. I don't think she was looking for it. Sometimes things happen. You meet someone and it's like a punch. There's not a lot you can do about that.'

'Was that what it was like for you and Robert?' he asks, missing the point entirely.

'No. He grew on me. He came along when I was at a low ebb, when all I needed was to feel safe and cared for.'

Tom's gaze has shifted to her knee. It's bouncing. She tenses it until it stops.

'Can I tell you the truth?' she says.

'I'd appreciate it if someone did.'

God, his eyes are beautiful. She pushes her hair back

and takes a deep breath. While she speaks he removes the pizza from the oven, slices it into wedges with a knife from the block, shares them on to the plates and puts one down in front of her. She picks up a piece and nibbles the end.

'I have never really been in love with him. I'm very fond of him and I'm truly grateful for what he's done for me, and for giving me Sophie, but I've never had that breathless feeling and I feel so guilty about that. I'm not a person who uses others; I've had to fend for myself and I'd do it again if it was necessary, but I don't like the part of me that agreed to be with him because of what he was offering. I hate that one day I'm going to hurt him. He's a good man. A lovely man. And he deserves better.' She chokes on her words and looks up at him, into his eyes. She almost believes it herself. 'I've never told anyone that. Not even Vicky.' To her surprise, tears spill on to her cheeks. She stands up abruptly. He must know, he must realize. She waits, her back to Tom, listening to her own breathing, to the light tap as he sets his empty bottle down, to the shuffle as he moves his chair. He puts his hands on her shoulders and she turns and buries her head in his chest.

'Oh, Tom,' she says.

She raises her chin, expecting to find him gazing down at her, but he's staring over her head at the darkened garden. She lets her hands slide around his neck and allows her fingers to touch his jaw, lifts herself up on her toes and tilts her head back, eyelids fluttering as she touches the corner of his lips with hers.

The gesture jerks him back to life. He lets her go and gently sits her down. Then he crouches in front of her and takes her hands.

'Amber, you're wrong. I think you really do love Robert, in your heart of hearts. Like I love Vicky. If you're looking to me to give you whatever is missing in your life, or to heal your wounds, it's not going to happen. I can't be there for you. Please don't mistake my caring about you for love.'

'But we . . .'

Her confusion and hurt are real. She stares at him, unable to move, unable to speak even. He touches her cheek and she leans into his hand, tears spilling.

'I thought we understood each other, Amber. Of course I find you attractive. You are incredible. But that doesn't mean I'm in love with you. It happened because it was late and we were both feeling miserable and vulnerable. You reached out and I was grateful. I didn't realize how strongly you felt. I thought we amused each other.'

Amused?

She closes her eyes but she can't stop that other man from entering her head. He's calling her to him, teasing her and making her feel scared and special at the same time. She imagines she's on the ice again, a child whirling round and round, her hands in his, her arms outstretched, and he's smiling, wolf-like, his teeth gleaming.

'Don't you want me, Luke?' she says in a small voice.

Tom frowns. 'What did you call me?'

She takes his hand and pulls it between her legs, into the heat of her crotch and he lurches away, horrified.

'Christ, Amber. Stop it.'

'Please don't call me that.' She stands up, crosses her arms and takes hold of the edges of her shirt and starts to pull it over her head. 'I'm your little girl, remember?'

He tugs at her top, struggling with her. At first she laughs and then she lets her arms go limp.

'You like this, don't you?' she says, arching her eyebrows and reaching for his fly. He grabs her wrist and holds her at bay.

'This is not funny. I think you'd better go.'

'That's not what you said in Spain.'

'I don't give a stuff about Spain.' He moves away from her and starts to stack the plates and cutlery into the dishwasher, banging them against each other, then grips the edge of the work surface, his neck drawn into his hunched shoulders. He doesn't turn round when he replies. 'Sorry. I didn't mean that. But Spain was a mistake. It never should have happened.' He bends to take out a dishwasher tablet from the pack in the cupboard under the sink, puts it in the dispenser and clicks it shut. 'I love my wife.'

'But what about me?'

He lets out a frustrated grunt and swivels round. 'You don't matter.'

She's left open-mouthed. He turns away from her again, and starts to scrub out a saucepan: anything to keep his hands busy.

Amber stares at his back, sees his dark hair and tall, wiry frame and her hand slides round the knife he used to cut the pizza. A scream rages up inside her and she rushes forward. He spins round but he doesn't have a chance to defend himself, to say anything at all, as she rams the knife into his abdomen. He cries out in pain, falls to his knees and doubles over.

June 1992

KATYA STARED INTO THE SHADOWS AS HER VISION adjusted to the night. Her digital clock read ten forty-seven. Something lingered in her mind, wisps of a dream that spun on its axis and changed direction mid-story. The taste of anger and disappointment. She had been dreaming about school; running through the corridors, late for a lesson, her hair not brushed and her new shoes falling off. Then suddenly she wasn't running any more and she wasn't at school, she was sitting in Maggie's car and Emily was ignoring her. Katya was telling her things about her life, about Linda's death and about being scared of Luke Bryant, but Emily just talked over her, jabbering away to Maggie as if Katya didn't exist. Then Emily was gone and Katya was sitting a couple of feet away from Linda, waiting, listening to the harsh drag of her breath, until it stopped. Then waiting, ears ringing, for it to begin again.

It wasn't Katya's fault. She had been neglected, hadn't she? And fed fairy stories where orphans had all the luck. If she had known that things would be worse after, she would have called 999 sooner.

'Go away,' she mumbled. Her mum was in her head now; Linda's eyes wide open and staring at her.

Emily's amber was under her pillow and she could feel it, like the Princess and the Pea, its jagged edges pressed up through the soft foam. She expected to be in trouble when Emily eventually noticed it was gone. She imagined being dragged in front of her to apologize. Emily wouldn't understand that she did it to be closer to her; she would think Katya was a thief. That made her start to panic. She fetched her compass from her desk, brought it back into bed with her. She pressed the point into her skin, piercing between the birdlike bones, feeling relief wash through her like a tide of warm water.

She needed the toilet. In the kitchen the television was still on but the gunshots and car chases had been replaced by canned laughter. She moved soundlessly and locked herself in, wincing at the scrape of the bolt as she slid it across. She didn't dare use the flush. Afterwards, she pressed her ear against the panels and listened, then edged the bolt back slowly, turned the handle and stepped out into the corridor. The laminate floor was bouncy beneath her feet and moonlight shone through the narrow, stained-glass windows on either side of the front door.

'Katya?'

She ran past the stairs into her bedroom and threw herself on to the bed, hoping he'd think he had imagined what he heard. Five minutes went by, then ten and just when she thought she'd got away with it, her door

387

opened. Luke stood on the threshold, his tall figure blocking the light, his eyes on the hump of her body. She regulated her breathing, keeping it shallow and audible, hoping to convince him. She felt his weight as he sat down on the bed beside her.

He stroked her hair. 'I know you're awake.'

His voice wasn't exactly slurred, but it sounded thicker than normal and softer-edged. He smelled of alcohol and sweat. She was too used to drunks not to know that they were seldom benign.

'I needed the toilet.'

'So you're talking to me now, are you? Come and watch the telly with me.'

'I want to sleep.' She yawned to prove it.

'Plenty of time for that when you're dead.' His smile wavered when he saw her expression. 'It's a figure of speech.'

'A what?'

'It's just something people say. You're not dying, not anytime soon at any rate. I'm sure you'll live to be a very old lady.' His tone was mocking but kind.

'I'm really tired. I don't want to get up.'

'Ten minutes then. You can fall asleep on the sofa if you like.' He sighed. 'What with Sally away and everything else that's been going on, I need cheering up.'

She assumed he meant the job interviews that never produced jobs. She felt some sympathy for him, but also mortification because no one wanted him. Then she remembered Emily's expression when she asked if she could stay; how embarrassed she had been because Katya was unwanted. How she deliberately turned her back on her. Katya knew how it felt to be rejected. She pushed the duvet off her legs and reached for her book.

He had been watching a boring chat show. On the coffee table there were four empty cans of beer, half a bottle of vodka and a plate smeared with meat juices.

'Why are you reading that book again? Aren't you too old for fairy tales?'

'I like them.'

Before she realized what he was up to, he had grabbed it off her, laughing at her dismay. He flicked through it, reading passages out in a creepy voice while she sat scowling with outrage, her chin jutted.

'Not exactly Disney, are they? Bloody hell, Katya. Listen to this, *"After some moments she began to perceive that the floor was all covered over with clotted blood, on which lay the bodies of several dead women, ranged against the walls."* Is this the sort of thing you like then?'

'Yes. So what?'

'So, I'm just surprised. You are a dark horse, aren't you?'

She wasn't sure what he meant but she didn't like the sound of it. 'I'm not. Give me back my book.'

'I think I might confiscate it,' he said. 'It doesn't seem very suitable.'

She got up on her knees and tried to snatch it, but he lifted it out of her reach. She tried again, standing up, wobbling on the sofa cushions in her bare feet. 'Give it to me! It's not yours.'

'But is it yours, Katya?' His eyes crinkled. Luke was beautiful when he laughed but she didn't like his looks any more. There was something wrong, something unsettling about the way those brown eyes examined her. As if she was food on the table. A nice juicy steak.

'It was my mum's.' She was close to tears now. 'You can't take it away. You've got no right.'

He lowered his arm and when she reached again, jerked it away so that she toppled towards him, involuntarily grabbing his shoulder to stop herself falling.

Luke put his hands firmly on her hips; hot hands that almost wrapped around her entire body. 'Steady. You might hurt yourself.'

She pushed him away and jumped off the sofa, furious. 'I'm not staying here any more,' she said sullenly. 'I'm going to tell Sally what you did.'

'You won't do that.'

'I will. You're horrible and I hate you.'

He handed the book to her with a smile and then turned back to the television. 'Sit down.'

'No.'

'Come on. I was only teasing. Sit.' He patted the cushions.

He sounded sad not hostile, so she sat, as far away from him as possible, and tucked her book behind a cushion. After that he appeared to relax; he even yawned. She hoped he would fall asleep.

In the commercial break, he spoke. His voice was soft, the words measured. 'You don't want to talk to anyone, Katya. You know they won't believe a word you say. I haven't hurt you, have I?'

He hadn't. Not exactly. 'No.'

He turned and smiled at her. 'There you are then.

There's no harm in a cuddle between friends. I don't want us to fall out. I like you. You don't nag me like Sally does, or make me feel I'm not good enough. And you're such a clever little thing. Now shift over and stop treating me like a leper.'

She could feel his eyes on her profile and with that the horribly familiar build-up. She didn't move a muscle, just kept staring at the screen, pretending to laugh at jokes she didn't understand, hoping he'd be more interested in the celebrities than her. It didn't stop him. He held out his hand and kept it there between them, opening and closing it in a quick, impatient gesture. When she didn't react he leaned over and took hold of her, pulling her towards him and trapping her under his arm. He pressed his nose into her hair.

Katya could hear the blood rushing past her ears; feel her heart thumping behind her ribcage. Up close, his smell was overpowering: stale yeasty beer and meat. When his fingers brushed her skin she flinched and scrambled away, but he moved as quick as a snake and before she could escape he was on her, pinning her down with his body, his hands groping between her legs. She screamed but he clamped his hand over her mouth.

It was different this time. She felt his loss of control, the escalation of desire. She closed her eyes tight. He sounded like the man she once found on top of her mother, the way the air rasped from his lungs in ugly pants and moans. She had thought he was attacking Linda and had taken a knife to him. She didn't do him much harm, but it was enough to need stitches and to get her noticed by social services.

She reached blindly and her hand touched glass. She nudged at the vodka bottle, stretching her fingers as far as they would go, walking them up to the neck. Then with one last effort she gripped it, swung it up and brought it down hard on his shoulders. He whacked it away with a curse and it smashed against the steel frame of the coffee table. When she cried out he gagged her, covering her nose and mouth with his hand. She thought she was going to suffocate. She was drowning again, underwater, a hand pressing her down and keeping her there. She reached and her fingers touched something cold, wet and sharp. She moved the piece of broken glass closer, tipped it into her hand, plunged it into his neck and held it there. Luke bellowed and lurched up, blood spurting between his fingers, his colour draining as he staggered around the room like a drunk. Finally, he fell, his head hitting the fake-marble hearth with an audible crack.

Katya covered her face and sobbed, cramming herself into the corner of the sofa, trying not to hear the noises Luke was making. His moans slowly became weaker until eventually he fell silent. When he hadn't moved for a while, she crawled over and crouched beside him. It was hard to tell if he was alive or not, even when she held the back of her hand near his lips. She could have imagined that there were signs; that his eyelid flickered, that a tiny thread of life still existed.

She shuffled back to the sofa on her bottom and found the phone lying in a pool of spilt vodka. She touched the keys then her fingers went slack and she let it drop on to the carpet. For the second time in her life, she did nothing.

It was the television programme finishing and the ads coming on that made her go in search of Luke's address book. She knew Sally's wouldn't have the number she wanted.

After she had woken Maggie and summoned her to the house, she brushed broken glass off her pyjama bottoms, retrieved her book from under the sofa cushion and went to wait by the front door.

39

JENNY'S SPARE ROOM IS ON THE TOP FLOOR AND HASN'T yet seen a paint roller. It isn't half as bad as Browning Street, but it's drab and dated, with yellow rag-rolled walls and white glossed woodwork. There's even a yellow basin set into a dilapidated vanity unit with a white plastic framed mirror above it. I looked in it earlier and saw shadows under my eyes.

I try to read but I can't stop thinking. I don't trust Amber, not after everything she's done lately. She may have taken back her demand for money and asked me to forgive her; but she hasn't done that out of love for Vicky Seagrave. She's done it for Amber Collins. I assume that Robert's trip paid off and he's got his contract. That at least would explain why the pressure is off. It doesn't mean I can suddenly rely on her again. The question is, what does she hope to gain by returning to where we were at the beginning of January when all this began? I'm not a fool, not a complete fool anyway. I'm not going to fall into that trap.

But what if I decide not to take Jenny's advice? I am still wavering. Tom and I would be in Amber's power.

My thoughts scatter as I panic. What if that man is arrested and tells Grayling what actually happened? What if I am charged with child abuse? Will she win? Will she take Tom? And what about when I got out? Would it be left to Mum to pick me up and take me with her to Bognor? Would my home be barred to me? Would I have access to my children? A tear dribbles down my cheek and I set aside the book with a groan of frustration. A. There is no point anticipating things that haven't yet happened. B. Jenny said it was unlikely I'd be imprisoned. C. I need to get some sleep. I switch out the bedside light and fall back on the pillow. When my mobile rings, it takes me a moment to work out where I am.

'Vicky, lovely. Thank God you're awake.'

From the sound of her voice it's clear Mum's been drinking. I sit up and rotate my head, stretching my neck, trying to ease the grogginess. I get out of bed and move the curtains aside. The street is very quiet, the night cloudless, London glowing as bright as the sprinkling of stars that prick tiny stitches in the night sky.

'There's something I didn't tell you.'

'OK,' I say slowly.

'I want you to know that I'm truly sorry for what happened, but it wasn't my fault. He lied to me.'

I yawn and rub my eyes. My body feels heavy. 'Stop being mysterious and tell me what's going on.'

'She killed him.'

My eyes widen. 'Who killed who?'

'Amber – Katya, I mean. She killed her foster father. I'm sorry; I know I should have told you.'

'Why didn't you?'

'Because I was ashamed. And there's something else. Katya's mother died of an overdose and Katya found her.'

'Oh Christ.'

'She said she was dead and that she called 999 straight away, but there was evidence that she waited. It was hushed up because she was so young. She may not even have realized Linda was still alive.'

I turn away from the window and let the curtains fall closed. I feel as though ice has entered my heart.

'Say something, Vicky.'

'Please don't tell me you were having an affair with him.'

The silence that follows kills me. Of all the things she could have done, this is both the most unbelievable and the most believable. I am not surprised and yet I am so shocked I want to scream at her, smash something. Instead I push it all down and try very hard to stay calm.

'You must have known it was morally wrong.'

'Of course I did.' Her voice wavers. She's like a child being told off by a teacher. 'I tried to stay away from him. But you never met Luke. He was so convincing, so charming, and I was lonely. I fell in love.'

'With Katya's abuser? With a man who preferred a little girl to you? Oh my God, Mum. How could you?'

My supper rises to my gorge and I lean over the basin and retch into it, dropping the phone. When I pick it up, I can hear Mum crying.

'Vicky, listen to me. Let me explain.'

'I don't want to hear it and I don't want to speak to you. I need to think.'

After I cut her off, I crouch in the middle of the room, my head in my hands, trying to understand. She was a defenceless little girl and he was a big man. She would have been terrified. She would have struck out with all the strength she possessed. No wonder Mum refused to believe her; she was too busy deluding herself she was in love with a decent man. What has it done to Amber's mind? And what the hell do I do now? Do I tell her I know? Do I ignore it and hope it goes away? Should I even tell Tom?

Tomorrow morning I'm going to find her and speak to her. This is a woman who has been hurt and let down and she needs my help, so the least I can do is talk to her; give her a chance to tell her side of the story. She's turned on me but she isn't to blame for what's happened. I've done that all by myself.

I crawl back into bed but a minute later my phone rings again. I should have turned it off. I groan and reach for it.

'Mum?'

'Vicky? It is Magda. I disturb you?'

'No. What's wrong?'

She wouldn't call at this hour without a good reason. Perhaps Tom has gone out and left her with the kids. Odd, but not impossible.

'I am not sure,' Magda says. 'I am worried.'

'Are you at my house? Are the kids all right?'

'No. I am babysitting for Mrs Boxer.'

'Oh. Is there a problem with her boys?' I have visions of them projectile vomiting over the dachshunds. 'Only I'm at Jenny's.'

'Ah.'

'What is it, Magda?'

'She has been there one hour now. I thought you have come home, but you know I have feeling in my bones that you don't yet. And I am right. You are not there.'

'What are you talking about?'

'Mrs Collins. I was in the sitting room watching telly and I hear something, so I open the curtains. I see Tom inviting her in. I do not wish to be involve but I worry for you and now you are not there I see I am right.'

I shiver. 'Do you know for sure that she's still in the house?'

'I think yes because I do not hear door again, but the baby wake up so I have not been always looking.'

'I'm on my way. Thank you.'

40

KATYA IS CONFUSED. SHE SITS UP AND RUBS HER HEAD.
She must have blacked out and in the meantime night
has fallen. She stands unsteadily, goes to the door and
switches on the light, wincing at the brightness.

Tom is lying on the floor, on his side with his face
pressed up against the base of the cupboard. She
approaches him but stops abruptly when she sees the
blood. She needs to think. She can see the handle of the
knife sticking out, so she takes some kitchen towel and
wipes it clean of her fingerprints. Then she washes up
her glass and plate and puts them away. It doesn't matter that every other surface has evidence of her presence
in the house. It's her home from home.

What else is there? She has to make it look like a
break-in. She goes outside and round to the French windows that lead into the sitting room and inspects the
door frame. The repair is invisible. She chooses a stone
from the edge of the flower beds and uses it to break the
glass, then listens in the darkness. Nothing. No sound.
No windows or back doors opening. She feels for the
key and turns it, but the doors don't open because there

are new deadbolts at the top and bottom. She considers her options and looks around for something to prise the whole thing open with, loses patience and kicks in the bottom panels. That should be enough space for a man's head and shoulders. She runs back into the kitchen, slides the doors closed and locks them. She should steal something. Vicky's jewellery will do. She knows where it's hidden.

I pull on my clothes, run down to the hall and grab my bag off the hook. Jenny and Simon are in the kitchen, Simon stacking the dishwasher, Jenny leaning back in her chair chatting to him. Night owls, the pair of them.

'Darling,' Jenny says when she sees me hovering in the doorway. 'You're as white as a sheet. Did I hear your phone ringing? Was it Tom?'

'Magda.'

'Why was she calling you? Is it the children?'

I shake my head. 'No. She saw Amber going into my house over an hour ago and she hasn't left yet.'

I turn and look behind me, anxious to be on my way, and she leaps out of her chair and rushes over. Simon watches us, pausing in the act of scraping food into the bin.

'Don't go rushing in, Vicky,' Jenny says. 'Think about it. There could be any number of reasons.'

I'd love to believe that, but I remember how he looked at her when we were in Spain, how he stuck up for her, how he cared for her after she deliberately threw herself into the pool. With me out of the way, he won't be able to resist. At the thought of them together I feel as though

I am losing control of my limbs. I bite down hard on my lip.

Jenny's voice is urgent, pleading. 'Don't do anything hasty. If you go charging in and they are together, you're the one who's going to be humiliated.'

'What do I do?' I remember Rose and Sophie and lower my voice. 'Jenny, what do I do?'

'You stay here,' she says firmly. 'And you talk to him in the morning. I very much doubt there is anything going on.'

'But you don't know that for sure, do you?'

I feel the impasse between us, the tension like a fishing line vibrating above the water, and I know that I cannot stay, even though common sense tells me she's right. If it hadn't been for the conversation with Mum I might have done as I was told, but everything has changed. Amber isn't the woman I thought I knew and I have no idea what might trigger her. My children are in that house.

'I agree with everything you say and I know I may live to regret this, but I have to go.'

With a brief hug, I plunge out into the night and start to run. By the time I reach the corner I have to stop to catch my breath and walk the rest of the way. In Coleridge Street all the lights at the front are out.

41

THERE'S NO SOUND COMING FROM THE DOWNSTAIRS rooms, nothing from upstairs. I stand in the middle of the hallway, puzzled. The silence is unnerving. I run upstairs but all three children are where they should be, tucked up in bed, sleeping peacefully. Polly is on her front, one arm under her head, the other cuddling her teddy bear. Emily always sleeps on her side. In his cot next door, Josh moves his mouth in his sleep and emits the occasional grunt.

On the floor below I glance into our bedroom. The bed is unmade, rumpled and tangled; the pillows crushed and out of place. The curtains are closed. A perfume that I associate with Amber lingers tantalizingly. She's been in here. In my bed. I stumble out of the room, my hand pressed to my mouth, images of Tom and Amber writhing naked lodged in my mind.

I run downstairs, flicking switches as I go, no longer caring if they hear me or not. Why don't they come out? Why would they hide from me? I sense something off. There's a distinct change in the atmosphere, as if what was rock solid is now unstable, shifting.

The reason becomes obvious as soon as I enter the kitchen. Tom is slumped on the floor, leaning against the cupboard doors with his legs stretched out, his head wedged to one side and his eyes half open. His arms are wrapped around his stomach, a knife protruding, and he's ashen. His shirt is soaked with blood that seeps through his fingers, trickles down through the dip between his hip and his ribcage and pools beside him. Didn't I dream something like this?

'Tom!'

I grab the roll of kitchen towel, kneel down beside him and try to staunch the bleeding but it keeps coming and I realize I'm going to have to remove the knife if I want to apply the necessary pressure. I whisper an apology and ease it out. Tom screams. I put my hand over his mouth and stare into his eyes. He stares back, his face contorted with agony.

There's a plastic basket of ironing within reach and I drag it over, pull out shirts and tea towels and wad them against his wounds. To my surprise I feel a sense of urgency but no panic. My training kicks in as I remember the drill. DR ABC.

D is for Danger – too late to assess. I can feel its threat but I'm beyond worrying.

R is for Response – there was none when I shouted his name. I say it again anyway, over and over.

A is for Airways. I check his mouth for obstructions; make sure he isn't choking on his tongue.

B is for Breathing. He is. I sigh with relief.

C is for Circulation. I hold his wrist and wait for a pulse. As I feel for it, his body starts a slow slide to the right. I consider pulling him into the recovery position but decide he's more likely to go to sleep that way, and he mustn't, so I pull him up and try to balance him against the cupboard door. I shake his shoulders when he starts to fall sideways again. There is blood everywhere, on the floor, on me, on the units.

'I have to leave you for a minute, Tom. I have to call an ambulance.'

The telephone isn't in its cradle and my mobile is in my bag in the hall. I calculate how many seconds it'll take to find my phone and get back to him, how many pumps of his heart that would mean, how much more blood he can afford to lose.

'Stay with me, darling. Don't pass out. I need your help. I need you to press down on this.'

I place my hand over his but when I release it, it slips to the floor and his fingers trail in the puddle of blood. I repeat the process and touch my forehead to his like I do with Josh when he's distressed. I want to give him my strength, let him know that I'm here for him.

'Amber,' he mutters.

'Where is she?' He doesn't reply, so I shake him gently. 'Tom. Where is she?'

His eyes open a crack and I hear something. It's a tiny noise. A bump. I put my finger to his lips to warn him and this time, when I lay his hand over the wound, it stays. I only have seconds before his strength gives out. I crawl across the cold stone, round the side of the island to the drawers, pull one open and reach in. My hand closes round the wooden rolling pin. Then the lights go out and the fridge is silenced, the green digital clock on the front of the oven goes blank and the house seems to expel the air from its lungs.

The fuse box is in the cellar. That's where she is.

There's a three-quarter moon, so even without electricity there's enough light to see. I cross the room, holding the rolling pin at shoulder height, wait for a moment at the door, then when I hear nothing, edge out into the hall.

'Amber. I know you're there.'

There's no answer. Outside the kitchen the yellow glow of a street light through the stained-glass throws the staircase into eerie relief. It feels like my house and yet it doesn't. It could be a film set; perfect in all respects and yet temporary, flimsy and incapable of keeping us safe. My gaze shifts to the front door, where I've left my bag. It's on its side, the contents scattered across the polished boards. My phone has gone. I hear something and whirl round.

'Where are you, Amber? You can't hide here all night. Tom's hurt. He needs a doctor.'

Silence.

'For God's sake. Do you want his death on your hands too? Talk to me. I know what happened to you. Mum told me. I want to help you.'

A shadow moves and I spin round but I'm too late. She comes at me from the sitting room, her hair wild, snarling as she lifts her arms and flings me backwards. I go down with a cry, hard on to the stone, and hear a horrible crack as pain explodes through my head. The rolling pin bounces across the floor and comes to rest out of reach.

'My . . . name . . . is . . . Katya!'

405

She pulls me up by the shoulders then flings me down. I struggle but I know what's going to happen. I wish it was over and done with. I send my last thoughts to my children and then my head connects with stone and everything goes black.

42

THERE'S NO MISTAKING THE SMELL OF DAMP, DIRT AND brick or the penetrating chill of our cellar. My body is bruised and grazed, and my skull feels as though someone has taken a chainsaw to it. My hands have been secured behind my back with a cable tie, my ankles bound the same way and there's some kind of rough linen fabric wedged between my teeth and tied at the back of my head. It's one of the rags I use for cleaning my tools. It has a nasty, bitter, metallic taste. At the top of the wooden staircase, a thin sliver of light outlines the door.

My situation, and Tom's, comes back to me in a wave of horror and I swear and shuffle forward, my feet dragging the rest of my body. The pain in my head is excruciating. I make tortuous progress but eventually get as far as the bottom of the stairs where I try to heave myself up, only to tip over. Once again my head hits the floor and fills with darkness.

The door opens. I twist awkwardly and look up. Amber is silhouetted by the hall light.

I grunt, 'Tom,' loudly at her, or an approximation of his name.

The door closes on my muffled shouts. What is she going to do with my children? Whereas I was reasonably calm and competent with Tom, the thought of them being in danger has the opposite effect. It's hard to control it, to stop the keening noise that's coming from deep in my throat, but I have to make the effort otherwise we are all in trouble. I control my breathing until my pulse stops racing and my mind begins to clear.

Once I get myself up I can't cross the room without support so I have to hobble, keeping to the wall, and even then I fall twice and it takes several minutes and an enormous effort of will to get up again. At one point I knock over Tom's skis and the clatter they make when they hit the ground is so loud I can't believe it doesn't bring Amber running.

I have no idea how long it takes me, but it feels like hours not minutes. I lean against the table with the edge of the work surface pressing against the tops of my thighs and bend over until my head touches the lid of my tool box. I press my cheek to the catch and keep trying until I manage to hook the edge of the gag underneath it. Then I pull up hard and it springs open, catching and tearing the skin on my lip. Blood seeps through the cloth into my mouth.

Arranged inside are screwdrivers of various sizes as well as pliers, a monkey wrench, a hacksaw, a collection of spanners and numerous useful small tools. I dip my head in, work my tongue around the gag and hook it into the handle of the hacksaw. It hurts as I strain the muscles in my mouth, but I get it to lean against the side of the box then tip it out with my chin. I nudge it to the edge, turn myself round and stand on tiptoes until I can get my fingers inside the handle. My satisfaction is short-lived. It hangs for maybe three seconds before dropping with a metallic clang to the floor.

I hear a noise and drop, slithering back against the wall. The door opens and Amber comes downstairs. In the darkness, her eyes look huge and haunted and out of nowhere I'm overwhelmed by a sense of déjà-vu. There have been few things I've done – or at least there were before David North and leaving Josh – for which I am truly ashamed, few things I've had to mentally block because acknowledging them makes it hard for me to respect myself. But this is one of them and now that fissure has opened, the memories spill out, one after the other, relentless and nightmarish:

Walking home, feeling miserable with a temperature and sore throat and Mum telling me that she was looking after a child for the afternoon and that the girl might be a little upset.

A little upset. That was an understatement.

Mum saying, *She thinks you're called Emily. It's best she doesn't know your real name.*

The girl hovering in the cramped hallway of our Streatham flat, shivering like a frightened rabbit.

Mum using all kinds of inducements to get her into the car.

Driving her to a prissy little bungalow in a dead suburban street that looked more like the set of a sitcom than real life.

The girl in the back sobbing like her heart would break.

409

Feeling embarrassed for her, repelled by the sheer volume of tears and snot that smeared her face. She didn't have a hanky and was using the sleeve of the cardigan Mum had lent her. My cardigan.

Mum going to the door and that man coming out.

The girl saying, *Help me.*

Looking away.

To my shame, I recognize that. I've done it countless times over the years. It's what I do when I walk past a homeless person.

Mum saying, *You'll be fine, Katya. You can phone me any time and come and see me. Don't worry, I'm not abandoning you. You are important to me.*

The man putting his hand on Mum's shoulder and moving her out of his way.

Trying to ignore what was going on.

Help me.

Pretending I didn't realize she meant me.

Why did I behave like that? It would have been so easy to hold out a hand, to add my pleas to hers.

Her pathetic, comic ungainliness as she fell out of the car into the road.

Him turning to wave us off as she yelled and kicked, flailing her fists at him.

Mum changing the subject when I asked questions.

Now I know what she did and who she did it with, those two hours when she left me alone in the flat take on a powerful significance.

Amber says, 'You remember me now, don't you?'

I try to speak and she pulls the gag out of my mouth. I spit out the filthy residue that has collected on my tongue.

410

'Yes, I do.' *Stay calm.* 'Amber, we need to get Tom seen by a doctor.'

'What has Maggie told you?'

'That you killed your foster father. But he was abusing you. You can stop this now. If you let Tom die, things will be so much worse for you.'

She gets up off the floor, brushes the dirt from her trousers and wanders round the cellar, touching our things, humming the tune to one of the children's favourite songs, picking up tools and bike pumps, twisting paint pots to see the labels.

'Amber!' I shout. 'Tom is dying.'

She keeps singing. She isn't going to respond to anything immediate. She's in the past. I have to keep her talking, to keep her conscious of me, of what's important now.

'What happened afterwards?' I ask.

She scratches at the work surface with a screwdriver and then puts it down. 'What do you mean, afterwards?'

'After you . . . after your foster father died. What did my mother do?'

She comes and crouches opposite me, stares straight into my eyes. When I look into them I can see that terrified child and my stomach turns over. My mother helped make her what she is, but I refuse to shoulder the blame. I was only ten years old and I was sick. And what could I have done anyway? The outcome would have been the same.

'I phoned her,' Amber says. 'I said, please come. Please come. So she came. She took one look at Luke and called the emergency services. Then she waited until

411

they arrived, gave a statement and left. I never saw her again. Nice, don't you think?'

'I'm sorry.'

'I thought you would click years ago. And Maggie as well. Shows how much I meant to you.'

'I only met you that one time and you were crying.'

'Pathetic, wasn't I?'

'Amber. Tom—'

'I expect you're wondering how I found you. The amazing thing is, I wasn't looking. Can you believe that? Bumping into you that day was a complete coincidence. I promise you, the penny didn't drop until you showed me your wedding photos.' She pauses. 'I shouldn't have come back to the class the next week.'

'Why did you?'

'Because I wanted to so badly. I thought I was strong enough.'

'Please, Amber,' I say wearily. 'Let me go to Tom.'

'We've had some good times, haven't we? Sophie and Emily are like the sisters we could have been.'

I make a sound between despair and exasperation and she pats my thigh.

'Why didn't you help me? You could have, but you didn't; you shrank away from me like I was vermin. Why? No, don't answer that. I know why it was. You were spoilt. So wrapped up in your own little world with your toys and your mum and your schoolfriends that you didn't want to acknowledge I existed in case you had to share. I didn't want your things. I wanted your help.'

I don't know what to say to her. Nothing is going to make it better.

412

'I've never been happy,' she says.

She lowers herself on to the floor and stretches out her legs, leaning back against the cold brick wall. Our shoulders touch but I don't shift. If she wants physical contact, she's welcome to it. I turn towards her. In the dimness of the cellar her profile is softened.

'Will you accept an apology?'

'It depends what you're apologizing for,' she says.

'For everything. For ignoring you. For not listening.'

'Listening was Maggie's job.' She twists abruptly to face me. 'I'm not evil.'

'I know that.'

'Maggie isn't very bright, is she? And she's so bloody vain. I thought I was important, but, actually, it was all about her.'

I bite my tongue. Am I as bad as my mother? I have looked to another man to give me a sense of self-worth. I am guilty of more than one act of pure selfishness.

Amber hasn't finished. 'I imagine Maggie went into social work because she had a picture of herself saving children, being a hero. But when things turned nasty, she wasn't equipped to handle it. She ran away.'

She smiles and reaches for my hand and I let her take it. She even raises it to her lips and kisses it.

'I wish I could turn back time,' I say. 'I wish I had said something.'

'What would you have said?'

'I would have told Mum that we shouldn't send you back, that it was wrong. I'd have said, Can't you see she's scared?'

'But you didn't.'

'No.'

'Instead you moved away and never thought about me again. You went to school and university while I was locked up. You got pregnant and you got Tom.' She pauses, then lets my hand go. 'I'm in love with him. We made love.'

'I don't believe you. Tom wouldn't do that.'

She laughs. 'Oh, Vicky, sometimes you are so naïve. Of course he would. And he did. We did it in the kitchen in Spain, on the table. It was beautiful.'

I launch myself against her. I'm not sure what it's meant to achieve, and in fact it doesn't achieve anything except to make my bruised body and head hurt even more. But even though I'm weakened, I am bigger and heavier than she is and I manage to pin her down with my weight. As she struggles out from under me I sink my teeth into her arm.

She yelps, shoves me off and jumps up. I lie in the dirt, panting, defenceless and angry, glaring up at her.

'If he means that much to you,' I say through teeth gritted against the pain, 'save his life. He's not going to be much use to you dead.'

She clumps up the stairs and switches the strip light on. Tom is slumped awkwardly at the bottom, rolled up, one knee under his chin, one foot wedged against the wall. She must have dragged him all the way through the kitchen, out into the hall and pushed him down there. God knows what damage that will have done.

'Amber, for Christ's sake! Call an ambulance.'

'Fuck off, Vicky. You don't understand anything.' She switches the light out again and slams the door.

Great.

It takes me a long time to get back into a sitting position. I allow myself half a minute to recover, then start to move, pushing through starbursts of agony, scraping my bottom across the brick floor until I get to Tom. I rest my head against him and catch my breath. I can't feel him breathing or hear anything and my face is sticky when I lift it away. I pass out for the second time.

43

AMBER OPENS THE DOOR TO THE GIRLS' BEDROOM. THE light beside Polly beams slowly revolving stars on to the ceiling. She's sound asleep, her fine blonde hair fanned on the pillow. She is such a darling. Emily's bed is empty, the covers thrown back. Not expecting this, Amber looks behind the door, then checks the wardrobe but she's not hiding there. She darts out again and into their bathroom, her foot snagging on a splintered floorboard. She swears under her breath and switches on the light. No Emily. She searches the whole floor, checking under beds and in Josh's room.

Then a small voice pipes up: 'Daddy? Mummy?'

Amber leans over the banister. The master bedroom light is on. She calls Emily quietly and listens in the stillness for her response. There's nothing at first, then Emily's voice again; more anxious this time, a tremor in it. She must have found the blood. Amber's mouth dries as she tries to think. She takes a deep breath and walks downstairs calmly, as if her being there in the dead of night is perfectly normal.

'Emily,' she calls. 'Where are you, sweetie? It's only

me. Daddy had to go out and meet Mummy, so I'm looking after you.'

There's a shuffle, the padding of small feet. But no sign of Emily. Amber frowns, irritated. 'Emily? Come out now, darling. You're not in any danger.'

Silence. Then from the shadows a frightened little voice asks, 'Why is there blood?'

'It was that burglar. The one who got in before. You remember. He's gone now. Daddy had to fight him. But don't worry. The police will be here soon.'

Emily steps out into the light. She stares, her mouth hanging open, taking in Amber's blood-smeared hands and face. Amber glances down at the knife in her hand and back at Emily, who turns on her heel and runs into the kitchen.

'Emily. Don't be scared.'

In the silence she imagines the child crouched behind the island, holding her breath, trying not to make a sound. She closes the kitchen door behind her and leans against it.

'You can't hide from me for ever, sweetie. Come out. I'm not going to hurt you.' There are red footprints everywhere; hers, Vicky's and Emily's, and long tracks of blood from where she dragged Tom.

She loses patience and steps forward, comes round the island and Emily backs away, puts the table between them and starts to scream her head off. Amber launches herself forward and grabs her, but Emily sinks her teeth into her hand and jerks out of her grip. As she tries to get by, Amber grabs her again and this time holds her securely. She feels a moment's anguished guilt. This is

417

how Maggie held her that time. Before she handed her over to Luke.

'Emily, it's me. It's Amber. For heaven's sake – I'm trying to protect you.'

'I'm scared.'

'I know.' What should she do now? She hasn't thought about this. When she left the flat her mind had been full of Tom. But that was fantasy and now she has killed him. What is she supposed to do with the child?

Emily starts to cry. 'I want my daddy.'

'Your daddy's in the cellar,' she says. 'He needs help. Why don't you go and find him?'

Emily wipes her nose on her sleeve and eyes her suspiciously. She's never liked the cellar. Not since Amber told her a scary story about it. Amber can feel her confusion, her desire to trust someone she's known all her life and her instinct to avoid danger.

'Bluebeard isn't down there,' she says in a wheedling tone. 'Just Daddy. He's hoping you'll help him. If you don't go down, he might bleed to death.'

'You said he was out.'

'No I didn't.'

'Yes you did. You said he went to meet Mummy.'

'Now why would he do that, Emily? They've split up. Daddy doesn't love Mummy any more because Mummy did something bad.'

'What?'

'I'll tell you later,' she whispers, pulling a reluctant Emily towards the cellar door. She flicks the light switch.

'There, you see. I'm telling the truth. Now in you go.'

Emily leans tentatively past her. She turns to Amber again and Amber nods.

'Go on. You'll be fine. I've rung for an ambulance. They'll be here soon. I'm going to make sure Polly and Josh are OK. I won't be far away if you need me.'

'Mummy?'

I open my eyes with difficulty and follow the sound to the top of the stairs where a small and familiar figure is gazing down at me.

'Oh my God. Emily. Where's Amber, darling? Does she know you're out of bed?'

'She's gone upstairs.'

Oh Christ. 'Can you come down here? Can you do that for me?'

'What's happened to Daddy?'

'He's going to be fine. I promise. I need you to look in my toolbox and see if you can find something to cut me free.'

She's very good, very careful as she clings to the wooden banister and swings herself round, stepping lightly over her father's body. She drags a stool across the floor and climbs up to the toolbox, delves inside and comes out with a pair of wire-cutters. I notice she avoids looking at Tom.

I bend away from the wall and she crouches down beside me and slices through the cable tie. I take the cutters from her and do the same to my feet.

'Mummy.' Her lower lip trembles.

'Shh.'

I put my finger to my lips, listening for Amber. I pull

off my shirt and use it to staunch Tom's blood, praying it's not too late. While I work, I issue instructions.

'I want you to listen very carefully, Emily. I want you to stay with Daddy and keep both your hands pressed on his tummy. Here' – I place her hands over the damp shirt – 'as hard as you can. That's right. I'm going to go upstairs and phone the police. I won't be far, I promise. Will you be very brave and do as I ask?'

'Yes,' she sniffs.

'Good girl.'

I fold Tom into my arms. His head lolls forward. I feel frantically for a pulse but I can't find one.

'Is he dead?' Emily cries.

'No.' I climb over him and go to the door, rattle the handle and push it. It's locked. 'Shit.'

The worst thing is happening: I'm beginning to break up in front of my daughter. I force myself to calm down. It's not as if I'm not spoilt for tools. I find a claw-toothed hammer and force it between the door and the frame.

Emily is leaning over her father. She looks like she's hugging him but she sits back up, slips her hand from under his hip and produces his phone.

'It was in his jeans pocket.'

My laugh sounds more like a sob.

'Good boy. Good Joshie.'

Katya bundles him up in his blanket and takes him downstairs. How has she got herself into this situation? She knows what's happening now. Emily will have cut her mother free and Vicky will make short work of opening the door. Then she'll come for her with some sort of

420

weapon. And even if she's too incapacitated to manage that feat, dawn is breaking and Polly will be downstairs before long, wondering where everyone is. And Tom said his sister was expected in the afternoon. She closes her eyes and hums a lullaby. Josh's weight melts against her. His warmth, his heartbeat, his gentle breath relaxing as he goes back to sleep, is a comfort to her. He at least trusts her. She must be doing something right.

Time to leave. She tries to unfold Josh's pram, fighting with it, pushing her foot on the hinge and tugging at the handles, but it's been four years since Sophie was in one and she's lost the skill. Josh's is one of those expensive, complicated affairs that are easy once you know how. She doesn't know how and she doesn't want to put the baby down.

'Amber!'

She swivels round. Vicky is standing by the kitchen door, a hammer in her hand. They stare at each other. Katya holds Josh protectively in front of her.

'You shouldn't have left him,' she says, reaching behind her to open the door.

'Give him to me.'

Katya shakes her head. 'You don't understand how precious he is. You don't appreciate anything.'

'Amber,' Vicky says slowly. 'Put him down or I will hurt you.'

Katya watches as Vicky suddenly slumps against the wall. Her fingers loosen round the hammer and it falls to the floor. Vicky takes a step forward but it's as though she's drunk. She holds out her hand, baffled, and slowly collapses to her knees.

Katya doesn't wait. She leaves the house with Josh wrapped in his pale-blue blanket and sets off at a brisk walk, only slowing to catch her breath once she's turned the corner. There's a mist hanging over the Common and the light is incredible. She looks back the way she came. Two people are following her; a man and a woman, their figures shimmering in the morning haze. A jogger runs past her with a muscular, whip-tailed Weimaraner at his heels. The dog stops and sniffs at Katya's leg then catches up with his master. She looks behind her. They haven't gone away. Their eyes are dark holes in their blank faces. Luke and Linda. She knows she's hallucinating, but even so it feels like a threat.

She picks up her pace, turns into Tennyson Street and half runs past the closed shops. Outside Johnson Lane she pauses to catch her breath and darts a glance behind her. They've gone. She sighs with relief. Josh is growing heavy, so she puts her foot up on the window frame and rests his weight on her knee. Her desk is tidy, nothing left out, anonymous, ready for whoever comes to take her place. Pity. She enjoyed her job. She moves away, past the bookshop and the off-licence, the new shop selling upmarket women's clothes and the children's shoe shop. She remembers when she first came here, parking the car and crossing the road on to the Common. Vicky had talked about buying a house in the area and Katya wanted to see for herself. It was pretty and much quieter than Streatham and it lacked the buzz she liked, but at least it was alive, unlike Hillside Way. She had sat on one of the benches and watched people going about their daily lives, and decided she could force herself to live here. She remembers telling Robert that it would be a great place to bring up kids; that young families were colonizing the streets near the Common, lured by the green space and the excellent transport links to central London. A line she's used on Johnson Lane's customers ever since.

She glimpses a reflection and turns quickly. They're just a symptom of stress and fear. Her mother – skinny, fine-boned Linda – stares back at her and for the first time Katya sees something of herself. It's in her eyes and the shape of her chin. She hurries on, crossing the road and taking the lane that leads to the station.

Josh is awake now, staring at her, his eyes big and bewildered. She can feel the tension gather in his body as she tries to reassure him.

A siren wails and she steps back, shielding herself from the road behind a parked van. Two squad cars race by, blue lights flashing, followed by an ambulance. She watches them until they turn at the traffic lights.

The station is open but the blind is pulled down on the ticket booth. She doesn't bother with a ticket but takes the stairs over the railway line, to the platform for London-bound trains. Josh is crying, working himself up, angry more than anything.

'Shh, Joshie,' she says. 'It'll be all right.'

Her ghosts follow her there too. There are three of them now because Tom Seagrave has joined them. She wants to tell him she's sorry, but what does it matter any more? They are dead. She scrunches her face against the threatening tears and sits on a cold bench. The place is deserted but ten minutes later the lights flicker on in the platform café and the earliest shift workers begin to drift down the stairs, ghostly themselves with their sleepy faces and disinterested glances.

Has she ever really mattered to anyone? Not to Maggie, certainly. Maybe Vicky, for a while, but she'd had to turn herself inside out to be the person Vicky needed her to be. That wasn't Katya. Katya hadn't been good enough for Emily Parrish – according to her mother. Not good enough even to know her real name. When she found that out, the thing she felt most was stupid, as if everyone had been in on the joke except her. Why had everything gone wrong for her and right for Vicky? Her life could have been so different if Maggie had become her mother. Maggie would have protected her from Luke instead of letting him get into her head and opening her legs for him. Stupid, vain, selfish woman.

What will happen now? She feels a moment's panic. Linda and Luke's deaths were avoidable, but she can justify them. She was a child. But Tom Seagrave? Katya had wanted to kill him. She had been angry but she knew perfectly well what she was doing, she was even aware that the blade had pizza on it, had thought enough to wonder whether the fact that it was dirty would affect the outcome.

She hums to Josh and bounces him on her knee. He's whingeing now, hungry for his breakfast, and people are beginning to look her way and wonder why he isn't in a pram, why his mother looks so fraught. Why there is blood on her clothes and in her hair. It occurs to her that they might think she's an asylum seeker or a homeless woman. She has that scent of defeat and hopelessness about her. A shaven-headed man in paint-spattered jeans and sweatshirt glances at a woman in nurse's uniform and surreptitiously reaches for his mobile.

The first announcement of the morning crackles out from the speakers. *Stand back from the platform: the approaching train is not scheduled to stop at this station.*

A car door slams and heavy footsteps pound towards the station entrance. The newest arrivals turn to watch them, interested in the unfolding drama, understanding that they are here for the woman and child. She hears a distant blast, long and mournful, from the train as three policemen take the stairs at a run. She stands up without thinking, moves towards the edge of the platform and waits. The train is coming now, getting closer, moving so fast it will be with them in a matter of seconds. The nurse suddenly comes to life and steps forward as the train rushes into the station. The last word Katya ever hears is, 'Don't!'

44

Friday, 23 April 2010

SHE'S TAKEN HIM. HOW LONG HAVE I BEEN OUT? I crawl to the front door, pull myself up and open it. I stare up and down the street. Keep it together. The Boxers' door opens and Magda comes out, shuts the door quietly behind her and sets off briskly up the road. I run down our steps, double over and fall on to the pavement like a drunk. I lift my arm and shout her name. She turns, sees me and runs back.

'Can you stay?' I gasp as she pulls me to my feet.

'Are you hurt?'

Yes, I'm hurt. I think my wrist is broken and my head has taken more than one blow. Nothing is quite in focus so I must be concussed.

'I'm fine. Tom isn't though. He's bad. He's in the cellar with Emily. Please, Magda. Can you stay with them while I go after Amber? She's taken Josh. She's taken my baby.'

'Do you want I go after her?' She places her hand on

my arm and starts to steer me towards the house but I brush her off.

'No!' I'm surprised I can inject that much force into my voice. 'I can't stay here waiting. Just go in and keep the door closed. The police should be here any minute.' I don't wait for her to try and stop me, I half run, half lurch up the street.

'Vicky!' Magda shouts after me. 'Vicky, this is not sensible.'

I keep going, crying with pain and misery. I am not going to let my son down again. At one point I vomit outside the house of someone I know from school, but I force myself on. I can hear sirens coming closer and at the idea that help is on its way, my legs begin to let me down. I fall against a lamppost and cling to it, trying to work out where I am. The lights all have weird halos and the trees are like children's paintings, black-green blobs on lollipop-stick trunks. I'm having trouble accessing my mental map of the area. I think Amber's road is close by. She must have taken him there. She doesn't have the pram, so what else would she have done?

A car screeches to a halt and someone jumps out of it and takes hold of me as my legs give way. I recognize Grayling even though his features are blurred.

'Vicky,' he says. 'What are you doing out here?'

'I'm trying to find Amber.'

I turn away from him and vomit again, then run, or do what ought to be running, but actually feels like a slow buckling of my muscles. He catches me and, with the help of another officer, gets me into the car where I sit shaking and speaking in tongues. I am incoherent even to myself. All I know is that Amber has Josh and I have to get to him. I try the handle but the locks are on and then we're moving and Grayling is speaking urgently into his radio. Then he goes quiet and listens.

After a moment, he twists round in his seat. 'One of my officers has Josh. He's safe. We'll get you seen to now.'

'You're going to have to prepare yourself, Vicky. He may not make it.'

'He will,' I blurt out. 'He can't die. Not now.'

Beside my hospital bed, Grayling is sympathetic but firm. 'He's lost a hell of a lot of blood. Your husband is in a critical condition. Do you understand what that means?'

I shake my head.

He speaks very gently but he doesn't spare me. He knows there's no point. 'It means that there are complications and that death could be imminent. It's what they say when they want to give loved ones time to prepare themselves.'

'But he isn't dead.'

'No. He isn't dead.'

Fairhaven Young Offenders' Institute

July 1992

DEAR MAGGIE

This place is OK I suppose but I don't want to be here. I get nightmares and sometimes I wake up and I've scratched myself so hard there's blood on the sheets.

I thought you would come to see me. Maybe you tried but they didn't let you. I've asked and asked but all they say is they can't get hold of you. Please come. I'm being good and going to my classes and this psychiatrist comes in most days and talks to me. He's called Doctor Adam Something. I can't remember his second name. It's foreign. I don't need one but they say I have to and he's all right. They keep saying it will help me to come to terms with what I've done and make the nightmares go away but they don't believe me when I say what he did. If you come you can tell them because you were there.

Please come. Or write. The other kids here call me all sorts but they're no better themselves. I've found out there's one who attacked her baby brother. I think that's worse because he can't have been upsetting her that much. I like Kam. He's funny and he doesn't pick on me. He's teaching me to play table tennis.

Will you phone me? I know they gave you the number but I've written it at the top just in case you lost it. I thought you wanted to help me.

Love from Katya.

'Who is Emily, Katya?'

She looked up at the psychiatrist and frowned. It sounded like a trick question. He held out a scrap of paper. On it were words in Katya's handwriting. She had written Emily over and over again and doodled babyish flowers and hearts around it. She flushed and pushed it away.

'Is she a friend?'

She shrugged. 'Not really.'

'So where did you meet her? Did she go to your school? Is she a neighbour or a family friend? Surely it won't hurt to tell me something about her.'

'Why don't you ask Maggie?'

'Why would I do that?'

'Because Emily is Maggie's daughter, of course,' she said with studied patience.

The wait felt very long before Adam eventually spoke. 'Maggie's daughter is called Victoria. There is no Emily.'

It was the final betrayal. Emily must have been in on the deception; Maggie must have explained: 'Don't tell

430

her your name because she wants to be your friend and she isn't good enough for you. She'll pollute you.'

She heard her mum talking to a friend once. She must've been about six years old. Her friend asked why she'd kept her. 'Why didn't you have an abortion, Linda?' And her mum said it was because she wanted to make someone who would love her whatever. Katya did love her but it made her cross to think she'd been made on purpose for that.

She asked Maggie that question after Maggie told her that she had her baby when she was seventeen years old. Maggie said it was because she wanted someone that she could love. Katya tried and tried to work out which was better: to make a baby to love or to make a baby to do the loving, but it was really hard. It made her feel that she had the bigger responsibility though. She had to love her mother even though when she got home from school sometimes she would have to wait to go in. It wasn't fair.

'You've got a visitor, Katya,' Yvonne, her supervisor, said. 'Up you get.'

It had to be Maggie. She had come for her. It was all going to be OK. She would go to Maggie's house and Maggie would change her mind and tell her that she loved her and would be her mum. She would have a sister. She might have to share a bedroom, because that flat was tiny, but she didn't care because it would be her home.

She followed Yvonne down the corridor and through the doors into the room with the friendly sofas and bright murals. It was supposed to make the kids feel happy. The sun was shining through the windows, straight into her face, and she stopped short.

'Here's Sally come to see you. Would you like some orange squash and a biscuit? Come on, love, don't be rude. Say hello.'

Katya stood with her hands down by her sides, her fists clenched, a cry growing like a tumour in her abdomen, pushing up her throat until she almost gagged on it.

She pressed it down hard as she was firmly propelled to a chair. Sally was sitting opposite. Her eyes were red and her skin was blotchy and she looked older. Katya wondered if the sister had died or if she'd had to leave her on her deathbed when she heard her husband was killed. The tumour was sucking all the space out of her insides till she felt like she was going to throw up her breakfast.

Sally pressed her forehead against her clasped hands and took a deep breath.

'I forgive you, Katya,' she said.

Katya heard herself scream like it was another person. It went on and on and on and people were rushing into the room and her arms were being held and she was being dragged out and taken back to her room through all these kids who stared at her. Some of them laughed. One lad shouted, 'Katya! Katya!' repeating her name even as she threw herself down on the bed.

'Tell me about Sally Bryant.'

'Why? Sally isn't important.'

'Isn't she? Well, Katya, why don't you tell me about her anyway and let me decide what's important or not?'

She sighed heavily and picked at her nails. The only thing good about these sessions was that they broke up the day, so she wasn't eager for them to stop. It was why she was talking now, telling her story. He recorded it all and wrote notes, but she didn't think it would make a difference. She was still stuck here.

'She was all right,' she said. 'She was out at work a lot.'

'A nurse, right?'

Katya nodded.

'How did she treat you?'

Katya shrugged.

'Did she get cross or irritated?'

'No. She was all right. I told you before.'

He clasped his hands and looked at her like he was reading the spines of books on library shelves. 'Why were you so upset when she forgave you?'

'Because I didn't need her to.' She scratched at her scabs. He was as thick as everyone else.

'Why not?'

'Because he deserved what he got, didn't he? He was a pervert.'

He gazed at her steadily, swivelling his thumbs slowly round and round each other. 'Were you jealous of Sally's relationship with your foster father?'

She laughed out loud but inside she felt uncertain. 'What?'

'Jealous. It would have been natural. He was a father

figure and vulnerable children attach themselves to father figures. Sally told me about an incident when he kissed her in front of you.'

'What about it?'

'She says you had a face like thunder.'

She glared at him. 'Well, I didn't and you can't say I did because you weren't there.'

'Katya, the police looked into this. There is no evidence to support your accusations, no witnesses, no other victims, no prior convictions. You were found guilty in a court of law.'

'But he started it. He took my book and wouldn't give it back.'

'*The Blue Fairy Book*?'

'Yes. It was my mum's. Then he tried to do it to me.'

'I'm sure you think that something like that happened. You were wound up and he took the teasing too far.' He glanced at his notes. 'At the police station you told the child psychiatrist that you had imagined killing him before that.'

He waited for her to contest this and sighed. 'Katya, you're only eleven years old and you have your whole life ahead of you. We are going to help you move on, but first you have to come to terms with what you did. Do you understand that?'

She didn't answer.

He clicked his biro and slipped it into his shirt pocket. 'Let's try again tomorrow.' His face softened as he stood up and moved towards the door. 'You matter, Katya. Don't ever let anyone tell you you don't.'

45

Tuesday, 4 May 2010

MUM BROUGHT THE CHILDREN TO SEE ME WHEN I FIRST
woke up after an operation to release the pressure on my
brain, but it wasn't a happy visit and we decided to spare
them any more. No child should see its mother in such a
frail, banged-up condition. Josh was the only one not
remotely bothered. He sat on my stomach and stared at me
before trying to pull the tubes out of the back of my hand.
Tom is in another ward on another floor, floating in an
induced coma, his body awash with someone else's blood.

Jenny told us that after Josh was brought home, carried in the arms of a police officer, he slept for three
hours solidly. The police said that he was bawling his
head off when they got to him. The nurse who picked
him up off the bench and missed her train was amaz-
ingly calm. She only broke down once they brought her
into the canteen and gave her a cup of tea. I am so grateful to her for holding it together for as long as she did.

Hannah stayed for a week and my life was made
bearable by Mum's stories. I couldn't hear enough about

how my sister-in-law ironed the girls' underpants and how her regimented rule over my household was constantly undermined by Polly. Since Hannah returned to the North, Magda has moved in temporarily. Mum thinks she's the bee's knees.

Grayling is coming this afternoon and I have made a decision. When I leave hospital I will have confessed everything, forced out every last drop of my story, laid myself open so that I can start again. Mum has already contacted the lawyer Jenny suggested and booked a provisional meeting for a week's time, assuming I'm out of here. The system will suck me into its deep embrace and hopefully disgorge me some way down the line, a better, wiser person. I am terrified.

When Grayling arrives, Mum gets up to go and I notice a subtle change in her body language. She fancies him. I'll have to tell her he is out of bounds. He sits down on the chair she vacated, twists it round so that he can fit his long legs between it and the bed, and drapes his big hands over his knees. He stays in that position until I've finished talking, then he leans back.

I reach for my water and clumsily knock it over. In the ensuing fuss, the nurse comes in and tells him it's time to leave.

'No,' I say firmly. 'Give us five more minutes.'

She treats us both to a disappointed glance, then leaves the room. I wait until her footsteps fade.

'What will happen to me now? What will the charges be?'

'Criminal neglect. Obstructing the police in the course of an investigation.'

On cue, my headache returns, right in the centre of my forehead. I rub at it with my forefinger. 'Will I go to prison?'

'I can't give you any assurances, Vicky. A good lawyer should be able to get you a suspended sentence. I'd hope you'll be allowed to stay with your children, but they'll probably impose sanctions. You may have to get live-in help.'

'I can do that,' I say. Maybe Magda could be persuaded to stay on.

'Vicky . . .' He eyes me warily, as if I might have a relapse. My stomach turns over. 'I am sorry, but you won't be able to teach. You do understand that, don't you?'

I take a deep breath and nod; it's no more than I expected, even though part of me hoped. Grayling sees that I don't want to talk about it and doesn't attempt to commiserate or explain.

'And I'll have to formerly charge you.'

'Are you going to arrest me right now?'

He stands up to go. His hands hang by his sides as he looks down at me, amused. 'Not if you can give me your assurance that you're not going anywhere.'

I raise my eyebrows and he smiles. He has dimples. I never noticed that before. No wonder Mum's smitten.

A month passes before Tom regains consciousness. I've been at the hospital every day, dropping the children at school and coming straight over. I've had a lot of time to think, but he hasn't. I'm not going to start rattling on about salvaging our marriage, or demand to know if

437

Amber was telling the truth about them. For the record: I don't believe her. Sitting at his bedside, watching his chest rise and fall, listening to the machines that keep him alive, I'm not intending to defend my own actions either. I have to be patient and give him a chance to catch up.

The worst has been the media interest. I've outdone the Pint-of-Milk baby by many column inches. Somehow or other they got hold of a family photograph and one of Amber, and have gone to town on the relationships between us. I'm only grateful that Tom hasn't had to read it, or felt under siege in his own house. The CCTV footage of Amber walking into the station with Josh in her arms is chilling. It even captures the moment the nurse jerks and steps forward, her hand outstretched, her face a mask of horror.

I was protected from the immediate fallout, but I did watch the news on television. I couldn't help myself. Mum and Hannah dealt with the initial door-stopping – separately they were pretty good, together they were dynamite. It didn't make much difference though. The journalists gleaned plenty of information outside the school gates, and a few choice headlines made the red-tops. The broadsheets ran with it too, how could they not? A nice, middle-class mother, a teacher to boot, leaves her baby alone in the house and sets in motion a catastrophic sequence of events. The story has everything: neglect, secrets and lies, historic child abuse, extortion, house prices and poor Amber's peculiarly urban death.

It's time to leave Coleridge Street and the area. I'm too much of a coward to front it out, even after the fuss dies down. I have half a mind to try the coast: Hove perhaps, or Shoreham. Not too close to Mum, but close enough.

Tom is brought out of the coma slowly, and I set off when the ward sister calls me. He is sleeping and I wait, sitting with my hands on my knees, listening to the hospital function, the snatches of conversation, the doors opening and closing. There is no hurry. He's pale and very thin, his eyes bruised, his lips chapped. His lashes curl on to his cheeks. His hair needs a cut.

His eyes open.

'Hello,' I say.

'I was dreaming about you.'

'What was I doing?'

'You were kissing me.'

'Did you hate it?'

His mouth twitches. 'No. I liked it.'

Did he sleep with her? I keep brushing the question away, but it intrudes whenever I let my guard slip. At any rate, I refuse to let it erode my happiness in seeing him on the mend. Because he fought not to die, I'll forgive him everything. If he won't forgive me, I'll forgive that too.

'What's happened to Amber?' he asks. 'Is she in custody? Oh shit, and Robert. Poor bastard. He must be devastated.'

'Robert and Sophie are in Suffolk with his parents. He can work from anywhere, so I doubt he'll be coming back.'

He narrows his eyes. He knows I'm keeping some-thing back. 'And Amber?'

There's no way of putting it that will soften its impact so I just tell him straight.

'She's dead, Tom. She threw herself under a train.'

'Oh my God. Why would she do that?'

'We don't have to talk about this now,' I say. 'You need to rest.'

He props himself up on his elbows. 'Was it my fault?'

'No.'

'Vicky, I have to tell you something.'

'No, you don't. Please don't.'

'I slept with her.'

Neither of us says anything. The man in the next bed moans quietly to himself.

'It was a mistake,' Tom whispers. He holds his hand out for mine and then drops it when I don't move. 'I told her she'd got it wrong. You know what happened after that.' His hand goes to his abdomen, lies across the wound like a mother protecting her unborn child. 'I am so sorry.'

'We've both made mistakes.'

Somehow that doesn't help.

I sigh deeply and stand up. 'I'll come back tomorrow.'

He nods and lets me go without a word. I turn and glance back at him through the glass panel in the door. He's staring straight ahead.

'Has there been a funeral?'

It's the next day. Despite everything, I can't not come and see him. Neither of us has mentioned his

440

confession. I nod. 'Yes. It was very small. Robert came. Sophie stayed with her grandparents. Grayling was there, and Sarah Wilson. And me.'

'Not Maggie?'

'She couldn't make it.'

He has no idea of their connection yet. One thing at a time. I thought she was wrong not to come. She is a woman with a lot to answer for but, fortunately for her, it looks like she won't have to do that. Unlike me.

There are a lot of things I haven't told him yet, like me leaving the teaching profession and my plan to move away and do something completely different. I'm thinking about setting myself up as a property developer. If we don't survive as a couple, I have my tools and my skills and I can look after the four of us on my own if I have to. I catch his eye and we both smile at the same time.

'I'm not angry with you,' I say.

It's odd, because I've been through a whole range of emotions in the last few days, and yet it's true: I'm not angry.

'I've written you a poem,' I tell him the next day, proffering my notebook. 'But it's nowhere near as good as yours.'

'Read it,' he mumbles, and closes his eyes.

'OK.'

I lift the book up and squint at my scrawl.

> *They said you wouldn't make it,*
> *When you were comatose,*

I thought I couldn't take it,
But then you twitched your nose.

'That's as far as I got.'

He chuckles. 'Very moving. I had no idea you were so talented.'

'Thank you, that means a lot, coming from the Coleridge Street laureate.'

I study his face as he drifts off. He is gaunt; his skin pulled taut over his skull, his eyes hollow. He speaks as I'm stooping to pick my handbag up off the floor.

'She hasn't been to visit me.'

I put it down again. 'Who, darling? Do you mean Hannah? She did come, but she's gone back home now.'

'No, not Hannah. Amber.' He gives me that small-boy look and I frown.

'Tom, I told you, Amber killed herself.'

'Oh?' he says. 'Yes. Sorry. I forgot.'

And that's how it is. Amber never quite leaves us because every so often, when he's distracted, or tired, or just plain confused, he asks me why she hasn't been to see us, and if we've fallen out. The doctor told me he died in the ambulance taking him to hospital that night. They lost him for three and a half minutes. It's affected his short-term memory.

Tom has fallen asleep. I stroke the hair away from his eyes and bend to kiss his forehead.

Robert emails me a photo a few days later. It was taken the Christmas before last in our sitting room. I'm about seven months pregnant with Josh, sitting deep on the sofa with my feet up on a pile of cushions, wearing a huge baggy green jumper and black maternity leggings. The girls were treating us to their interpretation of the Nativity, with Sophie Collins as a pontificating, self-important Joseph, Emily as Wendy, a pious scold, and Polly as an uncooperative baby Jesus. She wanted to be a king.

My hands are resting on my jiggling belly, my head rocked back with laughter and Amber is convulsed beside me, tears streaming from her eyes, gripping my arm.

I print out a copy, buy a frame for it and place it on my dressing table. We were true friends once, Amber and I. I hold on to that when I wake up at night, sweating from a recurring nightmare, her eyes staring at me through the darkness of the cellar. I wish I could have healed her.

Acknowledgements

Heartfelt thanks are due to Harriet Bourton and Bella Bosworth, both of them fantastic editors; to Tash Barsby, who inherited me and has been such a great support, and to Rosie Margesson, my publicist at Transworld; to Victoria Hobbs at AM Heath for her support and kindness, and her colleagues Pippa McCarthy and Jennifer Custer. Thanks to my lovely friend and neighbour Genevieve Quierin for allowing me to pick her legal brain; to the Prime Writers for listening, offering advice, having great lunches and making me laugh; to Detective Inspector Kate Balls of the City of London Police for patiently answering my questions. I am more than grateful to all the book bloggers and early readers who have been so generous with their time, reading and reviewing. And, of course, many thanks and loads of love to my family.

ONE LITTLE MISTAKE
Reading Group Guide

- In *One Little Mistake*, Emma Curtis explores the idea of trust in friendships and relationships. Are there people in your life you're more likely to trust than others? What is it about those people that causes the distinction? Does your history with someone dictate how much you trust them?

- Vicky compares herself to the Pint-of-Milk baby's mother throughout the novel. Is what she did worse? What do you think of Vicky's decision to leave Josh at home alone? Is this something you would do, or have done?

- Do you think Vicky is a good mother?

- Did you identify with any of the characters? If so, why?

- Early on in the novel, Amber says to Vicky: 'You mustn't take what you have for granted.' What does Vicky take for granted in her life? Why do you think she acts this way?

- What's the worst mistake Vicky makes throughout the course of the novel?

- Discuss the men in *One Little Mistake*. How do Tom, Robert, David and Luke impact Vicky and Amber, both individually and in terms of their friendship?

Special thanks go to the following bloggers
for their early support:

'A **riveting page-turner** of a book'
@Bbrilliantbooks

'A **gripping** and tense tale'
@TracyShephard (Postcard Reviews)

'This was my first read by the author
and it **won't be the last**'
@Lost815_Oceanic

'Gripping, **cleverly written**'
@Lizzy11268

'A **chilling** tense and indulgent, exciting read.
I honestly couldn't put this down'
@BookwormDH

'*One Little Mistake* is an **intense** psychological
thriller that **kept me turning the pages** long after
bedtime had come and gone'
@bethsy

'A thriller to **pull at the heartstrings of mothers** and,
perhaps, to make others question their closest friendships'
@rosieamber1

'You **can't help but get sucked in** as the story develops
and **secrets and twists** begin to unfold'
@Lauras_bookblog

'An absolutely **fascinating** read'
@tiny_ickle_jo

'It is **packed full** of story, twists and **punchy** characters'
@LynseyMummaDuck

'I'm **still reeling** from the finale of this book'
@gilbster1000

'In this **crescendo** psychological thriller, the truth is not the most important thing, it's the trust between you, your family and friends'
@Sweeet83

'A **compelling**, thought-provoking read'
@ShazBookBlog

'I can not and *will not* put this book down. For me, it was just **perfect**'
@Cupcakemumma11

'An **intriguing** and **totally engrossing** read'
@karendennise

'A **fantastic**, gripping thriller that will have you **guessing till the very end**'
@chazbookworm

'A **stunning** psychological thriller that is **thought-provoking, engaging and dramatic**'
@kraftireader

'Highly **addictive** and **absorbing**'
@JoannaLouisePar

'*One Little Mistake* is a chilling read and **an outstanding debut** . . . will leave you **reeling**'
@collinsjacob115

'**Frighteningly realistic** and relatable, particularly for mothers. Curtis's debut novel is incredibly written and **I can't recommend it highly enough**'
@deborahlsinger